Acknowledgments

First and foremost, I would like to thank the love of my life who put up with all my pouting every time I was offered a bit of constructive criticism. I truly do appreciate all of your wise advice. The reader may find this different, but I owe special thanks to my ex-wife who must have read five different versions of "Nameless" and cheered me on the whole way. Thanks to my ex-father-in-law who without his push, this project might never have been started. Finally, I would like to thank my editor Benee Knauer, whose counsel made "Nameless" a viable and veritable thriller definitely worth reading.

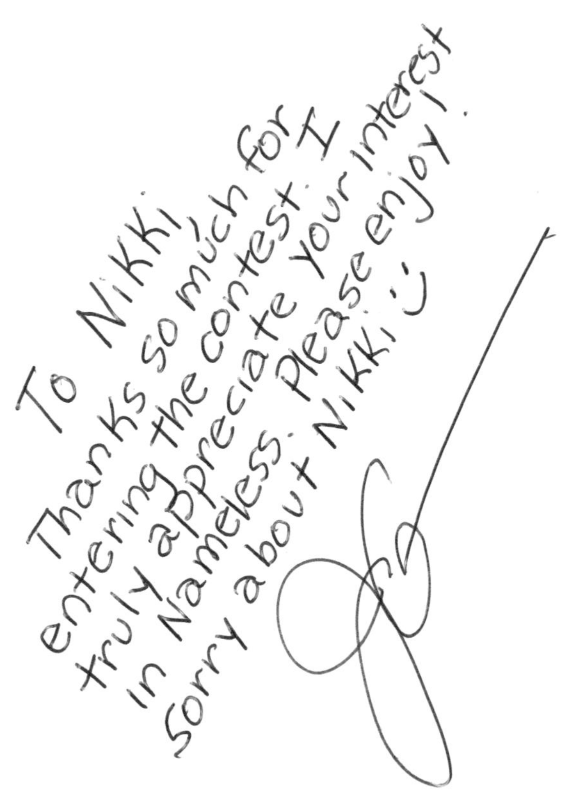

For Trey and Jill

Chapter 1

"This is bullshit," Nikki shouted out loud to no one in particular after her vain attempt to wave down a gray Chevy Silverado pickup. The middle-aged male driver slowed to a near stop then accelerated past her, almost running over her feet when she stepped off the curb. It wasn't an hour earlier; she decided this would be her last night on the streets. She was sick of it all; the repulsive, dirty, old men, the perverted degenerates of the world not to mention the constant danger to her health and life. She planned to make enough money tonight to get a bus ticket home and start over. There was a slim chance she could move back into her parents' house. Her stepdad was irrelevant. He would have no real say in the matter. She had burned bridges with her mother. "Burned" actually was an understatement. They were blown to smithereens. Nikki was hoping that time had healed some major wounds. Whatever happened, she was going to find a way to make an honest living and turn her life around.

The man parked in a Sports Utility Vehicle across the street on Biscayne Boulevard had been watching her for the last ten minutes. It was the first time he had seen her. Until only recently he was very familiar with all the whores working this strip. According to his calculations, this one was a runaway minor, new to the area, no older than seventeen. There was little doubt she was unfamiliar with local practice or was just plain stupid. There was normally a high police presence at this hour to protect and monitor patrons leaving the dollar movie theatre across the street. Most of the whores didn't show up until just after midnight. They knew it was when the theatre closed and the parade of johns driving up and down Biscayne kicked off. It was after 10:30pm and the infrequent passersby had no interest in what the girl was selling.

Just the way she shamelessly flaunted her body parts to draw in customers was enough to royally piss him off. Her willingness to screw any pathetic asshole prepared to pay put her on a level with the lowest form of blood sucking or shit-eating parasite. When she practically threw herself in front of the Chevy pickup, he knew it was time to act before she ruined everything and got herself arrested.

He started the SUV, pulled out of the parking space and made his way around the block. In the short distance he drove, he had to dodge a homeless man hoping to spit-wash his windshield for change and two derelicts selling crack. As he approached the prostitute, she stepped onto the street and flashed him a full breast. At that moment, he had the overwhelming urge to coax her into his truck, slit her throat, and be done with it. Instead, he took a deep breath and cleared his mind. The instant he stopped, she was at his passenger window.

"Can I get in?" she asked.

"It's not locked."

She hopped into the passenger seat without hesitation. Seemingly as an afterthought, she inquired, "You're not a cop or serial killer, are you?"

"No. I'm gonna pull outta here before we get arrested."

Satisfied with his answer, and more focused on making the money for her bus ticket, she replied, "That's fine. What are you into?"

"How much for the night?"

"One thousand." She thought that should be enough for the bus, plus a few extra dollars to live on while she looked for a job after she got back home to Macon. What luck to have a big pay-off with her first john of the evening.

"That's kinda steep isn't it?"

"I could make that in three or four hours. Take it or leave it."

He pulled out onto Biscayne Boulevard and said, "I like doing it outdoors."

"As long as you drop me off back where you found me, I'm ok with that. But I mean it. A thousand bucks."

"That's fine. I'll pay."

"I don't take credit cards."

He pulled a wad of cash from his pocket and waved it in the air between them.

"Satisfied?"

"No problem. Where we going?"

"Do you know Haulover Beach?"

"No, but it sounds fun. How far is it?"

Her answer confirmed she was a visitor to South Florida. That was a good thing. Any resident would be familiar with the clothing-optional beach. There was a great chance she had no real connections to the area. He replied, "It's a nude beach in North Miami. It'll only take about fifteen minutes to get there."

Haulover Beach was one of many park sites he had researched, visited and studied for a night like this one. In the midst of the big city, it afforded privacy from both the normally busy A1A and the beach itself. The five blocks it covered were lined by a dense forest of Florida sea grape trees. From personal observation and its reputation, he knew it was the site of daily sexual escapades along its self-guided nature trail. The beach closed at sunset. Having been there at all times of the day and night, he was confident they would have no company.

He parked in the large Haulover Beach lot in the space closest to the underground pedestrian walkway. There were no other vehicles. The only lighting was provided by street lamps and the barely visible crescent moon. A slight, land breeze made the cool winter temperature shoot a shiver up Nikki's spine as they passed through the tunnel toward the beach. Goose flesh popped up on her skin. The tunnel reminded her of the many nights she'd slept in places just like this. She'd left her parents' home when she was fifteen. Drinking, drugs, and a bad attitude were her M.O. since the age of twelve, when her father passed away and her mother married a deadbeat, gold digger who was after the insurance money. Luring her stepfather into her bedroom for sex was the last straw. Nikki's plan to remove the piece of shit from their lives had backfired. Her mom forgave her new husband and kicked her troubled daughter out of the house. For a year, Nikki lived with her twenty-three year old drug dealing boyfriend. When he had no more use for her, she hit the streets.

They emerged from the tunnel and turned north toward the forest and nature trail. Her client hadn't spoken a word since they'd arrived. She was starting to get the creeps and decided to strike up a conversation to ease her anxiety. It didn't give her much relief.

"You don't plan on spending the night out here, do you? It's kinda cold."

"Don't worry about it. I have blankets and sleeping bags in the backpack. You'll be fine."

Going silent once again, he led her down a path into the forest of sea grape trees. The trail was extremely narrow, barely wide enough for two small children walking side by side. The underbrush scraped at Nikki's bare ankles, shins, and calves. With the moon and streetlights almost completely obstructed by the treetops, she could barely see more than a few feet ahead of her. Following directly behind him, she couldn't fathom how he was able to make his way through the pitch-dark without a flashlight. By the time they advanced 50 yards along the tapered path, the chill up her spine had evolved into a full-scale, uncontrollable shiver. Having grown up in Minnesota, 50 degree weather normally didn't affect her this way. The blackness of the night and the dead silence weren't helping. Mostly, it was the vibe she was getting from her john. There was definitely something very bizarre, if not sinister about him. She was starting to regret following him into the deserted park. She seriously considered spraying his face with the can of mace she had in her purse, taking his roll of cash and running. If he wasn't about 220 lbs of ripped muscle, she just might have tried.

"Hey! There isn't enough room to walk through this shit, much less have sex. Where the fuck are you taking me?"

"Watch your fuck'n mouth, bitch." Before she could respond, he turned around and punched her square in the face with a closed fist knocking her off her feet.

In an instant, he was on top of her. She tried to maneuver her hands into her purse to retrieve the mace, but he was too fast. He snatched it from her grip and threw it into the sandy underbrush. Sitting on her chest, he leaned forward digging his knees deep into her armpits. Gravel, twigs, and mulch burrowed into her neck and shoulders and cut through the skimpy red Lycra Lame dress she was wearing. The pressure he applied sent bolts of pain up through her shoulders and down her arms. The extreme discomfort and her inability to breathe without difficulty were making it almost impossible to formulate coherent thoughts. Her sheer impulse for survival produced the only defensive response available to her. She kicked up and back as hard as she could with both legs and managed to connect hard with the nape of his neck and back of his head. He was stunned for just a brief moment, yet enough to cause him to lift his weight from her chest and arms and allow her to partially push him off her body. She immediately rolled over onto her stomach and clawed at the ground crawling to free herself from the remainder of his hold. Regaining his senses, he missed when he lunged toward her to grab the back of her dress as she stood.

Once on her feet, Nikki began to run as fast as she could although she had no idea which direction she was headed. She screamed at the top of her lungs for help then looked behind her to see that her assailant was right on her heels. Not 20 yards into her sprint, she tripped over a branch lying across the path, the same one he had helped her step over just minutes before. Her momentum vaulted her into the air. She struck the ground face first with a resounding thud that completely knocked the wind out of her and broke her nose. Blood gushed from her nostrils and down the back of her throat causing her to gag. Like a tiger in the final stages of the hunt, he leaped on her back, grabbed a fistful of hair and mashed her face into the dirt and mulch. Satisfied any further attempts at escape would be futile; he took several moments to listen to the sounds of the night. The distant hum of the surf and the girl's ragged breathing were all that infringed on its serenity. No one had heard her screams.

He released his grip on her hair then stood up and slipped the backpack off his shoulders. There were no blankets or sleeping bags inside. In their place were a butcher's knife, surgeon's scalpel, hammer, chisel, twine, flashlight, and several oversized plastic garbage bags. He lifted her head to assess her level of awareness. She was moaning, semiconscious at best, eyes closed. He stood up, reached into his backpack and pulled each item out of the bag. He turned on the flashlight and set his instruments in a neat row alongside her. Then he waited until she began to show signs of waking to full alertness. He wanted to look into her knowing eyes as he slit her throat.

In the interim, he tied her ankles and wrists. Moments after she was securely bound, her eyelids fluttered rapidly as if in R.E.M. sleep then opened wide. He picked up the butcher's knife and sat on her stomach. Instinctively, she struggled against the frayed string that constricted her wrists. Unadulterated panic consumed her. Seeing the look of terror in her eyes, he slashed the butcher's knife across her throat, from left to right. Warm, thick blood exploded out from the wound, spraying him about his upper torso and face. The pain felt like nothing more than the prick of a pin sliding across her neck. However, the sight of the copious amounts of her own blood soaking him elicited a terror that stung more sharply than any ache she had ever suffered. The blurring of her vision and the sensation she was floating into unconsciousness were not enough to spare her the realization of what was happening. In a matter of minutes, her life would be over. Tears welled in her eyes then overflowed leaving heavy mascara tracks down the sides of her face just below her temples. Then all went black.

* * *

Fourteen hundred miles north, while Nikki was taking in her last breaths, a winter storm was raging through Otisville, New York, home to one of the state's federal correctional facilities. Former FBI agent, Daniel Falcone, pulled the meager, jail-issued blanket tightly over his head, hoping beyond hope to achieve mindless sleep. It might as well have been a three inch thick, electronically heated comforter. It wasn't going to make a lick of difference. His failure to find warmth or sleep was the result of much more than the frigid weather. The relentless, nagging thoughts racing through his head were the real culprits. An unyielding, judgmental introspection brutally tormented his peace of mind and sense of well-being.

Daniel was having a hard time believing he didn't deserve everything that had happened to him over the past year and a half. Karma was a bitch and he was feeling its unabated wrath. In some ways he was waiting for something like this to happen his entire life. Other than the extreme guilt that plagued his thoughts each day and his dreams every night, he'd never truly paid for his brother's death so many years ago.

As if on cue, the shrill horn of a train sounded as it made its approach into the Otisville Metro North Train Station located less than a half mile southwest of the jail. Daniel was a sixteen year old boy again, back home in his family's brownstone in Chicago. It was a Friday night, December 3, 1993, his brother Peter's fifteenth birthday. Earlier in the evening, the family had celebrated by eating dinner at Peter's favorite restaurant, and then held a small party at home, just for the immediate family. Peter's big bash was scheduled for the following day. Friends and the rest of the family were invited for a night at the Navy Pier- ice skating and pizza- Peter's two great passions.

Later that Friday night, Daniel had plans for a special birthday blow-out of his own for his younger brother. At midnight, Daniel lay awake in his bed, fully clothed, waiting to be sure his parents were asleep. Normally, they went to bed early, around ten, and were well into the fifth and final stage of dream sleep by midnight. Delayed by the party, they hadn't gone to their room until eleven. Daniel waited patiently the extra hour, though sure they had probably conked out right after their heads hit their pillows. He was up, throwing on a jacket and on his way to his brother's room before the clock struck 12:01.

"Get up, Pete," Daniel whispered as he shook his snoring brother's shoulder, ready with his index finger over his pursed lips to keep Peter from making any loud noises.

Peter jumped up to a seated position. Seeing his older brother's indication to stay quiet, he fought his inclination to shout. "What the fuck? What are you doing?" he asked in a half-whisper.

"Just get up and get dressed. We're goin' out."

"No way. Get the hell outta here. I'm tired. I'm goin' back to sleep."

"Get your ass up. Don't be a pussy. It's time to really celebrate your birthday."

"I ain't goin' nowhere. Dad finds out he'll kick our asses."

"Dad's not gonna find out. Stop with the fuck'n goody two-shoes routine. Have some balls. Get up and let's go."

The roles between the two brothers were in some ways reversed from what would be expected of a first and second child. Peter was the structured one, mature, well-behaved, the caretaker. Daniel was much more likely to break the rules and challenge authority. They were typical in one respect. Peter idolized and adored his older brother. It took some doing, but Daniel could usually talk him into just about anything. That night was no different. After a few more curses mumbled under his breath, Peter got up and slipped into a pair of jeans and a sweatshirt.

It was an atypically mild night for December in Chicago. The temperature was in the mid-fifties and in the part of the city where the Falcones lived, the windy city was nothing of the sort. The trees were as still as a leopard lying in wait to seize its dinner. Before heading downstairs, Daniel grabbed a bag with two six packs of Bud Light from under his bed and they were on their way, tiptoeing as they descended the steps which lead directly to the front door. Daniel checked his pocket to be sure he had his house keys, then the two teenage boys stepped out into the quiet night, well-lit by the lights of the city and a full moon directly over their heads.

"Where we goin' and what's in the bag?" asked Peter as soon as they closed the door behind them.

"You'll find out. Let's go."

Daniel set out at a brisk pace in the direction of Lake Michigan with Peter at his side. The Falcones lived on the second and third floors of a brownstone built in the early 1950s, about a mile from the lake. On foot, it took them just less than fifteen minutes to arrive at Grant Park, a state compound covering three-hundred acres situated along the waterfront. They made their way directly to one of Chicago's most famous landmarks, the Clarence Buckingham Fountain. Distracted by the dancing, multi-colored spotlights reflecting off the surging water, Peter initially failed to notice his best friend, Ross, and Daniel's football teammate, Contrell, waiting for them on the lakeside of the fountain. Daniel's buddy was also carrying a bag with two six packs of beer. Together, the four teenagers crossed Lake Shore Boulevard in search of a secluded spot away from any potential, unwanted onlookers.

Once they were settled on the partition wall overlooking the black expanse of Lake Michigan, Daniel pulled out the first six pack.

"My baby brother didn't want to come out here. You think he's man enough to drink his first beer?" Daniel asked the group.

"Fuck you, Daniel. I'm here, ain't I?" replied Peter.

"You gonna drink or are you afraid you might get in trouble with Mommy and Daddy?" Daniel teased. Contrell found Daniel's goading hilarious, and laughed louder than the situation warranted.

"Shut up, Contrell. Why don't you keep on sniffing Daniel's ass? It's what you do best," quipped Peter. Now, it was Daniel who was bent over laughing. Contrell, defensive tackle for the football team, was 6'5" and weighed about two-sixty. He stood up and made a move toward Peter that Daniel quickly quashed by stepping between them.

"Knock it off, Contrell. I'm the only one that gets to beat his ass… So, what's the deal, Pete?" Daniel twisted the cap off a Bud Light and held it out to his brother.

Nervous, but not about to have his manhood challenged by the person he admired most in the world, Peter grabbed the beer and chugged several gulps. The other boys showed their approval with some hooting and hollering, breaking open their bottles and attempting to swallow bigger swigs than the rest. Peter's best friend, Ross, was the first to finish his beer. Unlike Peter, Ross didn't keep strictly to the straight and narrow. When Daniel called him two nights ago to invite him to the gathering, he'd agreed without hesitation. Ross had been trying to get Peter to party for more than a year.

It didn't take an hour for each of the boys to finish their respective six packs of beer. Peter was already slurring his speech and having difficulty keeping his balance when he stood. The other boys had more experience and were handling the alcohol a bit better.

"We need some more beer," commented Ross.

"I have a friend who can get us some," offered Contrell. "He's twenty-one. I can get him to bring it to us, but we'll have to pay him extra."

"I'm in," Ross raised his hand high in the air as if making a bid at an auction. "I've got twenty bucks."

"Me, too," said Daniel. "I'll pay for Pete."

Contrell walked the twenty yards to the bank of payphones east of the fountain and called his friend, who agreed to get them two more six packs. After notifying the group of his success, he pulled a small marijuana roach from his jacket pocket and held it up to Peter.

"I brought this for the birthday boy. He can probably get three or four hits from it. That'll knock him on his ass. It's really good kryp."

"Man, I don't know about that," Daniel said. Drinking was one thing for Daniel, but drugs were a whole other issue. He already had aspirations to be an FBI agent. Drugs were strictly off-limits.

"Come on," Ross replied. "It's his birthday. You're only fifteen once. He'll be fine. He's not gonna turn into a druggie."

"Gimme that thing," Peter slurred. "I'm a man. I make my own decisions."

Contrell handed the roach to Peter, who promptly put it in his mouth. As Contrell was lighting it he instructed, "Inhale real deep and hold it." Before Daniel could stop his brother, Peter sucked in a double-size dose then immediately started hacking uncontrollably. Daniel knocked the roach from his mouth and stomped it out, but his response was too late. A considerable amount of the potent kryptonite marijuana penetrated Peter's blood stream. The drug in combination with the alcohol resulted in a high that would have significantly impaired the capacities of a grown man with a strong tolerance for mind-altering substances.

"What the fuck, man," shouted Contrell. "That stuff is expensive. I could've smoked it."

"Then you should've. Don't be giving that shit to my brother."

Peter mumbled something incomprehensible then proceeded to vomit up his dinner and birthday cake. Ross and Contrell found it quite funny but Daniel wasn't as amused. "Serves you right," he said. Minutes later, Contrell's friend arrived with the beer and the incident with the marijuana was forgotten.

"You sure you can handle more beer, Pete? I'm not cleaning it up later if you puke all over yourself," warned Daniel.

"I'm fine, dude. I feel much better."

"If you say so. Just don't pass out."

"Let's get outta here," said Ross. "I'm sick-a-lookin' at the lake."

The horn of the Red line train blasted in the distance, giving Daniel an idea he would regret for the rest of his life. "Let's go check out the train tracks," he suggested. Near Michigan Ave., on the west side of the park, a series of bridges crossed over six sets of rails running north and south below ground level. From each trestle there was an unobstructed view of downtown Chicago, the train tracks disappearing into the base of the skyscrapers. By the time the teenagers arrived at the first bridge, they had each consumed two more bottles of beer and all had lost their holds on good judgment. It was Daniel's idea to climb down the trestle support to the tracks twenty feet below and follow them into the heart of the city.

Daniel was the first to reach the platform, followed by Contrell and then Ross. The three managed not to hurt themselves despite their inebriated state. Peter was not as fortunate. The instant he lifted his second leg over the railing of the trestle, he lost his grip. He was in free fall, his body perpendicular to the platform, feet first. To Daniel, it seemed as though it were happening in slow motion. His first instinct was to attempt to catch his brother before he hit the ground. He tried to make a move to the spot he calculated Peter would land, but it felt like his feet were glued to the cement. Looking up, he watched Peter's fall as if he were reviewing a film frame by frame, powerless to edit the outcome. Peter reached out for something to grasp with his right arm as his body bent at the waist with his hand outstretched. He clutched his fist catching nothing but air. Both arms began to flail. He looked down toward the platform and tucked his chin against his upper chest and placed his hands behind his neck in a learned protective maneuver. Due to an instinctive defensive reflex, his legs bent at the knee. His position shifted in midair as he performed a perfect half somersault in his descent, a torturous slow turn to first, parallel to the earth and then upside down.

When Daniel was finally able to respond, it was too late. He launched himself toward Peter without any real plan. The only purpose it served was to give him a close-up view of his brother's impact with the ground. Daniel landed on his stomach inches from the point where the crown of Peter's skull struck the concrete platform, smashing the brain's only protection into a hundred pieces.

While fragments of bone lodged into his parietal and frontal lobe, his neck snapped backward severing the spinal cord at the first vertebrae. Peter was dead before the rest of his body hit the ground.

* * *

Lying awake in his jail cell, Daniel wondered if he were finally paying for the terrible sins he'd committed back when he was a teenager, and all the subsequent mistakes he'd made as a result. Even his tendency toward overachievement could be traced back to Peter's death. It solidified his choice to pursue a career in law enforcement, driving him to dedicate just about every ounce of his energy to putting bad guys behind bars. Maybe it was a subconscious effort to cleanse his soul. At the end of the day, he knew it wasn't enough.

Before everything went wrong, he had taken great strides advancing both his personal and professional lives. Though his marriage was teetering at the edge of a cliff for some time, he and his wife, Deborah, had made a major breakthrough working toward reconciliation. Unlike his father, she was willing to try to forgive him for his previous transgressions. At the office, he was the best agent by far. His progression through the ranks of the FBI was on an unprecedented fast track. He was the youngest agent in the history of the Bureau to be appointed as a Special Agent in Charge of a field office. For his significant contribution to the resolution of several high profile crimes, he received national accolades and achieved worldwide notoriety. He established contacts with major players in Washington D.C. and was described by the Director of the Bureau as its "Golden Boy." Just two weeks before his arrest, he was invited to the White House to be honored by the President of the United States for his contribution to the war on drugs.

All that changed in a horrific twist of fate when he and Deborah decided to accept a gift to sail on the King Luxury Cruise liner, "The Joy of the Seas." The carnage was discovered by Chief Cabin Steward, Co Chi Cuyengkeng, who was having his usual difficulty sleeping that night. During his ritual early morning walk through his team's assigned territory, he found Daniel covered head to toe in blood, stumbling through the halls of the lido deck in a zombie-like trance. It was a massacre that made international news and dubbed Daniel the "Blood Boat Butcher." Charged with three counts of homicide by the very people he had called friends and colleagues, he couldn't deny that all of the physical evidence pointed to him as the killer. Although he was unable to explain his behavior on that infamous morning, even to himself, he was absolutely sure of one thing. He was innocent.

Chapter 2

Two years earlier.

The sun hung low in the western sky, splashing the clouds of the horizon with the spectacular fluorescent colors often seen after an afternoon of perfect weather. FBI Assistant Special Agent in Charge, Daniel Falcone, gazed out the window of his North Miami field office, admiring the stunning sunset as he packed up for the night. It was a beautiful South Florida evening and a fitting end to an amazing day. He would miss the view from this office, but was looking forward to facing the challenge the move to the second floor would bring.

Earlier that morning, the FBI's Assistant Director, Howard Evans, made an unannounced visit to Miami. Thirty minutes after Evan's arrival, Daniel was called to Special Agent in Charge Rick Suarez's office to meet with him and the Assistant Director. Of all the people at the North Miami office, Suarez was no doubt the agent Daniel admired the most. The Special Agent in Charge was more than a boss. He was Daniel's friend and a part of the family. Daniel looked up to him as a father figure; replacing the man he called Dad for most of his life. The head of the Falcone family was never really emotionally available and had all but disowned his firstborn after Peter's accident. It was a hard pill to swallow when Daniel learned that Suarez was diagnosed with lung cancer. What Daniel didn't know was that Rick had handed in his resignation and was planning to retire. Though the doctors had assured the Special Agent in Charge they had removed all the cancer, he felt it was time to turn the reins over to a young, talented agent and enjoy the remainder of his life with his family.

Daniel couldn't imagine why he was being summoned and was somewhat nervous as he turned the corner of the hallway leading to Suarez's office. Daniel knocked twice on the door then proceeded into the room where Richard and the Assistant Director were waiting for him. The S.A.C's large office was on the second floor of the Dade County FBI headquarters. Its rear wall consisted of four floor-to- ceiling bullet-proof, one-way windows with a less than inspirational view of the parking lot and industrial area beyond. There were two government issued chairs facing the large, polished, faux cherry wood desk and a cheap, pleather sofa against the wall opposite the entrance.

Evans was standing next to one of the chairs, extending his hand to Daniel. The Assistant Director was uncommonly tall, at least 6' 6" in Daniel's estimation. Evans towered over him though Daniel was not exactly short at 6'2". The Assistant Director was in decent shape for fifty-four, though he was beginning to show signs of a few extra pounds around the midsection, and was graying at the temples. The remainder of his hair was jet black, which was striking against his sparkling blue-green eyes. After the initial greetings and obligatory conversation, the Assistant Director sat in his chair and suggested that the Special Agent in Charge begin the meeting. He invited Daniel to take the seat next to him while Suarez assumed his position behind the desk.

"If I know you, Daniel, and you know I do, you've been makin' the rounds since the Assistant Director got here trying to find out what's up. Anyway, I'm not gonna keep you guessing. I made a decision a few weeks back that I haven't shared with anyone but my family and Assistant Director Evans. I've decided to step down."

Daniel relaxed for the first time since he was called to his boss's office. He didn't like the idea that Rick was leaving, but he had a feeling some good news was coming his way.

"I'm still gonna be around, not every day of course," Suarez continued. "I've offered my services to act as a consultant to the agent who takes my place. I've given the Assistant Director thirty days notice. As the Assistant Special Agent in Charge of the criminal division, you're next in line for my job. There are just a couple of issues we need to discuss."

Daniel had a good idea what his boss was talking about. It really didn't take rocket science to figure it out. He responded, "Ok, Rick. What's on your mind?"

"For the most part, it was an easy decision choosing you," Suarez explained. "Your work is exemplary and your leadership skills are exceptional for a man your age. We do have some reservations, however. First, your relationship with the media. You've made it pretty clear over the years they're not your favorite people. Telling Clifton Harris over at the *Herald* to shut the fuck up at a public press conference didn't help. Your communication skills with political officials are for shit too…at times, of course, not always. If you take this position, you'll have to work hard on changing your approach. It's imperative you treat members of the press and community leaders with the utmost respect if you're gonna lead an FBI field office."

"You're an outstanding agent, Daniel," Evans took over. "If that was all we needed to consider, we wouldn't be having this conversation. I don't like politicians or the media any better than you do. But, as leaders and representatives of the Bureau, we have rules of decorum. We're taking a bit of a risk offering you this position, considering these issues and your youth. On the other hand, we have confidence you'll work hard to correct it. What are your thoughts?"

Having guessed correctly regarding the topic of the discussion, Daniel already had a response prepared. He had to admit to himself that part of the job would be the most difficult for him. He'd had his share of run-ins with the media and wasn't a favorite of many public officials. Working on not letting them get on his nerves would require a great deal of self-control and discipline as he certainly felt justified about his feelings. He had seen too much corruption in politics and the press thought they were untouchable and above it all.

The seed of mistrust for both factions was planted long before he ever became a law enforcement agent. During his junior year at George Washington University, tragedy turned Daniel's young life upside down for a second time in a matter of five years. His beloved grandmother, who was seventy-five at the time, was run over and killed by a drunk driver while crossing the street. To make matters worse, the case against the guilty party was dismissed due to a legal technicality. Daniel wasn't so sure there weren't some shenanigans involved. The driver happened to be the son of the Mayor of Chicago. For Daniel, it was undeniable that evidence was hidden from the public. There were, suspiciously, no witnesses to an accident that occurred on a summer evening in broad daylight on a major street in Chicago. The Mayor was a media favorite. It was clear the story wasn't going to be given the normal attention worthy of an incident involving a major politician. Daniel took it upon himself to go to great lengths to get the police and the press to conduct a more in-depth investigation. His pleas fell on deaf ears. It became obvious to him there were times when the media wasn't interested in the truth. It was a lesson learned that he never forgot and a breach of justice he refused to forgive up to the present. Perhaps the time had come to put it all behind him, especially if his career depended on it.

"Well, I'll be the first to admit my attitude toward politicians and especially the press isn't great. You guys know I take my job very seriously. My career means everything to me. If you give me this position, I'll do everything in my power to improve my relations with them. You have my word," Daniel replied.

"You're definitely not afraid to call a spade a spade," Suarez added. "It's something that we respect about you, but in this position it can come back to bite you in the ass. Sometimes, you have to bite your fuck'n tongue. You know what I'm talkin' about?"

"I understand. Believe it or not, I do have a filter. I actually know when I'm saying something that's not exactly politically correct before I say it. I can be more discrete. I'll make sure I work hard on it. You know, Rick, better than anyone, when I make a promise, I keep it. I can do this."

"We're gonna take a chance on you, Daniel," replied Assistant Director Evans. "You've done amazing things for the Bureau and I'm sure there's plenty more to come. The position's yours." Both Suarez and the Assistant Director rose to shake Daniel's hand and congratulate him. He was notified that the official ceremony to bestow him with the rank of Special Agent in Charge would be held on Friday, which was only two days away. After Daniel expressed his gratitude and the meeting was coming to a conclusion, Assistant Director Evans turned their attention to one of the criminal division's most publicized cases.

"By the way, have we made any progress on the King Cruise Line honeymoon disappearance? I've been catching some flak from the director himself; he wants this resolved."

"Leland is the lead investigator in that case," Daniel responded. "I'll have to get back to you on the latest, Howard. I know that the cruise line is pushing for us to conclude it was an accident."

"Well, keep an eye on Leland. If at this point we haven't come up with any evidence this was a homicide, we should throw in the towel. Let me know by the end of the week what you hear from him. I've got a plane to D.C. to catch. Daniel, be sure Rick's secretary schedules an appointment for you to come up and meet with me within two weeks of the time Rick leaves." He wished the two men good luck as he rushed out the door.

* * *

On the way back to his office, Daniel was thinking there were going to be a few senior agents moping around the building with bruised egos and ruffled feathers. The promotion wasn't a total shock to the new Special Agent in Charge. Then again, it came a little earlier than expected. There were plenty of agents who could have been considered for the position who had many more years with the Bureau. That wasn't to say he felt he was undeserving of the role; Daniel was confident he was more than capable of judiciously performing its functions. It was his life's ambition to rise to the top of the FBI and he was ahead of schedule. Being the structured, obsessively organized person he had become since his brother's death, his career schedule was being planned when most other boys were preoccupied with fighting acne and chasing skirts.

His dream to work in law enforcement was originally conceived when he was just four years old and living in the home of his grandparents in Chicago. For the first two years of his life, Daniel and his parents lived with his maternal grandparents in the three storey brownstone not far from Grant Park where he would live again later with his brother Peter and the rest of the family. Daniel didn't have many memories of that initial time in his grandparents' home. One thing he could recall with exceptional clarity was the impeccably fitted, blue police uniform his grandfather wore to work every day. The brilliantly shiny silver badge and legion of medals decorating the lapel and shoulders of the jacket never failed to fill him with wonder and awe.

At the time they moved in, Daniel's parents, John and Maria, were recently married. John had just secured a position as night watchman at the Hancock building in downtown Chicago. Finances were tight for the newlywed couple. In order to be in a position to save money to purchase their own home, they decided to live with Maria's mom and dad temporarily. When John finally received a promotion from the security company to a supervisory position, they rented a small apartment near Wrigley Field. Two years later, Maria's father passed away suddenly from a ruptured brain aneurism. Maria's mom, Filomena, who was both devastated and lonely as a result of her husband's death asked John and Maria to move back to the house, offering the top two floors to the Falcone family. John, being a proud man, was initially resistant to the idea of living under his mother-in-law's roof again. Maria ultimately convinced him the move would be better for the family since they now had three young boys, were expecting a fourth, and were living paycheck to paycheck. Daniel's parents would end up living there until they divorced, years after the boys were grown.

Taking advantage of the opportunity of living with her mother, Maria decided to go back to school to become a licensed practical nurse, leaving Filomena the primary caretaker of the boys. Though she kept her feelings secret, Filomena always had a special place in her heart for Daniel and he responded in kind. During those years, they developed a very close relationship. He could still recount the stories she often told him of his grandfather's exploits as first a beat cop, then detective with the Chicago Police Department. What his grandmother always seemed most proud of was her husband's rise through the ranks of the force. Just before he passed away, he was promoted to leader and Captain of Chicago's metropolitan area and Southside. Daniel would never admit it to anyone, but it was his granddad who became his hero and role model. Though he wasn't proud of the fact, Daniel was embarrassed about his father's career and lack of education. Daniel had plans to do much bigger and better things. It was to his grandmother, rather than his dad, who he first announced his intention to become an FBI agent.

Daniel suffered from a severe state of depression for many months after Peter's tragic accident. Even the idea that the police were considering charging him with manslaughter didn't evoke any real emotion. He simply didn't care. Finding the motivation just to get out of bed in the morning was hard enough. His hope for a career in law enforcement became a non-issue. He received no help from his parents. Maria was in a deep depression herself and was of no use to her son. John made Daniel's condition infinitely worse. His father's words would haunt his dreams until the day he died… "You deserve to rot behind bars for the rest of your life. That beer you forced down his throat might as well have been a loaded pistol. You're a fuck'n murderer." Daniel's relationship with his father was irreparably damaged that morning, if not completely destroyed. The few words they spoke to each other when they happened to be in the same room were mechanical, empty, and superficial.

If it hadn't been for the love and support of his grandmother, the path Daniel chose after Peter's death might have been completely different. Daniel could remember the conversation that turned things around for him like it was yesterday. It was four months after Peter died. His parents and his brothers were visiting his grave site on a Saturday afternoon; Daniel wasn't invited. Lying on his bed, contemplating the advantages and disadvantages of living, there was a light knock at his door. He considered telling his grandmother to go away, then changed his mind and invited her in.

"Daniel, I'm gonna tell you a story that's just between you and me, alright?"

"I'm really not in the mood, Gramma. I just want to be by myself."

"I know you're feeling really bad, honey. I want you to listen to what I have to say. You keep on this road, I'm afraid what's gonna happen to you."

"I don't really care."

"Don't you say that, Daniel. You have to forgive yourself. It was an accident. You didn't set out to kill your brother."

"I might as well have. Dad wouldn't agree with you."

"I don't like to say bad things about him to you, sweetie, but your Dad can be a real jerk. He's wrong what he said to you. You're not a criminal. You're not a murderer. You did what millions of kids your age do. I'm not gonna say it was a great idea… It's what teenage boys do. Most of the time, by the grace of God, no one gets hurt. It's not like you decided to get behind the wheel of a car. It was just a horrible accident."

"Is that what you wanted to say?"

"No. I want to tell you a story about your father, just between us. I could throttle him for the way he's treated you. He knows better."

"Ok, Gramma, I don't think I'm gonna get rid of you anyway."

"No you're not. You just have to know we all make bad decisions. I feel bad you're so young and you have to pay so dearly for something most of us have gotten away with, including your dad. He was two years older than you are now when he got damn lucky. It was prom night. Of course, Maria was his date. He was too stubborn to rent a limousine for the night. He had to drive his Mustang his parents bought him for graduation. Spoiled him rotten-didn't have a pot to piss in and went into hock to get their eighteen year-old kid a brand new car and give it to him before he got his diploma. Anyway, he got his older cousin to buy him a bottle of vodka. He had a few drinks before the dance. Went back to the car with his friends a few times and finished off the bottle. Your mom had a drink or two. That's beside the point. John was half-crocked by the end of the night. Definitely had no business driving. They decided to go to some hotel afterwards where some kids were throwing a party. Damn parents, they asked for trouble. Gettin' their kids a hotel room thinkin' it's safer, they won't drive. Stupid, I tell ya. Your mom and dad made it to the party alright. John had a few more drinks…your mom too. Maria was still seventeen, so she had a curfew. I probably was kinda dumb lettin' her stay out as late as I did. They were supposed to be home by two. Of course, time got away from them and before they knew it, it was after two. Your dad thought he was ok to drive. The house was only a mile away. Your mom was drunk enough, she didn't know any better. They didn't make it a hundred yards from the hotel when a police car flipped on its red and blue lights to stop them. John was all over the road. Then he saw the lights and panicked. Instead of stopping, he got the bright idea to try to run. He actually thought he could lose the cop on the way here. To make an already long story short, he crashed into the next door neighbor's house- almost ended up in their living room. He's lucky he didn't kill himself or someone else and even luckier he didn't kill Maria. If your mom did get hurt, he woulda wished he got killed cause he woulda had to deal with your grandpa."

Filomena had Daniel's full attention. He couldn't believe what he was hearing. His mother was a saint and his father was a lawmaker not a rule breaker. Though he would experience significant guilt over his brother's death every single day of his life, Daniel could almost feel a heavy weight lift from his shoulders that day. He asked, "Did Dad go to jail?"

"Actually, he was extremely lucky he happened to commit the crime in your grandpa's jurisdiction. He did spend the night in jail, but charges were never filed. Luckily for John, our neighbors were good friends and were satisfied just to get the insurance company to do the repairs. My Tony did your father a huge favor. He could've have been charged with several felonies. Your mom begged your grandfather to drop the charges. She was already pregnant with you."

This time Daniel's jaw dropped. His whole concept of his parents was changing in a matter of minutes. Noticing his shocked response, Filomena continued, "Now you see why you can't repeat any of this. It's not something that I would ever have told you if it wasn't for what you're going through. I know it's gonna take a long, long time to heal and probably we never will totally. You have to use this experience to make you a better person, Daniel. You're being given the same opportunity your father was given so many years ago. The police chose not to charge you with any crimes.

They know you've suffered enough from Peter's accident. Whatever the reason may be, you're fortunate enough to have a choice. You can still be the FBI agent you always wanted to be. Peter would want it that way. You have an incredible opportunity. Now, are you gonna take it?"

Daniel answered that question in the affirmative and followed his grandmother's advice. He dedicated himself to being the best person he could be in memory of his brother. With a score of 1475 on his S.A.T. and the title of valedictorian of his high school senior class, acceptance to George Washington University in Washington D.C. was just a formality. His penchant for hard work and his innate intelligence rewarded him with a space in the 1996 freshman class at Harvard Law School where he ultimately graduated third in his class. In his final year at Harvard, Daniel didn't have to apply for a position with the FBI. They came to the college to recruit him.

* * *

News travelled like wildfire at the North Miami field office. It didn't take very long before Daniel was being approached by his colleagues to offer their congratulations. There were a total of seven-hundred Special Agents and support personnel at the facility and by 1:00 that afternoon, at least a third had offered their best wishes. With each new well-wisher, Daniel began to realize the magnitude of his accomplishment.

The North Miami field office was founded in October of 1924, as a satellite to the official Florida field office located in Jacksonville. As it became apparent that South Florida had a greater need for FBI presence, a field office was established in Miami in 1937. Since its inception, the North Miami office had been involved in many high profile cases, which included the largest bank fraud embezzlement arrest in FBI history. Daniel would proudly assume the role of the thirty-fourth Special Agent in Charge.

Daniel realized that with all the commotion he forgot to tell his wife his good news. Since he hadn't taken time out for lunch and was ready for a break anyway, he decided to deliver it in person. He advised the squad secretary he would be gone for approximately an hour, and three minutes later, he was behind the wheel of his government-issued 2003 Crown Victoria, bound for home in Hallandale Beach. The traffic on I-95 was unusually light even for that part of the day. Fifteen minutes later, he was unlocking the front door of his three bedroom, two bath condominium. He stepped into the small foyer then climbed the staircase of eight steps that lead to the main living area.

Deborah, who wasn't one to sit still for long, was busy fixing a broken ceiling fan in the boys' upstairs bedroom. She had aspirations of being an important psychologist one day, but her true passion was for fixing things. There wasn't a mechanical device that was beyond her magical powers of mending. Having two young, extremely active sons afforded her the opportunity to practice her reparative talents often enough. Pegging the fan with tennis balls was their most recent handiwork. Totally engrossed in her chore, she didn't hear the closing of the front door or Daniel's footsteps as he climbed the stairs.

If Daniel were to more closely scrutinize his motivations, he would be forced to confess there was a reason why Deborah wasn't the first person to receive news of his promotion. No question, she was one of the most beautiful women he had ever feasted his eyes upon. She was tall- 5'11"- with a long torso and athletic legs. Her hair was chestnut, her eyes the color of the crystal clear waters of the Caribbean Sea. Having a marriage proposal rejected by the love of his life less than a year before he met Deborah, his relationship with her couldn't be described as anything less than rebound. It took a long time for Daniel to admit to himself that was the case and he still didn't like the idea. Nevertheless, that spark for his wife was missing. As he caught a glimpse of her femininely muscled arms and shoulders reaching up toward the ceiling fan, he felt a twinge of familiar guilt. To avoid startling her, he knocked on the door of the bedroom. Despite his effort, Deborah nearly fell off the ladder that was positioned precariously underneath the red, white and blue helicopter propeller fan.

"Shit, Daniel, you scared the hell out of me. What are you doin' home in the middle of the day?"

"Nice greeting. I tried to be subtle."

"I'm sorry. You startled me." She climbed down the ladder and gave her husband a quick smack on the lips. "So, what are you doing here in the middle of the day?"

"I actually have some really good news. I wanted to come home and tell you about it. I've been promoted to Special Agent in Charge."

"Which office? We don't have to move, do we?"

"No, Rick's decided to retire. With the cancer and all, he wants to spend more time with the family. I'll be heading up the North Miami field office."

"Is Rick ok? It hasn't spread, has it?"

"Geez, honey, I thought you'd be a little more excited about this. Rick's fine. He just thought it was time to retire."

"I'm sorry, sweetie. You took me by surprise. This has to be the first time in five years you've come home before eight o'clock at night. I am excited. That's incredible news. I'm really proud of you."

Deborah did her best to be happy for Daniel and hide the fact she was already experiencing some mixed emotions. On the one hand, she was thrilled for her husband, knowing it was a huge accomplishment. Yet, the amount of time he spent at the office was becoming an issue in their marriage, at least for her. Now things were just going to get worse. Expressing those feelings would only serve to minimize his achievement. She decided it probably wasn't the best time to complain and threw her arms around his waist and gave him an extended congratulatory kiss. Daniel wasn't convinced.

"I get the feeling you're upset. What's wrong?"

"Don't be silly, honey. I'm fine and I'm thrilled about your promotion. Maybe now we can afford some new furniture for the dining room. Why don't I make something special for dinner tonight? Anything you want. We can celebrate together. We'll even make it a little romantic, just the two of us."

Daniel squirmed in his dark blue, Calvin Klein suit while picking at the tight collar of his white dress shirt. He knew exactly why Deborah's initial reaction to his promotion wasn't what one would expect. Just the previous night, she was complaining about his late nights at the office and how they rarely sat down as a family to share dinner together. His drinking was another bone of contention. If you asked him, he didn't think it was an issue. Two or three beers in the evening barely gave him a buzz. It could hardly be considered a problem. That didn't make it any easier to tell her he had already committed to going out for a drink with Rick Suarez and a couple of his closest friends at the Bureau.

He said, "That sounds great sweetie, but Rick and the guys are taking me out for a drink after work. I should be home by eight though. Why don't you join us?"

Deborah gave herself a moment before she answered. She knew if she reacted on emotion alone, Daniel's celebration for his promotion would be over. After taking a few seconds to calm herself and carefully consider her options, she chose to leave the drinking issue alone for the time being. She wasn't totally successful.

"Yeah right. Just what I want to do. Sit around and drink with a bunch of FBI agents. Besides, it's too late to get a babysitter and the boys have tennis drills tonight. Don't worry… I'll just wait for you to get home."

"You sure, honey? This is a special occasion. The boys can miss practice for one night. We can get your parents to watch them. I'd love to have you there." Daniel was pretty sure his attempt to make nice was going to be rejected. He was starting to regret coming home. There were certainly times she could be high maintenance. When she was like this, it was probably best just to listen and not say too much. He'd make it up to her later tonight.

"No thanks, I'll pass," she said.

"Well we can still have that dinner. I'll make sure I'm home before eight. I promise."

For a split second, Deborah considered not accepting that offer either, but instantly righted herself, feeling guilty she had already thrown enough of a dark cloud over his achievement. Continuing her efforts to exercise self-control she replied, "You go ahead and have fun. We'll celebrate when you get home."

"You sure honey? I can cancel with the guys. We can reschedule for tomorrow."

"No, don't worry about it. I'll make dinner for the boys before you get home. I'll be fine." Daniel figured it was best to not belabor the subject so he agreed to Deborah's plan.

Deborah inquired, "By the way, how did Leland take the news?"

"I have to give it to him. He was actually very polite and cordial."

"I'm sure he was. Now you really control his destiny."

Special Agent Robert Leland was one of Daniel's top agents in the criminal division. Deborah hadn't trusted him from the moment she met him. He was ambitious and made no bones about his interest in becoming the Assistant Special Agent in Charge of the criminal division back when Daniel was being considered. Leland didn't take the news well that he had been passed over. He was pleasant enough, but for Deborah, he was a fake.

Deborah was sure that Leland was responsible for some bad press directed toward Daniel when he was up for the Assistant

Special Agent in Charge promotion. Daniel and Leland were working together on a task force to eradicate gang activity in South Florida's tri-county area. After the arrest by the task force of a major leader of the Latin Kings, an article was printed in the *Miami Herald* by their senior journalist in the crimes division, Clifton Harris. Just before the story was released, Deborah went to Leland's home to return a book she had borrowed from his wife. As she pulled onto the cul de sac where the Lelands resided, she passed a silver Cherokee Jeep Wrangler. Having met Clifton Harris on several previous occasions, she could have sworn it was him driving the Jeep. At the time, she didn't really think twice about it. But, when the article came out several days later, she became very suspicious. It alleged that Daniel had been receiving protection money for years from the Hispanic gang. Direct quotes from the Latin Kings leader implicated Daniel in taking bribes in return for turning a blind eye to the gang's lucrative drug trafficking operations.

Deborah immediately notified Daniel of her suspicions. She even researched the type of vehicle Harris drove and had a match. Two days later, the gang leader was stabbed to death by a rival gang member inside the Dade County Jail. Since Daniel denied all allegations of wrongdoing and the gang leader was no longer around to verify his claims, the story fizzled out. A renowned and decorated federal agent's word against that of a deceased life-long criminal with a ten-page rap sheet wasn't much of a contest. Eventually, the *Herald* agreed to retract their support for the story. It didn't, however, quell Deborah's distrust for Leland. Though Daniel listened to what she had to say, he didn't seem to heed her advice when he made Leland his right hand man and supervisor overseeing the criminal division. Deborah hoped Daniel was just following the old adage, "Keep your friends close and your enemies closer." Now that Daniel was Special Agent in Charge, Leland would have to rely on Daniel even more to further his agenda.

"We've been discussing who's going to take my place as Assistant Special Agent in Charge of the criminal division and Leland is on the short list."

"You sure that's a good idea, Daniel? You know I just don't trust the man."

"Yes, I'm sure. One thing you can't take away from Robert is that he's an excellent detective and a hard worker. I've pretty much decided the position's his. I know how you feel about him.

And I'm not saying you're not right. Don't worry. I'll be keeping a close eye on him."

"I'll just have to trust you know what you're doing," said Deborah rolling her eyes.

Daniel took a glance at his watch, disappointed the visit didn't go as well as expected. If he had thought about it for a minute, he probably could have predicted Deborah's response. A more involved conversation about his career was going to be necessary, but now wasn't the time. "Shit, it's getting late. I gotta get back to the office," he said.

"Ok. Congratulations again, sweetie. I really am proud of you."

"Thanks, honey. I know you are. I'll see you around eight." Daniel kissed his wife, they exchanged I love yous, and he was out the door.

* * *

A minute after Daniel's departure, Deborah regretted the way she had behaved. He had been very clear from day one of their relationship about his dream to be an FBI leader. She was aware his career goals would require hard work and long hours at the office when she decided to marry him. Complaining would get her nowhere except maybe in divorce court. Her attitude about his job just wasn't fair. She dropped the screwdriver onto the bed and grabbed her cell phone from her pocket. In the middle of dialing his number to apologize, she pushed the end button. Rather than use words to express her regret, she would show him tonight by fixing his favorite meal and serving it by candlelight. Her regret was flowing full force now and she was well aware of the reason for it. She had spent years in therapy in search of resolution.

Throughout Deborah's childhood, she was plagued with weight problems. That combined with her well above average height made for a painfully shy pre-adolescence. Her poor self-image was magnified by amblyopia or lazy eye, which required that she wear glasses with Coke bottle lenses. She was an only child and had no real friends except for those naturally bestowed upon her such as her cousins on her mother's side of the family and the girl who lived across the street, Ally Schnyder. Deborah's and Ally's mothers were best friends and spent a good part of the day together. Ally was more like a family member than a friend or neighbor. During elementary school and most of middle school, though the two girls made somewhat of an odd couple, they were inseparable.

Deborah was the smart, fat girl while Ally was beautiful, athletic and popular. Fortunately for Deborah, it only took puberty to resolve her appearance issues. In the summer between eighth and ninth grade, she shed every ounce of baby fat, went from a training bra to a C cup and traded in her glasses for contact lenses. It seemed like overnight their roles had reversed. While Deborah blossomed from an ugly duckling to a beautiful swan, Ally began to put on weight and become withdrawn.

Initially, the newly discovered popularity had no effect on their relationship. For a while, the girls continued to spend most of their free time together, though Deborah noticed a distinct change in Ally's personality. Eventually, Ally started making excuses any time Deborah invited her over to the house to hang out. Confused and hurt, Deborah set out to find out what was up. Her efforts to pump mutual friends at their school for information resulted in a discovery that Deborah would have never imagined. Ally was seeing a boy who was a notorious drug addict. Even worse, she had become sexually active and was experimenting with drugs. When Deborah confronted Ally with the rumor, Ally admitted that not only was she using valium, she and her boyfriend were drinking alcohol on a daily basis. Deborah pleaded with her to end her relationship and to stop taking drugs but her appeal fell on deaf ears. The only thing Deborah could think to do, at that point, was to cut off all ties. It wasn't an easy decision, but she hoped it would bring Ally to her senses. She gave Ally a choice between her friendship or the boy and the drugs. Deborah came out on the losing end in a way she could never have anticipated or imagined. She could remember the night Ally died like it was yesterday.

* * *

Deborah had just received her final ninth grade report card. Not surprisingly, she had received straight A's and like always, her mom and dad, Kate and Jack Tyler, were thrilled.

"You take after your mom," said Kate, the same comment Deborah had been hearing for years every time she came home with a great report card. "You get to pick any restaurant for dinner tonight. Money's no object," she continued, the reward being another typical tradition in the Tyler household.

"I want pizza."

"Big surprise," quipped Kate. The apple didn't fall far from the tree. It was pizza just about every six weeks. "What's with the frown?"

"This'll be the first report card celebration without Ally."

"I'm sorry, honey. You did the right thing. You're being a good friend. She'll eventually come around."

"I hope. I'm really worried about her. You know, yesterday I decided to check out that creep she's seeing. I looked him up on the computer. He's been arrested six times for drug charges. A lot of them are still pending, but he has three convictions. I think he's spent time in jail."

"He's a dirt bag. I don't know what her parents are thinking. I'd keep her locked up in her room for a year."

"Right Mom. That would work."

"You know what I mean. They need to do something drastic and soon, yesterday, in fact."

"I just wish there was something I could do."

"It's not up to you, honey. That's her parents' job. So, wipe that frown off your face. She'll be alright. You'll see. Next week you guys'll be best of friends again. Now, go get your father. It's time for a celebration."

Deborah tried her best to put Ally out of her mind for the evening without great success. Telling her closest friend she couldn't hang out with her anymore hurt Deborah just as much or more than Ally. It had only been a few days since the conversation. The wound was too recent. All Deborah could manage was one slice of pepperoni pizza from her favorite Italian restaurant in all of Baltimore. On the way home, Kate continued her attempts to cheer her daughter up. It was starting to annoy Deborah rather than improve the situation.

"Mom, enough. I'll be okay. It's just all new. Going out without her tonight didn't help."

"Alright, sweetie. I was just sayin. You can't let someone else's problems take away from your accomplishments. But, I'll shut up now…What are those lights up there, Jack?"

The Tylers lived on a street that was more than a half a mile long. They had just turned onto their road when Kate noticed the flashing lights of police cars and what looked to be an ambulance.

"Something's goin on," replied Jack. "It looks like it could be near our house, across the street maybe."

Deborah instantly perked up in the back seat. She leaned toward the middle to be able to see through the front windshield.

"That looks like Ally's house," she said.

The closer they got the more obvious it became that the emergency vehicles were at the Schnyder home. When they pulled up along the curb beside their house, they saw Mr. Schnyder sitting on the sidewalk holding his head in his hands. Mrs. Schnyder was in her driveway in hysterics and being held back by a police officer and two EMTs. Jack didn't bother to park the car in the driveway. As soon as he stopped beside the curb, Kate jumped out and ran over to her friend, Terry Schnyder.

"Terry, My God. What's going on?" Kate almost shouted in her excited state.

"Ally's dead," Terry screamed.

By that time, Deborah was at the foot of the Schnyders' driveway. For several seconds, her mind rejected what her ears had heard. "What?" she shrieked. "What? No, no way. Where is she?"

Terry Schnyder reverted to crazed, incomprehensible muttering. Deborah calmly approached Ally's dad, a man whom she considered a second father. "Mr. Schnyder, what's going on? Where's Ally?"

Mr. Schnyder, without looking up, responded in an even tone seemingly barren of any emotion. "It's true, Deborah. She's dead. It was an overdose. She took a whole bottle of pain pills. She didn't go to school today. She was home alone all day. They said she's been dead since early this afternoon."

Deborah collapsed to the ground next to Ally's dad. The tears began to flow freely. After several minutes, she put her arms around Mr. Schnyder and tried to hold him. Uncharacteristically, he pushed her away.

Deborah would find out just several hours later why her best friend took her own life. Unable to sleep as it approached midnight, she couldn't help obsessing over the potential reasons. Earlier in the evening, a Baltimore Police Department detective had paid the Tyler's a visit. It quickly became clear he was looking for a suicide note. Deborah had told him she hadn't received any correspondence from Ally. Now, as she lie awake, slumber a laughable objective, an idea occurred to her. She jumped out of her bed, carefully made her way through the pitch black house toward the front door and opened it. Just to the right of the door attached at shoulder level to the house's façade was the family mailbox, the vessel of many a clandestine communication between the best friends. She reached inside with her right hand and extracted an envelope with her name written in Ally's unmistakable cursive. Deborah switched on the porch light and read. By the time she finished, violent sobs ravaged her body. She vomited half-digested pizza onto the greeting mat.

The letter explained that Ally was being molested by her father since she was eleven years old. She saw death as her only path to freedom. Deborah felt like her heart couldn't hurt anymore without bursting to bits when she read Ally's apology for destroying their friendship. Her words couldn't be more untrue. Deborah was convinced she was the cause of it all. The signs were there as plain as the nose on her face. Afterwards, she withdrew into an impenetrable cocoon. For weeks, it was all her parents could do just to get her to come out of her bedroom. Much later, through therapy, Deborah learned that the tragedy had destroyed her ability to trust the opposite sex. The realization that Mr. Schnyder, a man she truly loved, could commit such a horrendous act, blasted at the very foundation of her belief system. Many boys were interested in her over her four years of high school. The few she decided to date never lasted more than a few days. Any attempt at physical contact, even a simple kiss, and the relationship was doomed.

If Ally's death wasn't enough to plant a seed of distrust in men, the revelation of her father's extra-marital affair in Deborah's senior year in high school certainly sealed the deal. Prior to Jack Tyler's indiscretion, the man could do no wrong in his daughter's eyes. Her mother was able to forgive him long before Deborah finally put it behind her and then only with the assistance of her therapist. If there was one thing she should have learned from her sessions with her counselor, it was the injustice of punishing the men in her life for the transgressions of men in her past.

Deborah decided that tonight she would do whatever she could to make up for her lack of excitement about Daniel's announcement. As she picked up her tools to continue her repairs of the ceiling fan, she thought about how her mom always said the best way to a man's heart was through his stomach. She knew just what she was going to cook up later and it was going to involve much more than just a meal.

Chapter 3

In the final quarter of 2003, King Cruise Line had become the largest and most profitable cruise company on the planet and the parent company of six major cruise lines. Its fleet of over seventy luxury ships sailed all five oceans and visited the seven continents of the world. Its net worth was the sum of the gross national product of several medium-sized countries. It employed over one hundred thousand people from more than seventy-five nations. Over the last decade and a half, the cruise line industry and King Cruise Line, in particular, had become a powerful international political force.

Their corporate headquarters were located in the 110 Tower in downtown Ft. Lauderdale, where they occupied three floors. Annie Bryan was fighting traffic on Broward Blvd. as she headed to work at King. She used the rearview mirror to refresh her lipstick while stopped at a red light that had already gone through its cycle three times. She fumbled in her purse for her cell phone so she could warn her secretary, Rachel Bloom, she was going to be late, and took advantage of the delay to collect her thoughts about the Anderson case. She was hoping to once and for all convince Special Agent Robert Leland to close the file and classify the incident as a tragic accident.

Though Annie's official title with King Cruise Line was Director of Security and Press Liaison, her functions were many. Besides being the filter for any information released to the media, she was responsible for all communications and operations with the United States and foreign governments. She was the Vice President of security and the liaison between the cruise line and all policing agencies around the world. She was the undisputed best at her profession.

The Anderson file had become a thorn in her side. Most, if not the great majority of the public was unaware that deaths occurred on cruise ships on a fairly frequent basis. This could be attributed in great part to Annie's excellence at her job. On the average, there were ten-to-twelve deaths a month on King Cruise Line's ships. Before every cruise, a calculation was made regarding how many body bags were to be stored in the medical department. The number varied depending on the length of the cruise and the average age of the passengers. Many of the fatalities were attributable to natural causes. On the other hand, too many, in Annie's opinion, were of a suspicious nature. The great majority of the dubious kind was the result of losing passengers overboard. Most of those cases were deemed either suicides or accidents. On rare occasions, a death on a cruise ship was ruled a homicide. The Anderson incident was unfortunately for Annie and her company, not so easy to call.

* * *

Paul and Alyssa Anderson were married in Hicksville, Long Island the week after New York was struck by its worst blizzard in twenty years. Their timing couldn't have been better to temporarily escape the miserable Northeast winter. For their honeymoon, they had chosen a ten-day Caribbean cruise on the King Diamond. Upon boarding the ship on a balmy Ft. Lauderdale Sunday afternoon, they dropped their carry-on bags in their balcony cabin and headed directly for the Seafarer's lounge located on the Promenade deck. Amongst her friends and family, Alyssa was renowned for her passion for partying. She wasn't planning on being sober for much of the cruise. Paul rarely drank alcohol, but promised his new wife he wouldn't be a party pooper. For the next nine days, the newlyweds had the time of their lives.

The ship visited seven ports of call along its voyage, with two full days at sea. The weather couldn't have been better; the service was fit for royalty. Paul's parents purchased the bride and groom a week's worth of spa treatments, which included their choice of massages, acupuncture, facials, scrubs, or body wraps. The food was plentiful and delicious. Alcohol was available twenty-four hours a day. Paul and Alyssa met several other couples their age, with whom they caroused on the ship until the wee hours of the morning and participated in land excursions. The newlyweds couldn't have been happier with their choice of honeymoon. At least that was the case until the night before the ship was scheduled to return to Port Everglades.

* * *

The penultimate day of the cruise began quite normally. Paul and Alyssa enjoyed breakfast on their cabin balcony. An ocean spray, the cloudless sky, and the fresh fragrance of the sea air were the perfect romantic setting for the beginning of their final full day of the vacation. Paul fed Alyssa a strawberry. One thing led to another and before they made it halfway through the meal, they ended up making love on the floor of the cabin beside the open sliding glass doors of the balcony. Afterwards, they made a bee-line to the Polynesian spa and spent the remainder of the day at the pool, perfecting their tans.

Having plans to join their friends for drinks later that evening, they decided to have the last dinner on their own. Before the first course was served, Alyssa was on her third cocktail, counting the one she had in the cabin as they prepared for their evening meal. The drink tally didn't include the two Manhattans she downed at the pool earlier in the afternoon. Paul knew his wife well. Based on numerous prior experiences, he figured the odds were great she would drink heavily that night, so he thought it best to limit his consumption of alcohol. By the time they joined their friends at the Seafarer's lounge at 10:30pm, Alyssa was on her way to a major bender.

Their friends weren't in much better shape. Consequently, when the ship personnel and FBI agents interviewed them after Paul's disappearance, they couldn't contribute much helpful information. By two o'clock in the morning, Paul was the only member of the group capable of walking a straight line. He suggested to everyone that they retire to their respective cabins for the night and meet in the morning in the atrium to say their goodbyes. They wished each other goodnight and went their separate ways.

Alyssa was so completely snockered that Paul had to assist her to their cabin. Since the halls were essentially deserted at that time of the morning, there were no witnesses who reported seeing them after they left the lounge. In fact, neither of them was seen until five hours later when deckhand, James Price, found Alyssa passed out on a lounge chair at poolside. There was blood in her hair and on the right sleeve of her blouse. James attempted to arouse her several times without success. Following ship protocol, he immediately called security on his portable phone.

Chief of Security, Landon Jenkins, arrived at the scene within minutes, accompanied by the ship physician, Dr. Frank Gunther, who did a precursory examination of her body, finding no obvious anomaly. As he was calling for a stretcher, Alyssa began to stir. When she was awake enough to speak, the doctor asked her several questions about her condition. Based on her responses, he concluded that she hadn't suffered physical injury. She had no memory beyond leaving the Seafarer's Lounge earlier that morning and couldn't explain the presence of the blood. Worried for her husband, Alyssa asked the doctor and Chief of Security to escort her to her cabin. There was no reasonable explanation she could fathom for why her husband would have abandoned her at the pool, alone and unconscious.

The cabin was on the same level as the pool. In less than five minutes, the group had arrived at its door. Alyssa unlocked it with her key card, allowing Chief Jenkins to enter first and then Dr. Gunther. She followed closely behind. There was a bathroom and closet area to the immediate left. The bathroom door was ajar. Chief Jenkins poked his head inside and found no one and nothing unusual or out of place. Beyond the closet, two twin beds were set side by side to create one queen-size. It appeared as if no one had slept in it that night, although the bedspread was somewhat ruffled. On the far side of the bed, there was a night stand and desk, and then sliding glass doors leading to the balcony. As Chief Jenkins proceeded through the room toward the balcony, he noticed the carpet in front of the desk was soaked through with a dark red, liquid substance. He held his hand up to stop Dr. Gunther and Alyssa from moving forward. The coppery odor that had just assaulted his sense of smell instantly convinced him it was blood. The sliding glass doors were open and a blood trail lead from the carpet to the edge of the balcony. From where he stood, he could see four bloody footprints on the blue rubberized carpet of the balcony, advancing from the cabin to the rail's edge. His first instinct was to order Dr. Gunther to remove Alyssa from the room and secure a crime scene. Alyssa refused to leave the cabin and demanded an explanation. The doctor placed an arm around her waist to assist her out the door, but she released herself from his grip, ran to the other side of the bed and caught sight of the gory spectacle. She promptly passed out in a heap into Chief Jenkins' arms.

Dr. Gunther would need that stretcher after all. He called his medical staff and Alyssa was transported to the infirmary. By that time, the hallway had drawn a crowd of onlookers. Chief Jenkins called his people for back-up and announced to those gathered that the area was being evacuated. The curious spectators reluctantly dispersed, while Jenkins closed the door to the cabin and placed two strips of quarantine tape across the threshold, diagonally from top to bottom to form an X.

Since they were currently in United States' waters, the FBI would have jurisdiction over any potential capital crimes committed onboard the vessel. Before he made a single report to a governmental agency, pursuant to company protocol, he'd conduct a thorough search for Paul Anderson and call Annie Bryan at headquarters.

* * *

Annie finally arrived at the office just five minutes before her scheduled meeting with Agent Leland. Paul Anderson's parents were making a lot of noise and on the edge of accusing King of failure to provide proper security. This incident had to be put to rest and classified as a tragic accident over which the ship's staff had no control. Her argument to Leland needed to be convincing.

Knowledge of the file wasn't the problem. Annie had read it more times than she cared to remember and knew exactly how she would structure her presentation. She had assigned her best security personnel to investigate the Anderson incident and neither they nor the FBI could come to any reasonably solid conclusions as to what took place the night Paul Anderson disappeared. There were several alternative theories, none of which could be substantiated by hard evidence. Unfortunately for the investigation, but perhaps best for the cruise line, the body was never recovered, meaning no autopsy results were available.

Entering her building, Annie was able to catch an elevator at the normally busy 110 Tower with relative ease. She took it to the 17th floor, where her office was located. As she passed her secretary's desk, Rachel notified Annie that Special Agent Leland was already waiting for her in the 15th floor reception area. Annie instructed Rachel to have Leland escorted to the conference room, where she would meet him in five minutes. She hurried into her office and checked herself quickly in her private restroom mirror to make sure everything was in place. She was an impeccable dresser. This morning, she was wearing a Cavalli tuxedo-inspired black pant suit with Prada black patent leather pumps. She was stunningly beautiful and the suit accentuated the curves of her tightly muscled body in a very tasteful way. Satisfied with her appearance, she returned to her office, grabbed the Anderson file from her custom-made Huntington exotic wood desk, and headed straight to the conference room.

When Annie opened the double doors, Agent Leland was staring out the wall of windows on the far side of the rectangular-shaped room, with his back to her. His broad shoulders covering the width of one of the large glass panes and his short stature gave him a Boris Badenov look. The only items missing were a pencil-thin moustache, a fedora and a tall, slender sidekick named Natasha. Leland was in his late forties, yet his full head of hair was devoid of gray. Annie was pretty sure he dyed it. She was of the opinion that the man suffered from a Napoleon complex. His ego was twice the size he was and he paid great attention to his appearance. For a man, he was a good dresser and rarely did one find a hair on his head out of place. The sound of the doors opening alerted him to Annie's presence.

"Good morning, Ms. Bryan. It's good to see you again." They shook hands. Leland was always surprised by the strength of her grip. He could tell she was in excellent shape and most likely exercised regularly. Still, she couldn't be more than 5'5" and one-hundred ten pounds soaking wet. He fantasized about what a tiger she would be in bed. With Annie, that could be a mistake, especially if she had something that he wanted.

Though Annie had every intention of taking advantage of this meeting to pursue her company's agenda, it was Leland who requested they get together. "Good morning Agent Leland, have a seat. How can I help you?" Annie sat in the chair at the head of the table and motioned for Leland to take the seat to her right.

"I was wondering if your investigative team has come up with anything new. I have to tell you, I'm not comfortable closing this case. I was also hoping I could get a copy of your file."

Annie had to be careful about the way she responded to Leland's request. As a matter of official Bureau procedure, it was the investigating agent's ultimate decision to close a homicide investigation when there was a lack of evidence to prove a crime was committed. She didn't want to risk pissing Leland off by refusing to turn over King's file. He was enough of an egomaniacal ass to let such a thing affect his judgment. On the other hand, there was no way she was going to allow him access to private corporate records. She hoped the firm but pleasant approach might help. She wanted to maintain a good relationship with Leland since she had a feeling he was going places at the FBI. Annie had many connections in the political world, including the Director of the FBI himself. She had already attempted to apply some pressure on the powers that be within the Bureau to wind up the Anderson case. The easiest and most convenient way to get what she wanted was to just persuade Leland to drop the investigation.

"Agent Leland, if I could I would hand over everything we have, but my hands are tied. I'm sure you know our corporate file is protected by the work product privilege. I'd be unemployed if I gave it to you but I will answer any questions you might have. As far as updates, we have nothing new. We've concluded this was a tragic accident and I think we've provided your office with a summary of our report."

"You're an intelligent woman, Ms. Bryan. There's no way in hell you can convince me you're completely at peace with the accident theory. The amount of blood in that cabin was consistent with an injury to the jugular vein or carotid artery. It's a humungous stretch to believe he accidentally slit his throat. It's ridiculous, actually. And there's no way it's just a coincidence that the surveillance tapes on the ship malfunctioned right at the time we believe the incident happened."

"What I believe or am at peace with is irrelevant. I'm sticking with the law and the facts. And neither one is on your side if you're trying to prove Paul Anderson was murdered." Annie decided it was time to apply some of the skills she'd learned in law school to bring her argument home. This was when two years on Harvard Law School's moot court came in handy. Cite the facts and apply them to the law, employing a clear and concise line of reasoning. Taking advantage of the sentiments of the victim's family could also be useful.

She continued. "Both your experts and ours agree it was entirely possible the amount of blood was also consistent with an injury to the radial or ulnar artery of the arm. We know Mr. Anderson and his party were drinking heavily that evening. There's strong evidence he was using a pair of scissors to cut one of our coupons from the "Diamond Daily" when the accident occurred. His blood was found on the scissors and the coupon, which was partially cut. We know Mr. Anderson fell based on the analysis of our forensic experts. It just takes common sense to come up with the rest. In his inebriated state, he fell on those scissors and lacerated either the radial or ulnar artery at the inside of the elbow."

Annie wasn't citing any facts Leland didn't already know. She was hoping that hammering on the weaknesses of the case one after another would have its desired effect. There was no question she had his full attention. She could almost detect a defeated look in his eyes. It was time to close. "The bloody footprints on the balcony were Mr. Anderson's. Considering the major blood loss and the effects of the alcohol, he had to be delirious. He staggered onto the balcony, lost his balance, and fell over the railing. We haven't found any suspicious fingerprints in his cabin, nor have we identified any particular motive why anyone would want to murder him. As far as the surveillance tapes, the security officer manning the control room admitted it was possible he accidentally shut the recorder off. The FBI and the King team conducted an exhaustive investigation. These were some of the most talented forensics experts in the world. Regardless of how you or I feel, it's time to put this case to rest. The family deserves closure."

"I don't agree. I can't get rid of the nagging feeling we're missing something. We know Mr. Anderson wasn't much of a drinker. Records from the ship and witness statements confirm that every other day of the cruise he was the only one in his group who controlled his alcohol intake. Unfortunately, we have no idea how much he drank on the night he disappeared, since his wife and friends were all too wasted to remember. And we're still missing a statement from one of the crew members of the Diamond who seems to have conveniently disappeared. Have you been able to locate him?"

"I get what you're saying, Agent Leland, but that doesn't make a case for murder. No, we haven't found Damien Drysdale, but crew members disappear every day. He's not a United States citizen, so the chances of finding him decrease significantly. We gave you his HR file. You guys have much better resources for finding him. In the end, I don't think it matters. We can't legally prove a crime was committed."

Leland wasn't about to give up on getting the corporate file that easily. His gut was telling him there was foul play. He knew the cruise line conducted extensive interviews with all employees on the ship. He had done the same, but sometimes employees were more willing to give up information to their employer than a law enforcement agent investigating a murder. He said, "I'd still like to get a hold of that file. You never know. It could help both of us. If you guys are so sure this was an accident, maybe there'll be something in there that'll convince me to close the case."

"I'm sorry Agent Leland, but there's no way I can release the file. Again, I'm willing to answer any questions you have and produce any witnesses we have control over. Beyond that, I can't help you."

"I would've hoped for a little bit more cooperation from you people. We're talking about a devastated young widow and a mother and father who lost their only son. I think they deserve justice."

"I don't disagree with you. But both our organizations have been over this with a fine tooth comb. There comes a time when you have to realize the evidence isn't there to prove your case in a court of law. What the family really needs is to be able to move on. If you keep this file open, it'll just prevent them from being able to work through their grief."

"I see I'm getting nowhere here. I have to say I'm disappointed. I'm on the fence about this. I'm gonna take my time. When we make a decision, I'll have the squad secretary contact you."

Annie didn't believe him for a second. She had a special knack for reading body language. She was fairly certain he was just being stubborn and had every intention of closing the case sometime in the near future. Out of spite, he could delay it a week or two. That was all fine and good. In the end, her company would be satisfied with the result. Besides, she knew the people above him would be pushing for a quick resolution. She thought it best to change the subject at that point. "By the way, how's Daniel Falcone? It's been a while since I've spoken to him. I'm sure I told you we went to college together."

"Daniel is actually doing great. Just yesterday he was promoted to Special Agent in Charge of the North Miami office."

The jealousy in Leland's voice was palpable. Evidently, she'd chosen the wrong subject. She'd leave that one alone. "I hope Special Agent in Charge Suarez is ok?"

"He's doing fine. From what I understand, he's cancer-free. He decided to spend more time with the family."

"Well good for him. Give him my regards, if you will."

"I'll do that. Since there's nothing else I can do here, I should be on my way."

Leland rejected Annie's offer to walk him to the elevators and made his way out of the office.

***

During his return trip to North Miami, Leland couldn't stop rehashing thoughts of his most recent conversations with Alyssa

Anderson. He'd deliberately left out the content of those talks at the meeting. It made no sense to him that Alyssa was found at poolside with bloodstains in her hair and on her clothes. It would follow that she was in the cabin when her husband was injured. The cruise line's theory purported that Paul was cut by the scissors then Alyssa, in her drunken stupor, went to get help, got lost and never made it to the purser's desk. That argument didn't compute. Common sense told Leland that Alyssa's first instinct would have been to pick up the phone to call for assistance. Yet, he had to admit to himself that drunk people didn't exercise the best of judgment and perhaps initially neither she nor Paul were aware of the gravity of the injury.

Alyssa had related to him a recurring nightmare she was having several times a night. She dreamed she was being carried through the hallways of the ship by a man dressed in a King Cruise Line uniform. Robert asked her if she had any conscious recollection of such an event. Alyssa was forced to confess she still had no memory of anything that happened that evening, past their time at the Seafarer's Lounge. Without invitation, the words of Annie Bryan invaded his contemplation as if responding to the dream. But that didn't make a case for murder.

* * *

As soon as she sat down behind her desk, Annie picked up the phone and dialed Daniel's cellular number. He answered on the second ring.

"Annie Bryan. To what do I owe the honor?"

"I think you know exactly why I'm calling. You're not a Special Agent in Charge of a major FBI field office for nothing. Congratulations, Daniel. I have to say, I'm not surprised."

"Thank you. I was. I wasn't expecting Rick to retire. I don't have the greatest track record when it comes to communication skills either. You know that as well as anyone. Can't say I'm not ecstatic though. I'm sure you must have gotten the scoop from Leland. How did the meeting go this morning?"

"I'm not a hundred percent sure. He seemed pretty peeved I wouldn't give him my file. He kinda threatened to keep the case open for a while longer. I'm pretty sure he was just bluffing. You never know with him. I'm a little bit worried he's letting his personal feelings get in the way. I know he's been speaking fairly often with Alyssa Anderson. We keep an eye on those things.

There's just not enough evidence to prove Paul Anderson was murdered. I think he knows that just as well as I do. I'm hoping he closes this case sometime soon for the sake of the family."

Daniel was thinking she would probably soon get her wish based on his recent conversation with Howard Evans. He said, "I'm sure Leland will take a look at everything and make the right decision. He's a good agent and a smart man."

"That's a perfect place to move on then. What are you doing next week? I want to have you over for dinner."

Daniel started to fidget in his seat. If he were to be perfectly honest with himself, the idea of going to Annie's apartment for dinner was extremely enticing. In fact, the thought caused a stirring between his legs. His face turned three different shades of red before the guilt set in. He abruptly stood up and paced around his office then responded after an awkwardly long pause. "Annie, I couldn't do that. I don't think it would be appropriate."

"Daniel, we've been friends forever. I can't invite you to my apartment for dinner? I don't see the problem. Does she have you on that tight a leash?"

"Come on. You know it wouldn't be cool. We almost got married."

"That's ancient history."

"Right, Annie. That really makes a difference."

"Alright, Alright then, how about lunch at a public place? There's nothing wrong with that. I want to celebrate your accomplishment with you. It's my treat. Or would that put her nose out of joint too?"

"I don't know. Deborah has issues with us. She worries I chose her on the rebound. I don't want to cause any problems."

"You don't have to give her a detailed account of everything you do. What she doesn't know won't hurt her. This is perfectly innocent. C'mon, what day is good for you?"

Daniel always had a difficult time saying no to Annie. Parts of his body were urging him to say yes, while his head and morals were shouting no. If it weren't for Deborah's insecurities, his response would have been quick and easy. There was no question Annie still held a very special place in his heart. She was his first true love. In the end, it was his overactive sense of guilt that dominated. He'd be beating himself up afterwards if he were to accept.

"I'm gonna have to pass. I usually have a hard time getting out of the office for lunch anyway. Let's get together when Deborah can be a part of it, too."

Annie decided to leave the absurdity of that comment alone. There wasn't much of a chance Deborah would agree to do anything if Annie were a part of it. It was pretty clear to Annie that Deborah didn't like her from the first time they'd met at Daniel's last birthday party. For now, she would let him off the hook.

"Alright. Well congratulations anyway. It was a promotion well-deserved. If you change your mind about lunch, let me know."

"Sure thing, Annie. Thanks for the offer."

When Annie hung up the phone, she was a little flushed in the face and felt a hot tingle from head to toe. It seemed to happen just about every time she spoke to Daniel lately and it annoyed her to no end. For five years, he was hers. It was she who rejected his marriage proposal. Now eight years later, he was married, had two kids and she badly wanted what she couldn't have. She had no business pursuing him, whether her reasons were just sexual in nature or something deeper. On the surface, she couldn't even decide exactly what she was feeling. She had no real desire to explore her motives either. She was pretty sure she wouldn't like what she found.

Like Daniel, Annie had a plan for her life at a very young age. Being a child of mixed race, she was the victim of young children's cruelty and flat out prejudice. It wasn't exactly a great environment for developing a healthy self-esteem. This was especially true since some of the offenders were members of her own family. Instead of wallowing in self-pity, she'd used those experiences to make herself a better person. She certainly had the tools to accomplish her goals as she was gifted with exceptional intelligence and born into a family of practically limitless wealth.

Her father, Walter Bryan, was of African American descent. Her mother, Cassie, couldn't be whiter. She was born and raised in Dublin, Ireland. They met in Boston in the early 1960s while working on the presidential campaign to elect John F. Kennedy. It was Walter's side of the family that was affluent. He was one of three grandchildren who inherited his grandfather's multi-billion dollar estate.

Annie's great-grandfather made his fortune in the automobile industry. A talented and savvy businessman, he got his start when he opened a used car lot on Cambridge Street in Boston.

Unlike the typical used car salesman, his emphasis was on honesty and customer service. One lot soon turned into two, and then three. Within seven years, he opened a new car sales center which was ultimately expanded to a second location in Logan County. His business ventures didn't stop there. After making his first million, he began to invest in real estate and acquired full or partial ownership of several major commercial centers and high rise buildings in downtown Boston. By the time he passed away at the ripe old age of ninety-eight, he had accumulated a net worth in excess of three billion dollars and was considered one of the wealthiest black men in America.

Annie had no recollection of her father. He died suddenly and unexpectedly of a massive heart attack when she was just eight months old. Growing up, most of Annie's relatives in close proximity were from the Bryan side of the family. Cassie had a spinster aunt, who lived in New York, but they rarely visited her. To expose Annie to a family environment, Cassie remained close with her mother-in-law, the matriarch of the Bryan family. Annie spent most special occasions and holidays at her paternal grandmother's home, where all the family members would gather. Though it was the site of some of her fondest memories, it was also there where she fell victim to the most painful variety of prejudice.

Hearing the insults coming from strangers was unacceptable and hurtful, but much easier to brush off her shoulder. When it came from friends and neighbors, it was often devastating. Being subjected to racism at the hands of her own family was almost impossible to handle for such a young girl. This was especially true when that child was smart enough to understand the hatred behind it. It only took one bad seed and in the Bryan family that came in the person of the man Annie referred to as Uncle Byron. He wasn't related by blood to Annie- he was married to Walter's sister. Nevertheless, he did his best to spread his poison to many of Annie's closest family members. If Annie had just known what a slime he was back then, she might have avoided a lot of heartache.

Uncle Byron's unabashed use of all the racial slurs against white people and those of mixed race was unrestrained. He was insufferable in his attitude toward Annie and her mom. As a toddler and then preteen, Annie was fine with Uncle Byron's refusal to acknowledge her. He scared the hell out of her anyway. His treatment of Cassie was another matter. The hate seemed to ooze from his pores whenever the white woman entered the room. Most often, he would get up and leave immediately, mumbling horrible insults under his breath. Other times, it wasn't so subtle. At one Christmas family gathering, when Uncle Byron had overindulged with the spiked eggnog, he spit in Cassie's face for offering his children gifts.

What hurt Annie most was Uncle Byron's refusal to allow his children to speak to her. Byron's two daughters and three sons had become almost as intolerable as he was. Annie was excluded from any games in which her cousins participated. She was cursed at, teased, and tormented at every opportunity. Even worse, her cousins born to Walter's other sister chose to hang out with Byron's five children. They told Annie it was better to have five cousins to play with than just one.

As Annie grew older, she became aware of the true reason for Uncle Byron's behavior, though it certainly was no excuse. He had worked for Walter's father for thirty years as his right hand man. In Byron's not so humble opinion, he was a major contributor to the old man's fortune. When it came time to divvy it up, he didn't get a penny. His wife received an inheritance not nearly the size of Walter's. Then upon Walter's passing, his share belonged to Annie and her mom. Byron's greed and jealousy bred and nurtured the deep hate and prejudice he directed with great vengeance against Cassie and Annie. It wasn't a pleasant experience, but at least something good came of it. Annie's need to succeed propelled her to an exceptionally successful academic career. She followed in her father's footsteps and attended Harvard Law School. It also helped her advance to the position she now held with King Cruise Line. When Annie set a goal for herself, she aimed high and almost always achieved her target. She was a woman who sat comfortably in the driver's seat and controlled her own destiny. At least it was what she wanted to believe.

Chapter 4

He was nameless. His mother, Cherie Tucker, gave birth to him on an arctic, late November Chicago morning without assistance, in the rear cargo space of a Chevy van. She cut the cord with a pocket knife she kept in the front seat console. Taking the newborn infant to the hospital to be examined by a physician was out of the question. They would admit her and there was no way she'd go without a fix for several days. His arrival into the world wasn't registered with the Illinois State Census and therefore a birth certificate was never generated. As far as the United States government was concerned, he didn't exist.

His cradle was the floor of the van for the first eight months of his life. The fact that he survived his first Chicago winter could be considered a minor miracle. On several occasions, Cherie pondered throwing him in a garbage dumpster when she woke up in the morning to find his skin the deep blue color of a berry. She was both disappointed and exhilarated when she checked his breathing and found he was still alive. The child was a nuisance to her, but giving him to the state would have been too easy a solution. For an offer of one day's crack dose, she would probably admit she took pleasure in making her child suffer.

His feedings were sporadic and without the benefit of the advice of a practicing pediatrician. Nursing him was not an option. It would interfere with her business. To keep the infant from shrieking when he was hungry, she would fill his bottle with whatever liquid food substance she had at hand. Some days, the child's only sustenance was water mixed with coffee creamer. On his lucky days, he would get cow's milk. The inconsistent and inappropriate nourishment for a child his age provoked a variety of digestion and lack of nutrition problems that caused him serious illness. It would bring joy to his mother that the child seemed to have the resiliency of a superhero, always surviving for another day of her torture.

Several months before his first birthday, Cherie had become her pimp's number one whore, earning her an apartment in a low rent housing project on the south side of Chicago. For the next decade and a half, the home became the nameless boy's prison. Cherie treated her son like her personal outlet for a dark side that rankled in the pits of her corroded conscience. His confinement was intentional, his torment, an amusement. Even in the early months of his life, whenever she had business outside of the apartment, she would leave him alone for up to five or six hours. In order to avoid the interference of nosy neighbors, she would lock him behind the thick, oak door of her bedroom closet. At first, his wailing could last up to half the time she was absent. Despite his infancy, eventually, he habituated to the dark space, lack of company and nourishment, his body finding a way to survive against all odds.

By the time the boy was two years old, Cherie felt comfortable leaving the apartment for days at a time. Periodically, she left boxes of cereal or crackers on the dining room table for him, though she always made sure her cat's food dispenser was full. Most of the time, he was forced to live on water and what rotten food he could find in the refrigerator. If Cherie had known the boy would turn to her pet's food for sustenance, she might have let the animal starve too. Fortunately for his development, the cat food provided the protein and minerals lacking in the human fare at his disposal.

There was no television, toys, or any form of entertainment for a young child in the apartment. Kitchen utensils, his mother's cat, the cockroaches, and other vermin that infested the apartment became his playthings. He named and communicated with them in a language he invented on his own. His interaction with his mother was too limited for him to learn the English language at the age most children began to speak. His audible conversations with both the inanimate and living objects in the home embarrassed and infuriated Cherie, especially when he rattled off his gibberish in front of johns she invited to the apartment. This behavior would always be punished by imprisonment in the closet, and often a merciless beating that left him black-eyed and bruised.

The physical abuse stopped one day though not through any act of love, sympathy or generosity on Cherie's part. She had discovered a way to profit from her son and to help foster her drug habit. If it had been up to the boy, in all likelihood, he would have chosen to continue with the thrashings. One of Cherie's wealthiest clients offered her a substantial amount of money to have sex with her son, just five years old at the time. From that point on, she didn't hesitate to exploit his body for all kinds of perverse and aggressive sexual acts, including, when requested, having incestuous sex. At first, the act of fornicating with his mother repulsed him. His small frame didn't discourage him from fighting fiercely to resist the violation. When he eventually resigned himself to the idea he was powerless, he withdrew into a silent panic. As his body was sold with increasing regularity to the degenerates of the neighborhood, his panic transformed into a smoldering rage.

Unable to direct his fury toward his aggressors, he began to fantasize, using his playthings for more sinister acts. He considered using a butcher's knife to decapitate his mother's cat. Knowing this would only bring about severe punishment, he came up with more subtle ways to release his wrath without being discovered. One of his favorite games was to strangle his mother's pet until it lost consciousness. The look in its eyes as they bulged from their sockets made him shiver with excitement. The occasional rat that had the misfortune to stray into the apartment found the cat to be the least of its worries. With the speed and dexterity of a seasoned hunter, the boy was able to catch them with his bare hands. Then he would take his time to dismember and eviscerate the creature. Cutting off its head was always his final act.

* * *

The man without a name grabbed his binoculars, stuffed them in his backpack along with the other equipment he would need for the day, and walked briskly out the door of his new apartment. He was happy with his decision to settle in Ft. Lauderdale after abandoning his position with King Cruise Line. The security job was one of the best things that had ever happened to him. It had given him the ideal opportunity to perfect his craft. No question, he had a good run on the Diamond. The time had definitely come, however, to move on to bigger and better things.

Paul Anderson wasn't his first kill, though it was the most complex to date. It was hardly a product of genius but good progress. His mother, who he preferred to call the Tucker slut, had been his first. In his mind, she was nothing but a crack-addicted, two-bit whore who didn't deserve to breathe the same air as a shit-eating fly. It was an easy decision to make her his initial victim and an easier murder to plan. She was always falling asleep either in her bed or on the living room sofa with a lit cigarette in her mouth. His idea to cremate her alive didn't take an Einstein. That night of his liberation and salvation, as the Tucker slut slept peacefully on the couch, hot embers from her cigarette falling to the floor, the fifteen-year-old boy collected the few personal items from his room he had packed for this occasion. Just before he left the apartment, he detached the pipe from the wall that supplied gas to the oven, allowing the propane to flow freely into the open air. Within five minutes there was a deafening explosion. The boy waited outside in the back courtyard for several minutes more, carefully listening for any screams of pain. He was rewarded for his patience with much more. He saw his mother's frantic attempts to open the window to escape the burning apartment. His body tightened with the intense pleasure of an orgasm as he watched the flames engulf her. When the screams stopped and the sirens of fire trucks and ambulances carried by the brisk Chicago winds became louder, he smiled for the first time in his life.

The opportunity with King Cruise Line came more than ten years later. During the time between the death of his mother and his employment with King, he began to fantasize about killing again. As time passed, the fantasies became more regular and gruesome. His favorite was to imagine slitting some whore's throat and bathing in her blood, while pleasuring himself. It would always end with the most intense orgasms. He used his first killings on the ship to hone his skills. A master of falsifying documents, he specifically applied for a security position claiming on his resume he was an expert in video surveillance. After extensive research both on the Internet and at the library, his knowledge of the profession was as strong as anyone experienced in the field. Impressing his interviewers, he was offered a position to man the ship's surveillance monitors.

In the beginning, he preferred to keep it simple. He chose his victims after carefully observing their behavior over a period of days. The first was a sixteen year-old British girl who had a habit of sneaking out of her room in the wee hours of the morning, in search of young men. On the monitors he had seen her enter several boys' cabins and giving a teenager a blow job in the Jacuzzi. Most evenings, it was clear she had been drinking. For several nights, he fantasized about slitting her throat then using her blood as a lubricant to fuck her but that would be too risky. So, he continued to watch her for the next few nights, waiting for the perfect opportunity to arise.

That happened at around two o'clock in the morning on an overcast and rainy night. Setting out on his endeavor, he wasn't concerned he would be identified by any surveillance video. He had studied the ship's placement of cameras and become adept at avoiding them. With no moon to provide natural light, the sea and the pitch black sky in the distance couldn't be differentiated. In certain areas of the ship, where human traffic was sparse at that hour, the shadows cast by the cruise liners own lighting created some eerily dark spaces. One of those places was the children's playground located at the bow on Deck 16, where teenagers up to no good had a tendency to gather. That night, he waited at the playground on the port side of the ship in a corner hidden by silhouettes created by the playground equipment. At the time he arrived, there was no activity, a situation he had been waiting on for several nights. When she walked through the automatic glass doors onto the playground alone, stumbling and staggering from too much to drink, the stir in his loins told him it was time to act.

Disappointed to find the boy she hoped would be there was not, she made her way to the port side of the ship to gain access to the walkway which led toward the stern and Jacuzzi. As she passed into the dark area, he grabbed her by the upper arm and pulled her to the deck. In the shadows of the playground, he sat on top of her chest, placed his hands firmly around her neck and began to squeeze in a downward motion. The gesture completely cut off her air supply preventing her from screaming or calling for help. He applied all of his weight and formidable strength against her throat. The increased pressure he exerted allowed him to feel the blood coursing through her carotid artery, until the flow was ultimately completely obstructed. Initially, the pulse was strong and it gave him an erection. As it weakened, so did his sexual response. Disappointed about his inability to climax, he dragged her to an area of the ship where he knew there were no surveillance cameras and tossed her over the side. Her body quickly disappeared into the warm, dark water of the Caribbean Sea.

On subsequent cruises, he murdered an eighteen-year-old American and a nineteen- year-old Brazilian girl in similar fashion. Each time, when he returned to his cabin to masturbate, he failed to reach orgasm. It soon became obvious to him it wasn't easy prey he was after. In order to receive complete sexual satisfaction from the kill, there had to be blood. To feel intellectually fulfilled, he needed a challenge. The time had come to progress to a new phase of killing. His job as a security officer qualified him to leave the ship on most port days. During the winter months, the Diamond sailed the Caribbean. From mid-May to early September, it repositioned to Europe and sailed the Mediterranean. It was the perfect chance to become an international murderer.

* * *

Getting a job required a name. He chose Damien Drysdale for his employment with King Cruise Line. Having changed his name on countless occasions, he was an expert at obtaining falsified identification. He had fourteen fake passports with corresponding driver's licenses, seven of which bestowed him with American citizenship; the balance from several different foreign countries. He prided himself as a master of accents, English being one of his favorites. In his estimation, it gave one an air of sophistication. The name he chose for himself when not conducting official business was Shem Chassar. He believed Israel was the epicenter and origin of the most prevalent religions in the world, where good and evil was born, and therefore its language would provide him with his identity. He elected to embrace his mother's failure to recognize him as a human being rather than allow it to defile him. It's translation, "without a name."

Shem Chassar would not leave the ship on one of his deadly shore excursions unless he was sure to have a twelve hour window before the Diamond was scheduled to leave a particular harbor city. At most major ports, the ship remained docked long enough to allow passengers to spend the entire day and evening visiting its tourist attractions and enjoying its night life. Extended port stays were also typical when the city of interest was a significant distance from the port. There was no lack of opportunity to get the job done.

Planning and executing a kill in a foreign country was much more gratifying than the murders he committed on the ship. It gave him the freedom to kill in a manner he chose, not to mention, it actually required some thought. He calculated he could travel up to five-hundred miles roundtrip and return to the ship with time to spare. Approximately five months before he slit Paul Anderson's throat and threw him overboard, the Diamond was moored in Venice, Italy. It arrived at seven o'clock on a Saturday morning and wasn't scheduled to set sail until five o'clock the following evening. Just after his shift ended that Saturday afternoon, he rented a Fiat Grande Punto van from Venezia Autonoleggio and set off on the 215 kilometer trip to Innsbruck, Austria. Before hopping on the autostrada, he stopped at a department store to purchase some necessary provisions for his trip. Two and a half hours later, he lured Christina Becker from an Innsbruck brothel then raped and murdered her by decapitation. He sliced through his victim's neck with a razor sharp butcher's knife, achieving orgasm as her blood spewed with great force on his face and neck. Hearing the crack of the vertebrae as he severed the spine with a hammer and chisel was music to his ears. For good measure, he sliced off both her nipples and stuffed them in the mouth of her detached head. He was back onboard the Diamond before midnight.

Chassar would add to his body count in Karpenisi, Greece, Karabuk, Turkey, Frosinone, Italy and Aix-en-Provence, France before the Anderson murder. His shore excursion homicides were a step above his previous killings. Still, they weren't the challenge to his genius he had hoped. Up to that point, all his victims were women. It was time to change things up. He wanted to try something riskier, a mystery that would keep the authorities on their toes. To create such a scenario, he would have to be sure to involve the FBI and truly baffle the company's supposed cracker-jack investigative team.

* * *

The hand of fate can sometimes flex its dexterous fingers to deposit its chosen subject in a given place at a specific time changing the course of his or her life forever. At times, fate's tricks are very generous. It can also be the diametric opposite. Such was the case for Paul Anderson on the second evening of his Caribbean cruise. Shem Chassar was on the surveillance monitors that evening. He decided to allow his next victim to seal his own fate. Camera 127 was trained on the entrance to the gym located on Deck 14 aft. The security guard fixed his gaze on the screen of the monitor reflecting that scene. The next man who walked into the gym would die before the end of the cruise.

* * *

The security guard followed his chosen victim and the woman accompanying him to their cabin the first day he was off duty. He wanted their cabin number so he could look up their information on the Diamond's computer data base. Sound preparation was essential. Any information he could gather about the Andersons could be helpful in planning a successful murder. The Diamond kept a virtual file on each of its passengers, with information that could assist them to lure customers back for future cruises. It was in this file where Shem Chassar found what he needed. Three days into the cruise, Paul Anderson and his wife visited the purser's desk to inquire about prices for Mediterranean cruises. It was noted in the file by the Assistant Purser who fielded their questions that he recommended some great coupon offers coming out in the Diamond Daily on the last night of the cruise.

While the Andersons were off on a shore excursion the following day, Chassar thoroughly searched their cabin. There was no chance he would be seen on any of the ship's surveillance cameras because he conducted the search while he was on monitor duty. He simply shut the monitors off and locked the door behind him. It wasn't unusual for the monitors to be left unmanned for short periods of time. A cruise ship wasn't exactly breeding grounds for high crime. Leaving the surveillance center for something to eat or drink was typical. In the Anderson's bathroom, he found a pair of scissors in an overnight toiletry bag. When he returned to the surveillance center, he found it as he had left it. His mission was a success. He had located his murder weapon.

In order for the FBI to have jurisdiction over the crime he planned to commit, it would have to be done while the ship was bound for a U.S. port. The only opportunity to meet that condition would occur on the last day of the cruise. The night before the final sea day, while Shem was staking out the Andersons and their friends at the piano bar, he overheard their plans for their end of vacation celebration. His shift at the surveillance monitors would end just before their scheduled meeting. He would be waiting for them in the Seafarer's Lounge.

* * *

The lounge was designed in the shape of a half-moon, with an entrance that gave direct access to the Promenade deck. On the far side of the bar, there was a Filipino band performing fifties music. Shem chose a seat at a table near the entrance so that he had a view of the entire lounge and the people approaching from both ends of the promenade. He was wearing a baseball cap with its brim pulled low over his forehead and eyes. He didn't like large crowds- they made him tense. Avoiding attracting attention helped him relax. The feeling of being inconspicuous was his comfort zone. It would be better if he could just focus his thoughts on the matter at hand. The notion that he was planning to brutally murder a human being in cold blood usually had the calming effect he was seeking.

He timed his arrival so he didn't have to waste much time before the Andersons' scheduled meeting. Within minutes, he saw them approaching from the bow of the ship. Their friends came stumbling into the lounge as the Andersons were choosing a table halfway between the entrance and the stage. It was obvious the entire group, except for Paul Anderson, had been drinking heavily. Paul seemed to be the only member of the party in control of his faculties. That was fine by Shem. Anderson would be more aware of what was about to happen to him.

The drinking continued throughout the evening and into the early morning hours. By 1:30am, it appeared to Shem that the festivities were winding down. Everyone in the party, save Paul, was in danger of passing out at their table if they didn't return to their cabins in the very near future. Anticipating their departure was imminent, Shem purchased two sodas from the bar and headed to the monitor control room.

Before entering the surveillance center, he ducked into the crew quarters section of the ship in an area where he knew there were no cameras. On one of his more recent shore excursions, he had purchased the liquid tranquilizer, Restalex. He poured an exact dose into one of the colas, having previously tested the drug on himself on his day off. It took five minutes to render him unconscious for a period of one hour and twenty minutes, more than a sufficient amount of time for what he had in mind.

Chassar entered the control room and as expected, his colleague, Ken O'Brien was seated at the desk in front of the monitors. In preparation for this evening, so that his gesture wouldn't seem out of the ordinary, Shem had stopped by the office twice that week during his co-worker's shift with two Cokes in hand. O'Brien was addicted to the beverage, and known to drink at least a twelve pack a day. Shem expected his effort would be interpreted as a proffer of friendship. O'Brien wasn't the sharpest tool in the shed. His ploy had worked, perhaps too well. Over the past few days, O'Brien had become a little bit too chummy for Shem's liking. Shem offered his colleague the drugged soda which O'Brien accepted gratefully. O'Brien invited him to sit and chat a while, but Shem made his excuses, graciously declined and left the room. He returned five minutes later to find O'Brien slumped over his desk. Being of similar height and weight, Shem figured the unconscious man would be that way for a while. Glancing at the monitors, he saw Paul Anderson was just leaving the lounge. The wife could barely stand on her feet. Just before he left the control room, he planted a virus in the surveillance system computer that would stop the recording of the cameras for the remainder of the shift.

On every cruise ship, there is a crew area with restricted admittance to paying passengers. Employees of the cruise line had their own elevators, staircases, and hallways where they could access each deck without having to walk through territory reserved for passengers. The control room was located on Deck 5. The Andersons were staying on Deck 14. Shem entered the crew area at Deck 5 and slipped into the elevator. Five minutes later, he was peering out of one of the circular windows of the double doors that led to a passenger hallway on the Lido Deck. The Anderson cabin was across the hall and approximately thirty feet to the left, clearly within his field of view when standing in the right position. Seeing no one, he stepped away from the doors and stood in the corner to wait.

For him, the anticipation of the moments before the kill was one of the best parts of the experience. It invariably caused him to have an erection. Beneath his uniform, he was wearing a full body rubber suit with a buttoned fly. To pass the time until the Andersons arrived, he unzipped his pants, unbuttoned the fly and began to stroke his penis. He wouldn't allow himself to climax, however. That would be saved for when he felt his victim's warm blood against his naked skin.

As soon as he was through pleasuring himself, he removed his outer clothing and placed them in a neat pile on the floor. In his jacket pocket, he had a rubber mask with holes for his eyes, nose and mouth, and a pair of rubber gloves. After donning the mask and slipping his fingers into the rubber gloves, he heard the bell signaling the approach of a passenger elevator. Several seconds later, he peeked out the circular window and saw Paul Anderson practically dragging his wife down the corridor. When they finally made it to their cabin, Anderson propped her against the wall, holding her up with one hand and unlocking the door with the other. He then picked her up and carried her into the room.

With the Andersons safely behind their closed door, Shem looked through the circular window directing his gaze to either side of the hallway as far as his vantage point would allow. It appeared to be vacant. He picked up his clothing, exited the crew area through the double doors and walked the short distance to their cabin. Due to the late hour, he was fairly certain he wouldn't run into any passengers or crew members though he never let down his guard. He placed his ear up against the door and heard the sounds of someone rummaging about the room, assuming it was the husband. Approximately five minutes elapsed before the lights of the cabin were extinguished. Shem expected the wife would pass out immediately. He went back to his corner on the crew area side of the double doors and waited an additional fifteen minutes for the husband to fall asleep. When the time expired, he returned to the cabin and placed his master key in the lock.

From the days he lived with his noise-hating mother, Shem had learned to be very light on his feet. Without making a sound, he entered the room and immediately turned left into the space between the closet and the bathroom. The sliding glass doors were partially open and the roar of the ocean drowned out the creaking of the bathroom door as Shem opened it. He stepped up into the bathroom and closed the door behind him. The toiletry bag was hanging on a hook on the back of the door. He reached into the compartment where he had previously found the scissors, removed them then placed his clothing on top of the toilet seat.

With his murder weapon in hand, he proceeded into the bedroom, where he took note that Paul Anderson was sleeping on the side of the bed nearest the balcony. The wife was lying on her back, snoring thunderously at his side. Shem silently crept to Paul's side of the bed and stood over him, watching the rhythmic rising and falling of his chest as he drew in his last breaths. In one swift, sudden motion, he shoved Anderson facedown onto the floor. Dazed and disoriented, Paul looked back to see the tall, muscle-bound man in a black rubber body suit standing over him with a pair of scissors raised high over his head. In the split second before Chassar jumped on his back, his mind had not yet registered that he was in grave danger. With no time to react in self-defense, he was helpless to avoid the stab of the sharp point of the scissors. It penetrated through his Adam's apple and into the carotid artery. Shem then savagely dragged the scissors through flesh, tearing across the throat to puncture the jugular vein. Paul's entire body convulsed, reacting to the searing heat where the scissors ripped through muscle and tendons. It felt as though his neck were being shredded by a white hot poker. He tried to scream. Instead, he exhaled a barely audible squeak no louder than a whimper. The scissors had punctured through the neck deeply enough to sever his vocal chords. Warm, thick blood gushed from the open wound. The blood loss was quick and unrelenting. Within seconds, Paul lost all strength and power to fight for his life. As he faded into oblivion, his blood saturated his assailant's hands.

The orgasm that sent spasms through Shem's upper torso made his head spin. Through a cloud of disoriented ecstasy, he could hear his victim making a bizarre gurgling sound. As he recovered from the intense climax and the blood flow slowed, Shem pulled Anderson's head up by the hair to allow the crimson fountain to spew more freely. Meanwhile, the wife continued to sleep soundly without the least bit of a stir. Shem rolled the body on its side so that a pool could collect and absorb into the carpet. Satisfied with the large puddle that had accumulated, he wiped the scissors clean of any fingerprints with a bathroom towel. He placed them carefully in Anderson's hand, making sure to apply pressure on the circled grips and the upper parts of the blade with the tips of the corpse's fingers. Then, setting the scissors aside, he picked up the body as if it were the weight of an infant, carried it to the balcony and tossed it over the railing. Before it crashed into the water, he had already turned to reenter the room. He would have watched but time was short.

Avoiding the gore, he passed through the bedroom searching for the pair of shoes Anderson wore that evening. Unconcerned it would affect the woman's sleep, he switched the light on in the bathroom. The shoes were lying on the floor of the closet underneath a pile of dirty clothing. He placed them on his feet, walked back to the far side of the bed, stepped into the pool of the already stagnating gore, and made a trail of four bloody footprints leading outside to the edge of the balcony. He feigned losing his balance as he made the tracks. While on the balcony, he removed the shoes, mask, towel and blood spattered body suit, and threw them overboard.

In the event he was unable to find their issue of the *Daily Diamond*, Shem had one ready in his inside jacket pocket. Their copy was resting on a stack of papers on the wife's nightstand. Still wearing the rubber gloves, he leafed through the pamphlet to locate the ten percent off discount advertisement. He partially cut the coupon out with the scissors, being sure to smear it with blood from the carpet. He then placed both items on the floor in front of the desk.

The next part of his plan would truly baffle the authorities. It involved his intentions for the wife. He would have liked to have slit her throat and thrown her over the balcony too, but creating confusion was necessary for the overall effect. He threw the rubber gloves into the sea, made his way to the bathroom, got dressed, put on a spare pair of plastic gloves from his pants pocket, went to the front door, and opened it a crack to peek into the hallway. Seeing no one, he went back to the wife's side of the bed and lifted her. She stopped snoring for an instant, but didn't wake up. He carried her to the saturated carpet and rubbed her head and arm in it before heading toward the door. Having left it slightly ajar after cutting the coupon, he pushed it aside with his foot to exit the cabin. Since it opened toward the inside, it was a struggle to close it behind him without dropping the woman. He ultimately succeeded quickly enough to avoid lingering in the corridor too long, pulling the knob with his stronger, dominant right hand, while resting her head in the crook of his arm.

Before entering the crew area, he looked through the circular windows and as he expected, it was also deserted. One good kick and the swinging door opened inward, allowing him to deftly continue on his way through the crew hallways. He peered around corners before proceeding, making sure they were devoid of any late night wanderers. Arriving at his preordained destination on the same deck as the Anderson's cabin, he passed through the exit leading directly onto the pool deck. He set her down in a lounge chair, still sound asleep then quickly disappeared through the door he had entered.

He had one small task to complete. He used the crew area route to the Anderson's cabin and re-entered. Inside, he made the bed and sat on the edge to create a ruffled appearance. With that final installment of his plan checked off his list, he casually strolled back to his sleeping quarters. The instant he closed the door behind him, he looked at his watch. It had taken him exactly one hour and four minutes to execute his entire plan from the time he left his colleague sleeping in the control room. Ken O'Brien would awake from his slumber ten minutes later. Concerned that he would be fired, he never admitted to either the internal investigative team or the FBI that he'd fallen asleep on the job the night of the disappearance.

* * *

On his way to Annie's, Shem thought about the last morning on the Diamond, when he made the decision to stay in Ft.

Lauderdale. He didn't sleep after returning to his cabin. He knew he had committed the perfect crime, risky as it was, but intentionally made the circumstances ambiguous. He was certain it was time to call it quits and move on. The only downside was giving up his opportunity to see Annie when she periodically visited the ship.

The first time he met Annie Bryan, she came to the Diamond to conduct an inspection of their security systems and procedure. He instantly became fixated on her. She was a vision to behold, with her beautiful African American, cream-colored skin and emerald green eyes. She stayed on the ship for a full week. Grossly unfamiliar with the feelings he was experiencing for her, he never marshaled the nerve to speak to her. The desire to have an intimate relationship with another human being was both confusing and intriguing to him. She made a total of four visits to the ship over the two years he worked for King and not once did he approach her. He may not have been ready yet, though there was one thing about which he was absolutely certain. One day, she would be his.

He packed his bags at four o'clock on that final morning on the Diamond. At 5:30am, the ship pulled into Port Everglades, Florida. It cleared Immigration and Customs before seven. By 7:15, he slipped off the gangway, using the crew exit, never to return. He found it fateful that the end of his run on the Diamond would come in the city where Annie Bryan resided. Six months later, he was still living in the small apartment he'd rented in Pompano Beach, just ten miles north of Port Everglades. Parked across the street from Annie's condo on Ft. Lauderdale Beach, he waited for his first glimpse of her of the day.

Chapter 5

It was the dead of winter, but one would never know it by the record high temperatures roasting the South Florida coastline. Though Annie Bryan had her air conditioner running at full blast in her penthouse condominium on Ft. Lauderdale Beach, a bead of sweat trickled down her spine as she rooted through her over-sized walk-in closet, searching for something suitable to wear for the French Quarter restaurant. Michael asked her out for dinner and a movie and she was regretting having accepted his invitation. The combination of the oppressive heat and her aggravation over his persistence was putting her in a bad mood.

Annie had been seeing Michael Munez for the better part of three years, though she preferred not to refer to him as her boyfriend. From her perspective, it was a casual relationship with no strings. Despite countless conversations where Annie expressed her reluctance to any form of commitment, Michael, didn't see it that way. He was starting to get a little too attached for Annie's comfort. He was a nice enough guy, but she wasn't in love with him. She tried to break it off completely on several occasions. Each time Michael convinced her he had no problem with the lack of commitment. Deep inside, she knew it couldn't be further from the truth. One of these days, she'd find the courage to stick to her guns. She chose a red cotton Versace dress with black Gucci pumps. The garment was made of a light enough fabric to give her the best chance to avoid perspiring in the summer-like heat. Annie always looked forward to the South Florida winters. They produced some of the most beautiful weather imaginable and she enjoyed the relief from the brutal combination of sweltering temperatures and high humidity. She slipped into the dress and pumps, chose a Tiffany's set of diamond earrings with a matching bracelet and went directly to the kitchen to pour herself a glass of wine. If she was going to do something against her better judgment, she was going to have a good time doing it. She looked out at her panoramic view of the Atlantic Ocean while she downed two big gulps of the Chardonnay.

Annie's condo was 3,500 square feet of exquisitely decorated and furnished luxury. It included an immense master bedroom and two guestrooms, with a total of four full bathrooms. Floor to ceiling windows extended across the entire eastern façade. This afforded her views of Ft. Lauderdale Beach from every room. The master bath, the size of a studio apartment, had floors, walls and a roman tub that were constructed of polished white and beige Italian marble. The tub had Jacuzzi jets and ten adults could fit in the shower with room to spare. While Annie often felt guilty for the extravagance of her home, she conceded that she worked extremely hard for what she had and deserved a bit of spoiling. Besides, she did her part in assisting those less fortunate than she. She regularly volunteered her time and made large contributions to worthy causes. Generosity and charity were instilled in her by her mother from a very early age.

The resonating sound of the telephone interrupted Annie's peaceful contemplation of the gorgeous seascape. She placed her glass of wine on the family room coffee table and ran to the kitchen to check the caller I.D. It was Michael. She picked up the receiver.

"Hello Michael. Right on time as usual."

"Yeah, I try. Among many other fine qualities, I'm sure."

"You're a good man."

"Just what I was hoping you'd say. The words I've waited all these years to hear."

"I hope you're not starting Michael. I'm not in the mood."

"Geez, get up on the wrong side of the bed this morning? I was just joking."

"I'm sorry, you're right. This damn heat's been getting to me. I can't keep my place cool enough- it's so frick'n hot outside."

"Well maybe some good company and a great meal'll cheer you up. I'll be there in ten minutes. Do you want to meet me downstairs, or should I come up?"

"I'll come down. See you in ten."

Annie hung up the phone, guzzled down the rest of her wine, grabbed her black Gucci purse, and rushed out the door. By the time she arrived at the front entrance, Michael was just pulling up under the portico. He started to exit the vehicle to open the door for her, but she waved him off and hopped into the passenger seat. She gave him a quick peck on the cheek, evoking a grimace of disappointment. He pulled out onto Birch Street, turned left on Las Olas, and then drove the three short miles to the restaurant.

* * *

Shem Chassar had been parked outside of Annie's penthouse apartment since she returned from work at 6:30pm. He began the habit of following her to and from work every day just one week after settling in Ft. Lauderdale. He spent most of his nights until nine on the beach facing her building. When Annie's curtains were drawn, he had a perfect view inside the apartment using his high-powered, night vision binoculars. In the evenings, she spent most of her time in the family room overlooking A1A and the ocean beyond. The lights from the apartment created the perfect conditions for feasting his eyes on the woman who would someday soon belong to him.

In the entirety of Shem's life, there was only one other instance when he felt any sense of desire for closeness to another human being. It happened upon his very first opportunity to venture outside of his mother's apartment when he was nine years old. In a drugged and drunken stupor, Cherie Tucker forgot to lock the door when she left the apartment to meet with her crack dealer. The boy, aware of his mother's mistake, took full advantage of his opportunity, though not without trepidation. He felt a nervous excitement as he opened the door and walked out into the dark, dank hallway of the seventy-year-old building. When he encountered the staircase, he almost turned back. Instead, his curiosity got the best of him and he descended the steps in a deliberate manner, keeping a firm grip on the banister, taking excessive care not to fall. It took him several minutes to reach the ground floor. With a mixture of apprehension and thrill, he exited the front entrance into the broad daylight of a Chicago late morning. Blinded by the bright light, he immediately sat down on the front stoop to orient himself and survey the area. His apartment overlooked the rear of the building where public access was denied. As a result, before this occasion, the only people he had ever seen were his mother and her customers. Once his eyes adjusted, he saw children his own age for the first time. There was a group of boys in the middle of the street playing some type of game with a ball and a club. As he watched the scene, a young black woman came out of the entrance of a neighboring apartment building with two toddlers following closely behind. He was immediately taken aback by her stunning beauty, though it wasn't her appearance that ultimately won over his interest. He observed the woman as she played with her children and affectionately gave them hugs and kisses. Shortly thereafter, she called to one of the boys playing the game to inform him it was time for lunch. The family sat on the stoop of their building while the mother served them a picnic-style meal. The loving way she interacted with her children introduced the young boy without a name to an idea completely obscure to him. In spite of his total lack of experience with anything of a social nature, he could tell this woman was to her children what his mother was supposed to be to him. After observing them for a few more minutes, his understanding of the situation incited two diametrically opposing emotions. In that moment, he loved the mother for the way she loved her children. At the same time, a fury broiled somewhere deep within the recesses of his soul. It was an anger bred by jealousy for how a mother was meant to relate to her children and a hatred for the Tucker bitch.

The woman noticed the strange, skinny boy sitting all alone with his head bent down and forward in his hands. Having never seen him on their street, she walked over to ask if he was lost. Frightened by her approach, he turned to run. A tenderness in the tone of her voice calling out made him stop in his tracks. In a brief discussion with him, she discovered he lived on their street, hadn't eaten a thing all day, and didn't know where his mom was, nor when she'd be coming back. Though it angered her, she didn't express those feelings to the boy either with her words or her manner. She considered calling Child Protective Services, but recognized their response to cases in this neighborhood was a joke. The only way she knew to help was to offer him some fried chicken from her picnic basket. Unsure how to react, the boy ultimately accepted the strange, warm food. He had never eaten anything that wasn't stone cold and was reluctant to put it in his mouth. She had to encourage him to try it. When he finally did, it was the most delicious food he had ever tasted.

The nameless boy's mother became increasingly careless about locking the door as he grew older. Each time he had the opportunity, he would go outside to sit on the stoop in hopes of catching a glimpse of the beautiful mom across the street. With mixed emotions of rage, envy, and compassion, he watched her devoted and nurturing ways with her children. Every time she saw the boy, she would come over to greet him and give him a treat. When he wasn't able to go outside, he would listen for her voice when she called her children at meal times and the end of the evening. When the family moved out of the neighborhood two years later, it was the last time Shem could recall experiencing any kind of a curiosity toward another human being; until the moment he met Annie Bryan.

Everything about Annie, from her mannerisms and body type, to her facial features and disposition, reminded him of that woman. Why such a superior person like Annie continued to see Michael Munez was beyond his comprehension. She was way too good for him and he could plainly see she wasn't in love. What pissed Shem off the most was Munez's constant interference with his nights with Annie. The minute Shem saw her standing in her living room window in a beautiful red dress, he knew she was going out with him. As soon as the lights went out, he rushed to his car parked directly across from her building's front entrance and waited for her to come downstairs.

Like clockwork, several minutes later Shem saw a charcoal gray Porsche 911 approaching Annie's building through his side mirror. He often considered ridding the world of this waste of humanity driving his fancy car. It hadn't happened yet because of a rule he did his best not to violate. To kill in his own backyard was to be avoided at all costs. It also worked in Michael's favor that Shem didn't see him as much of a threat. Shem was confident Annie would eventually dump him. He would just have to wait a little longer and patience was one of his greatest assets.

After Michael pulled into the driveway, Shem started the engine of his Ford Expedition. He waited for several seconds after the Porsche headed south on Birch Street, then pulled out onto the road. To avoid detection by Annie or anyone else, he purchased four different ordinary cars for a total price of three thousand dollars. His plan was to never drive the same car on consecutive days. It minimized the wear and tear on the vehicles and more importantly, the odds of him being noticed when he was following Annie. So far, it was working. Maintaining a distance of approximately ten car lengths behind, he implemented some calming exercises he had learned on the Internet. It helped to relieve some of the agitation he was feeling from another night trashed by Munez. He could almost physically feel the anger bubbling its way to the surface. Overactive emotions bred mistakes and any missteps on his part were unacceptable.

The Porsche pulled into the valet parking line of the French Quarter. Shem maneuvered the Ford Expedition into the pay parking lot directly across from the restaurant. He placed two dollars in quarters in the meter, giving him a total of four hours. With time to pass, he sat on the hood of the SUV thinking that he would observe the cattle as they strolled down Las Olas Blvd.

* * *

Walking the streets of Miami was beneath her. She had more talent in her pinky finger than most of the drag queens that were making it big these days. At least, it was what Glamorosa Champagne was thinking as she reapplied her blood orange lipstick that was smudged by the blow job she'd performed on her previous client. When in drag, she was an extraordinarily beautiful woman. There weren't too many people who could tell she actually had a penis between her legs. It got her in trouble at times, but nothing she couldn't handle. Learning the fine arts of self-defense was a must for any man that dressed in women's clothes. Glamorosa never left her home without her portable can of mace and the derringer revolver given to her by her best friend. She also did her best to limit her services to oral and anal sex, without revealing her private parts.

It wasn't the most productive of nights. At that point, she had only earned sixty dollars for her oral talents. That wasn't even enough to cover her bar tab from earlier that evening with her friends at the Cathode Ray on Las Olas Blvd. She was actually lucky she still had her purse with her rent money and a small amount of extra cash. If it weren't for that nice, good looking gentleman sitting in the parking lot across from the French Quarter, the juvenile delinquent who was about to rob her would have gotten away with it. How the nice man grabbed her and placed his body between her and her attacker was nothing less than heroic. She tried to give her savior a tip, but he refused. As a substitute demonstration of gratitude, she gave him her business card with her home address and offered him free service any time he chose.

Heroes were scarce in Glamorosa's life. Villains were the norm. Her father left her and her mother when she was just a little boy. At the age of fifteen, she was kicked out of the house by her mother's new husband for being gay. At first, she lived on the streets. Then they became her place of employment. She couldn't count the number of times she was severely beaten by johns, usually when they discovered her true sex. The number of beer bottles pegged at her head from passing cars was anyone's guess. The never-ending insults and curse-outs were hardly worth mentioning.

Leading a life replete with scoundrels and lacking good guys, Glamorosa was pleasantly surprised when she returned home at the end of her night. She noticed a Ford Expedition parked in front of her apartment with that evening's hero sitting behind the wheel. Without hesitation, she jumped in the passenger's seat, scooted toward her rescuer and laid a big wet one smack on his lips. Before Glamorosa realized it and could prevent it, his hand was in her crotch. The look on his face and in his eyes when he became aware what was in his hand was unmistakable and very recognizable to Glamorosa. Only this time, the intensity of the look of fury was one that she had never encountered. Her initial reaction was to reach for her can of mace. His response was lightning quick. Glamorosa barely had time to grab for the zipper of her purse when he shoved a rag soaked with ether in her face. She struggled bravely but with futility. As she drew in an overdue breath of air and everything went hazy, she chided herself for not expecting that her hero would turn into a villain.

* * *

Despite his employment of all the calming exercises that normally set him at ease, Shem couldn't shake an underlying feeling of unsettled discomfort. This should be his time with Annie. If something didn't give soon, he was going to do something stupid. His frustration was a result of his jealousy over Michael. Relief for feelings this powerful would only come with a kill. He had no intentions along those lines that night. Though he could come up with a plan for murder at the spur of the moment, choosing a victim could be time consuming. It required a certain feel. These things should never be done impulsively.

Shem didn't subscribe to the theory of fatalism and believed that the idea of destiny was a load of crap. Yet, he had his fair share of experiences where he seemed to be in the right place at the right time. A business card wielding prostitute strolling down Las Olas Blvd was far from an everyday occurrence. It wasn't often that a person witnessed an attempted purse snatching in that neighborhood either. Whether or not someone from above or below was looking after him, he didn't have a choice but to take full advantage of the opportunity that presented itself.

Earlier in the evening, he saw the teenage boy dressed in baggy shorts that hung halfway down his ass whiz by some lady on his skateboard and snatch a bracelet from her wrist. An hour later, the kid had the balls to return to the scene in search of a second victim. Shem knew exactly what the young hoodlum was up to when he saw the garish, excessively decorated, but strikingly beautiful prostitute. She was stumbling toward the French Quarter parking lot, swinging her purse like a bolo whip. On his skateboard, the thief sped toward the prostitute at break-neck speed. The boy was lucky his spine wasn't severed when Shem pulled the woman off the sidewalk at the last second. Surprised at the disappearance of his target, the thief took a nose dive directly into the hard cement, his head snapping backwards as if on a spring. With blood spewing from his broken nose, the teenager grabbed his skateboard and fled the scene as fast as he could run in his oversized shorts.

Shem had no intention of leaving his spot before he was sure that Annie was safe and sound at home. So when the prostitute gave him her personal card with her home address on South Beach, he knew that later, he would have his peace. His problem of choice had been resolved. The absolute disgust, repugnance, and rage that overcame him because he popped a boner upon touching the prostitute were just confirmation. Miami wasn't as far from home as he would have preferred, but it would have to do.

Fifteen minutes after the averted theft, Annie, obviously upset, walked out of the restaurant talking on her cell phone. Munez plowed through the doors shortly after. It soon became evident they were involved in a heated argument. When the valet brought up Michael's car, Michael had to convince Annie to get in. Ten minutes later, he was dropping her off at her apartment building. With binoculars in hand, Shem waited on the beach for several minutes to be certain that Annie was in for the evening. The instant he saw her in her nightgown, he jogged to his car parked on Birch Street, made a quick stop at home to pick up a few necessary provisions then headed straight for Miami.

He sat for three hours in front of the prostitute's dingy efficiency apartment, waiting for her. When he first arrived, he peered into the front window ineffectively dressed with a bed sheet. The one room of the residence was clearly vacant. He considered the possibility the prostitute might not come home at all. Influenced by a hunch telling him his patience would pay off, he decided to wait it out. It wasn't a matter of believing in the destiny of the night. He had unwavering confidence in his intuition and often relied on it. It rarely let him down and it didn't disappoint him that night. In his rear view mirror, he saw her approaching his vehicle, this time with a sure and balanced posture. Evidently, she had sobered up. That was a good thing. He always preferred his victims alert.

The shock when he placed his hands over her genital area nearly sent him over the edge. Fighting his instinct, a rational head prevailed. Instead of slitting her throat impulsively, he reached into the space between the driver's door and seat and grabbed the ether-soaked rag he had stashed there for later use. After his discovery, he had no desire to postpone matters for sex. As soon as Glamorosa lost consciousness, he started the engine and made his way south along the coast toward Coconut Grove and Matheson Hammock Park. He had made himself familiar with most of the outdoor recreational parks in the Miami metropolitan area. One never knew when the disposal of a body would be necessary.

It took him less than a half hour to get to his destination. Since the park was closed, the parking lot was empty. Shortly after he maneuvered his car into an available space, Glamorosa mumbled a few incoherent words. He gave her an extra dose of the ether-soaked rag. Then, with his backpack strapped tightly over his shoulders, he exited the vehicle to choose a location for the deed.

The park's nature trail covered 630 acres, most of it lined by mangroves. He had no intention of carrying her a great distance, so he selected a spot approximately thirty yards off the nature trail in an area dense with foliage. The site chosen, he left his backpack with his supplies against a tree and returned to the SUV to collect the drag queen. With the muscles of a man, she was much heavier than he expected, though Shem's exceptional strength allowed him to carry her the short distance to the site without much effort. He laid her on the ground on her back then fetched the rope from his backpack and tied her hands and ankles. While he waited for her to wake up, he emptied the backpack of the remainder of its contents, including a butcher's knife, hammer, and chisel.

The heat and heavy air along with the excitement of the anticipation of the kill were causing him to sweat profusely. The annoying sheath of perspiration that covered his skin from head to toe distracted him. He failed to notice Glamorosa had suddenly regained consciousness. Her previous experiences with aggressive and violent men gave her a momentary advantage. Ignoring the horror of her predicament, it took only a few seconds to gather her wits and assess her strategy. As he was pulling his shirt over his head to remove it, she lunged for the hammer he had placed on the ground next to the backpack. If Shem didn't have the butcher's knife in a casing on his belt, he might have been in grave trouble. Confident she could overcome the rope that tied her ankles together, she hopped to her feet, moving with surprising dexterity closer to the hammer. Sensing something was amiss, Shem threw his T-shirt off his body in time to see the prostitute grab the hammer. The idea she was going to fight for her life magnified his exhilaration.

"This is interesting," he said. "Do you really think you have a chance?"

"Try me, motherfucker. I've gotten away from guys twice your size, you fuck'n pussy."

Shem howled with laughter, but it didn't divert his attention from her this time. She pounced toward him with the hammer held high over her head and the intention of burying the spiked end deep into his skull. Shem easily averted her obvious attempt by stepping to the side and swiping the razor sharp blade of the butcher's knife across the full length of her throat. Blood shot out from the carotid artery like water from a fire hose. Glamorosa dropped to her knees, stunned by her reversal of fortune. Losing pints of blood by the second, she didn't have the strength to hold the hammer, which dropped harmlessly to the ground. Meanwhile, Shem continued his hysterical laughter, placing his naked chest in the path of the blood flow. The warmth and texture of the life sustaining liquid against his naked skin and nipples caused him to have an instant orgasm.

In a matter of moments, the prostitute lost consciousness once again. Knowing she was still alive, he began the process of cutting off her head, hoping the pain would wake her for one last look in her eyes. Instead, her heart stopped beating and the flow of blood reduced to a trickle. Refusing to be disappointed, he expertly wielded the butcher's knife to saw through to the third vertebrae of the cervical spine. Next, he grabbed the chisel and picked up the hammer from where Glamorosa had dropped it. Two more orgasms racked his body as he chipped through the bone until the head rolled off to the side. For a coup de gras, he castrated Glamorosa and stuffed the penis up her anus. He roared at the thought that he had given her what she always wanted.

* * *

Annie's date with Michael turned out to be a complete disaster. She broke her pledge to herself to make the best of the evening before it ever really got started. Everything was going fine until he decided to have a couple of cocktails and suggested they see each other more often. That was never a comfortable conversation for Annie and always led to the same result. She protested addressing the issue to no avail. Ultimately, she had to repeat herself for the umpteenth time; she wasn't interested in taking the relationship to another level. To make matters worse, he couldn't help but notice that throughout the dinner, Annie was somewhere off in her own world. The reason- she was thinking about re-extending her offer to Daniel for lunch and daydreaming about having a closer relationship with him. He pressed her to tell him why she was so distracted. Finally, against her better judgment, she revealed her plans. A terrible argument ensued and their trip to the movies was cancelled. As they left the restaurant, Annie pulled out her cell phone to call a taxi. Michael convinced her to let him drive her home, apologizing for his jealous behavior. Not a word was spoken during the ride to her apartment.

When she had time to sit and contemplate the disagreement, she had to admit she'd behaved badly. There was no excuse for being out on a date with one man and thinking about another, especially when the other was married with children. She recognized there was something terribly wrong with the situation, though she had no desire to analyze it any further at the moment. She decided she would call Michael first thing in the morning and apologize.

The next day, Annie woke from a deep, dreamless sleep to the sound of what she thought was her alarm. For an instant, she was confused, wondering why she had set it on her day off. When the cobwebs cleared, she realized it wasn't her alarm after all. The telephone was ringing. She reached for the receiver on the night stand and without checking the caller ID, put the phone to her ear. In a thick, morning voice she barely managed a "Hello."

"Hi sweetheart, it's Mom. I didn't wake you up, did I?"

"Don't worry about it, Mom. I needed to get up anyway. I thought you might be Michael."

"Why were you still asleep? It's late, honey. Don't you need to leave for work soon?"

"No, I took the day off. But, I didn't want to waste the morning in bed," Annie lied as she had every intention of sleeping in.

"Were you expecting Michael to call?"

"Well, not really. It's just…we had a pretty bad argument last night."

"Oh sweetie, not again. What now?"

"Same old thing. Where our relationship is going."

"You have that poor man on a string."

"You don't need to take his side. Besides, I know. I don't know how many times I've tried to break up with him. He won't take no for an answer."

"You're giving the poor guy mixed signals. You say you want to break up then you sleep with him again. He's gonna see it the way he wants to, you know. Every time you show him affection, it gives him hope."

"I know, I know. I have no excuse for playing with his feelings. I know it's not fair. I'm just gonna have to set my mind to doing something about it."

Annie had an exceptionally close relationship with her mother. She shared almost everything about her personal life with her, sometimes too much. Her mom didn't think twice about lecturing her thirty-four-year-old daughter if she felt it was necessary. In this case, it didn't make Cassie happy that Annie would allow herself to be in such a relationship.

Raised without a father, it was just the two of them against the world. From an early age, Cassie instilled in Annie the importance of an education and respect for other human beings. Cassie especially wanted to do everything in her power to prevent her daughter from developing an entitlement attitude. There weren't many human characteristics that Cassie found more repugnant. From the time Annie was in elementary school, Cassie worried that their financial status could affect the way her daughter perceived the world. They had enough money to last their lifetimes, the lifetimes of their children and grandchildren, and still have money left over.

In spite of their wealth, Cassie expected her daughter to be a person who contributed positively to society. She didn't want Annie to get a skewed view of reality having everything handed to her on a silver platter. She taught her that most of the rest of the planet had to struggle from week to week just to pay their bills and put food in their children's mouths. To give her firsthand experience, they took several trips to Africa during Annie's childhood. With UNICEF and other charitable organizations, they visited some of the more poverty-stricken countries. Seeing the horrible conditions under which people lived and sometimes starved had a profound impact on young Annie. It certainly taught her not to take anything for granted. Why she didn't apply that lesson to her relationship with Michael was an issue she needed to explore.

"I think you should just make him go cold turkey," said Cassie. "You can't see him anymore. You've got to give him a chance to get over you."

"You're right, Mom. I'll have a talk with him."

"I'd make it sooner than later. Anyway, to change the subject, you have plans for your day off? I'm not doing anything, if you'd like to stop by."

Annie was actually thinking about going ahead and following through with her plan to invite Daniel to lunch again. There was no time like the present, especially since she had taken a personal day. Without thinking, she revealed her intentions to her mother.

"Annie, sweetheart, what are you doing? I'm sorry I'm giving you such a hard time first thing in the morning…I just can't keep my mouth shut. Honey, he's a married man. It's not healthy to keep him in your life when you still have feelings for him. It's the same situation with you and Michael, just in reverse. You do still have feelings for him, don't you?"

"I don't know Mom. I've always been confused about my feelings for Daniel. But, this is just a lunch. He was promoted to Special Agent in Charge. I want to treat him. It's nothing more than a celebration. We've been friends for almost ten years now."

"Famous last words, but I've said my piece. I know you're a grown woman. I trust you to make the right decisions. Just be careful."

"I will, Mom. I promise."

"Ok, sweetie, I'm glad we got the chance to talk. I'm gonna go grab some breakfast. Don't be a stranger. I love you."

"Love you too, Mom. I'll call you this weekend. Bye."

After hanging up the phone, Annie considered rolling over and trying to get another hour or so of sleep. Knowing herself and the nearly impossible task of falling back asleep once she was awake, she decided it wasn't worth the effort. Her thoughts turned toward Daniel. She knew he was an early riser and rarely got to the office after 7:00am. Totally ignoring her mother's advice, she picked the phone back up and dialed his cell number. After six rings and no answer, she ended the call. Refusing to be discouraged from her plan, she dialed Daniel's work extension, thinking his secretary would be there. Karen usually arrived before her boss. Annie wasn't disappointed. Karen answered on the first ring. Aware Annie was a long time friend of Daniel's, Karen told her he was in Ft. Lauderdale for the morning. Annie saw it as the perfect opportunity to convince him to meet her at J. Alexander's, his favorite restaurant, after his business meeting was over. She was about to try his cell phone again and leave a message when it began to ring. To her pleasant surprise, the caller I.D. indicated it was Daniel.

"What's up Annie?"

"Hey Daniel. I was just lying here in bed thinking maybe we could get together for lunch today. I have the day off. What are you doing?"

"I have some meetings I have to attend. I don't think I can make it."

"Where are you?"

"I'm on the road."

"Daniel, I know you're spending the morning in Ft. Lauderdale. I called your office. Karen told me. You're not gonna reject my invitation for a third time, are you? You're gonna give me a complex." Since the initial congratulatory call to Daniel, Annie had sent him an email offering lunch again. In his typical sweet manner, at least when it involved her, he responded he would love to, but his schedule was prohibitive. Annie wasn't about to let him get away with it this time. She continued, "How long is your meeting this morning?"

Daniel considered telling a little fib. Truthfully, the meeting should be over before noon and he had plans to stop for lunch in Ft. Lauderdale anyway. His desire for her was screaming for him to say yes to the invitation. His head was telling him to lie through his teeth. Before he had a chance to respond, Annie added, "You're hesitating. You're considering it. Come on, Daniel. It's just a meal…completely innocent. We'll take separate cars. I'll meet you at J. Alexanders. It's not every day you get promoted to Special Agent in Charge. There's no reason why we can't be friends, is there?" Annie knew just where to hit the man she almost married. Making him feel guilty rarely failed.

"I don't know," said Daniel fidgeting in the driver's seat of his Crown Victoria, his fingers furiously tapping on the steering wheel. "When you put it that way, it's hard to say no."

"Then don't say it. What time do you get out of your meeting?"

"What about Deborah?"

"What about her?"

"You know what I mean. You know how she feels."

"Daniel, you're one of the smartest men I've ever met, but when it comes to relationships, you can be dumb as shit. Sometimes, things are just best left unsaid. If it's gonna cause conflict, don't tell her. It's not like you're doing anything wrong."

"You don't consider going to lunch with your ex behind your wife's back doing something wrong?"

"Not when it's innocent and not when you're wife is being unreasonable controlling what you do. A relationship is supposed to be built on trust. Anyone comfortable in their marriage wouldn't have a problem with this."

"Aright, ok, I'll go. My meeting should be over by 11:30 or so. I'll meet you there at noon."

* * *

Annie met Daniel at a fraternity party when they were sophomores at George Washington University. For both of them, it was love at first sight. What followed was an intense and torrid love affair that lasted over five and a half years. In May of 1997, they both received their Bachelor's Degrees in criminal justice. At the time, it was Annie's plan to apply for Harvard Law School then pursue a political career later in life. Since Daniel was also interested in getting a law degree, she convinced him to apply to Harvard. When they were both admitted and Daniel made his final decision to accept, they rented a small, one bedroom apartment in Cambridge. For all intents and purposes, they lived as a married couple during the three years required to obtain their law degrees and loved every second of it.

After graduation from Harvard, Daniel, being the traditional, old-school type, was ready to settle down, get married, and start a family. Annie had a very different notion about the first few years in the real world that didn't include wedding bells or snot-nosed brats. Being the career-oriented poster girl, she wanted them to become established in their professions before even allowing the idea of nuptials to enter her thought processes. She accepted what she considered the perfect career opportunity with King Cruise Line. The job offered worldwide travel and the ability to forge relationships with V.I.P's in the U.S. and internationally. It wasn't something she was willing to give up. Another major conflict arose in that the position required her to move to Ft. Lauderdale.

Meanwhile, Daniel was following his dream to be an FBI agent and was to start training at Quantico in Virginia.

Daniel was crushed when Annie rejected his marriage proposal. Although they tried to maintain a long-distance relationship, they soon began to grow apart. The miles that separated them proved to be much too difficult. Within seven months of graduation, they decided to call it quits. Annie spent many nights crying herself to sleep when the final decision was made. There were times she even considered quitting her job and flying up to D.C. to be with Daniel. Each instance of doubt was eventually smothered by her unrelenting drive and ambition to strive for a successful career. The fact that she seemed to almost have a phobia to committing to marriage didn't help either.

Annie plunged into her work head-first, trying not to look back. A workaholic, her job and career truly became her life. Several years later, Daniel was transferred to the North Miami field office. The profound feeling she experienced when they reconnected struck her like a freight train head on. The realization she had made a terrible mistake and it was now too late was a crushing blow. If she had explored deeper into her psyche, she might have to admit there was something attractive about a man who wasn't available. At the time, Daniel was married and already had a child. The misery and sadness of those weeks after their separation came flooding back like a river breaking through a faulty dam. What she was telling herself on the surface was that her career was always a priority. It prevented her from ever truly considering a realistic compromise. The idea of marriage and a family spooked her and she fled. Maybe, her judgment wasn't the best. In the end, it didn't matter. She ultimately decided she'd rather have Daniel in her life than not at all and settled on a friendship. Thereafter, she dated men and finally conceded to a longer arrangement with Michael, but her heart was never in that relationship.

A burst of chilly air rushed through Annie's bedroom causing goose bumps to rise on her arms and down her back. The air conditioning wasn't running, leading her to believe, just maybe, a cool front finally swept through South Florida during the night. She rose from the bed and hurried to the bathroom to grab her terrycloth robe. Before she had a chance to put it on, she heard the creaking noise made by the front door when opened or closed. Michael and her mother were the only people besides the building's administration who had a key to the condo. She knew it couldn't be her mother since she just ended the telephone conversation with her ten minutes ago. And Michael would never use the key if he knew she was home. Nevertheless, she called out his name. The lack of an answer and a second creaking of the door sent a bolt of panic up her spine.

Being ultra-security conscious and a woman who lived alone, Annie was the owner of a semi-automatic Baretta 92F. She retrieved the pistol from the drawer of her nightstand and made her way to the front of the apartment. Holding the gun with both hands out in front, she listened carefully as she approached the door. The field of vision covered by the peephole gave her a view of the entire hallway to the elevators on the opposite wall. She looked through the lens and saw no one. She continued her search around the entire condominium, checking every room and closet, keeping the gun poised and ready as she opened each door. Convinced there was no one in the apartment, she released a huge sigh of relief and lowered the gun. On her way back to the bathroom to begin her morning ritual, she couldn't expel the eerie sensation that an unwelcome intruder had been in her home.

* * *

Shem Chassar pulled into one of the many parking spaces on Birch Street that gave him a view of the front entrance to Annie's building. That day, he was driving his 1996 Ford Mustang. He'd arrived early in order to catch a glimpse of Annie preparing for work. He was hoping to get lucky. Once in a while, Annie would open the curtains of her bedroom, allowing him to see her in various stages of undress. There would be no cheap thrills that morning, however. She was usually up by 6:00am and driving out of the covered garage by no later than 7:30. At 7:15, an hour and 15 minutes after he arrived, there was not a single Annie sighting. It was time for a mini-panic. He immediately considered what for him would be the worst case scenario. She made up with Munez and spent the night at his house. It was always most difficult to control his rage when she slept with him. If she didn't break off the relationship sometime soon, he was going to take matters into his own hands and end it for her. For the moment, he had to know what was up.

Throwing discretion out the window, Shem decided he must enter Annie's apartment. He had done it before though his purpose on that occasion was much different. Disguised as one of the construction workers re-carpeting the hallways, he broke into Annie's apartment while she was at work. Running his hands through her sexy, laced unmentionables gave him unprecedented erotic pleasure. He lay naked in her bed, masturbating to climax multiple times. The orgasm he achieved fantasizing bathing in Annie's blood could have been the most intense and gratifying of his life.

It was rather easy getting past security the first time. The guard on duty waved him through without even looking up from the sitcom he was watching on his portable TV. This entry was going to be a bit more complicated. The construction workers usually didn't show up on the job before 8:00am. Shem sprinted to his Mustang and gathered his construction clothing, lunch box, and tool belt from the trunk. He changed quickly inside the car then jogged to the front entrance of Annie's building, entering through the revolving doors. An older, portly security officer was manning the desk. When he saw the construction worker approaching he said, "Hold on, buddy. Isn't it a little early for you guys to get started?"

"Yes, sir, you're right. But, the work isn't progressing as fast as the boss would like, so I thought I'd get a head start this morning."

"You can say that again. This project was supposed to be done four months ago. I don't see you guys finishing before February. But, you know the rules. The residents don't like any construction noise before 8:00am on the weekdays."

"I know. I promise I won't make a peep. What I'll be doing doesn't require any banging, hammering or noisy machines. I give you my word."

The security guard studied Shem's face for a moment, hesitated then responded, "Alright, young man, I happen to admire early birds. I'm gonna trust you. It's my ass if you piss off any of the residents, so keep it down until 8."

"Yes, sir."

The guard allowed him to pass. Shem walked beyond the security desk to the elevator bank and pushed the call button. In order to throw the old man off, in case he was watching the floor indicator, he hit the button for the fifth floor. He knew they were re-carpeting there, but wasn't sure if they had reached the penthouse level yet. When the elevator arrived at the fifth floor, he exited, waited a few minutes, re-entered, and took it up to Annie's floor.

As soon as the doors opened, he peered out from the front corner of the elevator toward the apartments to check to be sure neither Annie nor the other tenant on the floor was in the hallway. Seeing no one, he quickly walked the thirty yards straight ahead to Annie's door. He placed his ear up against it and listened for signs of activity. There was dead silence coming from within and there was no light streaming from the crack underneath the door. Feeling secure the apartment was vacant, he opened his lunchbox and pulled out the fourteen- piece lock picking kit he'd purchased online. It took him less than two minutes to disengage the deadbolt and knob lock. No sooner had he stepped inside when the telephone began to ring. He stopped in his tracks. Two rings later, he heard Annie's voice from one of the back rooms of the condo. From his position just fifteen feet from the front door, he heard every word she was saying.

After learning Annie had taken the day off, Shem's first thought was that he had been mindlessly rash taking such a risk. That notion was forgotten the instant he realized Annie was talking to some man he didn't know. He heard her make plans to have lunch with him, intensely irritated by the way she was flirtatiously coaxing him to accept her invitation. There was a definite tone of seduction in the way she was speaking. It was obvious to him she admired this one. A rage began to sprout its roots in the pit of his gut that he quickly had to squelch. The conversation was coming to an end.

He purposefully left the door open in the event a quick getaway became necessary. Before he had a chance to make his exit, a breeze from the corridor blew the door closed to a position too narrow to pass. His feet moved over the marble floor in complete silence as he hastily glided toward the threshold. He barely heard the creaking of the hinges as he opened and closed the door on his way out. Hoping Annie didn't notice, he ran to the elevator and pressed the call button. It was a stroke of luck that no one had used it since he arrived on the floor. The doors opened instantly. He wasted no time stepping inside and pushing the button for the lobby. Two seconds after the door closed, Annie looked through her peephole.

His exit from the lobby was much less eventful. The guard who granted him access to the building was involved in conversation with one of the residents. Shem strolled toward the revolving doors at a normal pace and left the condominium without being noticed by the officer or the man with whom he was speaking. Outside the building, he accelerated his step on his way to his parked car. He unlocked the door, threw himself into the driver's seat, and proceeded to bang his fists against the steering wheel for a full minute. Before he was through, its steel casing was completely destroyed.

He had been angry many times in his life, but couldn't recall a time when he'd reacted in such a manner. The fury he felt when he thought Annie spent the night with Michael and the fit of rage over this new man was not acceptable. It caused him to take unnecessary risks and lose his ability to accurately assess a situation. His intuitive abilities were rendered useless under such circumstances. If he had just checked the covered garage, he probably would have discovered Annie's car was still where she parked it the previous night. He made a solemn pledge to himself. From this point on, he would always act with a clear and reasonable head. He did have to acknowledge that he came away from this experience with one useful piece of information. He would follow Annie to her lunch and find out what this man was all about.

Chapter 6

Interstate 95 was jam-packed as Daniel drove north to Ft. Lauderdale for his 8:00am appointment. Since the previous Wednesday when he received the promotion, his schedule had been as congested as the freeway. The transition process required fourteen hour days. While he was training his replacement for the Assistant Special Agent in Charge of the criminal division, he was going through orientation with Rick Suarez for his new position. That was not to mention the process of doling out responsibility for the files he was handling personally. He barely had time for his family. For the moment, they weren't giving him too hard of a time about his absence and he was grateful for it.

This morning he was meeting with the Chief of Police of the Ft. Lauderdale Police Department. A task force was created several months back to handle the resurfacing of gang-related crimes in Broward County. It included members of Daniel's squad, officers from the Ft. Lauderdale Police Department, troopers from the Florida Highway Patrol, and deputies from the Broward County Sheriff's Office. Daniel was a member of the task force despite his supervisory position at the Bureau. The severity of the problem called for his expertise as a director and educator for the Florida Gang Investigator's Association. To date, the task force had arrested more than two- hundred gang members and confiscated narcotics and stolen goods with a street value of over $750,000.00. Two of the most dangerous gang leaders were still at large, but they were hot on their trail. Since Daniel would no longer be available for the task force, he wanted to personally meet with the Captain to provide him with some important updates and answer any questions he may have.

That was his official business for being in Ft. Lauderdale, yet his date to follow was what was niggling on his mind. He was looking forward to seeing Annie, maybe a little bit too much. Convincing himself it wouldn't serve any good purpose, he followed Annie's advice and didn't mention his plans for lunch to Deborah. Now, a few hours from his rendezvous with his ex, he was beginning to feel guilty. Secrets weren't normally his style and he was sure Deborah wouldn't appreciate his lack of confidence in her. His true reasons for keeping Deborah out of the loop were probably much more carnal in nature than he was willing to admit. He had actually gone through a mental exercise convincing himself he loved his wife dearly, cherished his boys, and would never do anything to harm his family. The excuse wasn't exactly working. He was relatively certain Deborah would be more upset over his omission than the actual lunch, though neither would make her happy.

His meeting with the Captain took his mind off his guilt over the several hours it lasted. As he left the Ft. Lauderdale Police Department, those feelings came flooding back. He seriously considered phoning Annie to make some excuse and call it off. Just when he thought he had made a firm decision to do the right thing, his cell phone began to squeal. Annie's ears must have been ringing. She was calling to express her excitement about seeing him.

"I've been looking forward to this all morning," she said. "It's been a while since we were able to catch up. It'll be nice to have you all to myself."

Whether it was because he chickened out or he was feeling the same way, Daniel changed his mind as quickly as he entertained the thought of cancelling.

"Me too, Annie. I always enjoy spending time with you. I'm on my way to the restaurant now."

Annie's heart leapt as she felt a warm sensation in the pit of her stomach. She was thinking she was a big, hot mess, but said, "That's so sweet. You know I feel the same way. I'll see you there."

"Sure thing," said Daniel, who snapped his cell phone shut. After all the second- guessing, those words seemed to flow a little bit too easily from his lips. This couldn't be healthy for his marriage.

* * *

During Annie's morning telephone conversation with Daniel, Shem overheard they would be having lunch at J. Alexanders. An hour before their scheduled meeting, Shem pulled into the parking lot of the Krispy Kreme doughnut shop located just south of the restaurant, and waited. Daniel arrived first in his Crown Victoria. It was obvious to Shem it was some type of unmarked police vehicle. He already knew Daniel worked for the FBI, being familiar with the term Special Agent in Charge. It had the potential to make things interesting. Browsing through the FBI's Miami field office website, he also came across a picture of the agent with a caption indicating his former position. It was always helpful to have a last name. It allowed access to so much more information.

Five minutes later, Annie arrived in her fire-red BMW M6 convertible and parked next to the agent's car. Through the rearview mirror of his Mustang, he watched as the agent held the door of the restaurant open for Annie. He could feel the rage simmering beneath the surface watching both Annie's and the agent's body language and facial expressions. It was clear to him that not only did Annie have feelings for this man, but the agent was more than just interested in a friendly relationship with her. He waited several minutes after they entered and then made his way across the parking lot toward the restaurant.

* * *

When Annie turned into the parking lot of J. Alexanders, she saw Daniel standing at the front entrance waiting for her. She gave him a quick wave then parked in the available space next to his Crown Victoria. She took a glance at herself in the rearview mirror, unnecessarily adjusted her hair, and exited the vehicle. After they passed through the double doors of the restaurant, Daniel greeted her with a small kiss directly on the lips. A sudden, but not unexpected sensation of heat flushed through her head, causing her face to turn a bright shade of red. She rapidly turned away from him to conceal her body's betrayal and proceeded toward the hostess's podium. Her argument that this lunch was completely innocent could have been thrown right out the window if Daniel had noticed.

The restaurant wasn't very busy, so they were seated immediately at a booth along the rear wall. For the next hour, they talked about their professions, their families, and the good old days. They reminisced about their time together in college and joked about their near miss at the altar. They were so totally engrossed in each other that they didn't notice within a half an hour of their arrival, the restaurant had filled to capacity. At the table directly across the aisle, the tall blond, well muscled man wearing a baseball cap and thick lens glasses also escaped their attention. If Annie had just taken a hard look to her left, she may have realized the man was the spitting image of Damien Drysdale.

To Shem, they were acting like two teenagers in love. The idea that Annie had that type of passion for another man was almost more than he could bear. There was no mistaking Daniel's look into her eyes, either. Falcone was in love with her. When he heard that they had a serious relationship which nearly culminated in marriage, in his mind his suspicions were confirmed. It took every ounce of his self-control to keep himself from stabbing the FBI agent in the heart with the eight inch pocket knife tucked in his sock. He would have ended this disgusting display a long time ago if he wasn't gathering some very useful information. He discovered that the agent was married, had two children, and that they lived in Hallandale. Falcone was very well educated, exceptionally smart, and resolutely ambitious. He would make for an extraordinarily formidable foe.

Shem had reached a point where he could handle no more regardless of the intelligence he was collecting. There was no way he was going to allow this love fest to continue. He got up from his table, found his server, and paid the check. On his way toward the exit, he scanned the restaurant, the wheels in his head furiously churning. A crowd had gathered at the bar and waiting area. The consistent high volume chatter and sheer number of people made for a chaotic scene. It was just what he needed to maintain a low profile. He stood among the flock for several minutes to observe. His eyes were drawn to a young mother standing toward the entrance with an empty stroller. She was involved in an animated conversation with what Shem assumed was her friend. Neither of the young ladies was paying a lick of attention to the two and a half-year-old girl who had become enamored with the stained glass decorating the entry doors. Taking advantage of the opportunity, like a phantom he glided unnoticed toward the exit, opened the door, grabbed the child by the hand and walked out. Once in the parking lot, he wasted no time whisking the crying baby into his arms and carrying her to his car. By the time the mother realized her child was gone, Shem was pulling out of the parking lot onto US1.

The high pitched screams of the horrified woman was the first thing outside of their own world they had created that Daniel and Annie finally acknowledged. Daniel immediately jumped from his seat and ran toward the direction of the commotion. He showed his identification to the distraught mother and the restaurant employee attempting to handle the situation. They informed Daniel that the woman's child was missing. The mother, her friend, the manager and several restaurant employees had already searched the entire restaurant over the past five minutes. Daniel asked her a few quick questions about the girl's description and where she was last seen then enlisted the assistance of the manager to check the parking lot. Together, they burst through the front double doors.

Two cars, a Cadillac Escalade and a Nissan Altima were in line waiting to pull out onto the road. Daniel sprinted toward the driver's side of the front car with his ID held up in plain view, motioning the woman behind the wheel to stop. He ordered her to unlock the doors then searched inside the vehicle. Finding nothing, he moved on to the second car with no better results. Since there were no others leaving the parking lot, he instructed the manager to stand at the restaurant's only exit to the street to prevent anyone else from leaving. Daniel then began a systematic search of the surrounding area including a visual check inside each parked car. As he combed the lot, he detached his cell phone from his belt to notify the field office of the missing child. He gave them the brief description of the toddler obtained from the mother and the circumstances behind the disappearance. During his search, employees and patrons from inside the restaurant joined him to provide extra eyes. An initial circuit of the parking lot proved fruitless.

* * *

Waves of heat bounced off the pavement, creating an illusion of oasis-like water puddles floating over the road surface. No cool front had passed through South Florida. Quite the contrary, the relentless heat wave continued to oppress in full force. Shem's car's air-conditioning seemed to have little effect, if any. Perspiration soaked his skin from head to toe. Every few seconds, he had to wipe the dripping sweat from his brow with a paper napkin to keep his vision from blurring. His state of mind was also playing a big role in his body's failure to regulate its temperature. From the time he left his table at J. Alexanders, a fury had been festering in the bowels of his demented soul. Images of Annie's lovelorn gaze whenever she looked into the eyes of the FBI agent persistently assaulted his thoughts. His efforts to suppress them had no more than a superficial effect.

The toddler provided little distraction. The instant he saw her, his plan was formulated. The ruckus caused by her disappearance would force the agent into action. Shem wasn't prepared, however, for the intensity of the baby's response. Her annoying shrieks weren't what the doctor ordered for his volatile frame of mind. After leaving the restaurant, he picked her up, tucked her legs around his right hip and let the child instinctively grab behind his upper arm like the many fathers he had seen carrying their babies. At a normal pace, he walked to his to his car still parked in the Dunkin Doughnuts' lot. He threw her in the back seat like a sack of potatoes, locked the door then assumed his place behind the wheel. The girl was now out of control. Her wailing filled the car and pounded against his temples. His screams to shut her up only made matters worse.

He checked the surrounding area to be sure they were not attracting any attention. The lot was packed with vehicles, but the closest people were on the other side of the restaurant. They were paying no mind. He started the car and pulled out of his space and onto Federal Highway. The child's cries had reached a pitch that seemed to pierce through his skull to wring his brain. This could not last much longer. He had to put an end to it. He turned off the road into the parking lot for the California Pizza Kitchen and took the alley to the rear of the building. Seeing no signs of human presence, he parked his car beside one of two large dumpsters. There was no time to waste. It was one of the busiest hours for the restaurants in the area and an employee could show up at any moment. He grabbed the baby from the back seat, jumped out of the car leaving his door open and tossed her over the side of the dumpster. The shock of flying through the air momentarily shut the girl up. Shem felt instant relief from her silence but didn't wait to listen for her landing. He was already back in the driver's seat.

Minutes later, the hysterical child already erased from his thoughts, Shem was driving southbound on Federal Highway with no real destination. Cool blasts from the Mustang's air-conditioner turned up to its maximum setting finally began to clear his mind of the stress of the afternoon. It was unusual and totally unacceptable that he had taken so long to calm himself. He had always been proud of his ability to modulate his anger and control his emotions in order to work through an issue with a sound mind but without mistakes. Now was not the time for it to desert him. Shem couldn't afford to let the FBI agent get to him if they were going to be mortal enemies. His confidence in his ability to outwit the most brilliant of law enforcement officers was not enough. Being even-keeled, well-prepared, and at least one step ahead was absolutely essential. Before long, he would know everything there was to know about Falcone's private and professional life. Maintaining the upper hand was more important than ever. While he remained nameless and unknown, he would be able to read the agent like a book.

* * *

Daniel had swept the parking lot of J. Alexander's twice with no better success finding the toddler who had disappeared into thin air. The agency had already sent several more agents and representatives of the local police department to assist in the search. Daniel was about to begin the interrogation of potential witnesses inside the restaurant when his cell phone rang. The squad secretary for the FBI's kidnapping division called to inform him that a child matching the missing girl's description was found alive in the dumpster of the California Pizza Kitchen. Their head cook had called the Fort Lauderdale Police Department to report finding a screaming baby in their dumpster. They in turn notified the FBI who had put out the initial APB. The secretary was not sure if the victim had suffered any injury.

After sharing his intentions only with a colleague, Daniel hopped in his car and drove the short trip south to the California Pizza Kitchen. He wanted to be sure the victim was in a condition her mother could handle before he notified her that her child had been found. The head cook was standing just outside the restaurant's entrance holding the hand of the crying girl who was standing on her own two feet- a good sign. Daniel quickly exited his vehicle looking closely at what appeared to be a perfectly healthy two year old toddler, though he called for an ambulance for confirmation. She had red stains covering her Kids-R-Us polka-dotted dress and pizza sauce on her face and in her hair, but otherwise she seemed unharmed.

The head cook explained that he had stepped out back for a cigarette break and heard the child's echoing, ear-piercing wails. He knew immediately they were coming from inside one of their two dumpsters. A man well over 6 feet tall, he was able to step on the edge of its air vent and look inside. The child sat crying at the top of a pile of restaurant garbage filling the container to nearly ¾ its capacity. Luckily, the garbage men weren't due until later that afternoon or the bin would have been empty. The girl was just outside of his reach and his footing on the slanted vent top was unstable. He quickly jumped down to the ground and ran back inside to grab a step stool from the maintenance closet. The couple of feet it elevated him was enough to allow him to lift the baby to safety.

Daniel immediately called his colleague at J. Alexanders to request that he escort the mother to the California Pizza Kitchen. When the agent notified her of her baby's location, he didn't have time to offer a ride. She was already on her way, sprinting almost faster than the agent could keep up. Being no more than one hundred yards from J. Alexanders, it took her well less than a minute to arrive. Once inside, she found her precious baby unscathed, in the arms of the restaurant manager, chomping on a big slice of cheese pizza. An indescribable wave of relief washed through her when she saw her daughter's broad, tomato stained smile. They chose the perfect pacifier. It was her favorite food in the world.

For the next hour and a half, Daniel interviewed the mother, her friend, the head cook and potential witnesses at both restaurants. There was not one person who could say they saw the child leave J. Alexanders, nor did anyone see her at any time between her disappearance and when she was found by the cook in the dumpster. Though the mother indicated her child had an adventurous spirit and could climb like a monkey, Daniel didn't believe she was capable of getting into the dumpster on her own. Fortunately, he could leave the resolution of that mystery to the kidnapping division. At least the paramedics then Imperial Point Hospital emergency room staff had determined the girl was in perfect health and not abused or sexually assaulted. It was probably some nut trying to teach the mother a depraved, perverse lesson for not keeping an eye on her child. He had seen crazier things. As for Annie, she left shortly after the child was found. Daniel never even got the chance to properly thank her for the lunch.

* * *

The heads of three construction workers turned in perfect unison as the beautiful woman in tight Donna Karan jeans and a red Michael Kors tank top strolled through the lobby of the Maya Marca Condominium. Annie Bryan felt as though she was walking on air. Having lunch with a gorgeous, intelligent, well put together man could have that effect on a woman, especially, she thought, when she was in love with him. Yes, she had to admit to herself she was still head over heels for the guy. For today, she wasn't going to let the fact he was married with two beautiful sons bother her.

As she passed the security station and waved to Harry, the overweight security guard, she noticed her next-door neighbor, Hannah Richards, was waiting at the elevators. Annie's mood was more than obvious in her cheerful greeting.

"Hi Hannah, beautiful day isn't it?"

In her heavy New York accent, Hannah replied, "Well, hello sweetheart. I like your positive attitude, but it's way too hot and sticky out there for me. It doesn't do much for my hairdo. What do you think of it?" she asked as she felt along the side of her beehive with the flat of her palm.

Annie's eccentric neighbor and dear friend always had a dome of perfectly quaffed, bright auburn hair rising about six inches above her head. For an elderly lady, she had unusually smooth skin and a trim, athletic body. Left widowed and filthy rich at the tender age of twenty-nine, she'd never remarried. She was now in her early seventies and living alone in a 5,000 square foot ocean-front condominium. She could thank several very expensive encounters with one of America's most talented plastic surgeons for her youthful look. Annie thought that, at times, she dressed and applied excessive make-up like a common hooker. In spite of her appearance, she was one of the sweetest ladies on Earth and Annie adored her.

Thinking her hairdo looked the same as always, but not daring to say so, Annie responded, "It looks gorgeous, Hannah. Don't tell me you were at the beauty parlor again. Doesn't that make three times just since Friday?"

The elevator door opened and the two women stepped in. Annie pressed the button for the 14th floor as Hannah retorted, "Yeah, honey, they were havin' trouble getting the color right and you know how picky I am when it comes to my hair. Do you like the color?"

Again, Annie noticed no difference. She said, "It's perfect, Hannah. You look absolutely stunning."

"Thank you darling. It takes a lot of work these days. More than I care to admit to. But you keep that beautiful mouth of yours shut. That's between you and me."

"Mum's the word. My lips are sealed."

They arrived at their floor, exited the elevator, and continued up the hallway. Hannah's apartment was on the right. Annie's was at the opposite end across from the elevator bank. Placing her key in the door, Hannah asked, "Annie, what are you doin' for dinner tonight? I'm fixin' a nice brisket. I'd love to have some company."

Annie's memory of Hannah's previous brisket dinner was all too fresh in her mind. It tasted like braised shoe leather. Hannah wasn't the greatest cook in the world and that was a monumental understatement. Annie politely declined, lying that she already had plans for the evening.

Disappointed, Hannah entered her apartment. Just before she closed the door, she said, "By the way, I'm going to New York this weekend to visit family and maybe catch a show. Would you mind keeping an eye on the apartment?" Hannah travelled quite frequently and Annie had a key to her apartment and mailbox.

"Sure thing, Hannah. I'll pick up your mail too and leave it on your dining room table."

"You're a doll. I'll see you later."

"Bye. Take care. And if I don't see you before you leave, have a great time in New York."

Annie entered her apartment, threw her Cross bag on the kitchen counter, and decided she was going to treat herself to an afternoon nap. Lying on her favorite sofa in the living room, she daydreamed about her lunch with Daniel. Inevitably and quite intrusively, it led her to think about her conversation with her mother, regarding Michael. She had to admit it was getting old justifying her actions by telling herself she had always been excessively clear with him. It was obvious the man was very much in love with her. She tried to break it off several times, but Michael was so stubborn. He always assured her with the lie that he was happy with the way things were.

She knew if she were to be honest with herself, her mother was right. She wasn't being very nice. In fact, she was probably stringing him along. She was sure Michael had hopes that some day she was going to have feelings for him. That just wasn't going to happen. As she drifted into sleep, she made a commitment to herself and Michael. She would break up with him and be firm this time. It was best for both of them.

* * *

Shem sat across from the Maya Marca condominium entrance in his Mustang with the engine running. He didn't dare go out onto the beach in case Annie left the apartment again. Though he was doing a fairly decent job keeping his anger under control, he was still experiencing a deeply unsettled feeling in the pit of his stomach. It was happening much too often lately. He was frustrated that he continued to have difficulty composing himself. In recent days, there was only one fail-safe way to completely alleviate the condition. As he kept his eyes fixed on the revolving doors, his remedy was injected into the brilliant Ft. Lauderdale afternoon. Hannah Richards shot out from the exit like an arrow from its bow. The woman always seemed to move in ultra-accelerated motion. The first time he saw her, it was like being struck by the blast of a hand grenade. He had just settled on the beach after following Annie home from work when the woman came barreling toward him on her evening power walk. At first, he thought he was seeing a ghost. The resemblance to his mother was uncanny. As she drew closer, he realized she just seemed to be an older version of the Tucker slut. For a fleeting moment, he wondered if she'd survived the fire. Observing her for several days thereafter, he discovered she was a resident of the Maya Marca condominiums.

One week later, he followed Annie to work. Once he was sure she was safely inside the 110 Tower, he returned to her building. He found a free space across from the entrance, parked his vehicle and waited patiently for the postman to arrive. Five hours passed before the mail was finally delivered. Shem waited another thirty minutes until after the mailman left the premises to enter through the revolving doors and make his way over to the mailbox station. Since that area wasn't visible from the security desk, the chance of being noticed if he lingered was minimal. Within fifteen minutes Hannah exited the elevator at the main lobby and headed straight for the mailboxes. She unlocked hers leaving the door open just long enough for Shem to catch the apartment number. That afternoon, when he checked the building's layout on his Iphone, he found she was Annie's next door neighbor. He was also able to procure a list of residents and their apartment numbers by working his magic online. By the end of that night, he had uncovered a mountain of information about the woman who resembled his dead mother.

Annie's neighbor offended every single one of his senses and yet, he realized she was actually exactly what the doctor had ordered. From the instant he saw her, he knew she would have to die. Living in the same apartment complex with the object of his desire had saved her up to that point. There was no better time than the present to find a way around that obstacle. A well-planned murder with adventure and deception would be the perfect distraction, the more complicated, the better. It was what gave him the greatest fulfillment and satisfaction. It was what he lived for. It was his peace.

Proving to the authorities he was smarter than they was essential to his self-worth. If he were to search deep inside his psyche, something Shem would never consider, he would understand his acceptance and endorsement of having no name was just a farce. He longed to be someone, to show everyone he could even have more than one identity. He could be whoever he wanted. Surely, this kill would get him back on track.

Watching the Maya Marca over the past six months, he got to know a lot about its residents. He was aware that Hannah Richards travelled quite a bit. At least twice a month he would see her waiting for a taxi at the building's entrance, surrounded by a collection of suitcases that could serve an army. A malevolent design began to take root in the murky abyss of his admittedly demonic mind.

Chapter 7

If it had been up to Cherie Tucker, her only son would have remained an uneducated dunce for as long as he lived. School had always been out of the question. If the boy ever told his story to a teacher or school official, she would probably spend the rest of her life in prison. It wasn't until he was 15 years old that he got his first opportunity to learn. The subject matter wasn't one that would be taught in any public or private school. At that stage of his life, his mother had become increasingly careless about leaving the door unlocked when she left the apartment. Shem's many excursions outside his home hadn't ventured beyond his building's front stoop since he first met the beautiful black woman. With a late-blooming physical maturity, he finally garnered the nerve to pioneer beyond his own street. After several months of exploration, he felt secure enough to approach other boys his age. Inevitably, he crossed paths with his neighborhood's more than fair share of juvenile delinquents. They ultimately served a valuable purpose in his young life. They taught him how to burglarize homes and perform other various nefarious jobs for the local underworld crime bosses. For the several months before and years after his mother's murder, it offered him the means to a livelihood but not without risk. Other street kids would often get themselves arrested or even killed. Shem never had such problems. By drawing on his exceptional intelligence, he was able to survive his life of crime without a record and more importantly with a heartbeat and all four limbs.

A love affair and fascination with computers followed shortly after his 18th birthday when he obtained his first false identification and registered for night school. It was Shem Chassar's steadfast opinion that the worldwide web was man's most ingenious invention. At the age most boys were graduating from high school, he was just learning his ABC's. He caught up quickly, picking up the written English language as though he was learning a nursery rhyme. His initial encounter with a computer was at the public library where he would practice his newly acquired skill. He spent hours in front of the monitor reading, soaking up as much information as his physical stamina would allow. His powers of retention were extraordinary by any standards. Within one year of his first reading lesson, he was devouring textbooks written by Ronald M. Rivest, Adi Shamir and Leonard M. Adelman, world-renowned forerunners in the field of computer science. He consumed every book he could get his hands on regarding computer hard drives and software. At the age of 21, he probably knew more about computers than Bill Gates, himself, and could build his own fully functioning computer from scratch. He continued his self-teaching of the computer sciences throughout his adulthood. There wasn't a hacker in the world that was more adept than he.

After accumulating a relatively sizeable nest egg through his employment with the mafia and later completing the first years of his self-education, Shem wanted to find a way to make his money grow. He did his initial research on the Internet then went to the library to borrow Masters and PhD level textbooks on financial investment. They gave him a solid base of comprehension of the machinations of the New York Stock Exchange that he needed to get started. For the first several years after he began investing in the Market, he was able to support himself rather comfortably without the need for a formal job. At twenty five years old, he struck gold. He purchased ten thousand dollars of a penny stock selling at .39 cents a share for a new Internet based company. In a matter of months, the company's profits exploded increasing the price of the stock to over $100.00. His ten thousand dollars turned into millions. By the time he was thirty, he had invested so wisely, he amassed more money than he could spend in several lifetimes. He held many offshore accounts in several Caribbean municipalities. Some of his more significant holdings were kept in the same Swiss banks used by the richest people in the world. His fortune had grown so large that it required constant management. Trusting no one to oversee it, his homes always had an extra room for a fully equipped office. For Shem it was a pleasure to invest and invent ways to increase his wealth. His net worth could never be too great.

On the Wednesday evening of the day he saw Hannah Richards bolt through the Maya Marca revolving doors, he sat before his computer and hacked into the airlines' database. He knew it wouldn't be long before she was travelling again. Within ten minutes, he discovered she would be flying American Airlines flight 262 to LaGuardia Airport that Friday at 4:00pm. He purchased his first- class ticket in the name of Dwight Adelman, resident of Jerusalem, and booked the seat beside her. Next, he hacked into the Manhattan hotel computer information bank and found she would be staying at the Four Seasons Hotel New York in Manhattan. He then made reservations for a rental car at the airport Avis.

During his research of Hannah Richards, he discovered an article written about her husband, a practicing Orthodox Jew. On the Thursday before his scheduled trip, Shem went shopping at several different specialty shops and the Galleria mall. He purchased a long black cloth jacket, black trousers, black shoes, black yarmulke, white shirt and white socks. No matter how much it disgusted him to his very core, it was essential that he exhort the woman to trust him.

* * *

The yellow cab pulled up to terminal three of the Ft. Lauderdale/Hollywood International Airport and parked at the curb directly in front of the American Airlines sky-cap. The driver exited the vehicle, jogged around to the other side, and opened the back passenger door for his client. As was typical for travel days, Hannah Richards was gussied up to the nines, her idea of it anyway. She was wearing tight gold satin pants with a skin-hugging bright green sleeveless blouse. She had rings on all ten fingers and oval earrings approaching the size of a hula hoop. On each arm, she wore a train of bangle bracelets that made a clinking noise whenever she moved.

When she was safely up on the curb, the taxi driver unloaded two of her bags from the front driver's seat and placed them in front of the sky-cap stand. He then removed three of the largest and heaviest suitcases he had ever seen from his oversized trunk one at a time, struggling to set them in a row next to the others. Hannah paid him the fifteen dollar fare plus a twenty dollar tip for his efforts. After tagging the luggage, the sky-cap handed her the receipts along with her boarding passes, and instructed her the flight would be boarding at Gate 5. She handed him a twenty and entered the terminal.

Hannah loved to travel, but didn't care to do it alone. She was a social creature by nature. People were her fascination. The traveling part of her trips back home to New York was never her favorite. She was usually on her own and never looked forward to the hour and a half wait in the airport, then the two and a half hour flight to LaGuardia without anyone to chat with. Most times she'd strike up a friendship with her neighbor on the plane who would have to suffer through several hours of incessant chatter. She was a seasoned conversationalist with an effortless ability to chew through ear cartilage directly to the eardrum.

On this particular journey, her problem was solved when she met a nice young Jewish gentleman who sat directly across from her at the gate. She first noticed him when she was making her way through security. He was three people behind her in line. Her attention was initially attracted to him because of the black suit and yarmulke he was wearing. It was obvious he was an Orthodox Jew. She didn't think much more about it until it appeared he was on her flight. It was odd he would be traveling so late on a Friday evening. It was their custom, if not strict law to be indoors before nightfall. When he sat down, her curiosity got the better part of her. She decided to get to the bottom of the issue.

"I like your watch. Is it a Rolex?"

"No Ma'am. Just a fancy Timex. Thank you."

Hannah instantly recognized a foreign accent and was pretty sure he was from Israel, having visited the country numerous times. She responded, "It's beautiful…My husband was an Orthodox Jew. I used to be, but I've mellowed over the years."

"Your husband too?"

"He passed away a long time ago."

"I'm sorry."

Hannah smiled then extended her hand across the aisle. "I'm Hannah."

"Rabbi Dwight Adelman. Pleased to meet you, Madam."

"Rabbi…hmm. It's nice to see a young man devoted to his religion. Is that an Israeli accent?"

"You have a good ear. I am from Jerusalem."

"How interesting, I've been there many times. It's my favorite part of the world. I wish it was more peaceful, but it's a captivating city."

Shem nodded his head in agreement.

"You know, when I first noticed you in the security line, I was surprised you'd be travelling so late," she continued. "Then I figured you must be on a short flight. You're not on this flight to New York, are you?"

Instantly realizing what she was talking about, Shem had to think quickly on his feet.

"Actually, I am. I am going to have to break the rules tonight. There has been a family emergency. My mother is very ill and it was the earliest flight I could get out of Ft. Lauderdale. I guess I will just have to do a little extra praying tonight."

“Now it’s my turn to be sorry. I’m so nosy. Sometimes, I don’t know when to mind my own business.”

“Don’t worry, Hannah. There was no way you could know.”

Over the public address system, the gate agent announced American Airlines flight 262 would be boarding in five minutes. Shem squirmed in his thick cloth coat, cursing the Orthodox Jews for dressing in such a ridiculous manner. He couldn’t conceive of a reason why any sensible person would wear this type of garb in Florida or the heat of the summer. To him, custom and tradition were a ludicrous notion. They had no basis in logic or reason and were an obstruction to the evolutionary process. Anyone who restricted their behavior based on those tenets was just a complete moron in his opinion.

At least his plan was working as well as he had expected considering the one small glitch. He was quite pleased he was able to rectify the problem, though it wasn’t like him to make such mistakes. Forgetting the Orthodox Jews were required to be indoors before the sun set on Friday evenings could have been a crucial error that caused him to have to scrub the whole plan. He attributed it to the edginess he was experiencing over Annie and the FBI agent. Otherwise, it seemed as if she really took a liking to the rabbi. By the end of the flight, he was sure he would have her eating from his hands.

The gate agent called for the boarding of passengers holding first class tickets and those people needing special assistance. Hannah Richards was pleasantly surprised to see her partner in conversation rise when the announcement was made. When she realized they were sitting next to each other, she greeted him with a broad smile that turned his stomach. It was going to be a long flight. He reminded himself that his reward would be well worth the effort.

* * *

Shem’s head felt like it was going to explode. The crazy, obnoxious bitch found the words to talk throughout the entire flight, barely taking the time to breathe. Though the persistent rage loitered beneath the surface, his demeanor remained balanced. He was courteous and pleasant while listening attentively to her incessant ranting, even managing to smile when she did and laugh at her stupid jokes. It wasn’t easy maintaining the discipline to keep from shutting the bitch up permanently by shoving the silver fork served with his meal through her jugular vein.

His plan to use the family emergency excuse was working to perfection. He told the woman his mother was fighting a ten year losing battle with breast cancer and was admitted to the hospital in critical condition earlier in the day. According to the doctors, her prognosis was not good. They were giving her two weeks at the most. The Tucker slut look-alike seemed to fall for the whole story hook, line and sinker. She even shed a few tears.

After what seemed like an eternity to Shem, the plane finally landed at LaGuardia airport at 6:16pm. Continuing his role as the perfect gentleman, he removed Hannah's carry-on bag from the overhead compartment and carried it to baggage claim. While they were waiting for their luggage, he stepped aside to feign making a telephone call to the hospital. When he returned, he reported to Hannah the gist of his fake conversation.

"Evidently my mother is resting and visitation doesn't resume for another couple of hours. I reserved a rental car with Avis. Do you have a ride to your hotel?" On the plane, she had told him she was staying at the Four Seasons.

"That's very kind of you, Rabbi, but I couldn't impose on you like that. You have enough to worry about tonight."

"Nonsense. The Four Seasons happens to be right on the way to my sister's apartment. And actually, I could use the company. It's been a pleasure having you to talk to. It's distracted me from reality for a while."

"Are you absolutely sure? I have no problem taking a taxi. I don't want to be an extra burden. And what about all my luggage?"

He had already considered that the woman travelled with half her wardrobe and was well prepared for it. He responded, "You will not be a burden in the least. In fact, you'll be the opposite. It will be a pleasure. I insist. I have rented an oversized SUV, so there will be plenty of room for your bags."

"You're so sweet, Rabbi. In that case, I accept. But you'll have to let me pay you for your trouble."

"Don't be ridiculous, Madam. Your company will be sufficient."

They had to wait twenty minutes before their flight's bags were loaded onto the delivery conveyor belt. Shem placed them and his one suitcase on a cart, then walked the short distance to the Avis counter. With no one in line, they received immediate service. The entire process of signing the papers lasted less than fifteen minutes. The walk to the Avis shuttle bus stop across the street from the terminal building while pushing the cart stacked five feet high with huge, heavy suitcases took just as long.

* * *

Shem, keeping the brim of his hat low across his forehead and eyes, avoided the look of the shuttle bus driver as they were driven to the Avis parking lot located on airport grounds. Upon arrival, he allowed the driver to load the crazy woman's bags onto a cart while he located their vehicle. The lot attendant barely looked at Shem's face as he pointed out the location of the space where the SUV was parked. After returning to collect the woman and her luggage, Shem led the way to the vehicle. He helped Hannah into the front passenger seat then loaded her bags in the hatchback trunk space, strategically arranging them so that her view of him standing behind the vehicle was obstructed.

In an easily accessible front pocket of his suitcase, he had packed a rag and small bottle of ether. He placed the bag on the asphalt directly behind the open hatchback then returned the luggage cart to a stand located at the end of the row of cars. Before locking it in place, he wiped the handle clean with a handkerchief as he had done while the woman wasn't looking with the cart he used at the airport terminal. Staying alert to his surroundings, he doubled back to the vehicle, picked up his bag and placed it in the trunk so the front side was accessible. He unzipped the pouch and removed the cloth and bottle of ether, aware his actions were being captured by a surveillance camera mounted on a pavilion just behind him. Careful to keep his face or profile from being recorded, he opened the cap and poured a generous portion onto the rag. With the sedative tucked safely in his left pocket, he slammed the hatchback shut. He walked to the driver's side, checking in each direction to make sure he wasn't being watched, always maintaining his vigilant attentiveness to the camera. The parking lot attendant was nowhere to be seen and there were no other customers in the vicinity. He opened the door, stepped into the vehicle, slipped the rag out of his pocket and forcefully shoved it into Hannah's face. She let out a muted groan that was inaudible outside the car. Her eyes expressed a deep confusion, shock and terror that sent a shiver of ecstasy through

Shem's loins. Seconds later, her eyes rolled back into her head and she lost consciousness.

* * *

A blanket of fresh snow shrouded the rolling hills of the Hudson Valley. Dark clouds to the north and west threatened more precipitation. Shem was travelling north on Interstate 87, currently passing through the city of Newburgh. Hannah Richards was tied by a rope across her lap in the front passenger seat. For the first hour of the trip, he made sure she remained unconscious. Each time she began to stir, he reapplied the ether soaked rag to her breathing passages. At the moment, the effects of the tranquilizer had passed. She was sitting bolt upright and wide awake.

About a half an hour ago, he pulled off onto a deserted country road, grabbed some rope from his suitcase, and tied her legs to the seat. For further guarantee she didn't do anything stupid, he kept a sharp butcher's knife within her view, but out of reach. She wasn't talking much now. Instead, she was doing quite a bit of whimpering and it was really starting to get on his nerves. He warned her that if she didn't sit perfectly still and quiet, he was going to cut her tongue out. Every few minutes, he glanced over at her to take pleasure from the look of sheer horror on her face. He would allow her to speak later when they were far from the populated cities. He was very much looking forward to hearing her vain pleas for her life.

Tears streamed down Hannah's face as she did her best to remain stationary and silent in her extreme discomfort. The ropes tying her legs to the seat were so tight, they felt as though they were penetrating through her pants and shredding her skin. The inability to shift in her seat sent jolts of pain across her lower back and down both legs. She could hear her heart pounding in her chest and her head throbbed with such torturous pain, she thought it was about to implode. The unadulterated terror she was experiencing caused her stomach to spasm with waves of intense nausea. She strained every muscle in her body in an effort to keep from vomiting.

Hannah had feared for her life on one previous occasion- when she was mugged while jogging in New York's Central Park. The fright she experienced at that time was a trifle compared to the utter dread that now coursed through her veins. The gentleman who she thought was a holy man of God had transformed into a monster from the bowels of hell. She wondered how she could have been so stupid and gullible. Never in her life had she ever accepted a ride from a stranger. But, he was a rabbi, a man of faith who seemed so kind and courteous.

She struggled to fight through the panic and pain to think about the possibility of finding a way out of this nightmare alive. Perhaps she could offer him a lot of money to let her go. So far, there was no reason to believe he was going to hurt her. For all she knew, this was a simple kidnapping for ransom. That just reminded her of her sister who was expecting her call when she arrived at the hotel. Robin was going to be worried sick. Rather than dwell on the negative, Hannah tried to convince herself that the man just wanted money. After all, it was the root of all evil. But then every time she ventured a furtive peek over at her abductor, an ice cold chill raised the hair on the back of her neck.

Chapter 8

Robin Stein was trying to enjoy her after-dinner cup of decaffeinated coffee in the family room of her home on Long Island. She was beginning to worry herself sick. It was 8:30pm and her sister, Hannah, had not yet called from the hotel. She checked the American Airlines website and the flight supposedly took off from Ft. Lauderdale and arrived at LaGuardia ahead of schedule. Hannah should have had plenty of time to check into the hotel by now. Robin picked up the phone and dialed the Four Seasons number her sister gave to her. The receptionist answered on the fifteenth ring.

"Four Seasons Hotel New York, front desk."

"Hi. Could you connect me with the room of Hannah Richards?" Robin heard the hurried tap dance of fingers sprinting over a computer keyboard. A few seconds later, the receptionist answered, "I'm sorry Ma'am. Mrs. Richards hasn't checked in yet."

"Are you absolutely sure? Her flight arrived over two hours ago."

"Yes, Ma'am, I'm positive. Once a guest is assigned a room, it's entered into the computer. Hold on a sec. There are a few women waiting to check in. I can ask if any of them are your sister."

"Thanks so much."

In the background, Robin heard the front desk clerk address the women in line. Several seconds later, the clerk put the phone back up to her ear and said, "I'm sorry, Ma'am, your sister isn't here. But, I wouldn't worry yet. I'm sure you know traffic in the city can be horrible. It's taken our guests up to several hours to get to the hotel from the New York airports."

"Well, I hope that's the problem. She's never been this late."

"I'm sure it is. Would you like to leave a message for her?"

"Yes, please. Could you have her call me at 516-555-2422 as soon as she gets there?"

"Sure thing. I'll give her the message. Thanks for calling the Four Seasons."

Robin hung up the phone and cursed her sister for being so stubborn for refusing her offer to pick her up at the airport. She couldn't fathom any reason why Hannah couldn't have stayed on Long Island with her. Hannah always had to stay at the finest hotels in Manhattan. To make matters worse, the pig-headed woman still hadn't purchased a cell phone. Now Robin had no alternative but to sit home and worry herself into a migraine. She thought about calling Hannah's friend in Florida, to see if the neighbor knew anything. Looking at her watch, Robin reconsidered, deciding she'd wait a while longer before she bothered Annie.

* * *

As Shem Chassar approached the village of Tannersville, New York, he could hardly contain his excitement. It wasn't a matter of losing control of his emotions. Quite the opposite, he was as calm as a cool, clear mountain lake on a windless day. The sensation he was experiencing was pure exhilaration. Not being able to satisfy his sexual arousal was the only downside at the moment. They were on the road for more than two hours and the time of reckoning was rapidly approaching. The thrill of the anticipation of the kill was a difficult sentiment for him to describe. There was no doubt in his mind it was one of those extraordinary feelings that made life worthwhile.

He decided the deed would take place on the outskirts of a village with a population of less than five hundred people. As such, the woman's screams of agony wouldn't be heard by anyone. Heading west through Tannersville on 23A, he decided it was time to have a conversation with her. In a monotone voice devoid of emotion, he said, "You can speak."

Hannah, whose body was in a state of shock, hesitated. She was confused by his comment and didn't know how to respond. He repeated in a much more threatening manner, "I'm not going to say it again. You can speak."

Hannah began to sob, but managed to blurt out, "I don't know what you want me to say."

"It's your ass, lady. I can't help you with that."

"Why are you doing this to me? I've never done anything to you."

"You've done plenty. You're nothing but a rich, ugly, repulsive cunt that makes me want to vomit."

Hannah cringed at the intensity of disgust and revulsion in his delivery, more than the words. An unfathomable hatred exuded from every pore in the fiend's body. His stare was steady and it seemed to her there was no soul behind his bottomless black eyes. She didn't think she was going to make it out of this predicament alive. Somehow, it didn't completely suppress her survival instinct.

She wasn't going to just lie down and die. She asked, "Who are you? Do I know you?"

"That's irrelevant and you're making me angry."

"I don't mean to make you angry. I'll do anything you want. Please don't hurt me. I have lots of money. I can make you rich."

"I'm not interested in your filthy money."

Hannah's heart dropped into her stomach. She wanted to believe he couldn't really be serious. The alternative was too scary to consider. In spite of her efforts to suppress them, the terrifying possibilities running through her mind like scenes from a horror film threatened her ability to maintain control. She considered rape, rejected kidnapping, and prayed he wasn't planning to torture her. He found her ugly and repulsive, so rape hardly seemed probable. On the other hand, it was an exercise of power and dominion over the victim. It had nothing to do with attraction. She said, "I won't fight if you want to have sex with me."

Shem laughed in a loud, uproarious, and mocking howl. "I wouldn't touch you with a ten foot pole."

Hannah's options were running out. She was beginning to understand that her situation was desperate. She pleaded hysterically, "Please don't kill me. I don't want to die. I'll do anything you ask. Please let me go. I have family."

"I couldn't care less about what you want. And I know you don't have any children. Your pleas for your life are pathetic and selfish."

Hannah began to weep uncontrollably. She rocked back and forth in her seat banging her head forcefully against the headrest. She cried out in an ear-piercing scream. Shem backhanded her with a closed fist breaking her nose and rendering her unconscious.

* * *

Robin Stein was beside herself. Two more hours had passed and Hannah still hadn't phoned. She called the hotel on several occasions and each time the end result was the same. Her sister had not yet checked in. The last time she called was just five minutes ago. She was able to convince the agent at the front desk to call her himself, the instant Hannah showed up at the hotel.

Again, she considered calling Annie, but she didn't want to impose or make her worry if Hannah happened to be somewhere safe and sound. She stretched her imagination to the limits in an attempt to explain under what circumstances Hannah would neglect to call. There was the possibility she changed hotels. If that were true, it didn't make sense Hannah wouldn't have called to notify her. On the other hand, her sister was a scatter brain at times and could have forgotten her number or her personal phone book. Robin had an unlisted number, so she wouldn't be able to get it from information. She thought about whether it would be worthwhile calling all the finer Manhattan hotels. Deciding it would make her feel better to do something rather than nothing, she ran to the kitchen pantry to fetch her Yellow Pages.

Hannah had previously stayed at the first five hotels she called. The response was the same at each of them. She didn't have reservations nor had she checked in. For the next hour, Robin called hotels randomly from the phone book with no better luck. Now, almost five hours after Hannah's plane landed, Robin's panic was in full bud. She wished her husband was still alive. He would have known what to do. There was no way she was going to be able to handle this on her own. The only thing she could think to do was call her son, Steven, in California though she couldn't imagine what he could do from so far away. She picked up the phone and dialed his number. His wife, Dory, answered.

"Hi Mom, what are you doing up so late? Is everything alright?"

"Oh honey, I'm worried half to death. Aunt Hannah was supposed to call me when she arrived at her hotel and I haven't heard from her yet. Her plane landed almost five hours ago."

"Are you sure she got on the plane?"

"Yes, Yes, I'm positive. She called me a half hour before she was supposed to leave for the airport. If she didn't get on the plane, she would've called me by now. I can't believe that stubborn woman still doesn't have a cell phone. When I finally talk to her, I'm gonna give her the what for."

"Let me let you talk to Steve." Dory handed the phone to her husband who was standing next to her listening to her side of the conversation. He said, "Hi Mom, what's Aunt Hannah done now?"

Robin repeated the story to her son. When she finished describing everything she had done to that point, she was dangerously close to breaking. In a trembling voice, she said, "I don't know what else to do. Should I call the police? Don't you have to wait twenty-four hours before they'll do anything about a missing person?"

"Mom, you watch too much TV. I'm not sure that's actually the case in real life. We don't have to assume the worst yet. Maybe her taxi was involved in an accident either on the way to the airport in Ft. Lauderdale or the hotel in Manhattan. She could be in a hospital somewhere in Florida or New York. You call the police in New York and I'll call Florida. They should know if there were any 911 calls for an ambulance. We can also ask if they can find out if she boarded the plane."

"This is a disaster. I can't stop shaking. I'm so worried about her. I hope I can manage to dial the phone."

"Mom, it's not gonna help if you have a nervous breakdown. Try to calm down. There are plenty of potential explanations. Don't assume the worst. This doesn't mean that she's dead."

"Steven, don't even say that."

"I just want you to try to relax. You know how crazy Aunt Hannah can be. She'll probably wake up in the morning and call you with a thousand apologies."

"I hope you're right, honey. I just don't know what I'd do if something happened to her."

"Let's get started with the calls. I'll call you back when I know something. I love you, Mom. I'll talk to you in a few."

"Bye sweetie, I love you, too."

Robin leafed nervously through the Yellow Pages to find the number for the New York State Police Department. Despite her son's admonition to stay calm, she had a sinking and unnerving feeling something terrible had happened. On her first attempt to call the police, she dialed the wrong number. She cursed her unsteady hand and tried again. The staff sergeant answered, "New York Police Department, 115th precinct, Sergeant Patrick O'Reilly speaking. Is this an emergency?"

"Well, I don't know." Robin muddled through the events of the evening for a third time. By the end of the story, she was crying. She asked, "Is there any way you can tell me whether she's been in an accident or taken by an ambulance to the hospital?"

"I'll do what I can to help you, Ma'am. First, you need to try to get a hold of yourself. People go missing every day and more than ninety-nine percent of the time they show up in one piece without realizing the trouble they've caused their loved ones. I can check the computer for any accidents after 6:00pm. I'll also contact Emergency Services and find out if an ambulance was dispatched to take her to the hospital. I won't be able to require the airlines to give me information about whether or not she was on the plane. I can't start a missing person's investigation either until twenty-four hours has passed since her disappearance. Please hold on, Ma'am. I'll be back in just a few minutes."

Robin waited anxiously for the Sergeant's response. She was annoyed that for once, the TV and movies got their facts straight. After what seemed an hour, she heard the fumbling of the receiver as the officer picked up the phone. "I have some information for you, Mrs. Stein. You'll be happy to know your sister wasn't involved in an accident this evening. At least she wasn't transported by ambulance to any New York hospitals and there were no accident reports turned in referencing her name. I'm sure that doesn't totally resolve your concerns considering the circumstances. If you haven't heard from her by 6:16 tomorrow evening, give us a call and we'll start our investigation immediately. Hopefully, they'll be a happy ending to this story before you have to make that call."

"From your mouth to God's ear. Thank you so much for your help, Sergeant. Goodnight."

"Goodnight Mrs. Stein and good luck."

Robin felt as though her heart was going to burst through her chest wall. When the phone rang, she almost jumped out of her seat. She picked up the receiver and said, "Hi Steven. What did you find out?" Without waiting for a response, she continued, "The New York police said she wasn't in an accident and there were no ambulances called to take her to the hospital. But, you were wrong about the missing persons rule. They can't do anything for twenty-four hours."

"I know, Mom. I got the same story from the Ft. Lauderdale Police Department. She wasn't taken to the hospital as far as they could tell. The only thing we can do now is wait and hope and pray we get a call from her either tonight or some time tomorrow. Otherwise, we'll have to report her missing."

"There's only one other thing I can think of, son. She has a neighbor in Florida she's very friendly with. It's late, but she may know something."

"This is no time to worry about imposing on people. I'm sure she'll understand. I think you should call right now and call me back."

"You're right, I'll do it. I'll call you back in a few minutes."

Hearing the concern in her son's voice didn't help Robin's already lurid state of mind. She rushed to the kitchen to get her personal phone book. She was given Annie's number in case of emergencies. There was no question in her mind this qualified now. She opened the book to the A's. The tears were acutely flowing causing her vision to blur. She wiped them away with a handkerchief long enough to read Annie's number and quickly dial it. Annie answered the phone in a thick, disoriented voice. "Hello."

"Hello, Annie, this is Robin Stein, Hannah's sister."

Annie sprung to a seated position in her bed. Before she responded, she took a quick look at her alarm clock and saw it was after midnight. She inquired anxiously, "Is everything alright, Mrs. Stein?"

"I'm sorry to bother you at this time of night, but no, I'm worried sick. I haven't heard from Hannah and her flight landed at 6:16. She was supposed to call me when she got to the hotel. She hasn't even checked in yet. I was hoping maybe you heard from her."

"No need to apologize. Of course you had to call me…I wish I could help. The last time I talked to Hannah was Wednesday when she asked me to keep an eye on her apartment. I do happen to know she left in a taxi for the airport this afternoon. Todd, our maintenance man told me he helped her with her luggage. Have you called the hotel? Have you notified the police?"

Once again, Robin repeated all the steps she had taken to locate her sister. By the time she reached the end of the story, she was weeping irrepressibly.

"Mrs. Stein, I know you're scared, but we don't know that something horrible has happened. You know how eccentric Hannah can be. The only thing you can do at this point is try to get a good night's sleep. Hopefully, tomorrow we'll all be laughing about some crazy thing she did. In the meantime, I have a friend who works for the FBI. I'll give him a call and see if he can help. Maybe he can find out if she actually boarded the plane in Ft. Lauderdale."

"Are you gonna call him tonight?"

"Yes, as soon as I hang up the phone."

"Will you call me if he comes up with anything?"

"Of course, Mrs. Stein, I'll call you back right away."

"Ok, bye Annie and thank you."

* * *

Annie was wide awake. Trying to get back to sleep was pointless, probably for the remainder of the night. That was the least of her worries. Hannah was no doubt a woman who marched to the beat of a different drummer. She was guilty of strange behavior on a regular basis, a good deal more than the average person. The one instance in which she did conform was when her consideration for others was at issue. It was very unlike her to be irresponsible. Annie was sure something was amiss. She was somewhat apprehensive about calling Daniel at home, worried Deborah might answer. She didn't think about it twice. These were extenuating circumstances. Hannah was a very dear friend and even the possibility she could be in trouble was good enough reason for her to disturb Daniel. She picked up the phone and dialed his cell phone number. When Daniel answered, he sounded as alert as if it were twelve noon rather than twelve midnight.

"Hello, Annie, I'm not liking this. Something's gotta be wrong. What's going on?"

"I'm sorry to bother you at this time of night, but yes, something is wrong. I'm really worried about my neighbor, Hannah Richards." She explained everything she was told by Robin Stein. Afterwards, she continued, "I'm very concerned something terrible has happened. It's very unlike Hannah to be this thoughtless. They're not even sure whether she's in Florida or New York. Is it possible for you to find out if she was on the plane to LaGuardia?"

"I don't know, Annie. I'll see what I can do. Do you happen to have the flight number?"

"Damn it, I forgot to ask her, I was so upset. I know it was an American Airlines flight scheduled to leave Ft. Lauderdale at 4pm. It arrived at LaGuardia at 6:16. From what I understand, they left a little bit ahead of schedule."

"That should be good enough. I'll call you right back."

Daniel opened up a new tab on his laptop computer he had been working on and typed the web address for American Airlines. Navigating through the website, he located their toll free number and dialed it on his FBI issued cell phone. He explained to the American Airline's representative that he was the Special Agent in Charge of the Miami field office and needed information about one of that day's passengers. The call was passed to several different departments before he was finally connected to an on-call manager from corporate headquarters. Daniel repeated his request in more detail providing Hannah's name and her flight number given to him by the previous representative. The agent asked for Daniel's FBI identification number which he spouted off by memory. After placing him on hold for ten minutes, the supervisor returned to inform Daniel that Mrs. Richards did, in fact, board American Airlines flight number 262 which arrived at LaGuardia ahead of schedule with no reported complications.

For Daniel who didn't know the first thing about Hannah, there could have been any number of explanations for her failure to contact her sister. Nevertheless, for some unknown reason, like Robin Stein and Annie, he was having a very bad feeling. He wouldn't express that to Annie, but when he had a premonition like this, he wasn't often wrong. He used the kitchen phone to call her back. Annie answered immediately, "Hi, Daniel. Were you able to get any information? In the meantime, I went over to Hannah's apartment to see if by chance she might be there. No such luck."

"She was on the flight. There's not much of a chance she's in Florida unless she turned around and went straight back."

"This isn't good. I'm very worried. Poor Mrs. Stein is gonna have a nervous breakdown."

"There's not much more we can do tonight. When I get to the office tomorrow, I'll contact our field office in New York. I have some friends I trained with at Quantico who work up there. Maybe we can get an investigation started a little bit quicker than normal. I always hated that twenty-four hour rule. But, I have to say the overwhelming majority of adults do ultimately turn up safe and sound. It's just not helpful for those who are victims of foul play. Try to get some sleep and I'll call you in the morning when I know more."

"That's easier said than done. Anyway, I knew I could count on you. You're always there for me. Thanks a lot, Daniel. I really appreciate it."

"You're welcome. I hope they find her. Make sure you let me know if they do. Goodnight Annie."

"Sure thing. Goodnight and thanks again."

Annie called Robin Stein and told her what she had learned. She repeated Daniel's statistics about the happy resolution of most missing persons' cases although Annie was not, herself, convinced. She assured Mrs. Stein that Daniel would be following up in the morning and they would keep her updated. After Annie hung up the phone, she crawled into bed and turned on the TV. Fortunately, she thought, it was Friday night and she didn't have to work in the morning. She was certain this was going to be a sleepless night.

* * *

The temperature plummeted below ten degrees after the sun set over the Catskill Mountains. It was after midnight when Shem reached his final destination in the woods northwest of Tannersville. He parked his vehicle on a dirt road off of 23A and had to carry the still unconscious Tucker slut look-alike for more than a half mile through the thick forest of sugar maple trees. The moon and stars were hidden behind a substantial layer of low-lying clouds. If he didn't have his flashlight, he wouldn't have been able to see more than a few feet in front of him. To keep his body warm, before he left the SUV, he put on a pair of thermal underwear, ski bibs, gloves, and a thick parka. Hannah Richards was still dressed in the outfit she wore to the airport in Ft. Lauderdale. She did bring a mink coat with her on the trip. There wasn't a chance he would allow her to use it.

He chose a tree at the end of the trail that was streamline enough to tie his rope around securely. He set Hannah in a seated position with her lower back and butt flush against the trunk then wound the rope tightly around her chest, abdomen and the sugar maple. Once he was satisfied she was firmly bound, he jogged the mile long roundtrip to the rental car and back to retrieve his provisions. He was hoping to find Hannah awake, but she was still out cold when he returned. Allowing her to remain passed out during the process was inconceivable. It would take away all of the fun. He picked up a pile of snow from the side of the path and threw it in her eyes and down her blouse. When it didn't wake her, he smacked her across the face several times in succession. Fresh blood oozed from both nostrils forging a path to the bottom of her chin through previous blood that had already dried. She began to stir and moan, but her eyes remained closed. To finish the job, he reluctantly performed a crushing sternum rub between her revolting and disgusting, sagging breasts. He had read that healthcare providers would execute this procedure to wake an unconscious patient. It worked like a charm. Hannah sprung into an upright position.

She instantly felt the extreme chill of the night causing her entire body to shutter convulsively. A bolt of excruciating pain exploded across the bridge of her nose while the ropes tied around her chest and abdomen restricted her breathing. In the pitch-black darkness, it took her several seconds to become oriented. When she started to scream, he pulled the butcher's knife from a sheath connected to his belt, and bellowed, "If you don't shut your fuck'n ugly trap right now, I'll slice your lips off."

Barely talking lucidly through a series of fitful sobs and wracking shivers, Hannah cried, "Please let me go. Please, I'll do anything, anything you ask. Just let me live. You can have every penny I own. What did I do to you? Why are you doing this to me?"

"You exist. That's enough for me. I told you I don't want your stinking, putrid money."

"What do you want from me, then?"

"I want you dead."

Hannah wailed, screaming at the top of her lungs. He calmly walked over to his suitcase, opened it and removed three plastic, gallon-size milk jugs he had filled with lighter fluid. He took one of the jugs and began to pour the incendiary over Hannah's head. He splashed a good bit on her face and soaked her top. The piercing sting of the caustic liquid as it penetrated her eyes only served to increase the volume of her cries. When the jug was empty, he grabbed the second and drenched her satin pants. With the third carton, he saturated the rope and doused the trunk of the tree with what was left. Meanwhile, Hannah howled her protest shaking her head back and forth stretching and straining the muscles of her neck to their limit.

He stood in front of her for several minutes to enjoy the spectacle. Then he picked up the butcher's knife he had temporarily placed on the ground. Grabbing her head by the hair, he sliced off both ears with two quick, clean strokes and placed them in his suitcase. Hannah let loose a deafening shriek breaching the thick, black silence of the night for miles, blood flowing from the open wounds down the sides of her neck. Shem figured he better get on with things before the bitch screwed everything up and passed out. He pulled a box of matches from his suitcase and knelt approximately fifteen feet from her. He wanted to be able to look directly into her eyes when her body went up in flames. He lit the match and threw it in her lap. The satin pants ignited with a whoosh like the coals of a propane barbecue grill when the gas is left running too long. The flames scurried up her shirt and lit her face and hair afire. Her skin crackled like kindling for a campfire while her restricted body writhed in harrowing agony. The epidermis bubbled like boiling water. Blisters formed then burst spitting fiery drops of blood in all directions.

Despite the high temperature of the blood, he wanted to feel the red liquid on his bare skin. He moved slightly closer to the burning body allowing it to speckle his face and arms like some nightmarish variety of freckles. It left burn marks that wouldn't heal for several days thereafter. The more the droplets covered his skin, the harder his fully erect penis strained against the several layers of his clothing to reach its ultimate orgasm. As Shem screamed out in ecstasy and snow flurries began to float down from the heavens, Hannah Richards mercifully passed on.

Chapter 9

Driving on very little sleep wasn't a problem for Shem as he headed north on Interstate 87 toward Albany. The adrenaline coursing through his bloodstream manufactured an alertness that normally resulted from a restful, full night's sleep. The thrill and euphoria he was experiencing since the kill also helped and definitely made the entire trip worthwhile. He lived for the intricate, detailed and ingenious planning and execution of each and every step of the process. From his studies, he knew that most serial murderers killed within a restricted, preferred area. He didn't want to limit himself. The traveling provided an aspect that just made the adventure that much more complex and exciting. There was no better sense of satisfaction than what he received from a successfully staged murder and escape.

His getaway plan was to spend the night in a hotel in Albany then fly back to Ft. Lauderdale in the morning. After the woman was dead and the fire had fizzled to a few sizzling embers, he collected his belongings, returned to his car and drove back into the village of Tannersville. By that time, it was well into the wee hours of the morning. While passing slowly along the main thoroughfare of the small town, he spotted a dark colored pick-up truck in the parking lot of the Boarding House Bar and Restaurant. It was one of three vehicles in the lot but the only one that wasn't visible from the hotel's reception desk. Extinguishing his headlights, he pulled into the lot and parked next to the passenger's side of the truck so that he would simply be able to turn around to try the passenger door. It was locked. Deciding to minimize the risk of being seen and not waste time, he didn't bother to move around to the other side to try the driver's door. Having broken into countless cars during his adolescent years with whatever gadget he could find, it was child's play unlocking the truck with the fancy tools of his lock picking kit.

Leaving the passenger door in a mostly closed position to prevent the overhead light from switching on, he went back to the SUV and stored the kit. He then grabbed a rag from the suitcase and thoroughly wiped down each of the Tucker slut look-alike's bags. Having worn gloves the entire time he was in the SUV, it wasn't necessary to erase any fingerprints from the interior of the vehicle. Once he was sure he had left no traces, he threw his suitcase into the passenger seat of the truck, hotwired the ignition and was on his way.

During the quick one hour and ten minute ride to Albany, he played the murder of Hannah Richards over and over again in his mind. His memory of the event was always the sole souvenir he took away with him. Normally, it didn't matter how much gratification and sexual stimulation a kill would bring him- keeping a trophy was never part of the plan. He read of many serial killers who were caught and convicted because they were stupid enough to retain keepsakes. He wasn't about to make the same mistake.

The ears were not for his personal use. He had a plan for them. They would accompany him to Ft. Lauderdale. In order to transport body parts without raising suspicion, they would have to be disguised. It wouldn't be convenient for a security official at the airport to search his suitcase and find a pair of human ears. During the planning process for this murder, he did some research on the Internet about rubber and urethane coating. He discovered a company that manufactured a product that could be used to mold or cast just about any shape and it was available at your local Home Depot.

Shortly after the sun rose on the following morning, he laid in his hotel room bed with his eyes wide open. He wasn't able to sleep well during the night. It wasn't unusual for him to lose sleep after one of his kills. In reality, it wasn't an insomnia he minded. Remembering the life ebb from his victim's eyes produced an exhilaration that electrified every nerve ending from head to toe. It was this sensation that kept him awake and he wouldn't have it any other way.

The Home Depot in Albany where he intended to shop opened at 6:00am on Saturdays. He was waiting at the entrance when the store manager unlocked the doors at two minutes after the hour. He purchased the coating product then returned to the hotel. He had already read and memorized the directions for its use online. After fetching the ears from his suitcase, he carried them out to the lake behind the hotel and meticulously scrubbed them. He returned to the room, carefully dried them with disposable towels then began applying the rubber coating compound to the first ear. With exquisite precision, he painstakingly worked the chemical so that it would leave no seams. The final product resembled a gag toy one would purchase from a novelty store. He repeated the process with the second ear.

By the time the job was finished and the coating completely set, it was time to leave for the airport. He carefully placed the ears in his suitcase along with the clothes he wore the previous night. He had already disposed of his rabbi clothing in the forest where Hannah Richard's corpse was now rotting. Once his bag was closed and locked, he performed a quick check of the room to be sure he didn't leave anything behind. Carrying the suitcase in one hand and the used can of rubber coating in the other, he walked out the door. He tossed the can in the lake, made his way to the parking lot, hopped in the truck and pulled out onto the highway. A wry smile contorted his face as he realized the flight back to Ft. Lauderdale would be much more pleasurable and peaceful.

* * *

The blazing heat wave that singed the South Florida coastal area over the past few days finally broke during the night. Deborah Falcone, who fancied herself an amateur meteorologist was always on top of the day's forecast, well-informed regarding approaching fronts, atmospheric pressure, relative humidity, and upcoming storms. She warned Daniel it was going to be chilly with record lows as he prepared for the day. Cold weather always made her reluctant to get out from underneath the warm, toasty covers in the morning. She was still relaxing in bed as she watched Daniel pull a pair of wool pants over his thick, muscular thighs. In the eight years she knew him, he hadn't lost a thing. He was as sexy as ever. She stared at his bulging eight- pack while he buttoned up his white dress shirt. If it wasn't time to get the boys up, she might have tried to entice her handsome husband back to her side.

She reluctantly threw her legs over the edge of the bed and slipped her ice cold feet into her bear claw slippers. "Did I hear your cell phone ring late last night?" she inquired.

Already feeling guilt over the surreptitious lunch, Daniel wasn't about to lie about the identity of the previous night's caller. "Yeah, Annie called."

"What did she want?"

"She was worried about her seventy-two year-old next door neighbor who went missing. Her flight landed in New York just after six and no one's heard from her since. Evidently, she was supposed to call her sister on Long Island when she arrived at her hotel. The sister was a nervous wreck. Annie asked me if I could help out, maybe find out if she actually boarded the plane."

"You didn't do it, did you? I mean, you can't conduct your own little investigation outside of an official one, can you?"

"Honey, if it were your mother or sister, would you care about the rules?"

"I'm just sayin, sweetie. I wouldn't want you to get in trouble."

"I don't think it's a problem. Besides, the airlines gave me the information. She was on the plane."

"Boy, you just jumped right on it, didn't you?"

"What's the problem? I don't get it. Why would you be upset that I'm doing what I can to find a missing woman?"

"Daniel, don't be naïve. You're a brilliant man, but sometimes you can be so dumb. It's not the woman. It's Annie. I have a huge problem with her. It's not that I don't like her. She's nice enough, not to mention beautiful and intelligent. Think about it. You were in love with her for a long time. You asked her to marry you for Pete's sake. How would you like it if I started hanging around with my ex-boyfriend, Justin?"

"Jeez, is this High School or what? Sweetheart, I'm very secure about your love for me. I trust you. That's what relationships are based on. I'd never tell you who could be your friend and who can't. Who the hell is Justin, anyway?"

"I just made up a name to make a point. I don't care what you say. It's not normal for a married man to have a close relationship with his ex-almost fiancée."

"I guess I'm not normal then. Are you saying you don't want me to help this woman? Do you want me to end my friendship with Annie?"

"No, honey, I wouldn't do that. I just want you to understand how I feel. I can't help getting jealous. When I get sarcastic, you should let me get away with it. I'm confident you love me and I trust you. I just get a little insecure every once in a while."

"I'm not your father. I'm not your professor friend from college. I'm your husband. I'm not going anywhere."

Daniel always had a way of getting the upper hand in a conversation. Suggesting she was comparing him to her dad and her first love was almost a low blow. It was something he knew she worked hard on with her therapist to avoid. In the end, she had to concede he was right, as usual. She probably wouldn't have as many insecure moments if it hadn't been for the extra havoc the professor wreaked on her ability to trust men.

In her first couple of years at Georgetown University, Deborah's total focus was on her studies. She did go out on occasion with fellow students of the opposite sex, but rarely accepted an invitation for a second date. Receiving inspiration from her therapist and incentive from the tragic experience involving Ally Schnyder, it was Deborah's goal to get her PhD in Psychology. Throughout her years in high school, Deborah volunteered her time to programs for neglected and mistreated children developed by her therapist. Her dream was to someday open her own center for kids who were victims of sexual abuse. It was during her time at Georgetown's College of Psychology that she met her first love.

Toward the end of her junior year, Deborah registered for Anatomy of the Brain, a class required for her major. When she walked into the classroom for the first time, her attraction for the professor was both immediate and powerful. She wasn't a believer in the concept of love at first site, but the feelings that struck her like a lightning bolt that day compared to nothing she had ever experienced. It was apparent the feeling was mutual. Embarrassed, yet enjoying every second of it, she noticed he didn't take his eye off of her until she chose her seat. Two weeks into the class, she received a note from him tucked into a returned paper asking her out to dinner. Being a woman with principles and morals, she rejected that invitation and the several overtures that followed. She refused to get involved in a romantic relationship with a professor while she was taking his class.

It wasn't until the following semester she finally gave in to his advances and agreed to a date. For the next several months, they saw each other on a regular basis. He was the most handsome, intelligent, sophisticated man she had ever known. There was no question in Deborah's mind she was at the precipice of the love abyss and was about to fall over the edge. She was so smitten by the man that finally, she had to confide in a fellow psychology student that she was having a secret romance. She was shocked, mortified, humiliated and devastated when the friend informed her that her lover was married. Deborah's classmate had attended a department function the previous year where the professor was being honored. In his acceptance speech for the award presented to him, he thanked his wife in the audience. Deborah confronted him with the information and he was forced to admit the truth. Disappointed, hurt and furious just skimmed the surface of describing the emotions she experienced for quite some time afterwards. She had let her guard down only to get involved in another relationship that would foster her mistrust in men. She immediately cut off all ties with him and didn't date another man until she met Daniel.

Daniel finished dressing then went into the bathroom to comb his hair. He truly never thought about Deborah's feelings about Annie. It didn't take a genius to know a woman's claws came out when they felt their relationship was being threatened by another woman. Perhaps, he was subconsciously avoiding the subject. He wasn't so sure it would be easy to cut Annie out of his life if Deborah had answered the question differently. At least, he didn't have to go there for now. His marriage and especially his children were on the top of his list of priorities, but there was no way he could deny that a piece of his heart would always belong to Annie.

After saying his goodbyes to Deborah and the boys, Daniel stepped outside into the cool, crisp morning. The sun shone brilliantly through the cloudless sky, though the strong wind gusts carried a penetrating nip that motivated Daniel to put on his black overcoat. In his hometown of Chicago, this may have been a day for short sleeves. Having lived in South Florida for the past five years, when the temperature dipped below sixty, it was time for the heat. He cranked it up as he pulled out of his parking space. At the first red light, he pulled his cell phone out of its case and dialed Annie's number.

"Good morning, Daniel. I've been waiting for you to call. I didn't sleep a wink last night."

"I take it there's no good news? They didn't find her?"

"No. I spoke to her sister ten minutes ago. Still nothing. She's a mess and so am I. I'm almost positive something terrible has happened to her. I would think if she fell asleep early last night, she would've called by now"

"I'm sorry to hear that. I'm on my way to the office right now. I should be there in about twenty minutes. As soon as I'm through with the morning briefing with my people, I'll call the New York field office."

"I appreciate anything you can do. So does the family. Call me when you can."

"Sure thing, Annie. If she turns up, or God forbid, the family receives a ransom call, let me know right away."

* * *

Shem Chassar exited the plane into the covered jet way leading to Ft. Lauderdale airport Terminal 3. There was an extra skip in his step as he made his way to baggage claim to collect his prize. The edge he was feeling over the past few days had completely dissipated. Everything had gone smoothly at Albany's airport. His suitcase passed inspection. Otherwise, they would have removed him from the flight before it took off. Not that he was ever really concerned. If he wanted, he could probably get a homemade bomb past the numbskulls. Arriving at baggage claim, he checked the monitors which indicated his flight's bags would be delivered at Carousel 4. He waited at the entrance to the conveyor belt at the point where the luggage exited through the plastic verticals. He wanted to be able to snatch his suitcase as soon as it emerged into the terminal.

There was still one more task to complete before his plan was fully executed and time was going to be an issue if he wanted to get it done that day. If he hurried, he could make it to the post office before it closed at noon. Having also ridden in first class on the return trip, his suitcase was among the first to spew out onto the conveyor belt once again. With his bag in hand, he exited the terminal and took the shuttle bus to the remote pay parking lot off airport property where he left his car. When he sat in the driver's seat of his 1997 Acura Integra, he took a second to calculate whether it would be worthwhile trying to get the job done before the post office locked its doors. He would have a little bit over an hour. Deciding he absolutely didn't want to have to wait until Monday, he headed for a stationary store he knew was open on Federal Highway just down the road from the airport. Before he entered the shop, he placed a pair of driving gloves on his hands. He purchased a manila envelope, paying close attention to the surveillance cameras at the entrance, behind the counter and at the rear of the store.

Back behind the wheel of the parked Acura, he rummaged through the console compartment to find a pen and razor. He scribbled an address on the front of the envelope, reached into the backseat to grab the suitcase then set it in the passenger seat. The ears were sealed in a plastic bag inside the lid's zipper pouch. He opened the bag and removed one of the ears. With the razor, he carefully peeled off part of the rubber coating to expose the human skin of the lobe. Next, he put the ear back in the plastic bag, fastened it, placed it inside the manila envelope and sealed it.

The post office on Las Olas Blvd. was just a five minute drive. It was now 11:40, so he would have plenty of time to get there before it closed. He didn't trust placing his precious package in a mailbox. He wanted to personally deliver it to the post office. There was a line running from the counter all the way out the door when he arrived. Since it was approaching closing time, the postmen manning the desk worked quickly. Ten minutes later, his envelope was placed on a scale to determine the price for postage. Shem gladly paid the fee then strolled out of the building whistling one of his favorite rock tunes, "Every Word is a Knife in My Ear."

Chapter 10

Daniel's morning briefing was over by 8:30am. Accompanied by Rick Suarez, on his way to grab a cup of coffee, Daniel described the events that took place the previous evening involving Hannah Richards.

"I'm going to call the New York field office to see if they can get a head start on this. Obviously, timing is crucial if she was abducted. You don't think they'll have a problem if I ask them for help, do you?"

"Absolutely not. In fact, you should also call TSA over at the airport and get a hold of their surveillance tapes. They could be a tremendous help. I would have them do that up at LaGuardia, too. As Special Agent in Charge, it's our responsibility to determine which cases are within our jurisdiction. I'm sure you know that. Since this incident is a multi-state affair which could include kidnapping, I can't see a problem starting an investigation, at least until we know more. Later, we can get the local police involved."

"I was thinking along those lines. I just wanted to check with you first. I was also a little bit worried about stepping on someone's toes, not waiting the full twenty-four hours."

"That's what I'm here for, at least for the next couple of weeks. And even when I'm gone, feel free to call me any time you have a question... Fuck'em if they get their nose outta joint. It's completely within your discretion to take this kind of action right away. Don't hesitate, Daniel. Get right on it. Waiting the full twenty-four hours can have disastrous results. We've seen it enough."

"I hope for the family's sake that isn't already the case. Thanks, Rick."

"My pleasure. Just don't spend your entire Saturday in the office. If you need any more help with the Richards woman, let me know."

Daniel headed back to his office preoccupied by his jam-packed schedule. He was still in a transition period handing his former responsibilities as A.S.A.C. of the criminal division to his replacement Supervisor Charlie Atkins. After careful consideration and caucuses with Rick and Assistant Director Evans, Daniel ultimately decided to pass over Leland for the job. Everyone agreed Leland was too valuable an investigator in the field and wasn't quite ready for the next level of management. Daniel had a meeting with

Atkins in twenty minutes to go over some details of the A.S.A.C's involvement in the task force for the prevention of juvenile crimes and gang activity. He decided to use the time to call the New York field office to recruit some help with the Hannah Richards disappearance.

At Quantico, Daniel trained with several of the agents who were now working in the criminal division of the New York office. Being a part of the Bureau's career development program, he also had the opportunity to visit the New York field office for inspections and established a good rapport with many of the agents there. He developed an especially close bond with Special Agent James Mancini, now working in the Violent Crimes Task Force in Manhattan. He picked up the phone and dialed Mancini's extension.

"Hello, Special Agent James Mancini."

"Jim, it's Daniel Falcone. How are things up there in the jungle?"

"Dan, shit, I haven't heard from you in months. I couldn't be doin better. I have some great news. I finally knocked up the old lady. We've been trying for five years now. She's expecting in November."

"Congratulations, Jim. That is great news. Although, it wouldn't have surprised me if you were shooting blanks."

"Go to hell, pretty boy. You wish you were half the man I am."

"Yeah, my life's ambition, to be just like you."

"So, what do I owe this call to? I'm sure you're not calling to shoot the shit."

"Actually, I do have a favor to ask. A neighbor of a personal friend of mine is missing." Daniel described the details of the disappearance.

"They're really concerned for her. They say it's not like her to be this irresponsible. Do you think you can check the New York area for any women fitting her description that may have turned up at one of your hospitals? I guess there's the possibility she could be dazed or confused and forgotten her name. It's happened before. So, include unidentified women in your search. She's in her seventies, red hair, blue eyes, about 5'3". I understand she looks a lot younger than her age though. I suppose we should also check for any bodies found since last night. I'd like to get my hands on the surveillance tapes from LaGuardia, too. What do you think?"

"Sure thing, man. It's been a slow morning here. I'll get on it right away. I'll give you a call this afternoon."

"Thanks a lot, Jim, I owe you one."

"And don't forget it. I'll talk to you this afternoon."

"Take care and give my regards and congratulations to the wife."

Next, Daniel phoned TSA at Ft. Lauderdale Airport and made a request for the previous day's terminal three surveillance tapes. They advised him they could have copies available by noon. Since time could be of the essence, he decided to pick them up at the airport, himself during his lunch break.

* * *

Shortly after noon, Daniel hopped in his car and headed north on Interstate 95 toward Ft. Lauderdale's international airport. When he arrived, he parked his Crown Victoria alongside Terminal 3 in an area reserved for police vehicles. He walked into the building and descended one flight on the escalator located just inside and to the right of the entrance. The TSA office was adjacent to baggage claim on the far side of the security check station. From across the room, Daniel could see the door to the TSA office was closed and the reception area dark and deserted. He peered through the narrow window that ran along the side of the door to find there was a room toward the rear with its lights on. He knocked. Several seconds later, a middle-aged man the size of an NFL linebacker in a TSA uniform opened it.

"Are you Agent Falcone?"

"Yes, I am." They shook hands.

"It was me you talked to on the phone earlier, Agent Spencer."

"Good to meet you."

"Likewise. You wouldn't mind showing me your credentials, would you? Better to be safe than sorry."

Daniel pulled his identification from his inside jacket pocket and held it up at eye level.

"Perfect," said Agent Spencer. "Why don't you follow me back to my office."

The two men walked through the dark reception area into the lit office on the opposite side. Rather than take the seat being offered by Spencer, Daniel told him he preferred to stand. He wanted to make this meeting as short as possible, hoping to get home at a reasonable hour. He inquired, "Were you able to make copies of the tapes?"

"Yes, I was. I assume they haven't found the woman yet?"

"No, unfortunately, they haven't."

"I hope you don't mind I took the liberty of watching a portion of the tapes this morning. I thought maybe I could be of some help." Actually Spencer was thinking about covering his own ass. A kidnapping at the airport under his jurisdiction would require some reports and explanations. "I was able to identify the subject pretty easily based on your description. On the tapes I watched, the only interaction I saw between her and persons not employed by the airport was with a young man. I'm pretty sure he was an Orthodox Jew. I guess he could have been a priest or rabbi of some sort. They seemed to be getting along really well. They had a long conversation then boarded the plane together.

Funny though, I never got a good look at his face. I almost got the impression he was avoiding looking into the cameras. I could be totally off-base. I didn't get a chance to see all the tapes. I just stuck to the ones at the gate."

"I appreciate the input. Will you be available later if I have any questions? There may be other TSA agents we might want to talk to also, to see if they witnessed anything that could be important."

"I'll be on duty until nine o'clock tonight. Call any time. After that, you can talk to Agent Steele. He'll be here till the last flight of the evening lands. That should be around midnight."

* * *

It didn't seem as though Daniel was going to be able to heed Rick's suggestion to not spend his entire Saturday in the office. He had been watching the surveillance tapes for the last two hours and already collected a fair amount of disturbing information. Thus far, he observed the young Jewish man described by the TSA agent recorded on at least six of the cameras located in Terminal 3. He was captured entering the terminal, descending the escalator, making his way through the security line, passing through the food court, seated at the gate and boarding the aircraft. It was obvious to Daniel the man was aware of the location of each camera and was deliberately avoiding looking directly into them. Even more disconcerting, he was following Hannah Richards from the time she entered the airport until she took a seat at the gate. He didn't have to see much more to pick up the phone and call Special Agent James Mancini.

"Jim, it's Daniel. I've been looking at the Ft. Lauderdale Airport surveillance tapes. I don't think we should waste any more time. We need to open up a full-scale investigation. Before I explain, have you gotten a hold of the LaGuardia tapes, yet?"

"I'm expecting them to be delivered any minute. I sent a runner to go pick them up more than an hour ago. I do have some information for you, though. I haven't had any luck with the hospitals. As far as I can tell, no unidentified women were admitted in the last twenty-four hours. There have been no reported deaths of anyone fitting her description, either. What have you got?"

Daniel described what he had observed on the tapes. He continued, "We need to get an all points bulletin out…for Mrs. Richards and the suspect…the entire state of New York. Hell, let's make it the entire Northeast. He's got closely cropped blond hair, a muscular build, approximately 6'2" tall and at the time, he was wearing traditional Orthodox Jewish clothing. We also need to send out an abduction team over to her sister's home on Long Island. There's always the chance they're going to get a ransom call. I'll handle the call to Mrs. Stein."

"I can get right on it. And I'll call you as soon as I get a chance to look at the tapes. The time frame they would have been at LaGuardia should be much shorter, so I hope it won't take me that long."

Daniel wasn't looking forward to his next call. He dialed Annie's number.

"Daniel. I've been a nervous wreck waiting for you to call. Have you found anything?"

"I can't be one hundred percent sure of anything yet, Annie. I can tell you Hannah met a man on her flight and had a long conversation with him. The part that has me concerned is that he was obviously following her from the time she entered the terminal until she sat down at the gate. It was also pretty clear he was avoiding looking directly into the cameras. We should know more once we review the New York tapes. You remember James Mancini. I trained at Quantico with him. He's expecting them any minute."

"That doesn't sound promising, Daniel. Who was the guy? Were you able to identify him?"

"It's gonna take a while before we'll be able to get a name." Daniel explained what had been done so far.

"I can't believe this," said Annie. "Hannah's been missing now for more than twenty-one hours. I can't imagine what she might be going through. Do you think this was a kidnapping?"

"I can't answer that question right now. The longer we go with no word from her, kidnapping becomes a best case scenario. I don't want to speculate on that yet."

Annie began to cry softly. She said, "This is awful. I don't even want to think about Mrs. Stein. I don't know if she can handle all this. Does she know, yet?"

"I haven't called her. I wanted to talk to you first. I'll call her right after we're done. We're sending a team over to her house in case she receives a ransom call…or note."

"Who would want to hurt that sweet woman? It would have to be a monster. Wouldn't he have been in touch by now if it was a kidnapping?"

"First of all, Annie, don't assume the worst. There's a lot we don't know, yet. If it is a kidnapping, there's still a chance we'll get her back unharmed. To answer your question, sometimes they'll wait a day or two… to let the family stew."

"You know, Hannah's husband was an Orthodox Jew."

"I didn't know that. That's very interesting. Hmm…If this guy is involved, he obviously did his homework. You're pretty close to her, right?"

"Yes, she calls me her best friend."

"I want you to take a look at these tapes. You may recognize something or someone that could be helpful. It's certainly worth a shot. Do you think you can come to the office?" Daniel hesitated before expressing his next thought out loud. Throwing caution to the wind, he offered, "I guess I could come to your place. Do you have a VCR? They still record this stuff on tapes."

"I'd really rather not drive, Daniel. I don't think I'm up for it. Do you think you can come here?"

Daniel thought seriously about what he was suggesting. Several times, he had resisted Annie's invitations to come to her apartment. Tonight, he almost preferred it. Dangerously, it had been a while since he last had sex with Deborah. The reasons were varied. He could truthfully say that a good part of it was due to his chaotic work schedule. By the time he got home late in the evening, he was exhausted. If he wanted to be real with himself, he would have to admit the more accurate explanation involved his sexual attraction for her. It wasn't what it used to be. He would never dare talk about it out loud or even really give it much opportunity to germinate in his thoughts. Just entertaining it as a possibility made him wriggle in his office chair. Though he loved her dearly, he wasn't in love with her. Now, thinking about going to Annie's, he felt a stiffening and tightness in his groin. If he went through with it and she was receptive, he knew he wouldn't be able to resist. He always knew it would be impossible to just say no to the woman who stole his heart so many years ago.

As quickly as he invited the idea of sex with Annie into his head, his self-critical, guilt-ridden side took over. He would have to be a real dick to try to take advantage of a woman in grief. Sex would be the furthest thing from her mind. Fighting against his male hormones now flooding through his system, he decided he would go to Annie's apartment, but exercise the discipline to behave like a normal human being.

"I'll come to your place. You do have a VCR, right?"

"Yes, I still have my old one. Are you coming now?"

"I have a few things to do before I leave the office. Would it be ok if I show up around seven o'clock?"

"That's fine. I won't be going anywhere. Thank you so much for everything you're doing. I'll see you at seven."

Daniel was about to make his next call to Robin Stein then thought better of it. The poor woman deserved much more than an impersonal phone conversation to notify her that her sister could be in serious trouble. He decided to request that New York send an agent to her home to deliver the news. As worried as Annie was about Mrs. Stein's reaction, someone should probably be there. He called Mancini back and voiced his concerns. Jim agreed he would have one of the ransom team members explain everything to Mrs. Stein. He didn't want to leave the office because the LaGuardia tapes had just arrived. He promised to call Daniel back shortly to brief him on his findings.

It actually took Agent Mancini one hour and sixteen minutes to watch the tapes showing Hannah and the suspect from the time they disembarked the plane at Gate 24 of Concourse B to the time they left the counter of the Avis rental office and exited the terminal. He called Daniel immediately after the last tape ended.

Mancini explained, "I just finished watching the tapes. There's no question you were right. This bastard knew the location of every camera from the arrival gate to the point when he left the terminal at the baggage claim level. We don't get one good look at his face. I can't give you any more of a description of him than you gave me. Either he put his arm or hand in front of his face or some other object he had in his hand or simply turned away. Mrs. Richards was with him the entire time, except for a short stretch when he separated himself to make a phone call. It's possible there are others involved.

We'll need to get a hold of Avis's parking lot surveillance tapes. I think we're getting closer to being able to at least call this a kidnapping. There's a minute chance he dropped her off somewhere, but his avoidance of all the cameras can't be coincidence. I've already contacted Avis and they're working on getting me the tapes. I'm hoping to have them by this evening. Oh and one final thing. Avis tells me he rented the vehicle under the name Dwight Adelman. I'm sure it's got to be an alias. Do you want me to stick around?"

"That would be great if you could, Jim. If this is our guy, he's a pretty cool customer and extremely well prepared. He went to great lengths to develop a complicated plan to abduct Mrs. Richards. I'm starting to wonder whether he was playing games with us in the process. A smart, calculating criminal doesn't expose himself to so many surveillance cameras without an ulterior motive. He may be challenging us. Obviously, that's not a good sign. Hopefully, she's alive and being held captive somewhere in the New York area. It's still possible this was a kidnapping for ransom. I think we also have to consider he may have had worse plans for her.

You mentioned he made a phone call. We need to act quickly. I know you have a pregnant wife at home, but, if you could wait for those tapes or have someone else from the office take over, I'd appreciate it. I'm going to talk to your A.S.A.C. and see if we can get you assigned to this case for now. Once we know what we're dealing with, we can come up with a more detailed plan."

"Donna is having dinner with her mother and then they're going baby shopping. They won't be home until later tonight. I don't mind waiting."

"You're a good man, Jim. Thanks a lot. Let me know when you have the Avis tapes."

"Will do. I'll get back with you."

Chapter 11

The aroma of Italian sausage and garlic wafted through the apartment as Annie prepared Maria Falcone's secret, family recipe for spaghetti sauce. Maria shared it with Annie during the years Annie lived with Daniel. Annie developed a close relationship with his mom, who seemed as devastated as Daniel when she refused his marriage proposal. Annie figured that since he was scheduled to arrive at dinner time, the least she could do was to fix him a decent meal. His mom's spaghetti was one of his favorites and it would keep her mind off of Hannah's disappearance for a while. She added a pinch of red pepper flakes and a handful of grated Romano cheese to the sauce, then retreated to the dining room.

Annie was never really the domestic type. She always appreciated good food, but until she met Daniel, she had no real experience in the kitchen. He was a much more skilled cook than she, his specialty being Italian food. In their first several years of dating at George Washington University, Daniel often cooked dinners for her and her roommates. It was usually Annie's responsibility to find a fine wine that suited the meal he was preparing. They both liked to think of themselves as amateur connoisseurs.

As Annie waited for Daniel, she scanned her dining room wine rack and chose a bottle of red she had procured on her most recent visit to the Santa Inez Valley. She uncorked the bottle of Sangiovese to allow it to breathe having decided it was the perfect compliment for a spicy Italian tomato sauce. Since she had a moment to relax, she poured herself a glass of Cake Bread Chardonnay from a bottle she opened earlier in the evening. When she sat down to enjoy it, the events of the last eighteen hours came charging back to the forefront. Thoughts about what Hannah might be feeling turned her mood south in an instant. She prayed her good friend was still alive and unhurt. As the tears welled and threatened to spill over, the telephone rang rescuing her from her morose reverie. It was Daniel. She picked up the phone and greeted him.

"Hi Annie, are you alright? You don't sound great."

"I'll be ok. Are you on your way?"

"I just left the office. I should be there in about fifteen minutes."

"Any more news?"

"You sure you don't want to wait till I get there?"

"I'm alright. It'll make me more stressed to wait and wonder."

"Ok, well Mancini reviewed the LaGuardia tapes. I'll fill you in on the details when I get there, but it's looking more and more like an abduction. It seems Hannah accepted a ride from the man she befriended at the Ft. Lauderdale airport. If we don't hear anything from her soon…and the chances of that are getting less and less likely, we have to figure out if this was a kidnapping for ransom. I don't want to jump to conclusions, though. Just in case, I sent a kidnapping team out to Mrs. Stein's several hours ago. No calls yet."

"I know. I spoke to her a little while ago. She's a mess."

"I called to assure her we were doing everything we could and to explain procedures. She was sobbing through the entire conversation. It's good she's not alone."

"I guess it's just a waiting game now. How long will you wait before you give up on the kidnapping theory?"

"It can take up to three or four days. On very rare occasions, it's taken more than a week to hear from the perps."

"Damn, I don't think I could handle that. And I know for a fact Mrs. Stein can't."

"Like I told her, Annie, we're doing everything we can. Hannah even gets the benefit of an investigation that was started earlier than normal. Besides the APB, we got a photo of Hannah from Robin. It'll be scanned so every law enforcement official in the New York area and northeastern United States will be on the lookout for her. It's also been distributed to all airports, train and bus stations. We're working on getting a photo of the suspect from the tapes that'll at least show his size, body type and maybe a profile. Once we have one, we'll put it out."

"Thank you so much for getting things going right away. I'm sure the family really appreciates it too. By the way, have you eaten?"

"I'm famished. I've been so busy today I haven't eaten a thing since breakfast. Maybe we could order something while you watch the tapes."

"Not necessary. I fixed your Mom's spaghetti."

The idea that Annie had cooked for him sent another erotic charge directly to his loins. "Annie, you didn't have to do that. I'm sure you were in no mood to cook."

"Don't be silly. It's the least I could do. Besides, it took my mind off things for a while."

"Well, I can't say I'm disappointed. Thanks. I should be there in a few minutes."

"Ok, Daniel. See you then."

* * *

The crisp, invigorating fragrance of a blast of arctic air was a welcome stimulant to the sleep-deprived Shem as he huddled against a palm tree on Ft. Lauderdale Beach. It was a good thing he still had the parka he wore on the trip to the Catskill Mountains. It would come in handy this evening. Ft. Lauderdale was under a freeze warning and the temperatures were expected to plummet below thirty degrees by the following morning.

The beach was as deserted as it was earlier in the day and the darkness afforded him cover he wasn't able to enjoy that afternoon. He replaced his daytime binoculars and camera with special infrared photographic equipment that allowed him to take pictures in spite of the blackness of the night. Annie hadn't left her apartment the entire day. He wondered if she were aware of the disappearance of the Jew slut. This wouldn't be her last experience with losing someone close to her. In the end, he would be the only person who mattered in her life.

Most evenings, Annie sat on her living room sofa opposite the picture, floor to ceiling windows to take advantage of the view of the beach below and the steady stream of pedestrian traffic. He had not seen her yet that night and was beginning to question whether she was at home. This time, he checked to find her BMW parked in the garage. Still, there was always the possibility that a friend or her nuisance of a boyfriend could have picked her up before he arrived. He was pretty sure that wasn't the case because he saw the lights in her bedroom switched off and the light in the kitchen was on since sunset.

His decision to stick it out was rewarded five minutes later when Annie appeared before her living room window staring out into the black emptiness that was the Atlantic Ocean. He gazed through his zoom lens to see her goddess-like silhouette as if she were standing on the beach directly in front of him. He absent-mindedly reached out with his left hand to touch her bare shoulder when he realized that Annie seemed to be dressed to go out. He snapped a picture, quickly packed his equipment then hurried to his parked car to wait for Annie to come down.

* * *

On a typical winter evening, it would be impossible to find a public parking space across from Annie's building. The Ft. Lauderdale Beach nightlife had resurged since the City Council cleaned up the area and did away with the traditional Spring Break night clubs and bars of the mid-nineteen eighties. That night, Daniel was able to parallel park in one of many available spaces. As he turned off the ignition to his vehicle and prepared to exit, his cell phone rang. It was Mancini.

"Hi Jim. What do you have for me?"

"It's not good news. I'll get straight to it. Mrs. Richards did accompany the suspect to the Avis parking lot. He was recorded speaking to the parking lot attendant and at various points, he and Mrs. Richards were seen walking together to the 2007 Ford Expedition the suspect rented. I called and got the number of the attendant working last night and the shuttle bus driver. Both were able to give a basic description of Mrs. Richards and height and weight guesses about the suspect. Neither got a good look at his face. I'm gonna have someone sent out there to show them a picture pulled from the tapes and see if it jogs his memory…to help with the police sketch artist. He just might be able to come up with something decent with the software and graphic arts they use these days.

Getting back to the tape, the suspect loaded six bags into the rear while the woman waited in the front passenger seat. Obviously, this confirms your hunch she accepted a ride. Of course, the camera was shooting his back as he stacked the bags. When he returned the luggage cart to its stand, he avoided the cameras like he did at both airports. None of them caught a frontal view of his face. The worst part happened after he put a final bag into the SUV. He opened the front zipper pouch and took out a rag and a bottle of clear liquid. Before he poured the liquid into the rag, the brazen bastard actually held the bottle up high for the camera. No question he wanted us to see him going through the process. When he entered through the driver's side front door, our view was obstructed. I don't think there's much doubt he's our man. The liquid had to be some type of anesthetic because cameras catching the vehicle as it exited the garage got Mrs. Richards slumped forward in her seat. They only managed shadows of the driver."

"Has anyone talked to Robin Stein?" inquired Daniel.

"Not yet."

"I'm just getting to Annie Bryan's place to show her the Ft. Lauderdale Airport surveillance tapes. She's Mrs. Richards' closest friend in Florida and an expert in security procedures. She has a sharp eye. I'm hoping she can help, maybe recognize someone in the tapes who could have been hanging around her building. We'll call Mrs. Stein to update her on the latest. Of course, I won't mention any particulars about the rag and clear liquid. I think we should keep that information to ourselves for the time being. Has her son arrived yet from California?"

"I believe one of the agents from the ransom squad is on his way to the airport to pick him up now."

"Great. She's gonna need all the support she can get. Thanks for your help, Jim. You've done some great work. Now go home and take care of that pregnant wife of yours."

"I don't think she's home yet from the mall, but I'm definitely ready to put my feet up and have a beer. Isn't Annie Bryan the chick you asked to marry you way back when?"

"Yeah, she's the one who called me yesterday, worried about Mrs. Richards."

"Oh ok. You didn't mention that. She works for a cruise line now, doesn't she?"

"Yes, she's their head of security."

"Hopefully she'll be able to help. I'm outta here. I'll talk to you tomorrow unless something comes up before then."

After ending the call, Daniel exited his vehicle and crossed the street to Annie's building. He approached the security station where Harry, the overnight security guard, was on duty. Annie phoned the front desk earlier to warn them she was expecting a guest. After Daniel identified himself, Harry gave him a nod signaling he could pass. Several minutes later, the elevator doors slid open on the 10th floor. He proceeded to the opposite end of the hall and knocked on Annie's door. When she opened it, his eyes were immediately drawn to the strapless Diane Von Furstenberg peach colored dress that clung to her skin showing every feminine curve of her body.

"Hello Daniel. Come on in. Make yourself comfortable. Can I get you something to drink? Maybe a glass of wine?" She gave him a quick peck on the cheek and led him into the living room.

"I'm not sure that's such a good idea. I have to drive. How much have you had to drink? I prefer that you have a clear head when you look at these tapes."

Annie, who was holding a half-full glass of wine, responded. "This is only my second. Don't get your panties in a bunch. I'm not drunk although I'd like to be. You've had a long difficult day yourself. You deserve to have something to relax you. I know how much you love a great Sangiovese. I opened up a bottle before you got here. One glass isn't gonna hurt you. You're gonna be here for a while and you're eating. You'll be fine."

"Oh alright. You twisted my arm."

"I didn't think you'd resist even that long."

"It smells great in here. I'm about to pass out from starvation."

"I'll get the water boiling. Dinner should be ready in about ten minutes or so. We can watch the tapes after we eat. Go ahead and have a seat. I'll be back in a minute."

Annie poured Daniel a glass of wine then retired to the kitchen. Daniel sat on the plush, brown leather sofa and took a sip of the Sangiovese. It felt really good to finally take a moment to sit back and unwind. As he took advantage of the spectacular view of the beach and dark sky fusing with the invisible sea, a red light flashed across his field of vision that seemed to come from the street below. He stood up to look down at the area where he thought it came from, but the beach was deserted. He dismissed it, concluding it must have been his imagination, sat back down on the comfortable sofa and put his feet up on the ottoman. Scanning the room, he thought about how Annie had done extremely well for herself. This certainly was the life. She lived in a beautiful, spacious apartment overlooking Ft. Lauderdale Beach and the Atlantic Ocean. He felt a hint of bitterness as he considered this was what Annie chose over him, then immediately quashed the idea.

Annie joined him in the living room several minutes later with her glass of wine and the remainder of the bottle. She sat on the sofa next to Daniel, positioning herself a little bit closer to him than what would be considered appropriate. Daniel joked though in reality, he was very serious. Suddenly his efforts at discipline were about to be thrown out the window.

"You're not going to try to get me drunk and take advantage of me, are you?"

"That wasn't nice. My friend disappeared, could be dead on the side of the street somewhere and I'm thinking about sex? I'm sure I'll be able to control myself and keep my hands off of you."

"I'm sorry, Annie. That was insensitive." For a moment, Daniel felt the bite of disappointment.

"I'll forgive you this time." She lifted the bottle from the coffee table and started to refill Daniel's glass. Refusing a drink or two in the evening was far from his normal practice. Tonight, he had to think about driving, but this time, he didn't have Deborah nagging him to take it easy.

"You keep pouring those, I'm gonna get hammered."

"Seriously, Daniel. It's not like you never drank wine before. If I know you, you have at least a couple of drinks in the evening after work. It's gonna take a lot more than a glass and a half of wine to affect you."

Annie's prediction was not exactly accurate. By the time they began dinner, he had a pretty good buzz going. The lack of any food in his system caused the alcohol to go straight to his head. Finally getting some nourishment in his stomach didn't help much as he downed an additional three glasses of wine during the meal.

After dinner was over, Daniel's offer to help with the dishes was summarily rejected. Annie insisted he relax in the living room while she straightened up. She opened a third bottle of Shoestring Sangiovese and poured a glass for Daniel which he accepted without complaint. While Annie cleared the table, he fumbled in his brief case in search of the surveillance tapes. He placed the first of the cassettes into the VCR then sat on the love seat facing the television set to wait for Annie.

Once she finished stacking the dishwasher, Annie returned to the living room with the third bottle of wine and an empty glass for herself. She grabbed the remote, turned the TV on and started the first of the tapes. She sat down on the love seat next to Daniel and over the next hour, watched Hannah's arrival at the airport and her meeting with the suspect. She did her best to focus a professional eye on the events she was witnessing. However, by the time the last tape was finished, she was stricken by such a terror and sadness for her dear friend she couldn't stop the tears from flowing.

She downed two glasses of wine in quick succession, which didn't dull the wave of emotion that invaded her spirit. As she continued to cry, she laid her head on Daniel's right shoulder. In an attempt to comfort her, Daniel put his arm around her and pulled her closer to him. They stared into each other's eyes and before Daniel had the time to think about what he was doing, he passionately kissed her familiar soft lips. As she stroked his face with her silky hands, a deluge of emotions from years past came rushing to the surface. Both of them lost all self control. The next thing they knew, they were tearing off each other's clothes. Standing before the picture window, naked, Daniel re-explored Annie's hard, velvety body from head to toe with his lips, tongue and fingers. The alcohol he consumed in addition to the sexual anticipation caused him to break out in a perspiration that covered his body. The sheen of his skin accentuated the tightly cut muscles of his chest, abdomen and legs. In the heat of passion, Annie fell back onto the carpeted floor pulling Daniel on top of her. For the next twenty minutes, they made love like they had never skipped a beat, the years of separation seeming to melt away. By the time it was over, Annie achieved multiple orgasms. It wasn't until Daniel rolled off of her onto his back directly in front of the huge window that the significance of what he had just done hit him like a ton of bricks. The idea of having sex with Annie was so enticing; he wasn't able to stop himself from following through with his plan to take her. Now that the orgasm was over, he was powerless to prevent the guilt from drowning him. In a matter of an instant, his feelings about his intentions and actions made a complete 180 degree about-face. He was in a tailspin in danger of going over the edge.

He took a few moments to catch his breath before he stood up to look for his clothes. Without saying a word, they both got dressed. After they sat down on separate sofas, Daniel was the first to speak.

"That was a mistake."

Slightly embarrassed by her behavior, taking into account the reason for Daniel's visit, Annie was struck silent. If she were to admit her true feelings, she would tell Daniel she had been waiting for that moment for a long time. It wasn't like she hadn't made it quite clear. Analyzing the situation on a more profound level, there probably wasn't much of a question she set the whole thing up. Adding Hannah's disappearance to the equation, Annie was figuring she had some serious soul searching to do. There were several characteristics about her personality and objectives that could be considered downright disgusting. Through it all, the fact remained she had wanted Daniel, wasn't over him and evidently his marriage and children weren't going to stop her.

"Are you going to say anything?" Daniel persisted.

"I don't know what you want me to say."

"I can't believe that just happened. This is a fuck'n mess."

"Well Daniel, we're the only two people who know. It's not like I'm gonna say anything."

"Is that all you're worried about? Whether anyone finds out? I've got a wife and kids. It's just fuck'n wrong. I don't know what got into me. Damnit. What a huge mistake."

Annie knew what Daniel was saying was true, but couldn't help feeling a twinge of hurt by his reaction. Somewhere deep down, beneath all the games, fronts and self-protection mechanisms, there was no doubt she still had intense feelings for him. Her behavior, however, had been no less than despicable, immoral and had gone way beyond the appropriate boundaries. Why she was considering all this now rather than before when it could have been prevented was anyone's guess.

"I'm sorry. I suppose this was all my fault. I don't know what else to say."

"I shouldn't have come over here. I knew it wasn't a good idea. I wanted it just as much as you did. Shit, what am I gonna do?"

Daniel's confession didn't go unnoticed though Annie smartly decided not to explore it at the moment. "Just relax, Daniel. I know you feel horrible. Shit, if the wind blows, you feel guilty. I'm not saying you don't have good reason. We just have to deal with it now. No one's gonna find out. I promise, and I mean it…I won't say anything to anyone, not a soul. Let's just get back to what you came for. We'll sort all this stuff out some other time. Here we are acting like two horny teenage kids while one of my best friends could be in the hands of some deranged maniac as we speak."

* * *

The smoldering fires of hell couldn't match the intensity of the fury that blazed in Shem's midsection, making his stomach feel like a furnace stuffed with glowing hot coals. He was crazed to the point that he was having trouble thinking with clarity. A thousand thoughts fought for supremacy at the same time. One repeatedly made it to the forefront- the idea that the mother-fucking, cheating cocksucker had the unmitigated gall to force himself on his Annie. The state of bliss he was experiencing for the past twenty four hours was already a distant memory.

He never expected his evening to come to this when earlier he waited in his parked car across from the Maya Marca entrance anticipating Annie would appear any minute. Instead, Daniel Falcone pulled into the parking space directly behind his Acura Integra. At first, he didn't realize it was the FBI agent. He strained his eyes squinting for a look through his rearview mirror, unable in the faded light of the lamppost to see the driver through the tinted windshield. Five minutes later, Falcone exited the vehicle and jogged toward Annie's building carrying a large briefcase.

Initially, Shem wasn't that concerned about the agent's arrival. He figured the authorities were aware of the Jew whore's disappearance by now and it was probable a representative from the FBI would be meeting with building officials. Though Shem didn't like the idea, he didn't doubt Falcone would stop by Annie's apartment. He had an inkling Annie might communicate with the agent after her neighbor was discovered missing. Not for one second did he permit himself to believe the visit would be for any other purpose except to discuss the Tucker slut look-a-like. After the agent entered the building, Shem reached into his backseat, grabbed his equipment bag then hopped out of his car. He hurried toward the beach and set the bag behind a large palm tree. Scouting the area, he confirmed that the street was still devoid of pedestrians. Vehicle traffic was light and the beach was totally deserted.

The stiff land breeze blowing in from the northwest pounded at his face as he looked up toward Annie's apartment hoping that the curtains were open. He ignored the sting of the cold on his naked face and eyes pleased to see not only was that the case, every light in the place had been switched on. His view into the living room area with his binoculars was nothing short of crystal clear. Looking through the high-powered magnifiers, he had a perfect perspective of the living room and an ideal sightline of the leather sofa, love seat and entertainment center. Fixing his gaze on the penthouse apartment windows, there was no sign of life for the first ten minutes. Shortly thereafter, Daniel sat on the leather sofa, giving Shem a full frontal view of the FBI agent. Shem saw that Annie's guest had removed his suit jacket, loosened his tie and was drinking a glass of wine. It forced him to reconsider his opinion regarding Falcone's motives for the visit and wonder about its true purpose.

Without thinking, Shem pulled his laser sight 9mm pistol from his bag and pointed it at the agent's temple. The urge to pull the trigger was so strong, for a fleeting moment, he didn't think he was going to be able to resist. At the last minute, he changed his mind, deliberately causing the target beam to quickly pass over both of the agent's eyes. The thought of exercising some power over Falcone helped calm him for an instant. With the agility of someone half his size, Shem ducked behind the palm tree making sure both he and his bag were completely out of sight. Seconds later, he could sense a pair of eyes combing the area from above. Allowing several minutes to pass, he peeked out from behind the tree up toward the apartment. If the agent had investigated the laser target, he had given up.

Checking the living room more closely with his binoculars, Shem saw that Annie had joined Falcone on the sofa. She was also drinking a glass of wine and had placed the remainder of the bottle on the coffee table. If knowing the agent was drinking wasn't enough to affect his peace of mind, seeing Annie indulge with him did the trick. His distress and anger increased ten-fold when they disappeared for more than thirty minutes. He was starting to regret not having pulled the trigger when he had the chance..

With his thought processes in overdrive, Shem tried his best not to pace or fidget while he waited for an opportunity to get an idea of what was happening in the apartment. Not knowing made him tense, a feeling he didn't handle well. His imagination wasn't being kind to him either. When the wait was finally over, it was the agent who entered the living room first. Falcone took what appeared to be videotapes out of his briefcase. Shem's tranquility was partially restored when the agent tested the VCR, showing the first few seconds of the airport surveillance tape. Perhaps this wasn't a social visit, after all.

Though Shem was very curious about his performance on the tapes, he didn't avert his gaze from Annie and the agent for more than a few seconds at a time. They were sitting way too close on the love seat for his comfort. At the conclusion of the tapes, he doggedly watched as Annie gulped down two glasses of wine. He zoomed in on her eyes and saw they were overflowing with tears. What happened immediately after tested the limits of his self control more than any experience in his entire life. When he saw the agent kissing his Annie, then ripping her clothes from her body, he seriously reconsidered going for his gun to blow the man's brains out. He boiled over with unparalleled rage. He struggled to control his impulses and emotions. It was a difficult battle that he came extremely close to losing. In the end, his calculating and reasonable self prevailed. In place of the pistol, he pulled his camcorder from the bag and began to record the horror as it unfolded. The wheels of his calculating mind were already furiously churning.

* * *

Daniel didn't leave Annie's apartment until well after 10:00pm. He wanted to be sure he sobered up before he got behind the wheel of a car and potentially faced Deborah. The idea of what transpired was somewhat surreal to him. Yes, he was sexually attracted to Annie, but he saw himself as a man of exceptional discipline. For the life of him, he couldn't figure out what made him so weak. At least that was what his guilt-ridden conscience was hypocritically coercing him to believe now that the deed was done. It was going to be a difficult struggle to stifle his shame and keep a secret from Deborah. Normally, they were brutally honest with each other. If he had any intentions of making his marriage work, she must never know.

Earlier in the week, he feared his wife would ask him to end his friendship with Annie. Now, he might have to consider the possibility on his own. It wouldn't be easy to completely cut her out of his life. To allow the maintenance of the status quo could and probably would risk his marriage. His boys were his life and he took his nuptials very seriously being raised a devout Catholic. He had to recognize the chance he and Annie could get weak again. It wouldn't be fair to Deborah to place himself in that position.

Just when everything seemed to be falling into place at work, with life in general, he had to go and complicate things. It seemed to be a recurring theme since his brother's accident. He wondered if he invited it. One of the FBI shrinks tried to tell him once that guilt was his comfort zone. It sounded like a bunch of psychobabble shit to Daniel at the time. Since then, he had seriously contemplated whether the psychologist hit on something. Now, he had a bunch of hard questions to answer. Was his love for Deborah strong enough to sustain the marriage? Could he be happy staying with her for the rest of his life? Was it good for the boys for him to work through the relationship if the necessary spark was lacking? Was he still in love with Annie? Why was it so difficult to completely cut her out of his life? Thinking about all the issues was giving him a premature hangover. His head was pounding. Things weren't going to get any better.

Daniel parked his car in his allotted space in front of his condominium. It was almost 10:30 and the kids were most likely asleep. He wondered whether Deborah was still awake. It didn't take long to get his answer. She was standing right behind the door when he opened it. He tried to greet her with a kiss but she avoided his lips, which pecked at the air beside Deborah's cheek.

"Daniel, where the hell were you? Why didn't you call me to let me know you would be this late? And why do I smell alcohol on your breath? Did you actually drive?"

"Hold on, Annie. One question at a time."

"Don't take that tone with me. I'm not the one who walked in at 10:30 at night with alcohol on my breath after spending time at my ex-girlfriend's house. And my name's not Annie." A tear forged a course down her right cheek as she turned to storm back to their bedroom.

"Oh, honey, I'm sorry. I made the mistake of having a little bit too much wine on an empty stomach. I didn't eat anything all day before I went to Annie's place. I let her talk me into having a couple of glasses of wine. Then, somehow, by the time we were done looking at the tapes, I downed three or four. I had to wait a while to sober up before I could drive home."

Deborah stopped at the top of the foyer steps with her back to him to listen to what he had to say. Without turning around she responded, "Gimme a fuck'n break, Daniel. Somehow? What the fuck are you doing drinking at her place anyway? I guess it was the wine that kept you from picking up the phone and letting me know what was going on so I didn't worry. That's a poor excuse. I'm really upset with you right now. I think you should sleep in the guest room." Daniel knew he was in deep trouble. Deborah rarely used the "F" word and never in their nine years of marriage had she banished him from their bedroom.

"Sweetie, I completely understand why you're angry with me. I was an idiot. I should've called. I shouldn't have allowed myself to get to that point. Please forgive me."

"Daniel, I'm not angry, I'm furious. You're going to have to give me a chance to cool down. The guest bed has fresh linens. Goodnight."

Daniel was left standing alone as Deborah stomped nosily up the steps. He hoped it wouldn't take her too long to get over this though he deserved the most severe of punishments. He didn't even want to consider what her reaction might be if she found out what actually happened. Most likely, their marriage would be destroyed. It was his intention to do everything in his power to avoid that. He cared for her too much and couldn't allow the boys to suffer through their separation and divorce.

Chapter 12

It was the Tuesday evening after Hannah Richard's disappearance and the family had not yet received a ransom call from the kidnapper. Annie was at her wit's end and beginning to lose hope. On the third day of the Hannah ordeal, she received a call from Steven Stein, informing her his mother had to be rushed to the hospital with chest pain. It turned out Robin wasn't having a heart attack, but was held overnight for observation. Annie's spirits and physical state weren't in much better shape. She had been feeling depressed and totally depleted of her normal high-energy. The chances Hannah was still alive were going from smaller to slim.

Being smacked in the face with what life can throw at you, Annie finally came to the realization her breakup with Michael was long overdue. Her decision was final. She would stop wasting her time and more importantly, Michael's, on a relationship that was going nowhere. She needed to end it with him for good. As she drove home from work that day, she dialed his cell phone number. He answered in his typical jovial manner.

"Hello beautiful. How are you today?"

"I've had better days, Michael. Hannah is still missing and we have no clue whether she's dead or alive. I can't believe I'm saying it out loud, but if you asked me, I don't think it's the latter. Anyway, I was wondering what you were doing tonight. Are you gonna be home?"

"Actually, I have no plans at all. So you're in luck. Would you like to go out to dinner? Maybe catch a movie. Get your mind off things."

Michael wasn't going to make it any easier on her. She said, "No, I'd like to just come by your house, if you don't mind."

"Not at all. I'd be glad to have you. Would you like me to fix something for dinner?"

"No thanks. I had a late lunch and I'm not that hungry. I just want to talk."

"Sure thing. What time is good for you?"

"How 'bout seven? Will you be home from work by then?"

"I'll make sure of it."

"Alrighty, I'll see you then."

An hour and a half later, Annie pulled into Michael's driveway at his waterfront home off of Las Olas Blvd. He had just arrived and was at the curb checking his mailbox. They walked into the house together while Michael rummaged through his assortment of letters, bills and advertisements. They passed through the front double doors onto the polished Brazilian cherry wood floors of the foyer. Curious about a manila envelope that had no return address, Michael held it up to the light coming in through the window above the doors to examine it. A bulge in the package led him to believe there was a product or gift inside. He tore it open and found what he thought to be some kind of practical joke. With a puzzled look on his face, he removed the two rubber ears from inside the envelope. Surprised to find there was no letter to explain the bizarre package, he inspected the ears more closely. The rubber had been scraped off of one of them. What he saw underneath caused him to inhale a quick gasp of air and a bit of saliva. It appeared to be human skin with a star-shaped mole on the earlobe. Annie, who was watching him open the envelope, noticed a look of disgust in his grimace before he started coughing. She asked, "Michael, what the heck is that? What's wrong?"

After a few seconds the cough settled. "I have absolutely no idea," he responded. "At first, I thought it was some type of gag gift. But, take a look at this. It actually looks like human skin."

Annie inspected the ears. When she saw the mole, her face contorted into an expression of pure horror and she passed out in a heap on the floor. Astonished by her reaction, Michael dropped the envelope and rushed to her aid. He picked her up off the floor, carried her to the living room and gently laid her down on the sofa. He considered calling 911 then thought it might be an overreaction. He hurried into the kitchen to run a dish rag under cold water, returned to the living room and placed it on Annie's forehead.

Within several minutes, she began to stir. When she completely regained her senses, she cried out, "Michael, that was Hannah's ear. I recognize the star-shaped mole on the earlobe." Tears streamed down her face leaving trace lines of black mascara.

"What? Are you sure about that? Why would anyone send such a thing to me?"

"I have no idea but I'm positive. That's not a mole you see every day and it's in the exact right location. I'm not wrong about this."

"Are you ok? You took a pretty good spill. I was worried you might have broken something."

"Physically, I feel fine." She stood up to test her bearings. Michael tried to get her to stay on the sofa but she was determined.

He said, "We need to call the police then. Let me get the phone."

Annie followed him to the kitchen suggesting, "I think we should call Daniel. The FBI is already investigating the case."

Michael handed Annie the phone and she dialed Daniel's cell phone number. She hadn't spoken to him since the night they made love and was feeling somewhat awkward calling him. Considering the circumstances now was no time to worry about her own well-being.

"Hello, Annie."

"Yes, Daniel, I'm sorry to call, but something terrible's happened. I'm over at Michael Munez's house. He received a package in the mail today... Oh my God, Daniel, Hannah's ear was in the envelope. It was coated with rubber except for a section on the earlobe that was scraped clean to expose her mole. It's very unique... unmistakable. It's star-shaped. There was a second ear in the envelope that I assume was Hannah's too. This is horrible. I can't believe it."

"Are you sure it was a human ear?"

"I can't be absolutely sure. It definitely looks like it to me. To Michael too."

"I'm gonna send a forensics team down there right away. Where's the package now? Be sure neither of you touch it again. Can you give me the address?"

She turned to Michael and asked him where the envelope was. Because of his panicked response to Annie's loss of consciousness, he couldn't recall what happened to the ears or the envelope. She relayed the information to Daniel and gave him Michael's address.

"Please leave the evidence exactly where it landed. I'm sure it's already been tainted with your fingerprints, but I want to minimize the contamination."

"We won't touch a thing...Daniel...I'm sure she's dead. This is just too sad...Oh my God. What kind of demented monster would do such a thing?"

"You can't jump to any conclusions yet. The abductor could be playing games with us. You never know. I've seen a lot of crazy shit. I'll send a team out right away. We shouldn't assume anything until we're able to do some tests. Before I hang up, do you have any idea why this package would have been sent to Michael?"

"It's a total mystery to me. It makes no sense whatsoever."

"For now, I know it's not gonna be easy...try to get yourself together. Maybe you shouldn't be alone. Why don't you spend the night at Michael's?"

"I think I'll just stick around till the forensics team is done. Then, I'm gonna go to my Mom's."

"So long as you're not alone. I'll give you a call tomorrow with an update."

"You're not coming?"

"No, I've assigned the case to Leland. He'll be there."

* * *

It was a crisp, brisk Wednesday morning in the Catskill Mountains just north of Tannersville, New York. There wasn't a cloud in the pristine, blue sky. The unfettered, bright sun shone down on the leaves of the sugar maple trees causing icicles to form that resembled the sharp tiny teeth of a moray eel. Frank Jensen and three of his buddies were up at the crack of dawn that morning for a day of deer hunting though there would be no fresh venison served at the dinner table that night. As Frank skulked stealthily down a backcountry trail in his bright orange hunting gear, he spied a charred shape low to the ground approximately twenty yards ahead. The tree just behind the object had burned also. The closer he approached, the more it became clear the object was the body of a human being. About twenty five feet from the horrific scene, he stopped in his tracks. Despite the frosty chill in the air, the stench emitted from the corpse caused a burning acid-like bile to rise into his throat. He vomited his pancake breakfast into the fresh, white snow.

After collecting himself, he moved downwind from the body and called to his friends who were lagging behind. Larry Costa was the only member of the party who had a cell phone with service. Frank warned the guys not to get too close to the scene. When Larry saw the scorched cadaver, he pulled his cell phone out of his backpack and called 911.

* * *

Sheriff John Freeman of the Green County Sheriff's Department responded to the scene of Hannah Richards' murder along with Deputy Sheriff Blaine Carter. Sheriff Freeman had been involved in police work for more than forty-five years, including working the homicide division of the New York State Police Department in Brooklyn. Never, in his entire career had he witnessed the remains of such a horrendous killing. With the collar of their sweaters covering their nose and mouth, they approached the body. Their efforts to protect their senses from the fetid stench were weak at best. While Freeman visually examined the body, Carter stepped off the path to expel his breakfast. Freeman followed suit seconds later.

Most of the victim's clothing had been burned off the body. There were some strings and rags remaining hanging from the legs and wrists. The epidermis was completely charred black from head to toe. Cracks in the skin on her face, torso, and legs revealed cooked flesh beneath. In some cases, the crevices were so deep they exposed the red, frozen, raw tissue that was spared the intense heat of the fire. Desiccated, frozen, over-boiled blood trailed down from the empty eye sockets like vampire blood tears. It also flowed, bubbled and dried into hundreds of odd shaped scabs that filled many of the other open fissures that covered the corpse. While inspecting the body, Freeman noticed what appeared to be some form of identification or driver's license nailed to a tree trunk ten feet behind the burned sugar maple. On closer examination, he saw it was in fact a Florida Driver's License belonging to Hannah Richards.

After calling the name into dispatch, he regrettably learned that the FBI had put out an All Points Bulletin for the alleged victim. The Feds were far from his favorite people, but since they were already involved in the Richards case, he was obligated to notify them of the discovery. He wasn't pleased to have to bow to the Bureau. In his opinion they were just a bunch of cocky, overconfident, snooty sons of bitches. On the other hand, he knew this type of crime didn't happen often in Green County and they were ill-equipped to evaluate a crime scene of this magnitude. It pissed him off when he called the New York field office minutes later and the agent working the case had the impudence to instruct him how to secure the area. He wasn't in law enforcement for almost half a century to have some young, punk, federal agent tell him how to manage a crime scene. He'd have Carter put up some yellow tape, though he wasn't going out of his way.

Once the area was cordoned off, Sheriff Freeman asked the four young hunters to follow him to the station where he planned to take their statements. It was his jurisdiction after all and hell if he didn't have every right to open up an investigation. There was also the slight possibility this wasn't the Richards woman. The license could have been used as a distraction by the murderer. He left his deputy at the scene and ordered him to call as soon as James Mancini and his team arrived.

* * *

The equipment in the computer room of Shem's apartment could have overseen a NASA moon voyage. In fact, his self-made computer was more complex than what NASA employed for their Apollo space missions in the late sixties and seventies. That day, he was performing a simple operation. He had downloaded pictures from his camcorder onto his hard drive and was printing them onto 13x8 Epson premium glossy photo paper.

After the Saturday night episode, his first instinct was to plan the murder of the FBI agent to make him suffer more than any person ever suffered in the history of humanity. Once he got to really thinking, he devised an ingenious plot that would make Falcone's torment last for the remainder of his life. The agent would rue the day he crossed Shem Chassar. This plan was going to be his piece de resistance, truly one for the books.

Before beginning the printing process, Shem placed a pair of rubber gloves on his hands. He removed five sheets of the glossy photo paper from its package and put them in the printer. Initiating the printing process with the click of his mouse, the images were etched onto the paper. After placing them carefully into a manila envelope, he addressed it to Deborah Falcone, setting the printer to type "for the addressee's eyes only." It was a joyous occasion the day Munez received his special package and Shem had the opportunity to be present. He watched the spectacle from afar, including the arrival of more than seven law enforcement vehicles. The asshole Munez should know now what he was up against if he had half a brain. Shem considered putting a note with the ears warning him to stay away from Annie or he'd be next. That was too obvious a clue for the investigators. If Munez didn't get the message that this was what happened to people who got too close to what belonged to Shem, there would be no doubt next time. Hopefully, this new special delivery would bring about even better results.

He drove his Mustang to the main post office on Oakland Park Blvd. It was important the package not have the same post mark as his previous delivery. In spite of his efforts, he knew there was the possibility the two packages would be connected. So, he was careful to avoid standing out or looking directly into the cameras. Not that he thought they were smart enough to find him even if they got a good look at his face. It's kind of difficult to catch a guy who doesn't exist.

* * *

Purples and reds painted the sky over the snow-capped peaks of the Catskill Mountains composing a sunset that on any normal day would inspire the soul. James Mancini experienced no such revelation as he oversaw the bagging of Hannah Richards' corpse. He and the Evidence Response Team, commonly known as the ERT, arrived five hours earlier to conduct the analysis of the crime scene and surrounding area. The lack of hospitality from the local authorities and plunging temperatures made for one miserable day for Mancini and his men. They were cold, wet, tired and more than ready to get back on the private jet back home to Manhattan.

When they arrived, the forensics team's arson expert, Logan Powell, was happy to find a crime scene that wasn't trampled over by firefighters, supervisory personnel, onlookers and property owners as usually was the case in an arson investigation. The scene was essentially in the condition it was found by the hunter. Ordinarily, the first issue Powell would address was the location of the origin of the fire. That wouldn't be necessary here. The intent was clear. The fire damage was concentrated around the charred body. For this particular crime scene, the most important question was how the fire was started. It was essential to collect any trace evidence that may lead to the identification of a suspect. He instructed his team to look for the presence of igniters, kindling, ignitable material, matches and other means of starting a fire emphasizing that ignitable fluids often ran into cracks and under objects. Any especially charred items or materials that appeared to absorb kerosene or gasoline was to be collected, marked, and identified to be later sent to the lab. The same instructions applied to any empty containers or broken glass jars found at the scene.

Logan collected samples of the tree bark, rope, the victim's clothing, charred skin and hair. There was always a chance such materials could have deposited on the suspect's clothing. Stick matches could be used in the same way to link an arson scene to a suspect. There had been cases where they were physically fitted into a matchbook later found in a suspect's possession. Any of these items could also be chemically processed for fingerprints.

A meticulous search of the entire area was conducted to locate any large or miniscule piece of evidence that would be collected at any murder scene. James Mancini and his colleagues combed the nearby trail and forest floor on hands and knees for pieces of clothing, hair, semen, skin, footprints, fibers, blood, paint, dye, tools, and any other item that could be linked to the suspect's world or environment. Hundreds of photographs were taken of the body, the surrounding area and individual items determined to be evidence. Aerial photographs were taken to clearly depict the geography of the area and to identify potential routes of ingress and egress.

All of the work was done in arctic conditions where the temperature never reached twenty degrees. Oftentimes, the more fastidious work was done without the benefit of gloves. Usually, the local police provided hot coffee and food to help cope with the conditions. Sergeant Freeman did show up at the crime scene. But, that was only to complain that the agents were blocking access to the main road into town with their helicopter and other equipment filled vehicles.

Finally, Mancini and the ERT were wrapping up their tedious inspection of the crime scene. The body was being loaded into the helicopter which would transport it to the medical examiner's office in New York. After the scene was finally cleared of personnel, Mancini called Daniel to update him on the day's findings.

"Hey Jim. What do you have for me?"

"Where do I start? Uh… first, I don't think there's much doubt the victim here is Mrs. Richards. Besides the driver's license, about twenty feet from the corpse, on the ground, we found a set of large hoop earrings that look identical to the one's she was wearing in the surveillance tapes. Also, her gold sandals didn't completely burn. Some of the paint on the toe support and heal of the shoe survived the fire. It matches what we saw on the tapes. The rings on her fingers were just further confirmation. Though some of them were charred and partially melted, they were still in good enough condition to identify. I'll have the sister take a look at them after the medical examiner does his thing. Obviously, we'll have to wait a few days to weeks for the DNA results or dental records comparison. As far as I'm concerned, they'll only be a formality.

Daniel, this woman suffered a horrible, unthinkable death. The fuck'n maniac who did this is evil in its purest form. The body's on its way to the coroner's office in Manhattan. It was barely recognizable as human. I'll spare you the gory details for now. Besides, you'll be able to read them in the autopsy report. It should be available later this evening."

"What about the ears?" Daniel asked. "Was the coroner at the scene able to determine whether they were amputated?"

"The ears were gone. Unfortunately, the head was too damaged by the fire for him to be sure whether they burned off or if they were cut."

"Maybe the medical examiner will be able to see some evidence of a dissection when he examines the body. What else do you have?"

"We cast several footprints in the snow. You already know that four hunters stumbled on her this morning. Luckily, they didn't get too close to the body. We also got lucky that it hasn't snowed since at least the time of the murder. The forensics team was able to differentiate between their footprints and the killer's.

The remnants of the rope she was tied with and some of her clothing was soaked with some type of combustible. We're sending them to the lab for testing along with the casts of the suspect's footprints and hairs that were located at the scene...

One other thing. A boarding house in Tannersville reported to the Sheriff's Department that an SUV was parked in their lot since at least Saturday morning. At first, the manager thought it belonged to a guest of one of the tenants. By Tuesday, when the vehicle wasn't moved for the entire weekend, the manager decided to conduct his own little investigation. It turned out it didn't belong to anyone staying at the house. Bottom line, he reported it abandoned and it's been confirmed as the suspect's rental. Mrs. Richards's luggage was in the back. The whole truck, inside and out, was dusted for fingerprints. It was obvious he wiped everything clean. Not even one partial was found. Oh yeah, that reminds me. More good news. His clothes were found thrown away about a half-mile from the scene. There were some solid partials they were able to lift from the buttons of the white shirt.

It wasn't easy to get information from the local sheriff. He was a real asshole. Ultimately, I was able to get the name of the boarding house and the manager and send an agent to interview him. The manager told him sometime between Friday night and Saturday morning, a pickup truck was stolen from that same parking lot. I put out an APB for the truck. Just for your information, Tannersville is no more than 15 miles from the murder scene. That about wraps things up."

"We're gonna have to get a task force together to get this investigation going," Daniel replied. "I'm gonna talk to your SAC and see what he thinks. I expect we'll include agents from the New York and Miami field offices. There's no question the Bureau has jurisdiction over this one. It was a kidnapping that crossed state lines. Although we don't have the DNA results available yet, we're just as sure the ears that were sent to Michael Munez belonged to Hannah Richards. It's at least confirmed they were human.

I think the suspect is most likely in South Florida. The postmark on the manila envelope was dated the day after the kidnapping from right here in Ft. Lauderdale. Unless he sent them Federal Express to an accomplice, he must have flown back on Saturday morning. We're checking with the post office to determine which branch it was mailed from. We're also looking into where the envelope was purchased and the rubber substance used to coat the ears. It could take a while for the envelope since that particular brand is sold in a lot of stores both in New York and Ft. Lauderdale. We'll start with Ft. Lauderdale because we suspect he bought it here. Once we have the coating substance identified, we'll know more about where it's sold."

Daniel had been doing a lot of thinking about the ears and the fact they were sent to Annie's boyfriend. She seemed to be a common denominator. It didn't seem like coincidence that she was close friends with the victim and the girlfriend of the recipient of the ears. He described his concerns to James.

"I had Annie take a closer look at the tapes," said Daniel. "Even though there was no way of recognizing the suspect because of the way he avoided the cameras, she said there was something vaguely familiar about him. Unfortunately, she couldn't pinpoint where she might know him from, or if she'd ever met him at all.

I've gone over this in my head a bunch, especially what could have motivated the suspect to send the ears to Munez and not Annie directly. I'm thinking there's a possibility he's a stalker. Someone with some type of infatuation or obsession for Annie. I had Leland assigned to lead the investigation. He's put a couple of men on tailing Annie. We'll see what we come up with."

"Anything you or Robert need, just let me know, Daniel. I'll do the same. As soon as I get a hold of the autopsy report, I'll fax you a copy. If the truck turns up, I'll call you immediately. It shouldn't take long with the APB unless he ditched it in some deserted rural area. Most likely, I'd say we're probably gonna find it at some airport if he was already in Ft. Lauderdale the next morning. The closest international airports to Tannersville are Albany, LaGuardia and Kennedy. I'll be sure to put security on alert at all of 'em right away."

"Perfect. I know it's really soon. No one wants to hear the words. I'm not saying it's what we have…This fucker enjoys killing. You know it as well as I do…"

"Spit it out, Daniel. Since when do you beat around the fuck'n bush?"

"You know this psycho has murdered before. I'll repeat. I know it's really early…If we're dealing with a serial killer and Annie is in his sights, she could be in danger."

"Yeah, yeah, I've thought about it already. With a murder like this, it's always in the back of your head. You know I'm on board. There's nothing more I would like than to nail the sick fuck."

"Ok, I'll have Robert look out for that autopsy report tonight. If you hear anything before that, I'll be in my office. Oh… Are you gonna notify the family? I'm sure you agree this is news that has to be handled in person."

"As soon as I get back to New York, I'll drop by her place. The woman is already in pieces. This won't be easy."

"I'm sorry. That's always the shit job. I hate it. Thanks for taking care of it, Jim. I'll let Annie know."

* * *

The forecast the previous evening called for high temperatures approaching the eighties, bringing an end to the South Florida cold snap that lasted a grand total of three days. Deborah Falcone figured sweaters would be appropriate for the boys as she helped them pick out their clothes for school. Daniel left for the office early that morning, so she would be responsible for dropping them off. Once the boys were dressed and eating their breakfast, she ran upstairs to put on her make-up and pack her gym bag.

Deborah wasn't one to stay upset for very long, but the previous weekend's incident was still weighing on her mind. She forgave Daniel the following morning after they had a long, serious discussion. It was obvious in his demeanor and expression he was truly sorry for making her wonder and worry. He admitted it was naïve to think she shouldn't be bothered by his friendship with Annie and even sincerely offered to cut off all ties with his ex-girlfriend. Regardless of Daniel's goodwill, Deborah couldn't help being concerned that her husband and Annie still had feelings for each other.

Deborah and Daniel met at a gym in Washington D.C. where she was giving spinning lessons to help her parents with college costs. From that point on, the course of her life changed dramatically. Despite her past experiences with men and her previous refusal to believe in lightning bolt love, for Deborah, it was truly love at first sight. Daniel was everything she ever wanted in a man. He was handsome, intelligent, caring, a true gentleman and had an old-fashioned way about him. She found herself with a diamond ring on her finger just six months after their initial meeting. Three months later, they were married. Two months after that, she was pregnant with her first child. Whenever she thought back on it, she felt their picture should be next to the expression 'whirlwind romance' in the encyclopedia.

Initially, Deborah didn't think her lifelong dream to create a center for abused children would have to be placed on hold. It became clear shortly after her pregnancy that her career plans would have to play second fiddle. Daniel wasn't present enough to assume a large role in the care of the child and he wasn't making enough money to hire a full time nanny. Even though it was without a doubt, more Daniel's idea to have children, Deborah harbored no resentment for the postponement of her professional aspirations. She was too happy and in love to let that happen.

Daniel confessed his former relationship with Annie shortly after he met Deborah. At first, Deborah feared that Daniel chose her on the rebound and voiced her concerns. He swore he was over Annie and would never consider marrying a woman unless he was head over heels in love. She believed him, though she didn't have much of a choice. She was already irrevocably in love with him and couldn't live without him.

As far as she was aware, for the first three years of their marriage Daniel had no contact with Annie. It wasn't until they moved to South Florida that her husband rekindled his friendship with his ex-girlfriend. At first, Deborah was extremely uncomfortable with their re-found connection, but didn't want to play the jealous wife. Though Daniel assured her he and Annie had no interest in anything except friendship, Deborah never really learned to become totally at ease with the situation. This past Sunday morning, Deborah voiced her honest fears and requested that he not see Annie unless she was also present. Once again, he offered to end the friendship if it would make Deborah feel better. She didn't want him to think she had no trust in him at all, so she settled for the compromise.

To keep in shape, Deborah continued to teach spinning classes at the Bally's gym around the block from her home. That morning, she had a class scheduled for nine o'clock. After she dropped the boys off at school, she headed straight for the gym. The class lasted one hour and by 10:10am, she was back at the condominium. She checked the mail before entering the house and found a notice from the post office indicating they attempted to deliver a package that was too large for her mailbox. It would be available for pick-up at her local post office after 2:00pm. She wondered if Daniel ordered something he neglected to tell her about since she wasn't expecting any packages. She would find out soon enough. After she picked up the boys from school, she planned to drop by the post office.

* * *

The remainder of the morning and early part of the afternoon passed quickly for Deborah. Reading novels of any genre were one of her favorite pastimes and never failed to make time fly. After returning from the gym and taking a shower, she sat down on the family room sofa setting out to finish the most recent Daniel Brown thriller. When she was through and looked up at the clock, school had already ended five minutes before. She grabbed her keys from the hook in the kitchen pantry and ran out the front door into a gorgeous South Florida winter afternoon. It was days like this that made her exceedingly happy to live in the state. It also had the effect of making her forget her problems. Her concerns about Annie couldn't be further from her mind.

She drove the two miles to the boys' elementary school, blasting the CD player while singing along at the top of her lungs to Kelly Clarkson's, "A Moment Like This." When she arrived at the school, there was a line of at least fifty cars waiting to pick up their children. Moving at a fairly quick pace, she reached the front in less than fifteen minutes. The boys, engaged in a heated discussion about a baseball card, jumped into the backseat. Deborah warned them they were going to the post office and had better behave while inside. By the time they arrived, the argument was forgotten. They were no trouble for their mom as she exchanged her notice for the large manila envelope the postman handed to her. She read the typed information on its face understanding that the package was intended exclusively for her. Intensely curious, she almost started to tear it open at the counter then realized she would hold up the line. She tucked the envelope under her arm, took the boys' hands and escorted them out to the SUV. Once the boys were safely belted in, she took her seat behind the wheel.

Before she opened it, she looked at both sides of the envelope to determine who sent it only to find there was no return address. The car was stifling hot, so she started it, turned the air-conditioner on full-blast and rolled down the windows. Then, with a pair of scissors from the glove box, she tore at the sealed portion of the envelope. Inside, she found a group of enlarged photographs. The moment she realized what the first one depicted, she had to stifle a scream. It felt as though a knife had pierced her heart. An overpowering feeling of nausea threatened to cast out the contents of her aching stomach. She quickly replaced the pictures into the envelope so the children didn't see them. For their sake, she tried her best to keep herself under control. The feelings she was experiencing were so intense, her body betrayed her and began to violently tremble.

The boys were getting restless complaining to their mom they wanted to go home. With an unsteady voice, Deborah told them she needed just a minute to read the mail and asked if they could sit quietly for a few minutes. She wasn't sure she could trust herself to drive in her condition. Both Dale and Timmy recognized the strain in their mom's voice and did as they were told.

Deborah took a few deep breaths as tears raced down her cheeks in rivulets. She grabbed a tissue from her purse to wipe her eyes and face, knowing she needed to get herself together in order to drive the kids home without killing or hurting them. She thought about calling her parents to ask them to come. But, their home in Pembroke Pines was at least twenty minutes away and there was no way the boys would sit still that long. She was going to have to find the courage to block the image of her husband's face in Annie's naked crotch from her mind for the short ride home. Using Dale and Timmy's welfare as her source of strength, she willed herself to stop shaking. Several minutes later, when her vision finally was no longer distorted by the tears, she put the car in gear and backed out of the parking space. She thanked God as she pulled into her condominium complex without incident ten minutes later. As soon as they entered the house, she sent the boys upstairs to do their homework. Still aware of their mom's state of mind, they complied without hesitation. After they left the room, Deborah sat down on the family room sofa and one at a time, painfully examined the explicit photographs of her husband having sex with Annie. With each flip of a picture, it felt as though the life was being sucked out of her and her heart was being torn from her chest. She wished she could pinch herself awake from this unimaginable nightmare. No doubt, she was going to be useless for the rest of the day. She picked up the phone to call her mom. She broke down attempting to explain the terrible package she received in the mail. Kate Tyler assured her daughter that she and her father would be there as quickly as the traffic allowed to take care of the children.

* * *

Daniel knew something was amiss when his secretary told him his father-in-law, Jack Tyler was on the phone. Jack rarely called him, period. Daniel couldn't imagine any reason why Deborah's dad would interrupt him at work other than an emergency. Daniel picked up his extension.

"Hi Jack. Is everything alright?"

"Let me say first no one is hurt or dead. But, things are far from alright. I think you should do your best to wrap things up at the office and come home."

"What's goin on, Jack?" Can't you give me a clue? It's not easy for me to drop everything and leave. It's only four o'clock."

"This isn't a subject either you or I would want to discuss over the phone. I suggest you find a way to get your ass home."

For Jack to speak in that manner was totally out of character. Daniel felt a huge lump developing in his throat. He said, "I'll be home right away, Jack. It should take me about fifteen minutes to wind things up and let everyone know I'm leaving for the day. I should be home in about an hour. I'll see you then."

Jack hung up the phone without saying another word. Daniel's stomach twisted into a wrenching ache that made him break out into a cold sweat. His analytical, detective's imagination immediately took over as he considered every potential explanation of what could have gone so wrong. One after the other, he eliminated each contingency until he arrived at the unthinkable. Major trouble involving the boys was unlikely. There was no reason why Jack couldn't at least give him a brief explanation over the phone. Jack was too angry with Daniel for that to be the issue. If there was a problem or health emergency affecting any other close family member, Jack wouldn't have responded with antagonism toward Daniel. He also explicitly said it wasn't an issue of illness, injury or death.

Daniel's heart began to pound so hard it felt as though it was going to burst through his rib cage. Beads of perspiration poured from his temples down the side of his face. Having suffered from a crushing sense of guilt over the past week, he couldn't help but wonder whether Deborah had discovered his infidelity. He couldn't imagine how she could possibly know, except there wasn't much else to consider. The only reasonable conclusion would be that Annie told her. That was even more implausible. He stood up from behind his desk, put his jacket on and rushed out of the office. He barked to his secretary he was leaving for the day as he raced past her desk. When he stepped outside of the federal building, he dialed Annie's cell phone number.

"Hello, Daniel. What's up?"

"Annie, you haven't spoken to Deborah recently, have you?"

"That's a weird question. I don't even get a hello or how are you?"

"I'm sorry, I'm outta my mind here. How have you been?"

"I'm fine. What are you talking about?"

"Have you spoken to Deborah?"

"You're scaring me, Daniel. I haven't had any contact with her since your birthday party. What's going on?"

"I didn't think you talked to her…Just a few minutes ago, I got a call from my father-in-law. He's at our condo right now." Daniel described his conversation with Jack in more detail. He continued, "The only thing I can think of is…Deborah found out about us."

"Daniel, I wouldn't ever think to tell Deborah about that. Not in a million years. I wouldn't mention it to anyone. I told you I meant it when I said I'd keep it a secret. I hope you didn't think I said something."

"I was almost positive you didn't, but I can't for the life of me figure out what else could make Jack so mad at me. Especially, to the point he asked me to leave work."

"Maybe it's your imagination. If neither you nor I told her, there's no way in hell she could know what happened Saturday night. It has to be something you're not thinking of."

"I guess I could be overreacting. I've been feeling extremely guilty."

"You and me both. We all make mistakes, Daniel. You're gonna have to forgive yourself for this one. For now, just get yourself home without crashing your car and call me later so I don't worry. I'm sure everything'll be alright."

"K, I'll let you know what happens. Sorry, I had to make this call."

"Don't worry about it. I'll survive. Just get this taken care of. I'll talk to you later."

Daniel's conversation with Annie didn't make him feel any better. His head was telling him she was right. His gut was leading him to believe the contrary. The only circumstances that would warrant taking him away from his job would be that something terrible happened to either Deborah, the kids, his brothers, her parents or his. He didn't believe it involved his parents or brothers. It didn't explain why Jack used that language or refused to discuss it over the phone. Excluding death, injury or illness, he was unable to think of any issue concerning his children that couldn't be discussed over the phone. He seriously doubted it had anything to do with Jack or Kate. That left Deborah.

Daniel flew north on Interstate 95. Normally, it took him twenty five minutes on a day of average traffic to get home. He walked through his front door just fifteen minutes after he left his office. Deborah and her parents were sitting in the family room. Deborah's eyes were bloodshot red. She had obviously been crying. When Daniel entered the room, Jack and Kate excused themselves saying they were going upstairs to help the children with their homework. Not only did they not greet Daniel, they didn't even look at him.

When Deborah and Daniel were alone, Daniel spoke first. "Deb, what the hell is going on?"

Though Deborah thought she had evacuated her reservoir of tears, a new stream scurried down her cheeks. For several seconds, she couldn't speak. Daniel couldn't hold back. "For God's sake Deborah, damnit, please tell me what's wrong. Why are you crying?"

Deborah picked up the manila envelope from the coffee table and handed it to Daniel without saying a word. He pulled the 13x8 glossy photographs depicting several stages of his passionate love making with Annie. He couldn't believe his eyes. It felt as though someone hit him in the gut with a sledgehammer. In the few seconds before he spoke, a thousand fleeting questions raced through his head. His first response was not the best choice as far as Deborah was concerned.

"Deborah, where did you get these pictures?"

"What does it matter where I got them from? How could you do this to me? How could you do this to your children?"

"It meant nothing. Both of us had way too much to drink. Annie was upset over Hannah's kidnapping and I was trying to comfort her. It all happened so quickly. When it was over, neither one of us could believe what happened. I love you, honey. It was a huge mistake and it'll never happen again. I'll never see Annie again."

"I couldn't give a shit how much you had to drink. How can I believe anything you're saying, Daniel? That's a really strange way for a married man to be comforting another woman. You swore to me you were over her. You lied to me. I can't ever trust you again. I want you out of the house. Please go upstairs, pack your bags and leave."

Daniel's initial reaction to the reality that he was losing his family hit him even harder than he ever expected. The guilt he felt over hurting Deborah was overwhelming. The thought of being without his boys was even more devastating. "Honey, please, let's talk about this. I love you. I can't live without you and the kids. This was just one big, humungous mistake. It'll never happen again. I swear. Please, let's think about this. You're very angry right now. Give yourself time to think things through clearly."

"I'm more than angry. I feel dead. I never, in a million years, thought you could be capable of such a thing. I don't know you anymore. Funny how you have to include the kids when you say you can't live without me. I don't need time to think. These photographs say it all. I can't even look at you. Please go."

"Oh come on, Deborah. You know you mean the world to me."

"I don't want to hear anymore. I'm done. Just get out.

"Can I ask how you got the pictures? Did you hire a private investigator?"

"I don't understand what that has to do with anything. But no, I didn't hire anyone. They arrived in today's mail. Now, I answered your question, so go upstairs and pack… Now."

"Sweetheart, please, we have to talk about this. I swear it meant nothing to me. Don't do this. We can work it out."

"You can't be serious. If you felt nothing for her, what would possess you to kiss her like that, to fuck her? You have to go, Daniel. I can't stay in this house with you. If I leave, I'm taking the children with me."

"Ok, Deborah, I'll go. But promise me we'll talk later."

"I'm not going to promise you anything. The least you can do is respect my wishes."

"Ok, alright, I'm going upstairs now. I'll do as you say, but I want to talk to the boys before I leave. Do you want me to explain what's going on?"

"Just do it and go."

The last time Daniel cried was the day Annie rejected his marriage proposal eight and a half years ago. As he climbed the stairs to tell his children he would not be living in the house with them for a while, he wept like a baby.

Chapter 13

"I don't believe it, Daniel. How is it possible? Who could have been taking pictures? Do you think she's telling the truth about not hiring an investigator?" asked Annie.

"I have no clue. I don't know which end is up right now. I don't think she was lying. I took a look at the envelope. It was delivered by mail. It had a stamp and postmark. Private investigators don't send that type of thing in the mail."

"I've been doing a lot of thinking about what happened the other night. I'm really sorry it's come to this. I am. I hope you don't take this the wrong way… It seems to me there's something missing in your marriage. I just don't get that you're happy."

"First of all, my relationship with Deborah is between her and me. You know me just as well as anyone. When I make a promise, I keep it. I have a great family. I love them. The boys are everything to me. It's where I want to be. I'm not gonna discuss my marriage with you."

"I know you love your family, Daniel. Maybe I should just keep my mouth shut. Your marriage wasn't the only thing I was thinking about. I've been doing a lot of psychoanalyzing myself. It's kinda been obsessing me. It's no secret I've been wanting you since you moved to Florida. I've been trying to get you alone in my apartment forever. Why now and not when you were mine?...I'm a mess. I think I'm only interested in men I can't have. If you ask me, it's a self-esteem issue."

"Really Annie, I have no interest in making this about you right now. I just got kicked out of my house."

"You're right. I'm an ass. A selfish one at that. Do you think she's gonna get over this?"

"She wouldn't even listen to me. Right now, she's obviously extremely upset. I'm hoping when she settles down, I'll be able to get through to her. What I'd like to concentrate on for the moment, if I can get my head together, is who the hell took those pictures."

"Over the past week, there have been some awfully strange things happening. I'm really starting to believe you may be right about someone having some type of fatal attraction for me. First Hannah, then Michael, now you. It can't be just coincidence. You would think though…the agents you assigned to keep an eye on me would have come up with something by now."

"Do you think Michael could somehow be involved in this?"

"No way. No question he's head over heels in love with me, but I don't see him coming up with such a devious plot. You don't suspect he had something to do with Hannah's murder, do you?"

"I'm not ruling out anything. It's something that's going to have to be explored."

"Well, there's no doubt in my mind he's not capable of murder, much less in the way Hannah was tortured. He wouldn't hurt a fly. He doesn't have a vicious bone in his body."

"Sometimes, people can surprise you. Obviously, he wasn't the man in the surveillance tapes. He could have hired someone to do his dirty work."

"I don't believe that for a minute. It doesn't make sense he would murder Hannah. What threat was she to him? And why would he have the ears sent to himself and open the package up in front of me?"

"You have a point. Still, the two incidents could be unrelated. Or, it could have been a ploy to distract us. Either way, I'm going to investigate further. You still seeing him?"

"No, I finally got up the nerve to end it for good last weekend. I still think you're barking up the wrong tree. You'll be wasting your time. Have you guys discovered anything from the post office where the package to Michael was mailed?"

"We're working on getting their surveillance tapes. The postmark was stamped at their office on Las Olas Boulevard. I'm pretty sure Robert Leland or one of his men is picking up the tapes tomorrow."

"Those tapes could be very important. I'll be curious to hear what you find."

"I'm going to check into a hotel close by the condo. I've had about as much as I can handle today. I know I'm probably not gonna sleep a wink tonight. Once I'm in the room, I've got a lot of thinkin' to do."

"Daniel, I know I've done some pretty shitty things… I'll support you in whatever you choose. You're a good man. I want to see everything work out for you. I guess we both made a big mistake. She'll eventually realize you're just human. You're not the first and sure as hell won't be the last. I'll do everything in my power to help you get things back in order. If there's anything I can do, please let me know."

"Thank you, Annie. I think this is something I'm gonna have to handle on my own. I don't expect anything to change any time soon. I fuck'n cheated on her with my ex. I'm just hoping eventually she'll find it in her heart to forgive me. I don't want to throw away nine years of what's been a solid marriage. I'm pulling into the hotel parking lot. I'll call you tomorrow with an update... Goodnight, Annie."

Daniel checked into the Hampton Inn on Federal Highway in Hallandale Beach, just three miles from his home. Once he settled into the room, he thought about returning to the office then quickly reconsidered realizing in his state of mind, he would be essentially useless. Instead, he decided to take a shower to help clear his mind. He was about to step into the bathroom when his cell phone began playing the ringtone for James Mancini. He didn't feel sharp enough to discuss business at the moment, so he let the call go to voicemail.

After a long, cold shower, he dressed in a pair of jeans and a navy blue FBI t-shirt, grabbed his briefcase and hopped onto the king size bed. He desperately craved a drink, but didn't dare. He needed a clear mind for at least his conversation with Mancini. The shower didn't do much for his stress level or morale, though it did have the effect of increasing his alertness. Inside his briefcase, he kept a file with notes he had gathered since the night he was notified of Hannah Richards' disappearance. He took a few minutes to review what he had written, picked up his cell phone and listened to Mancini's message then dialed his number.

"Hey, Daniel. I've been trying to reach you. I called your office, cell phone and home number. Where the hell are you?"

"It's a long story, Jim. I'll get to it in a minute. First, tell me what you've got for me."

"Alright then...We found the stolen pick-up truck. It was parked in the long-term parking lot at Albany International Airport. One of our agents was up in Albany, so I had him courier the airport surveillance tapes for Friday evening and Saturday morning to me. Three of us watched a total of a dozen tapes. We just finished. I'll summarize everyone's notes. Our guy took a US Airways flight back to Ft. Lauderdale on Saturday morning. I'm in the process of requesting a manifest of passengers for that flight. I doubt the bastard used his real name, but every little bit helps. You know we were able to determine he used the same name he used for the rental car, Dwight Adelman for his flight from Ft. Lauderdale to LaGuardia. Actually, it was Leland who came up with that information. He's been trying to get in touch with you, too. He spoke with an agent at American Airlines who told him the suspect used an Israeli passport for identification. Leland verified the passport was fake.

The prick is a true professional. He was caught by eight different cameras in the parking lot, garage and inside the terminal. We didn't get one good look at his face. I've done an NCIC and Interpol search to check for any wanted dangerous criminals fitting his description. I didn't come up with much. I also ran the particulars for the Hannah Richards murder through VICAP. Didn't get any clear cut matches. I'm really surprised this is the first time this guy's popped up on our radar screen."

Interpol and VICAP were tools regularly used by the FBI for the investigation and apprehension of criminals around the world. Interpol is an international policing agency that has member countries on every continent in the world. VICAP is part of the FBI's National Center for the Analysis of Violent Crime. The acronym stands for Violent Criminal Apprehension Program. Its computer software collects and analyzes information regarding victims, offenders, modus operandi, sexual activity, weapons, vehicles, forensic evidence, photographs and any other related case data. Details of the crime being investigated are input into the computer. It then provides criminal investigative analysis, potentially related cases and possible leads amongst a host of other valuable investigative tools.

"Have you gotten any results back from forensics, yet?" inquired Daniel. "Were you able to confirm the jewelry the victim was wearing belonged to Mrs. Richards?"

"We know the rope was soaked with a standard barbecue lighter fluid. Since the chemicals found in most of 'em are identical, forensics said it would be impossible to identify a brand name. We don't have any DNA or dental results yet. Mrs. Stein was able to positively identify one of the rings as a birthday present she gave her sister several years ago. It pretty much confirms what we already knew. What's going on down there? Where are you?"

"Right now, I'm staying at a Hampton Inn in Hallandale Beach, three miles from my place." Before calling Mancini back, Daniel reflected heavily on whether he should share his indiscretion with James and the other members of the investigative team. There was a significant chance that the taking of photographs of him and Annie were integrally intertwined with the Hannah Richard's disappearance. The murder, delivery of the ears and photographs seemed to revolve around Annie. To protect his reputation and personal life by holding back important facts from his colleagues who were attempting to solve this horrendous crime would be unacceptable. Especially, when he considered his family and Annie could be in danger. Ultimately, it was an easy decision to put the investigation first and suffer whatever consequences would follow. Daniel went on to explain what occurred on Saturday night, the photographs and his conversation with Deborah.

"Holy shit, Daniel. I'm sorry about that. I hope everything turns out alright."

"Thanks, Jim. I've made a mess of my personal life. I can't afford to lose focus at work. I only told you because I think it's most likely related to the Richards' case." Daniel described his common denominator theory involving Annie.

"This definitely thickens the plot," replied Mancini. "Do you have any idea who could have taken the pictures?"

"If my theory about a stalker is accurate, it would make sense he took the pictures. If that's the case, then he has information about me and my family. I've also wondered if Annie's boyfriend Michael Munez was involved. She's pretty emphatic he's not capable of murder or a devious plan to break up my marriage. She has a point. There's no motive there. He doesn't seem to be the stalker type who would wait outside her apartment spying through her windows, either. The person who took the pictures definitely used high-tech equipment. I asked Annie if Michael had an interest in photography. She said he doesn't even take a camera with him when they go on vacation.

Just thinking on my feet here, I'm leaning toward the stalker theory and I'm not likin' it. If the killer is the vengeful type and I suspect he's that and much more, it puts my family in danger. We've already entered the data into VICAP regarding all the details of the crime and the best photo of the suspect we could extract from the tapes. His description and photo are also being distributed to all policing agencies in the country. I would like to do the same with Interpol. I'd like to get a list from VICAP and Interpol of all unsolved gruesome crimes committed within the past two years. Do you think you could handle that or should I get Leland on it? I'm gonna talk to your SAC either tonight or tomorrow to get a team together for this case. Obviously, I'm going to highly recommend you be part of it."

"I don't mind doing it, Daniel. It'll just take a couple-a-phone calls."

"I really need to stay on top of this. I could never forgive myself if something ever happened to Deborah or the kids."

"Don't worry, man. I got your back. Let me get busy. I'd give Leland a call if I were you. Your office is kinda worried about you."

"Will do. Thanks for all your help. I'll be in touch."

"Any time, buddy. Take care. I hope everything works out between you and the Mrs."

* * *

Days passed, then weeks without Daniel hearing a word from Deborah. He left countless messages on the home and cell phones with no response. He wrote at least three emails a day to no avail. Deborah maintained her silence. In order for him to see the boys, he had to communicate through Jack and Kate Tyler. He begged both of them to persuade their daughter to talk to him. His pleas fell on deaf ears. He was at his wits end. How could he tell her he couldn't live without her and the boys if she rejected every attempt to communicate with her?

After a good deal of soul searching of his own, Daniel had to admit to himself his feelings for Annie were more than just a platonic love. That being the case, Deborah was the mother of his children and the woman with whom he wanted to spend the rest of his life. The first step in the process had to be the termination of his relationship with Annie. It was unfair to all parties concerned for it to continue. They both needed to get over each other once and for all.

The Hannah Richards investigation wasn't progressing any faster than his efforts with Deborah. The DNA and dental records comparison results came in confirming the corpse found in the woods outside of Tannersville was, in fact, Hannah Richards. Several of the hairs found at the scene were assumed to be the killer's. The same applied to the fingerprints found on the buttons of the white shirt. Michael Munez was for all intents and purposes, excluded as a suspect. Beyond that, the investigation had come to a complete standstill. The post office tapes were just more of the same practically useless footage seen at the airports. The DNA results of the suspect's hair sample was entered into the Combined DNA Index System known as CODIS. The program was developed as a national automated DNA information processing and telecommunications system to link biological evidence in criminal cases. DNA testing of forensic crime scene samples from around the country and sometimes around the world could be compared against a catalogue of known offenders. The DNA of the hair found at the Richards site didn't match any subjects already in the CODIS database.

Interviews of Hannah's family and friends weren't helpful in identifying the man in the surveillance tapes or any individual who had any reason to harm Hannah. Interpol was dragging their feet and had not yet provided any of the information requested. Daniel recently contacted several of the FBI's overseas agents to light a fire under the international policing agency. He was hoping for quick results. Nothing had come in yet. The stake-out to determine if anyone was stalking Annie hadn't yielded any results, either.

VICAP provided a list of recent gruesome murders committed in the United States and various agents were reviewing those cases to determine if there were any potential connections to the Richards murder. They hadn't come up with anything solid to date. The name Dwight Adelman also led to a dead end. There were several Israeli citizens with the name. They were all ruled out as possible suspects. None of them were in the United States at the time of the murder. Eventually, it was confirmed that Leland's conclusion about the false passport provided to American Airlines for the flight to New York was accurate.

Daniel felt like something had to give, though it wasn't going to happen all on its own. He was a firm believer a person created his or her own luck. It didn't make sense to him that they were unable to come up with any leads. It was improbable Hannah Richards was the suspect's first murder victim. It definitely didn't have the feel of an inexperienced killer. The murderer was too good at what he did. His method was almost impeccably professional. He also seemed to be challenging the authorities. The only thing keeping Daniel relatively optimistic was his confidence that this guy was going to make a mistake. When he did, Daniel planned to be there to nab the bastard.

* * *

The first real break in the Richards case would come the very next week. The FBI liaison at the American Embassy in Rome was able to match the CODIS DNA analysis to a killing that occurred in Europe more than a year earlier. The suspect's hair sample found at the Tannersville crime scene was found to have the exact DNA code as traces of blood found under the victim's fingernails in a brutal murder case that occurred in Frosinone, Italy. Immediately thereafter, Daniel assembled a team to travel to Italy to further confirm the two crimes were linked to the same killer. Jonathan Frazier, one of the Behavioral Sciences Unit's foremost profilers, was appointed to lead the team. Ordinarily profilers were employed to a specific crime or series of crimes to develop a behavioral composite of an unknown offender. In this particular instance, it was Special Agent Frazier's assignment to determine if sufficient commonalities existed between the crimes to be able to say with relative certainty that the cases were connected.

Accompanied by the lead investigator, Special Agent Robert Leland, and two men from the ERT, Frazier arrived at the American Embassy in Rome three days after the DNA match was discovered. With the help of the FBI liaison who spoke Italian fluently and Roman Carabinieri, they made an appointment for the following morning to meet with the local investigators in Frosinone. They hoped to review the investigative file and inspect the crime scene of the murder of Francesca Leone.

Francesca's mutilated, naked body was found in a wooded area just outside the property limits of a seminary for Roman Catholic priests. The cause of death was determined to be extensive blood loss due to a knife wound to the throat which severed both the carotid artery and jugular vein. There was some evidence of sexual penetration although no semen was found on the scene or anywhere in or on the corpse. It was assumed the suspect's blood under the victim's fingernails was a result of a defensive act against the rape. The victim's right middle finger was amputated and placed inside her vagina.

Frosinone was approximately ninety-three kilometers southeast of the center of Rome. On the day of the scheduled meeting, the FBI team hired drivers to chauffeur them on the one hour and ten minute ride to the office of the Carabinieri in Frosinone. When they arrived, the ERT members were escorted to the crime scene to take photographs and comb the area for any possible evidence missed by the original inspectors. Meanwhile, Frazier,

Leland and the FBI liaison stayed at the office to review the autopsy reports, lab analyses, crime scene photos, the method and manner of body disposal, witness statements and the victim's family history.

Using this information, Frazier developed a preliminary profile of the suspect. In his final report he estimated that the most likely perpetrator was in his late twenties to early thirties with a significant history of previous violent crimes. Frazier believed the murderer worked alone. The perpetrator's behavior at the scene demonstrated he was experienced, controlled and methodical. This probably wasn't his first kill. The mutilation spoke of his anger toward women and his need to humiliate the victim sexually. There was clearly a component of revenge and the expression of dominance in his method.

Special Agent Frazier ultimately concluded that the Leone and Richards murders were committed by the same killer. He based his decision on the obvious DNA match and the fact that he would assign similar character traits to both perpetrators. In his verbal report to Daniel, he pointed out many murderers who kill with a sexual theme often commit arson. Frazier was certain the suspect would continue to engage in post-mortem mutilation and that his behavior could even get worse. He strongly suggested they explore the possibility of other similar murders in Europe as he doubted Francesca was his only victim during that time frame.

* * *

It was a crystal clear March evening on Ft. Lauderdale beach. The moon over the Atlantic Ocean bounced off the horizon like an oversized, Swiss cheese colored beach ball. It cast a reflection off the water that made the crests of the waves sparkle like a child's Fourth of July fireworks. Shem Chassar stared at the display though his mood was something short of festive. He had been riding on a high over the past month and a half. As the exhilaration never lasted for more than a few weeks, a crash was overdue. The events of the past few hours had undoubtedly contributed to his decline.

More care and discipline were going to be absolutely necessary to the success of his new venture involving the FBI agent. Several weeks ago, he debunked the FBI's attempts to gain information through providing protection for Annie. He followed her home that day. As he was passing down Birch Street looking for a parking space across from the Maya Marca, he noticed an obvious unmarked police vehicle occupied by two men in dark suits. He couldn't believe the morons actually thought they were being inconspicuous. The only thing they managed to do was keep him from seeing his Annie for a few weeks. It made him extremely angry, but he knew they would eventually give up on their plan. When a stake-out wasn't rendering results, the government was too cheap to continue financing the project. Today was the first day he noticed their surveillance had been abandoned.

Earlier, he stood on this beach to spend a belated and much anticipated evening with his Annie. Gazing up toward her apartment through his top of the line binoculars, he wondered what she would think of his newly dyed black hair. He didn't have time to consider the possibilities. Annie was turning off all the lights in the apartment. Since it was only 7:45, this could only mean one thing. He gathered up his equipment and walked quickly back to his parked car. Sure enough, five minutes later, Annie's red BMW pulled out of the parking garage and turned north on Birch Street. Shem's vehicle was parked in a southerly direction, requiring him to make a hurried three point turn in order to maintain a tail on her.

He kept a safe distance behind as she made her way northbound on A1A. A mile and a half down the road, she turned left into an outdoor style shopping village and parked her car in a metered parking space. Shem scanned the area to locate a space where he could park without being noticed by Annie. He had to act swiftly. There were a number of stores, boutiques and more importantly restaurants in the area she could enter. She could be meeting someone for a meal. He didn't want to lose track of her. He found a space twenty yards up the road. Despite his rushed efforts, by the time he parked, grabbed his cowboy hat and hopped out of the vehicle, she was already out of sight. Until she disappeared, he had kept an eye on her through his rearview and side mirrors. He knew she headed back in the direction of A1A. It wasn't going to be easy trying to locate her before she potentially ducked into one of the several business establishments leading up to Sunrise Blvd.

He jogged to the beach road, then slowed his pace to blend in with the crowd. This time of year was considered the season in South Florida. Scores of college and high school students were spending their spring break on Ft. Lauderdale's famous beach. As a result, the sidewalk along A1A was packed with pedestrians. His height afforded him a view over the tops of most people's heads. Unfortunately for him, his advantage offered no benefit. Annie was nowhere in sight. He cursed under his breath at his bad luck. He couldn't afford for his search to be obvious. Nevertheless, if he wanted to locate her, he would be forced to enter each and every store along her anticipated path. Waiting for her to return was not an option. He had to know if she was meeting with anyone.

In spite of his misfortune, he remained calm, searching all shops along A1A to its intersection with Sunrise Boulevard. He doubted she crossed the street to the beach, so he turned left on Sunrise and checked the Splish Splash Bikini store on the corner. Still, no Annie. He continued west until he passed by the front window of the Starbucks Coffee Shop. What he saw inside stopped him in his tracks. Annie was seated at a table in a secluded corner involved in a deep conversation with the FBI agent. A familiar rage began to boil just beneath the surface. This time, he wasn't sure he'd be able to reel it in. He stepped away from the window and took a few deep breaths taming his anger at least enough to assess the situation. Knowledge of the topic of their conversation was much too critical. He wondered for a split second if his plan to separate them backfired. Refusing to believe it, his confidence in his intuition prevailed. He was sure the agent loved his wife or at least cared deeply for her. It didn't make sense he would continue to see Annie. With an ultra-peaked curiosity and the feeling that he was settled enough to refrain from doing anything rash, he weighed his options.

After a few minutes of careful deliberation, he decided there was no way either Annie or the agent would recognize him after the changes he made to his appearance. Besides dying his hair, he grew a full beard and moustache which he also dyed black. He placed the cowboy hat he was carrying on his head and entered the Starbucks, secure he could choose a seat close enough to eavesdrop.

His startled reaction to what he eventually overheard nearly blew his cover. Somehow, they had tied him to the killings in Europe. Evidently, an article had been written in the Miami Herald that evening linking Hannah's murder to the Italian whore he killed back when he was working for King Cruise Line. Shem had been outside Annie's apartment all day and had neglected to either listen to the news or purchase a paper. Falcone was furious that an agent on his team was leaking information.

After taking a few minutes to digest what he just learned, Shem's first thought was that he underestimated his arch nemesis in a major way. Then, as quickly as he gave credit to the agent, he took it all back. He refused to believe Falcone or anyone at the FBI was responsible for their breakthrough. Under normal circumstances, it wasn't his practice to admit to stupidity or sloppiness. This time, the proof he was guilty of both character flaws, if only temporarily, was very much stacked against him. According to the agent's description of the newspaper article, the authorities were able to tie the murder in Italy to that of the Tucker slut look-alike because of evidence he left at the scene. In Europe, he was practicing and perfecting his art, so he allowed himself the mistake of leaving DNA trace evidence behind. He had to concede however, he rushed into the murder of the Jew whore. There was absolutely no excuse for carelessness at her murder scene. It was obvious he didn't take the time to think things through sufficiently. Although he did it intentionally, he allowed the authorities to trace him back to Ft. Lauderdale. These were errors a reckless, overconfident novice would commit. In his mind, there was only one explanation. His overwhelming desire to make Annie his possession was blurring his ability to reason. He was acting like a school boy in lust. The more he thought about the issue, the clearer it became he had been exercising poor judgment since the day he decided to find an apartment in Ft. Lauderdale.

His lack of good decision-making was a problem, but he wasn't about to give up on Annie. His only other choice was to find a way to control his emotions and be patient. This was imperative if he was going to execute his masterpiece plan before he made her his own. That wasn't going to be easy when it seemed the agent insisted on carrying on with his relationship with her. An unsettled feeling continued to nag at Shem's sense of well-being. There was only one way he knew to recapture that high, though having arrived well into their conversation, he wasn't aware of a significant decision Daniel had made and already disclosed to Annie.

* * *

Daniel was waiting for Annie when she walked into the Starbucks dressed in a tight pair of Levi jeans and a hot pink tank top. He had to make a concerted effort to avoid looking her up and down. She was truly a stunning woman. He had been stewing about this meeting the entire day. It had been a significant and almost obsessive part of his thoughts since he had made up his mind. He certainly didn't need the drama of having two women in his life. A choice had to be made. The difficulty in finally arriving at a resolution was something he didn't expect. He made important decisions everyday sometimes involving life and death issues. This personal problem caused him more time, anguish, heartache and stress than any he had ever faced at the office. His future and happiness and that of the four people who meant the most to him in the world were on the line. When he finally made his decision, he knew he had made the right one. A peace and serenity immediately replaced the turmoil that had been relentlessly haunting him.

They each ordered a cup of black coffee then took a seat at a table in the back corner. Daniel would have preferred a little more privacy, but he wanted to meet in a public place, on neutral ground. After their initial greetings, Annie was the first to speak.

"I've been getting the feeling this isn't just a friendly get together. I haven't heard from you in a while. Every time I call for updates about Hannah, I'm rerouted to Leland."

"I'm not gonna beat around the bush, Annie. You know how much you mean to me. I'm sure you know you'll always have a special place in my heart. My number one concern right now is to save my marriage. So…our relationship has to end. I can't see you anymore."

Annie wasn't totally surprised by Daniel's revelation. Still, when he spoke the words, her heart sank into her stomach. She tried to not make it obvious through her expression. At that point, it didn't matter much since Daniel continued to ramble, looking down at his hands folded as if he was in prayer asking the Lord for forgiveness.

"I still have feelings for you. I'm not even sure what's going on. You have a way of confusing me. When you had me you didn't want me. Now that I'm not available, you have to have me. What I do know is if we keep hanging out, it's gonna happen again. I'll always love you. That's just the honest truth. You were my first true love. That being the case, I think it's obvious it's best for everyone if we stop seeing each other. It goes without saying it would be unfair to my wife to continue our relationship after what happened. It wouldn't be fair to you or me, either."

Annie listened quietly as Daniel said his piece. She took a moment to compose herself before she responded. She had done a lot of soul searching herself over the past few days. Several nights, she involved her mother discussing her romantic woes on the telephone until the wee hours of the morning. It wasn't unusual for Annie to use Cassie as her psychoanalyst. The idea that Annie had a habit of going after unavailable men wasn't a new concept. Ultimately, they both agreed it was a self-esteem issue. Annie simply felt undeserving. She could thank Uncle Byron in great part for that.

After all the discussion and self-examination, Annie was convinced she was still in love with Daniel regardless of the circumstances. At the same time, she knew there was no excuse for her behavior. There was no other way to describe herself. She had been a selfish bitch and that was going easy. She had her chance and she blew it. She would probably regret it for the rest of her life. If it was Daniel's choice to be with his family, she absolutely must learn to accept it. They had made enough of a mess of things.

The short period of silence made Daniel fidget in his seat. Annie recognized his uneasiness and decided to put him out of his misery. She said, "I can't say I wasn't expecting this. I do want to say one thing though. I do love you. I fucked up…in a lot of ways. I'm just sorry for acting the way I did. It was all about me…to hell with Deborah and your kids. I'm gettin' just what I deserve… a whole lot of nothin'."

"Annie, you gotta stop that shit. You're an amazing woman. You've got everything for Christ's sake. Beauty, intelligence, personality, a career, money. You deserve to love a man who's available to love and adore you right back. Maybe someday you'll finally get it through your thick skull."

"Yeah, I've heard a lot of that lately. I just want to make things right now. I wish there was something I could do."

"We'll see what happens. I can't even get her to respond to a fuck'n email, much less talk to me on the phone or in person. I'm not gonna give up."

"I have a question."

"Shoot."

"What about Hannah's case. Who do I talk to for updates?"

"We can only share so much with you, Annie. I'll talk to Leland and ask him to give you and update now and then. He'll probably give you about as much as you'll read in the papers. Speaking of the news, did you read Harris' article in the *Herald* this evening?"

They discussed the leak of information for several minutes. Daniel's anger was flagrant as he complained that one of his agents was evidently capable of compromising the case when Deborah, the boys and Annie could suffer the consequences. After a while, when there was nothing left to say, they drank the last of their coffee, wished each other well, and went their separate ways.

* * *

Henry Greenburg had lived on South Beach in Miami since long before it became the sunshine state's tourist Mecca and celebrity hang out. Being a man who always preferred a more culture forward and liberal city to settle in, it's resurgence in the late eighties and early nineties was a welcome change. He spent most of his earlier adult life residing on the east side of Greenwich Village in Manhattan, building his business as an interior designer. Once he made his name as one of the country's forerunners in the industry, he packed his bags and moved into his dream home one block from the world-famous Ocean Drive. He still dabbled in decorating homes, but for the last five years, he left the hard work to his younger prodigies managing his nationally renowned design business. He had every intention of taking full advantage of his golden years for living a life of leisure and doing what made him happy.

One of Henry's biggest weaknesses was young, muscular, gorgeous men and South Beach was teeming with them. During the early years of the beach's revitalization project, he was still young enough to attract men without having to spend too much money. His entourage of beautiful people of the male persuasion was consistently abundant. However, now that he was rapidly approaching his eighties, paying to spend time with a young, good looking man had become a weekly event. His favorite stomping grounds had become a private men's club well known for employing upscale male prostitutes. With the payment of a modest fee for a locker or small room, access to an anything goes gay man's wonderland was granted. The charge for a hustler was much steeper.

Henry was feeling especially lonely that night. The boys to and with whom he rented his guesthouse and shared meals had been away on vacation for the past week and a half. He had just been to the club three days before, but decided at the spur of the moment it would be the perfect remedy for his doldrums. Maybe, he could even convince one of the hustlers to come home with him and spend the night. Though it would cost him some extra cash, a young, muscle bound stud to cuddle against all night was unquestionably the right medicine.

He was pleasantly surprised when five minutes after he arrived at the club, a beautiful dark-haired man approached him with a very reasonable offer. He wasn't one of the regulars and his price was well below the typical fee charged by the gigolos sponsored by the club. It wasn't condoned by the management for free-lance male prostitutes to use the premises to find work. Henry wasn't about to say anything when he was going to save at least five hundred dollars. After the deal was struck, Henry invited the man back to his place. Since his hire claimed to have had a little bit too much to drink, Henry offered to drive. They left the club together under the watchful and suspicious eye of the manager, hopped into Henry's Mercedes and started on their way to his South Beach mansion.

* * *

The only thing that could rival Shem Chassar's hatred, abhorrence and ire for a female hooker was an elderly john in search of a male prostitute. They were more vile and putrid than the lowest form of scum living and breathing on planet Earth. Shem made it his business to know the establishments in Miami where he could find any number of old geezers trying to get their rocks off with a boy a quarter their age. He considered it his own personal form of charity to rid the world of as many of the slop suckers as possible. It was an easy decision to head directly to a private men's club he had read about on the Internet after overhearing the conversation between Annie and the FBI agent at Starbucks. The sense of accomplishment and exhilaration he would receive from preventing one less filthy, perverted, old fuck from ever being able to prey on a young boy would surely have the effect of erasing that irritating memory.

Scrutinizing his field of choices, he targeted Henry Greenburg as soon as he walked through the door onto the private club's pool deck. Shem knew instantly that Greenburg was a sleazy, ancient troll in search of young company. It was a cinch getting the old man to agree to his terms. He didn't like the idea of going to Greenberg's home, but then he had absolutely no intention of doing so. The plan was to get the degenerate to stop in some deserted parking lot before they ever arrived at his house. There was no way the old man could resist Shem's offer to give him a blow job on the way. As they passed a Publix grocery store off of Alton Road, Shem seized his opportunity. Henry gladly agreed to the proposition and parked his Mercedes in the alley behind the grocery store next to an oversized dumpster.

The instant Henry placed the car in park, Shem reached for his ether soaked rag hidden in a plastic bag in his jacket pocket. He shoved it violently over Henry's nose and mouth, applying as much pressure as he could to cause a maximum amount of discomfort without cutting off his ability to breathe in the fumes. Henry tried in vain to push Shem's vice-like grip off his face. After recognizing the futility of his efforts, Henry attempted to blast the horn. Shem was a step ahead of him. He grabbed both of his victim's wrists with his free hand and squeezed with such force, he could feel something snap. In fact, he broke the radius bone clean in half. Within seconds, Greenburg lost consciousness.

Behind the wheel of Henry's Mercedes, Shem's destination was a park located in the southernmost part of Dade County. Several weeks prior, he had studied an online map of the grounds of Coral Reef Park then visited the site to get a better idea as to whether it contained areas secluded enough for his special version of private work. On the property, just behind Coral Reef Elementary School, there was a jogging path that ran through a pineland preserve. It was the ideal spot to dispose of a body. The remainder of the premises was wide open space. The people who frequented that section of the park shouldn't have reason to enter the wooded area and joggers rarely strayed off the path into the preserve. Even if they did, he doubted they would find anything after he buried the body in the manner he had planned.

On the way to South Miami, Shem stopped to retrieve his bag of provisions at the garage near the private men's club where he parked his Ford Expedition. He had injected Greenburg with what he had left of the liquid tranquilizer he used on his former colleague, Ken O'Brien at the time of the Anderson murder. He knew Greenburg would be out for at least the ride to the park which would take about 25 minutes. The anticipation of what was soon to come was beginning to fill him with a healthy dose of excitement and euphoria. The rage he experienced earlier in the evening as a result of Annie's meeting with the agent was already just a low priority, buzzing, gnat-like irritation in the background of his consciousness.

It was after park hours and Shem didn't want to risk having the Mercedes noticed by one of the police officers who regularly patrolled the grounds at night. The parking lot of the elementary school was not an option either. It was against the law to trespass on school grounds after hours. That wasn't a risk worth taking. On his previous scouting trip, he found a poorly lit, hammock area leading into the park's preserve on a dead end residential street beyond the elementary school. The closest homes were approximately fifty yards away. Shem spent several hours that evening observing the neighborhood and saw that both pedestrian and vehicle traffic was sparse. His car remained parked at the edge of the hammock the entire time and was never noticed or reported by the neighbors. There was no routine police patrol on that street to worry about either.

Shem felt confident his operation would go unnoticed and without a hitch as he turned right onto the dead end street continuing the half mile to the edge of the hammock. With his window intentionally rolled down, he listened for the sounds of human activity. The neighborhood was deserted and exceptionally quiet. Even the crickets and tree frogs seemed to have taken the night off, their chirping and croaking eerily absent. The old man was still unconscious, laying in the backseat with his head up against the passenger side door. To be sure Henry didn't scream or make any loud noises, Shem had tied a gag tightly around his mouth and head.

Shem maneuvered the car off the road so that the passenger's side was parked along the hammock. After exiting the vehicle, he removed his bag of provisions from the trunk. Other than the slight noise he made raising the lid, one could hear a pin drop. With the bag in hand, he made his way into the trees to relocate the site he had chosen on his first visit to the preserve. He placed the bag against one of the larger pine trees in the area then returned to the Mercedes. The old man hadn't moved an inch. Shem opened the back door, placed his hands underneath Henry's arm pits and pulled him gently onto the ground beside the car. He wanted to be sure Henry didn't wake up just yet so that his transport to the site would be less complicated.

Twigs snapped under Shem's feet as he carried the dead weight of the unconscious old man through the tight spaces between the pine trees to his selected work site. He laid Henry down on a natural bed of pine leaves in a small clearing approximately the size of a broom closet. It had been more than forty five minutes since Shem gave Henry the tranquilizer injection. He should be waking up any minute. To expedite the process, Shem lifted him to a seated a position, placed his hands on the old man's frail shoulders and shook his upper body violently. Henry's neck snapped back and forth like a child's bobble head toy until he was finally startled into consciousness. It took him just a few seconds to become aware of the excruciating pain brought on by the broken bone and that he was gagged and bound at the wrists and ankles. The tight nylon string at the injured wrist felt as though it was cutting through flesh. When he saw Shem with a butcher's knife in his hand standing over him, he feebly attempted a scream. The most he could muster was a muffled squeal that couldn't have carried for more than a few yards.

Henry had read about the various serial murderers of gay men such as John Wayne Gacy and Jeffrey Dahmer. He was actually somewhat obsessed with their stories having, himself, engaged in the risky behavior of hiring prostitutes for many years. He watched multiple documentaries and movies made about these killers and feared one day he would become a victim. Now, his worst nightmares were about to come true. He desperately tried to focus through the fear and pain to think of a way to save himself. Getting to his feet was impossible. The only way he could move was to roll along the ground. With the trees and a healthy young man pursuing him, he wouldn't get very far. His sole option was to attempt to convince the man not to hurt him. As he looked into the vacant, charcoal-black eyes of his aggressor to address him, his bladder was instinctively stimulated causing him to wet his pants.

Fleeting thoughts and jumbled words raced through Henry's mind, but he was unable to come up with a coherent sentence. When he eventually tried to speak, the gag and his trembling voice made his statement incomprehensible. Consumed by a feeling of hopelessness and terror, he felt a crushing pressure and burning sensation in the center of his chest that travelled up into his jaw and down his left shoulder and arm. An instant later, his eyes glazed over as he clutched at his chest. At that moment, an infuriated Shem sprung into action. If the old man dropped dead of a heart attack, it would rob him of the pleasure and tranquility he was so passionately seeking. He grabbed Henry by the hair and pulled him up into a seated position. With one violent thrust, he shoved the knife into his throat then slashed through it dissecting both major blood vessels of the neck. Instead of receiving a constant flow of blood against his abdomen, it spewed in fits and spurts. After less the ten seconds, the surge stopped completely. The blood dripped slowly from the wound leading Shem to come to only one possible conclusion. The old man's heart was no longer beating.

Being deprived of the ecstasy of the orgasm derived from his victim's terror-stricken eyes and the texture of the warm blood against his naked skin was infuriating. It was his intention to dissect the body into small pieces when the deed was done, place them in small plastic bags and bury them in shallow holes around the preserve. Normally, he would have performed the task meticulously with precision, as he did with the drag queen he murdered in Miami. This time, he reached into his bag, grabbed the large machete he had packed for the job and started to maniacally hack at the body with no rhyme or reason. He fiercely chopped, slashed and sliced until his shoulder, back and arm muscles ached to the point it was physically impossible to continue. When he finally took the time to look down at the body to see the results, the flesh was butchered beyond recognition. The head was detached, but not before it was chopped into numerous pieces. Other body parts were strewn along the forest floor, some landing more than ten yards from what was left of the rest of the corpse. Standing above the completely annihilated body of the degenerate, Shem realized he was sexually aroused. He unzipped his pants, pulled out his hard penis, and masturbated to orgasm. As his frame of mind slowly returned to a relative state of calm, he started the long and tedious cleanup process.

Chapter 14

Special Agent in Charge Daniel Falcone immediately began to assemble a task force after receiving confirmation from Special Agent Frazier that the murder in Europe was perpetrated by the same suspect in the Hannah Richards case. He wanted his best and most experienced investigator to lead the team, so he appointed Robert Leland with James Mancini as his co-investigator in New York. Agent Christopher Frye would work side by side with Leland in the North Miami office. To ensure consistency, the ERT squad that inspected the Richards crime scene was made part of the task force. Members of other law enforcement agencies would be included in the future, if new murders were discovered in their jurisdiction. Daniel appointed himself as liaison with the media and would be available in an advisory capacity. He had every intention of paying very close attention to this case. He would also take on the responsibility of finding the leak. The guilty party's career with the FBI would be coming to an abrupt end if Daniel had anything to say about it.

With the help of the Italian authorities, three other unsolved murders in Europe were identified that could potentially be linked to the Leone case. The killings occurred in Aix-en-Provence, France, Innsbruck, Austria and Karpenisi, Greece. Once again, Frazier and the ERT packed their bags and headed across the Atlantic to review each of the files and inspect the crime scenes in the three European cities. James Mancini held down the fort in the U.S. in the event any local responsibilities arose.

It took nearly a month to meet with the local European authorities, review all reports, inspect crime scenes and interview any potential witnesses. In the final week, a fourth murder was discovered in Karabuk, Turkey. This extended their stay for another two weeks. The Turkish authorities were unwilling to cooperate initially. Daniel was forced to call in a few favors with his contacts in Washington to eventually convince the Turkish government to allow his team to review the file and visit the crime scene.

In the end, it was determined that the same murderer committed each of the crimes. Four of the victims were female prostitutes. The cause of death for each of the women was blood loss due to dissection of the carotid artery and jugular vein. They were then decapitated post-mortem. Analysis of the chips in the bone of the cervical spine revealed the detachment of the head was executed with the use of a hammer and chisel in each instance. In Aix-en-Provence, a teenage mother and her baby were the victims. The killer performed a crude mastectomy of both breasts. He placed the nipple of one of them in the mouth of the baby's severed head. Indisputable confirmation came when DNA testing was done on hair samples found at the Turkish crime scene which matched those found at the Richards and Leone sites.

Although Daniel was pleased the investigation was finally progressing, he was frustrated there were no leads regarding the suspect's current location or true identity. A tail was placed on Deborah and the boys, Annie and Michael Munez without any results. As far as anyone knew, the suspect was no longer in the Ft. Lauderdale area. Reports of missing persons in the South Florida area and around the country were consistently coming across his and Leland's desk. It didn't make sense to Daniel that, so far, there were no other victims found in the United States who could be connected to the killer. He feared it was only a matter of time.

The suspect had already broken some of the rules of the behavioral characteristics studies of previous serial killers. Experts warned that each serial killer was unique, however, they normally hunted and murdered in a comfort zone from which they didn't usually stray. There have been serial murderers who traveled great distances to kill, but the examples were few and far between. Another rule that didn't seem to apply to this suspect was that many serial killers follow a specific time pattern between killings. More often than not, patterns such as killing in a lunar cycle were exposed. Daniel knew it was a misconception to believe they couldn't stop killing. Frequently, they killed based on availability and opportunity. He had to resign himself to the fact that this guy wasn't going to make things easy on them. This maniac was operating with his own set of rules.

* * *

Officer Tanya Concord was one of fifty officers assigned to bicycle patrol for the Miami Dade Metro Police Department. It wasn't exactly her idea of the police work she had signed up for when she decided to go to the Miami Police Academy. Detecting was her dream. Finding clues, analyzing their significance and solving major crimes was her calling. One day, she hoped to be a homicide detective. Until then, she would have to pay her dues.

Riding on a bicycle eight hours a day around the residential streets of Miami had been her payment for the last year and a half. This morning she was checking out a complaint that had been lodged practically on a daily basis for the past two weeks by an inordinate number of patrons of Matheson Hammock Park. A rancid stench was reported to be coming from the forest of mangroves bordering the nature trail on the south side of the park.

Matheson Hammock Park wasn't ordinarily within her jurisdiction. The Captain of the bike squad must have had it in for her. She had evidently rejected his requests for a dinner date one too many times. Now, she was on stink patrol. Mostly out of spite, she barely pumped at the pedals of her black and red Schwinn ten- speed set at its lowest gear. She was in no hurry to get to the offending site, moseying at a leisurely pace into the park at its main entrance off of Old Cutler Road. It was 7:30am and already the trails were crowded with joggers getting in their morning exercise. Once she hit the path leading to the south side of the park, she increased her speed to avoid the risk of being run down by the serious joggers trying to work up a decent lather. As she got closer to her destination, the joggers were accelerating their pace, perhaps doubling it. Matching their speed to keep up, it only took minutes to discover the reason for their sense of urgency. The stink hit her like an invisible physical force field. She instinctively applied the handbrakes squeezing them with a vice-grip that almost sent her flying headfirst over the handle bars. Once she recaptured her balance, her first move was to pinch her nose as tight as possible. Then, she quite audibly cursed the captain as two joggers happened to be passing at sprinting speed. Tanya had never smelled anything as repulsive and offensive as the odor assaulting her nostrils at that moment. The several skunks she had come across during her childhood in North Florida smelled like a luxurious perfume compared to this. She was wishing she had brought a gas mask with her and was seriously considering heading back to the station to grab one.

Taking a moment to contemplate what could cause such a foul stench, she quickly changed her mind. Officer Concord had never smelled the odor of decaying flesh, but had read and heard it described hundreds of times. Though it could easily be a dead animal, she had the distinct feeling it was something more. Off to the side of the path, on a soft patch of weeds and dead mangrove leaves, she set the kickstand on her bike and secured the padlock around the wheel spokes. Without any clear search plan, she headed into the mangroves in a southwesterly direction covering her nose with a thick cloth she had taken from the first aid kit attached to her bicycle seat. Approximately twenty five yards into the thicket, she noticed a depression in an area of exposed dirt a few feet further ahead. As she got closer, it appeared to be a hole dug by an animal. Along the sides, she could see evenly-spaced thin lines as if made by claws. When she was near enough to look into the hole, two empty eye sockets of a half-eaten human skull stared back at her.

* * *

Less than ninety minutes later, the FBI's Evidence Response team assigned to the Hannah Richards serial murder case was scouring the grounds of Matheson Hammock Park at the site where Officer Concord made her macabre discovery. Most of the heavy work had already been done. They were meticulously searching for any trace evidence left behind by the killer. The head wasn't the only body part located by Officer Concord. In an area covering approximately twenty square yards, she found a partially dug up, half-eaten thigh, left arm and upper shoulder, right ankle and foot. After examining the head to be sure it was in fact human, she immediately called it in to dispatch who in turn notified Captain Kyle Fromberg of the homicide division. During his years as Assistant Special Agent in Charge, Daniel had developed a good working relationship with the captain collaborating on several anti-gang and drug task forces. When Daniel recognized they may have a serial murderer running loose in South Florida, Captain Fromberg was one of the first law enforcement officers outside the FBI he contacted. Other than the obvious reason for notifying the captain, Daniel was enlisting his help. He requested that the captain report any murders occurring in the Miami Dade Metro Police Department's jurisdiction to Special Agent Robert Leland, especially those involving decapitation and/or detached body parts. Captain Fromberg didn't hesitate to call Leland as soon as he received Concord's briefing from dispatch.

So far, Leland, Frye and the ERT had conducted a search for the remaining body parts with the help of three German Shepherds specially-trained for the task. Some serious digging was necessary. The torso was found buried at least four feet below the surface of the mangrove floor. In the end, most body parts were found however decayed or semi-eaten. The victim's penis was never located. Later, the medical examiner would find traces of it inside the severed head's mouth. It was assumed the remainder was consumed by a family of foxes. The claw marks found at the sites where body parts were dug up and eaten by animals were determined to be those of four separate Florida red foxes. It was assumed to be a mother and her three kits known by several of the park's rangers. Female clothes and a wig were interred with the torso though the M.E. on the scene came to the conclusion the victim was a man based on his bone structure. Two separate types of human hair were attached to the tube dress recovered and bagged for later DNA analysis. Leland examined the cut pattern of the spine at the level of the decapitation. Confirmation with the experts would be necessary though he was fairly convinced it was done with a hammer and chisel similar to the murders in Europe.

While the ERT was busy wrapping things up, Leland reached in his pocket for his cell phone. Daniel would be anxiously waiting for his report, even had the nerve to order him to call as soon as his inspection of the scene was complete. It was rarely a pleasant experience for Leland to deal with Falcone in his capacity as a boss. The kid was fifteen years his junior. Leland consciously adjusted his demeanor so that his frustration wouldn't be obvious then dialed Daniel's extension at the office. After discussing the items of evidence found at the scene, Leland offered his opinion.

"It looks like the victim might-a-been some kinda fuck'n freak. If the clothes found at the site were his, he was at least a transvestite. Poor fucker got his cock chopped off. Because of the advanced level of decay, the M.E. couldn't say whether or not it happened before or after death."

"You guys have any idea who the victim may be?"

"No, I got Frye checkin' on missing persons. I wouldn't be surprised if he…she…he-she, whatever the fuck it is, was a hustler. It's got that kinda feel. The dress was a flashy red, tight number. Bunch-a-rings on the fingers and other gaudy jewelry found here and there with the other body parts."

"Any useful fingerprints?"

"Nah…anything exposed to the elements woulda been washed clean by now. The buried stuff was useless...anything on 'em was long gone."

"What do you think? Any chance it's our guy?"

"I'd say there's a great chance. Definitely his M.O…. especially if it was a prostitute though this is his first he-she. I guess it's possible he might not have known what he was dealing with. Thing that got me was the decapitation. It looks like the same pattern as the others. I had the M.E. look at it. He can't be positive until he compares the cuts, but he agreed it could've been a hammer and chisel. Hold on. Frye's running up here with something."

Special Agent Frye handed Leland three pieces of a scuffed up and torn business card covered with dirt and other unidentifiable stains. He gave Leland a quick explanation that it was found by one of the ERT members amongst a pile of mangrove leaves a good thirty yards from the general area where most of the evidence was dug up. Despite its poor condition, the pieces, when put together made the victim's profession and perhaps identification quite clear. Leland dismissed Frye with a nod of his head then addressed Daniel.

"It looks like we might have a great lead to identify the victim. One of the evidence guys found a business card. It's got to be the he-she's. It's torn, lots-a-crud, but easy enough to read…Glamorosa Champagne, professional escort…Enjoy a taste of my bubbly."

* * *

With Glamorosa's address on the card, identification was just a matter of looking him up on the FBI's computer database. Christopher Frye was assigned to conduct the investigation of the victim's history and flamboyant personal life. Glamorosa's real name was Charles Ingram. Though he still had all his male parts, Ingram lived his everyday life as a woman. According to friends, he had every intention of changing his sex as soon as he was able to save the money for the operation. To earn the cash for his ultimate goal, Glamorosa did some freelance entertainment work at several of the gay night clubs on South Beach dancing and performing lip sync versions of pop and disco music. Her main source of income was prostitution. Both Frye's and Daniel's assumption was that it was the latter profession which lead to her demise.

Preliminary DNA results had come back indicating the testers could not exclude the killer's DNA profile as a potential match to some of the hairs found at the scene. It would take at least a month before the findings were conclusive. Daniel was fairly certain they were dealing with Hannah Richards' murderer. The autopsy results confirmed that a hammer and chisel were used to decapitate the victim. The cut patterns were compared to the photos of those in the European cases and were determined to be identical. Special Agent Frazier's opinion after his visit to the crime scene and analysis of the evidence provided further confirmation that the transvestite's murder could be added to the growing list attributable to the serial killer.

Daniel was hopeful the additional information collected would help develop a clearer picture of the subject. The obvious goal was to catch him. The disappointing truth was they were no closer to identifying him and he didn't seem to have any intentions of changing his occupation. As they discovered more murders, the pressure to resolve the case would increase exponentially. Clifton Harris of the Herald was already criticizing the FBI's lack of progress and specifically attacking Daniel as Special Agent in Charge. That was no surprise. It seemed to be Harris' favorite pastime. Daniel didn't expect it would be long before the killer provided more fodder to fuel the reporter's personal vendetta. He was right. Just seventeen days after Officer Concord's discovery, Leland received another call from Captain Fromberg.

* * *

Henry Greenburg could have gone missing for months if it hadn't been for his tenants who rented his guesthouse on his property in South Beach. His only living relatives were a brother and sister he barely spoke to or saw and their children and grandchildren some whom he had never met. His last contact with any family member was a call from his sister's son asking for a handout more than six months before the night of his disappearance. The boys living in the guesthouse got concerned two weeks after they returned from their vacation in the Caribbean. It wasn't unusual for Henry to travel and be gone for weeks without notifying them. What they found to be extremely bizarre was his failure to call them on the rent due date with instructions about what to do with the check in his absence. Henry was extremely diligent about money issues.

When the boys hadn't heard from him for five days after the rent due date, they decided to contact the authorities to report him missing. The officer who responded was initially resistant to open an official investigation. It took an effort on the part of the tenant to get the detective to at least check with family members and other friends. They explained their landlord had a habit of engaging in risky behavior. The argument was enough to convince the detective to call Henry's brother and sister and write out an official report.

Three days later, a pre-teen boy and his dad were building a fort in the woods at the end of their cul-de-sac bordering Coral Reef Park in southern Dade County. The father, while in the process of digging a hole in the ground to insert a two by four, scooped a full shovel of earth and threw it over his shoulder. More than just dirt landed in a heap at his son's foot. At the top of the pile, a section of scalp with dense white hair glistened in the beam of sunlight breaking through the tree's canopy. The fort building project came to an abrupt end. The dad called the emergency line of Miami Metro Dade Police Department who then notified Captain Kyle Fromberg. Within an hour of the discovery, Special Agent Robert Leland, the FBI's Evidence Response Team assigned to the serial murder case and profiler, Jonathan Frazier were combing the site for the remainder of the body and any other items that could be useful in identifying the victim and/or solving the crime.

Not much was found in the way of other body parts. Several rotting chunks of flesh were dug up within a forty foot perimeter of the scalp's location along with broken pieces of bone. They were bagged for later analysis by the Medical Examiner. According to the M.E. at the scene, the victim was most likely an elderly gentleman. He based his opinion on his inspection of the scalp and a chunk of bone he determined was part of a femur. At that point, the task force wasn't sure whether there was more than one victim though the amount of flesh and bone recovered would not normally lead one to that conclusion. To be absolutely certain, DNA testing would be necessary.

Scraps and shreds of clothing were found dispersed in the general area. It was assumed most of it belonged to the victim. Further analysis in the lab would be required to ascertain whether any of the other various items collected could be connected to the killer. No obvious hairs or other trace evidence were uncovered that could potentially be linked to him.

Though the detective who took Henry Greenburg's Missing Persons report had done nothing yet to investigate his disappearance, the filing of the report ultimately helped the task force identify the victim. It was actually through Daniel's persistence they were able to narrow down the list of missing persons and tie this murder in with the serial killer. Laboratory analysis set the age of the corpse between seventy-nine and eighty-five. That decreased the number of potential victims to just five on the Missing Persons list. Daniel attended a meeting of the task force after some of the lab results came back. Usurping Leland's position as lead investigator, Daniel directed the gathering.

"Ok guys, I want to move fast on this," Daniel said. "We've got five names. I want five teams of two sent out to look into each man's background. I want to know everything. His family, friends, habits, likes, dislikes, was he married, does he have a girlfriend...a mistress. You guys know the drill. Most important, I want to know everything they did for the weeks and especially the day before they disappeared. Anyone who came into contact with them during that time frame, I want them interviewed and investigated. So that you know, Frazier thinks we could be dealing with the same killer. I want to know as much as we can by the end of the week. I want this murder officially on the list or ruled out."

"What about the media?" barked Leland. The question was asked more to relieve his anger than for any significant purpose. Leland knew it would piss Daniel off and remind him that despite the intense investigation into the leak he was conducting, he had come up with zilch. The Special Agent in Charge had grilled every member of the task force himself. No one was admitting to anything. Not surprisingly, the Herald refused to reveal their reporter's source citing the first amendment of the United States Constitution.

"What about the fuck'n media? We discussed this. The answer to any of their questions is no comment. I don't want anyone talking to them Leland or I'll have their ass. I promise you that. I'm the only person authorized to talk to the media about the serial murder case. Understood?" Everyone in the room nodded their head in the affirmative including Leland. He had gotten what he wanted.

The fruits of the investigation were reaped just a week and a half later thanks to Special Agent Christopher Frye and his teammate. Upon interviewing Henry Greenburg's tenants, they learned that Greenburg was a regular patron of male prostitutes and often visited an upscale, private men's club not far from his mansion. Frye questioned the owner of the club who confirmed he had seen Greenburg several weeks earlier leaving with a young man with black hair never seen before that night. The owner hadn't seen Greenburg since. After getting a detailed description of the unknown man, Frye decided it would be best to get an FBI artist to sketch the subject and requested both a normal frontal view and profile. When together, he and Daniel compared the sketch to others derived from the airport surveillance videos; the resemblance couldn't be denied. The Greenburg murder was officially added to the list of serial murders.

* * *

The bright South Florida summer sun slipped behind a mountain-high cumulus cloud, offering Deborah a momentary respite from the oppressive heat. In a race against the reappearance of the sun, she walked quickly to her mailbox to retrieve that day's mail. It had been more than a month and a half since she and Daniel separated. Several weeks prior, she spoke to him on the telephone for the first time since he left the house. Until then, she had ignored all of his ceaseless calls and scores of emails.

For the first few weeks after Deborah received the infamous photographs, it was a monumental struggle just to be able to perform her daily activities. In spite of Daniel's history with Annie and Deborah's mistrust of his relationship with his ex-girlfriend, Deborah wanted to believe with every fiber of her being she could trust her husband. The reality that he was capable of infidelity was crushing. It caused her to retreat into a self-protection mode. She knew if she spoke to him, she would completely break down. With two young, innocent boys to look after, she wasn't about to let that happen. Her reflexive response was to feel as though she never wanted to see Daniel again. It wasn't until an issue from her past resurfaced that she began to wonder whether she was being unreasonable to cut off all communication with him. It was a subject that was normally taboo in the Tyler family and as far as Deborah was concerned until recently, for good reason. For years, she had been working on this problem with her therapist and though she was getting closer to a resolution, she never quite got there. Based on recent events, closure for Deborah for this long-term issue was going to be next to impossible.

Deborah first heard she really wasn't an only child when she came home to visit after her first semester at Georgetown. Her parents had kept it a secret because of her bad reaction to her father's infidelity. Kate knew how difficult it was to accept and forgive the fact that her husband's mistress was pregnant with his baby and refusing to have an abortion. She was certain her daughter would flip when she heard the news she had a two year-old sister. Kate feared it would damage Deborah's relationship with her father forever. She was right on both counts. After an initial tirade, Deborah rejected her father's pleas to forgive him and wouldn't speak to him during the entire break. She barely directed a word toward her mother. By the end of the vacation, she announced to Kate she didn't think she would be returning to college. It took a concerted effort by both Kate and the therapist to convince Deborah she was making a huge mistake. She did go back to school, but, was never able to totally forgive Jack.

The only way that Deborah would even consider trying to work on her feelings with her dad was if the child was never mentioned. Kate had no problem with the condition imposed by Deborah. The easier it was for Kate to forget the incident, the better.

For a good while, Deborah refused to deal with the issue at all during her quarterly visits with her therapist. Over the past three years or so, it had become a focus of her therapy. What Deborah didn't know until just recently was that her sister was born with Down's syndrome. Her previous rejection of any conversation about the scandal prevented her from learning anything about the illegitimate child of her father. Hearing about the disability managed to soften Deborah's unyielding stance. She became more open to discussing her half-sister. Her therapist knew they had made a major breakthrough when Deborah allowed herself to learn that her sister's name was Allison. It was also a very harsh reminder of her childhood friend Ally Schnyder and the mistakes she made in that relationship. Deborah was on the verge of attempting to arrange a meeting with Allison when the most unexpected of tragedies struck. Allison and her mother were killed in a head-on car collision. For the second time in her life, Deborah was being denied the healthy closure of a significant relationship. This time was very different than Ally, though the strong negative feelings Deborah was hoping to release forever regarding her half-sister could never have a proper burial. Her inner obsession and need to fix things born with Ally's suicide played no small role in her ultimate decision. She wasn't going to let the same thing happen a third time with Daniel.

The first step Deborah took to reestablish contact with him was to peruse some of the emails he wrote. In the first fifteen she read, he must have apologized and begged for her forgiveness over a thousand times. One week later, she accepted his call. The emotion in his voice when he realized Deborah actually answered the phone was heartrending. He was unable to speak coherently for the first five minutes. It took her another couple of weeks to finally agree to meet him for dinner. Daniel seemed as excited as the day she accepted his marriage proposal. She wasn't even remotely considering reconciliation, but made the conscious decision it was time to restore some type of relationship one step at a time. Whether she was going to be able to forgive him for something as inexcusable as infidelity was still up in the air.

Deborah returned to the comfort of her air-conditioned home as she rooted through her mail. The last letter in the heap caused her to inhale an extra gulp of air. Above the return address appeared the name Annie Bryan. Without a second thought, she tossed the envelope in the garbage. After a brief argument with herself, her curiosity got the better part of her. She rushed into the kitchen to get her letter opener, retrieved the envelope from the trash, tore through the seal, and sat at the breakfast nook table to read.

Dear Deborah,

I know that I'm the last person you want to hear from right now. You might have even thrown this letter in the garbage. But, if I've gotten this far, please hear me out. Before I get to the point of the letter, I want to apologize for all the pain I've caused you and your family. I'm not looking for forgiveness or to make excuses. I just hope you'll believe me when I say that I know I was wrong and my only concern now is to do what I can to try to make things right again.

Daniel has no idea I'm writing this letter. In fact, he instructed me not to communicate with you. I just can't stand by idly knowing that I'm directly responsible for your break-up. Not that you care, but I've been sick over it. And though you owe me nothing except for maybe your disdain, I'm going to implore you to please give Daniel a second chance. He is absolutely miserable without you. I can assure you he's done with me. Even though he felt hopeless when you refused to talk to him, shortly after you guys separated, he met with me to once and for all end our relationship. I haven't seen or talked to him for weeks now.

I would like to offer you and your family an all expense paid cruise with my company. Please don't take this as a gift to buy your forgiveness. That's not my intention at all. Perhaps, some time away, just you, Daniel and the boys, will be a start to your reconciliation. I pray that you accept this gift.
With best wishes,

Annie Bryan

Deborah absent-mindedly placed the letter on the table, stunned by what she had just read. She couldn't decide whether she was angry Annie had the gall to try to manipulate the situation or if she admired her courage. One thing she was absolutely positive about, she wasn't going to be accepting any gifts from her. She wondered what Annie's true motivation was. Deborah couldn't think of any advantage Annie would gain by sending the letter nor could she believe Daniel would have been stupid enough to enlist Annie's help. He would know that type of trick wouldn't work. There was only one response Deborah felt would be appropriate. She would ignore the offer.

* * *

Darting around the confined space of his temporary abode in preparation for the evening, Daniel was in an upbeat mood for the first time since his separation from Deborah. His dogged persistence had finally paid off. She agreed to have dinner with him and the boys. For the past two months, he had been living in a miniature studio apartment in Hallandale on a month- to- month basis. He barely had room to breathe, but the rent was cheap and the lease allowed him to vacate with only one week's notice. The arrangement suited him just fine considering his goal that his stay would be very short. Eventually, he was going to have to move into a more permanent home. He was hoping it would be the condominium he shared with his family. Now that Deborah was speaking to him, he could make his case for their reconciliation.

At the moment, he was rushing to get ready for his big date. He had left work as early as possible. Even with all the hustle and bustle, by the time he stepped out of the shower it was after 6:30pm. Deborah and the boys were expecting him at seven. He quickly threw on a pair of black dress slacks and a blue polo button-down nearly knocking over the flimsy night stand next to his bed and dislodging the white folding closet door from its track in the process. He specifically chose the shirt because it always drew compliments from Deborah. He even decided to spray himself with a couple of spritzes of her favorite cologne. The way he was bouncing off the walls while running around the apartment like a chicken with his head cut off made him feel like a teenager preparing for a first date. The $10,000 question was would his feelings for Deborah actually be different if only he could wipe the slate clean and start again from scratch. There was no doubt he was willing to make the commitment to do everything in his power to make it work and keep his family together.

When he arrived at the condominium, he saw Agents Tom Morehouse and Bill Menendez parked in the lot adjacent to his home. After he parked his vehicle, Daniel walked over to the unmarked car and advised the guys they could take a break until later on in the evening. Little did he know, he was setting himself up to make a fatal error that would change his life forever. He rang the front doorbell and was greeted by an overexcited Dale and Timmy. They attacked him from both sides almost knocking the wind out of him.

"Take it easy on the old man, kids. Are you guys ready for some dinner?"

"Daddy, are you moving back in?" asked Timmy.

"You know Dad is just here to take us to eat, stupid. Mom already told us," said Dale.

"Dale, don't call your brother stupid. Dale is right, Timmy. I'm not moving back in. Where's your Mom?"

"Here I am," said Deborah. She appeared at the top of the foyer steps wearing a Ralph Lauren bright yellow cotton dress with spaghetti straps tied over the shoulder. Daniel thought she looked absolutely gorgeous. His eyes were automatically drawn toward the bottom of the garment as it clung to her long athletic thighs. Even before they separated, it had been a while since they had made love. Taking in the perfection of her feminine frame and her beautifully chiseled face, he wondered if he had been out of his mind to lose his attraction for her. He said, "Hello Deborah. You look incredible. I've never seen that dress before."

"It was a gift from Mom and Dad. Do you like it?"

"Like it, I love it…I love the woman in it even more. You look gorgeous, sweetie."

Deborah squirmed at Daniel's profession of love and the use of a term of endearment. She was nowhere near ready to refer to him in the same way. "Thank you, Daniel. You look good. I see you wore my favorite shirt. Is that Dolce and Gabbana cologne I smell?"

"Yes it is. Thank you. I was hoping you'd notice…So, I thought we'd go to Dave and Busters in Hollywood. The kids can play video games. It'll give us a chance to talk."

"Sounds like a good idea to me. Are you kids ready?" The boys were more than happy to go to Dave and Busters. Mom and

Dad were always generous with the quarters for video games. They were practically out the door before Deborah had the chance to complete her question.

Inside the car, on the way to the restaurant, the conversation was spirited and enthusiastic. Daniel was genuinely excited to be with his family again. The same was true for Deborah and the boys. Daniel had come to realize he missed these times desperately. Directing his entire focus on his beautiful wife and children, his attention to other matters had become distracted. Had he been on his normal state of alert, he wouldn't have failed to notice a black Jeep Cherokee when it turned out onto Hallandale Beach Boulevard and followed them three cars behind. It wasn't until he was holding the front door of the restaurant open for his family that he thought to scan the parking lot. By that time, the driver of the Jeep had passed Dave and Busters intending to make a U-turn to return to the restaurant after a few minutes.

Once they were seated, the children immediately ran off to play video games. Deborah and Daniel didn't expect to see them again until after the food was delivered. They placed their orders and those for the kids with the server then took advantage of the moment to chat. After catching up on recent events and the health of family members, Daniel broached the more important subject matter of the evening.

"Sweetie, I don't want to push you into anything you're not ready for, but I have to ask. Does your willingness to take my calls and meet with me mean you'd like to work on our relationship?"

"Daniel, I'm taking one day at a time. I just don't think I'm capable of looking that far into the future right now. I can't even tell you what I want to do next week. What I can tell you is I've been doing a lot of work with my therapist on trust issues and forgiveness. Before I ever even think about our marriage, I have to learn to forgive you."

"So that means you're considering it… forgiving me?"

"It means I'm working hard on being a little bit more realistic about life and men. I'm not saying unfaithfulness is excusable. But, we're human beings and we make mistakes. Most people deserve a second chance. Don't take that like I'm saying I'm capable of giving you another chance. I'm working on the idea in therapy."

"Well, I'll settle for that. I'm gonna do my best not to rush you into anything. You know I'd move back in tonight if you'd let me. I've been a mess without you."

"It hasn't exactly been a party for me. I don't want you to get your hopes up, Daniel. I'm gonna take things very slowly. I think maybe we should get a little counseling. What do you think?"

"I'm ready to try anything. Like I told you on the phone and a million times in emails, I want this to work. So, whatever we need to get it to happen, I'm all for it."

"I think it's best. Even if, in the end, it doesn't work out, the therapist'll help us with whatever relationship we have after. We definitely have some issues we need to resolve. A relationship is nothing without trust. I can't lie to you. I'm going to have to work hard. There are definitely no guarantees. Geez, here comes the server with our food already. I better go get the kids."

"No, you sit, honey. I'll go get them."

Daniel headed for the game room to find the boys involved in a tense game of video tennis. They resisted their dad's request to wrap things up convincing him to compromise and allow them three minutes to be seated at the table. After the boys arrived, the Falcone family enjoyed their first dinner together in more than two months. They joked, laughed, talked about the boys' school and tennis and just appreciated each other's company. The angst that was Daniel's constant companion for many weeks was finally beginning to dissipate.

After the busboy cleared the table and the family ordered their desserts, Dale and Timmy ran off to get in a final video game or two. Deborah seized the opportunity to bring up a matter that was on her mind.

"Daniel, the other day, I received a letter in the mail from Annie." Daniel's eyes almost popped out of his head. Deborah, who couldn't help but notice his reaction, said, "Don't worry. It's nothing bad. I guess she felt the need to apologize to me though she claimed she wasn't looking for forgiveness. Not that I care how she feels, I got the impression she's truly upset that we're still having problems. She offered us a free cruise hoping it would be a start to us getting back together. I didn't respond."

"Honey, I haven't spoken to Annie in months. I told her I couldn't see her anymore. I asked her not to contact you."

"She mentioned that in the letter. When I realized it was from her, I was pretty mad. But, the more I think about it, I'm not so sure I want to give up a free cruise. It's not like she'll be on the ship."

Daniel felt that the best strategy would be to keep his opinions on the matter to himself. He said, "My only concern right now is for you and the kids. I'm sure Annie'll be fine. I appreciate her concern. This is our business. Whatever you want to do with her offer is fine by me."

"Even if I were inclined to accept, it wouldn't be something I'd be ready for any time in the near future. Perhaps down the road."

"Like you said, sweetheart, one day at a time."

* * *

Much earlier that same day, Shem Chassar had parked his Jeep Cherokee in the Ross Department Store lot located on the south side of the Diplomat Mall in Hallandale. The vehicle was positioned so that he had a view of both east and westbound traffic on East Hallandale Beach Boulevard and easy passage to the exit onto the street. The time had come to initiate the next phase of his masterpiece plan. Access to the agent's wife to gather information about her and her habits was essential to develop the final touches. He had spent the last few days waiting in this parking lot for hours at a stretch. His goal was to catch the wife passing without the protection of an unmarked police tag.

The Ross store was less than a mile from the Falcone condominium, directly across from the entrance to their community. East Hallandale Beach Boulevard was the only exit available to the residents of their building complex. If the wife drove out of her neighborhood, he would see her. Shem was only too aware the Falcone family's home was being watched by two undercover agents for the past few weeks. Falcone and his buddies had become a major nuisance. Shem could no longer rely on them to abandon their stake-outs. It was time to make something happen. His only option was to stay vigilant and hope that the wife found a way to slip past her constant companions. Everyone eventually needed a bit of privacy.

As he sat waiting patiently, his break didn't quite happen in that fashion. He almost couldn't believe what he was seeing when the agent's Crown Victoria occupied by the entire family passed directly in front of him. The fact that the undercover agents hadn't followed solidified his decision. It was a risk to tail them but an opportunity Shem couldn't pass up. After waiting several seconds to be sure they weren't being followed, he pulled out of the parking lot onto the street maintaining a distance of at least three car lengths behind the Crown Victoria. Though he was happy to have this chance, it infuriated him the wife would agree to be in the same car with her immoral, lying and cheating husband. He admonished himself to wait to see where this was leading before he jumped to any conclusions maintaining his pursuit until they pulled into the Dave and Busters in Hollywood. Shem continued to the next intersection, made a U-turn and made his way back to the restaurant. After cutting off the engine, he grabbed his bag from the back seat, pulled out a wig of long, disheveled hair and placed it on his head. To complete the disguise, he put on a Peterbuilt baseball cap and leather motorcycle jacket then exited the Jeep and entered the restaurant.

The building housing Dave and Buster's was immense. The bar, restaurant and gaming area covered more than forty thousand square feet. The bar alone sat more than two-hundred patrons. The structure, as a whole, held a capacity of two thousand people. He passed the reception podium deliberately ignoring the hostess who greeted him and scanned the part of the dining room visible from the bar. He spotted the agent and his wife engaged in an intense conversation at a table along the wall opposite the far side of the bar. He proceeded into the restaurant and chose a seat at the bar just fifteen feet from the couple with his back to them. Luckily for Shem, the restaurant was mostly empty making it easy to eavesdrop. The subject matter of their talk was less fortunate. Shem couldn't believe the woman was actually considering working on a relationship with the shameless philanderer. He wondered if all women were just totally fucked in the head.

Listening to the family's conversation was edging on the unbearable. Several times during the course of the dinner, he contemplated walking out of the restaurant. He was a hair's breadth from finally making the decision to get up from his barstool and spare himself anymore of their pathetic display when the wife made a comment that stopped him in his tracks. She had received a letter from Annie. Though Shem was pleased to hear Annie and the agent were no longer seeing each other, the most fascinating piece of information in the correspondence was Annie's free cruise offer to the Falcone family. The wife may have refused the gift, but her comments were suggesting and his fine-tuned intuition was telling him she would accept some time in the near future.

Sitting in his Jeep in the restaurant's parking lot ten minutes after the Falcone family left the premises, Shem was in deep contemplation. It was now just a matter of time. If he could maintain an even-temper, the light would be shining brightly at the end of the tunnel. He reminded himself that patience was always extremely important to a successful outcome. His lack of it almost cost him some very valuable information. The final piece of the puzzle would soon be in place. As the details of his course of action became clearer in his mind, the anger smoldering beneath the surface remained at bay.

Chapter 15

While weeks passed and more information was collected regarding the investigation of the Hannah Richards' murder, a sense of frustration continued to plague Daniel. After hours upon hours of time and manpower dedicated to the subject, there were still no leads to help identify the suspect. They had his genetic code and partial fingerprint. The videotapes and the witness description provided them with a fairly accurate composite sketch. Special Agent Frazier was able to develop a much more complete profile of the killer's probable behavioral characteristics with the discovery of the linked murders. The killer's file currently consisted of four accordion files stretched to their limits with more than one-thousand pages of evidence analysis. About the only piece of information they were lacking was a name.

It was determined that each of the victims, except for Hannah Richards, was engaged in prostitution. Teams were dispatched to the European cities where the other murders took place to interview the female prostitutes in those areas. The women were shown a detailed description of the suspect with the composite drawing of his face. A friend of Francesca Leone was able to recognize the picture claiming she saw Francesca with the man several hours before she was murdered. This information managed to confirm that the composite drawing was accurate and it was used for his photograph on the Ten Most Wanted list. To date, it didn't help lead to the suspect's identification.

Leland and Mancini scoured the streets of Miami and New York respectively, showing the composite picture to the prostitutes in those cities. New York was a bust. They had better luck in South Florida. One prostitute in the Ft. Lauderdale area and another in Miami thought they recognized the suspect as one of their previous clients. They described him as tall, extremely fit and handsome, though not much of a talker. The Miami girl recalled that when she gave him oral sex, he seemed to reach orgasm, but didn't ejaculate. None of the three women could say he came back as a repeat customer.

Agent Frazier wasn't sure whether the prostitute's identification of the suspect was accurate and if so, if his failure to ejaculate was significant. For purposes of the investigation, they had to recognize the possibility it was the serial killer. His sexual handicap was a fact they couldn't afford to ignore. Through the study of previous case histories, Frazier was aware of a sexual condition known as dry orgasm. There were several causes, including surgical removal of the prostate or bladder, exposure to radiation in the pelvic area and release of semen into the bladder. It wasn't an uncommon disorder, most often associated with older men. It didn't ordinarily afflict men of the suspect's age range. If the killer was, in fact suffering from the syndrome, it was well worth paying a visit to hospitals and urologists in Palm Beach, Dade and Broward Counties. Several investigators were assigned to the task and to accumulate a list of young men with the problem. As of yet, this line of investigation was no more successful than any other previously pursued by the task force.

A team to inspect records of men travelling outside the United States was assembled by Special Agent Mancini. It was their job to determine if they could pinpoint one traveler who had been to the countries in question at the times of the European murders. After weeks of examining thousands of passports and getting permission from the various nations to scour through their travel records, the search came up empty. Not only did the suspect seem to have no identity, but he was able to travel from country to country as if he were a phantom voyager.

Every night that Daniel returned to his studio apartment, he would spend hours reviewing piles of information collected by his investigators. He felt there had to be a clue locked somewhere inside the details and was a firm believer in the value of profiling. He always had a special interest in the subject. Crime analysis and the study of criminal behavior had intrigued him since he was a child. In his initial years as a rookie agent, it was his plan on his way to the top to someday become one of the exclusive group based in Quantico. He attended seminars offered by FBI profilers and conducted his own research. In the end, his career path led in a different direction, though he always kept up with developments in the field.

Frazier's most recent report was the last thing Daniel would read before he allowed himself a few minutes to relax before going to bed. His last updated profile indicated that the man they were looking for was intellectually exceptional, streetwise, and sophisticated and most likely considered himself a self-made man. With regard to his profession, he would be a business owner or highly placed executive in his company or firm. He was proud of his manipulative talents and probably committed crimes in the past involving deception or theft.

From a sexual standpoint, he would most likely have some disability or handicap. The women of his past with whom he had sexual relations mocked him and laughed at him for his inadequacy. This combined with an overbearing and perhaps even abusive mother fostered a rage that caused him to believe women were merely objects to be mistreated. He has an overactive sex drive and his fantasies associated with masturbation often are excessively aggressive. Power and dominance motivates him. He thoroughly enjoys beguiling and then controlling women. When he chooses his victim, he knows he's going to kill her and revels in the thought as he manipulates her. He was exposed to sex at a very young age and associates it with brutality.

Frazier believed there would be a salient resemblance in physical appearance between the women that mocked him, his mother and the women he kills. The murders provided him with short-term gratification, but would never alleviate the profound void that had grown exponentially since his youth. Nor would they ever correct the perceived transgressions committed by those women who offended him and the abuse suffered at the hands of his mother. In the meeting where Frazier presented his completed profile to the task force, he reminded everyone that serial murderers often develop a sense they can't be caught. This especially applied if the investigators have missed all the clues the killer either intentionally or inadvertently left at the crime scene. This mindset was the reason for his success. It would also be the cause of his ultimate demise. It offered him the motivation to continue to kill. However, in due course, he would get sloppy. Daniel was counting on it.

* * *

The obstinate South Florida summer usually refused to relinquish its grip to the Fall until sometime in late October or early November. That afternoon was as hot and muggy as a day in mid-August. It was Halloween and Daniel was deciding on what he would wear to escort the boys for an evening of trick or treating. Deborah warned him the forecast predicted rain though at the moment, there wasn't a cloud in the sky. Mindful of her near perfect record predicting the weather, he wouldn't even consider doubting her. He decided on a t-shirt and jeans and threw a windbreaker in the back seat of the car while he was thinking about it.

On the home front, Daniel couldn't have been more pleased with the progress he and Deborah had achieved so far in their work to rectify their relationship. They were seeing a marriage counselor two times a week for the past month a half and worked their way to having dates on Friday and Saturday evenings. His only disappointment was the lack of sex. He was forced to accept making love to her would be the last step before she allowed him to move back into the house. That was just Deborah's way. It was too significant an act for her to take any less seriously.

There had been one other obstacle along the road to reconciliation. For a while after he and Deborah separated, his father-in-law was being an asshole. At first, Daniel understood Jack was playing his role as the protective father. It didn't excuse his behavior one night recently when Daniel was picking up the boys from his in-law's place and he and Jack almost came to blows. Daniel remained as calm as he could throughout the argument, but Jack was so irritated at one point, he reared his fist. The loud altercation had attracted the attention of neighbors. Fortunately, no one had called the police. Daniel didn't need to give the media any more ammunition to abuse him, especially when it involved his personal life. In the past week, he and Jack had been getting along famously. Deborah must have said something about the work they were doing to repair their marriage. For the most part, the rapport between the two men had returned to the pre-affair status. Based on his father-in-law's marriage history, Daniel felt that Jack had huge balls to sit in judgment anyway.

Daniel drove the short distance from his studio apartment to his condominium, confident the day was coming soon when he would no longer be separated from his family. He was certainly more than ready to put this chapter of his life behind him. When he pulled into the parking space in front of his home, the boys were waiting outside in their costumes. As usual, they were thrilled to see their dad and were on top of him before he could extricate himself completely from the car. Deborah was standing in the doorway witnessing the assault with a big smile on her face. After granting the boys their due attention, Daniel made his way to Deborah. He had graduated to more than just a peck on the lips as a greeting. Although the kiss she planted on his lips was more a tease than anything else, he was happy to get the more passionate embrace.

It was a longstanding Florida tradition to wait until dark to commence trick or treating. There was still an hour before nightfall, so Daniel offered to take Deborah and the boys for a quick meal. He wasn't aware Deborah had prepared eggplant parmigiana for dinner, one of his favorites. In spite of the children's complaints for having to wait for the night's festivities, the Falcone family sat down to their first home cooked meal together in months. It gave Daniel a warm feeling inside and even more reason to be optimistic about the future.

After dinner, he helped Deborah clear the table and do the dishes. It was just like old times. Daniel washed and Deborah dried. They had always refused to have a dishwasher in their home. They enjoyed their time in the kitchen together after a meal, Deborah more than Daniel. Simply placing the dishes in a dishwasher diminished the experience for her. By the time she put the last dish in the china cabinet, the light from the sun had almost completely disappeared. Since the boys were bouncing off the walls by then, they decided it was time to hit the streets. Daniel grabbed his windbreaker while Deborah pulled a giant-size umbrella from the hall closet and they were on their way. The boys were trick or treating at their first house when Deborah decided to take advantage of the opportunity to speak in private.

"Daniel, I've been doing a lot of thinking about the cruise Annie offered us. I think I was being petty. I'm feeling like it's the right time for us to do something like that. Go on a vacation together. What do you think?"

"That would be great, honey. Do you mean you want to accept her offer or do you want to do something else?"

"I mean let's go on the cruise. I really don't think Annie was expecting anything out of this. If I'm going to forgive you, I should consider forgiving her too. At least, my therapist thinks it would be a good exercise for me. Besides, cruises are the best."

"I wouldn't know. I've never been on one. But, if you're willing, so am I. Maybe your parents can take care of the kids. That way it could be just the two of us."

"Actually, since you mentioned them, I was hoping you wouldn't mind if they came along instead of the boys. I was nervous about the kids being on a big ship in the middle of the ocean. We'll still be able to have quality time together. I'll just feel much more comfortable if my parents were there."

"I understand completely, babe. I would love to have them along. So, when would you like to do it and who's gonna talk to Annie? I'd prefer you do it."

"Well, since the gift was offered to me, I should be the one to accept. I'll send her an email. I'll take care of all the details. Let's do the Caribbean. It's the perfect time of year. If you can work it out with your job, I'd like to go within the next month or so."

"The serial murderer is our most pressing case right now. My role is more support than anything else. Leland is more than capable of handling things. I think they'll be fine without me for a week. Just give me a couple of weeks notice."

"Sounds like a plan. I'm really excited about this, Daniel. I don't want you to go packing your bags yet to come home, but I'm really starting to feel good about things, again."

"You don't know how happy it makes me to hear you say that, honey. So am I." As the boys joined them in the street to head for the next house on the block, the first drops of rain began to fall from the sky.

* * *

The night was his play time. Darkness energized him. Shem's most creative work was conceived and produced after midnight. His grandfather clock chimed the hour of one o'clock in the morning while he surfed the net in complete obscurity. There wasn't a light on in the apartment. The glow from the computer monitor reflected off his expressionless face resembling that of a demonic, candle-lit jack-o-lantern. This was a very exciting time for him. As he suspected, the wife decided to accept Annie's generous gift. Since he overheard the conversation at Dave and Buster's, he had been hacking into the King Cruise Line website on a daily basis. Just three days ago, he discovered the Falcones booked a cabin on the King Joy of the Seas for the week of November 28th. That was just two weeks away. He had already worked hard on the preparations for the execution of his masterpiece plan. Still, much work remained. He was going to be a busy man.

This particular night, he was checking the crew list of the Joy of the Seas. Many cruise line employees were transferred from ship to ship when they signed a new contract. There was a great chance there were at least a few who were currently working on the Joy who worked with Damien Drysdale on the Diamond. While on the Joy of the Seas, it would be essential to avoid those people even though he had plans to totally alter his appearance. He found that several boutique employees and a couple of the entertainment staff were on the Diamond during his tenure. They didn't have much contact with him at the time and he doubted they would recognize him. The only potential problem was that Ken O'Brien was now working security on the Joy of the Seas. Depending on his role, he could have access to the surveillance monitors. Even if he wasn't working the monitors, he would, no doubt, be patrolling the ship. Shem couldn't risk being recognized by his former colleague. This was going to cause him some extra work, nothing he couldn't handle with relative ease.

Another interesting discovery Shem had made was that the agent's in-laws would be onboard as opposed to the children. His plans for the Falcone family would have to be changed meaning the pleasure quotient would be drastically diminished. It was a disappointment he would have to get over. He blamed the wife. The pathetic bitch couldn't lift a finger without consulting or involving her parents. The weakness of her character disgusted him and made the disappointment that much harder to swallow. Her lack of maturity and independence was pitiful. He couldn't imagine what good purpose parents would serve anyway. If he had known he was going to witness an incident the very next day that would make his ultimate job easier, he wouldn't have wasted as much negative energy.

It happened on a Friday night. Daniel and Deborah had gone out to dinner for their first date of the weekend. Deborah dropped the boys off at her parents' place earlier in the day. Not long after, Shem decided he was going to pay the Tylers a visit, hopeful to get some idea of who these people were, their behaviors, their tendencies. When he first arrived mid-afternoon, two undercover agents were parked in a van across the street from the in-laws' house. Shem caught sight of their vehicle before he turned onto the Tylers' street forcing him to abandon his mission. Lack of persistence was never one of Shem's character traits. He couldn't imagine the agents were there to watch the old people. Either the kids or the wife must have been there. Under that premise, he returned later in the evening. He wasn't above or opposed to peeping in windows to gather the information he was seeking. His decision to persevere rendered better results than he ever expected. Shem arrived for the second time that day almost at the same time the agent stopped by the Tyler house to pick up his children. It was his weekend for visitation. Since Daniel had just dismissed his undercover agents responsible for keeping an eye on the children from further duty, they had left the neighborhood. Seeing no surveillance truck, Shem parked across from the house and approximately twenty-five yards up the road. Once settled, he pulled a pair of binoculars from his bag and watched as Falcone was having an intense discussion with his father-in-law. The light of the day had faded significantly, but with his high-tech equipment, Shem was able to observe the entire event with no problem. It was acutely obvious the agent was agitated, though focused on his mission. Sensing what was to follow could have some value; he turned his night-vision camcorder on and pointed it in the direction of the Tyler house.

Never once during the entire taping did the agent look in Shem's direction. From Shem's perspective, it appeared that the father-in-law wouldn't let the agent in the house and was evidently refusing to hand over the children. A heated argument between the two men ensued on the front lawn drawing neighbors out of their homes. Before the riff ended, the father-in-law raised his fist as if to strike the agent. Shem was disappointed the fight didn't escalate to the point of blows. At the time, he wasn't aware the video would become a valuable piece of evidence at the agent's trial.

Chapter 16

To make up for lost time, Daniel was working on the serial murder case late the night before his cruise was scheduled to set sail from Port Everglades, Florida. He had just returned from a trip to Washington D.C. where he was presented with the Ronald Reagan Freedom Award for his previous contributions to the War on Drugs. Though he was honored to receive recognition for his work from the President, the event took him away from the serial murder case longer than he would have preferred. He was hoping to have some kind of breakthrough before he left for his vacation. That didn't leave him much time and his chances were getting slimmer by the second. He had even refrained from having his normal three or four evening beers to keep his head clear.

As it turned out, the time constraints were exactly what he needed. He did some of his best thinking under extreme pressure whether self-inflicted or real. Following his routine of reviewing the updates of the case in his studio apartment before he retired for the night, the light bulb finally switched on bringing long-anticipated, brilliant clarity to the key that had eluded him for too long. For the past several weeks, he was working on what was known in law enforcement as geographical profiling. Computer software has the ability to map out the separate murder sites of a serial killer and through a series of calculations, provide information as to his probable home base. The European cities where the murders took place were plugged into the program and it was originally suggested that the killer's domicile was most likely somewhere in Central to Southern Italy between Rome and Naples.

Both the European authorities and FBI personnel searched the part of Italy recommended by the program, visiting small villages and big cities alike. They went into neighborhoods and showed the composite drawing of the suspect to the inhabitants in hope that someone would recognize him. From the onset, Daniel felt they were missing something in their mapping analysis. It was while repeating to himself the names of the cities where the killings occurred that he finally happened upon the missing piece of the puzzle. Everyone, including the software, was assuming there was only one central home base. Perhaps, that wasn't the case. It was never considered that the killer could have been moving with each murder.

Excited by the idea, he hurriedly flipped through the papers in his briefcase to pull out the map of Europe where he charted the cities in question. Staring at the map, he realized the answer that had been so illusory to that point was beautiful in its simplicity. Each killing occurred within a few hours' drive of a major port city. Keeping in mind that Annie was somehow involved, he went to the King Cruise Line website to research their European itineraries at the time of the murders. What he found made him want to shout out in celebration. Over the five months the murders were committed, the King Diamond was docked in each of the corresponding ports within driving distance of the murder sites. It was probable the killer's home was a cruise ship owned by Annie's company. Daniel immediately picked up the phone to call Leland. He answered after four rings.

"I'm sorry to wake you up, Robert, but I think I may have come across something that could be huge."

"No, not at all. I couldn't find the phone. What's up?"

"There was something about the geographical profiling that's been bugging the hell out of me, but I couldn't figure out why. I knew we were missing something. It finally hit me tonight. We were focusing on a central home base for the killer instead of considering he might be moving." Daniel went on to explain his theory that it was likely the killer was a member of the crew or possibly a passenger on the King Diamond, though the latter was improbable due to the time period over which the murders occurred. That particular ship had special significance for Leland who was the lead investigator on the Paul Anderson case.

"Daniel, that's the ship Paul Anderson disappeared from."

"Shit, that can't be coincidence."

"Motherfucker, I knew I was right. I've always suspected the security guard, Damien Drysdale, had something to do with Anderson's disappearance. You know he quit his job without warning anyone. He disappeared off the face of the earth just like Paul Anderson."

"Unbelievable. The answer was right there under our fuck'n noses. It sucks I'm gonna be gone for the next week. We've got to run with this. We need to get in touch with Annie Bryan ASAP and see what we can get on this guy. I'm sure they have an employee file for him. We need to get a hold of it. It would be great if they had a picture of him."

"I have a picture of him in the Anderson file. I requested it from Annie a long time ago. She wouldn't give me the entire employee file. I convinced her to give me a copy of the picture and any information they had about his residence. I was thinking about getting a court order to get her to turn it over, but I was getting all kinds of pressure to close the case."

"You were obviously on the right track. We should've trusted your instincts. Tomorrow morning we need to enter the photo into VICAP to see if we get any matches. You'll want to run it through the facial recognition software and databanks for driver's licenses and passports too. We could get a match if he actually applied for any of his identification documents…There's a good chance Annie knows him. She's the Vice President over security for King and this guy was a security officer. If she does, we'll want her to take another look at those surveillance tapes from Fort Lauderdale and LaGuardia. If you remember, she said there was something familiar about the suspect."

"I'll get right on it. It's a little late to call her tonight. I'll do it first thing in the morning. I'll call the office right now and get one of the night guys to enter that photo into system right away." Leland was peeved that Daniel was treating him as if he were a rookie though he was trying his best not to show his anger. The excitement of the possibility of having a real lead helped. Unaware of Leland's issue, Daniel continued to spout off instructions.

"I hope we're able to connect this guy to the killings. Otherwise, we have a lot of work ahead of us. We'll have to go through all the passenger lists for every cruise over the five months the murders took place and interview all crew members and guests on the ship. There might be a witness among them who saw something suspicious that could turn into an important lead. For potential suspects, we'll need to look at any passengers taking an extended vacation on the Diamond. If it doesn't turn out to be Damien Drysdale, you need to get a team set up right away to get all that information together."

Leland's attempts to maintain his composure had reached their limit. He barked, "Daniel, take it easy. I've been doing this for a long time. I know what I'm doing."

"Robert, I know you know what you're doing. I'm stoked we finally have something to work with. Sorry, if I offended you. I do have a personal stake in this."

In a feeble attempt to backtrack, Leland responded, "No, no I'm fine, Daniel. You know I'll take care of everything."

"Alright, well I'm gonna have my cell phone with me on the cruise. If you need anything, you can call me anytime. Definitely give me a call if you can confirm it was the security guard. I'm anxious to hear how that turns out."

"Will do. Have a great time on your cruise and I'll see you when you get back."

* * *

It was nine days before Daniel Falcone, his wife, and in-laws were scheduled to set sail for the Caribbean that Shem Chassar commenced the detailed preparations for his most complex mission to date. Late that Friday night, he drove his Acura Integra south on Interstate 95 to Overtown in Miami. Located just northwest of downtown, Overtown was considered one of the most dangerous communities in the nation. It had a higher murder per capita rate than the entire city of Detroit. Many of the murders were drug related due to the high amount of trafficking competition that took place on its streets.

His objective that evening was to obtain two hundred fifty grams of heroin. It should cost him approximately ten thousand dollars, though he was pretty sure he wasn't going to pay for it. He would make his final decision at the time of the transaction. If necessary, he had the cash on hand. Holstered in a shoulder harness just inside his blue denim jacket was an automatic Colt 1911 A1 pistol with silencer, if and when he chose the second option.

He merged off of I95 at NW 14th Street. It was 2:00am and the roads were deserted of vehicles. While waiting at a red light on the exit ramp, he removed the holster with the pistol and placed it underneath the driver's seat. When the light turned green, he slowly proceeded underneath the interstate's overpass with his driver's side window lowered halfway. Three emaciated figures emerged from the shadows cast by the streetlights below the bridge and approached the Acura.

"I'm looking to score some smack," Shem said.

A tall, lanky African American man with bloodshot eyes and yellowed sclera stooped down to the window level and inquired, "How much you lookin for?"

"About two hundred fifty grams."

"Fuck, man. You don't come drivin' down these streets for that much dope." Not wanting to lose such a potential lucrative transaction, the drug dealer thought quickly on his feet. He could walk away with at least 500 bucks. That could support his cocaine habit for almost a month. His ex-brother-in-law probably had that much heroin on hand. It was worth a shot to make a call. That is if the dumb ass cracker realized how much it cost and actually had the money. “Shit, I can probably get it, but not here.”

“I need it now.”

“I can get it for you, but you’ll have to give me a ride. It’s gonna cost you.”

“Where do we need to go?”

“We ain’t goin’ nowhere until you show me the money.”

“I’ve got the cash. Hop in, just you, not your buddies.” He flashed a roll of one hundred dollar bills to convince the man to get in the car.

“We’re goin’ to Carol City. You ain’t a cop, are you?”

“Do I look like a fuck’n cop? Hell no. Now, do you want the fuck’n sale or not? I don’t have time to waste.”

The two other men disappeared back into the shadows of the bridge while the spokesman of the group walked around the vehicle and climbed into the passenger seat. He said, “I gotta make a call first. I gotta make sure the stuff is available.”

“Fuck this, man. You said you could get it. Get out! I’m outta here.”

“Calm down, dude. I’ll get it for you. I just gotta make one quick call.”

“Do whatever the fuck you need to and hurry. I don’t have all night.”

The drug dealer pulled a cell phone from his pocket and dialed the number of his sister’s ex-husband.

“What you doin' callin' me at this hour, mothafucka?” asked the brother-in-law who was known as Candyman on the streets of Overtown.

“Hey Candyman, it’s Skinny. I’ve got a customer here for you that’s lookin’ for some big H. He wants two-fifty and he’s got the dough.”

“I know who the fuck you are dumb ass. Have you ever heard-a-caller I.D.? You sure this guy ain’t the heat? I’m gonna fuck you up if you get me arrested.”

“He showed me a roll of hundreds. He says he’s not a cop.”

“That don’t mean shit, dumb fuck. Check him for a badge and a piece.”

Skinny turned to Shem and said, "Dude, I have to search you for weapons or we can't do business with you. He has what you need."

"You want to do that right here under the bridge?"

"No man, take a right on 7th then a left on 10th and pull into the park on the right hand side. We'll do it there."

He followed Skinny's instructions and parked his car in a lot adjacent to a baseball field at Reeves Park. They exited the Acura so that Skinny could pat him down. When Skinny was satisfied he was unarmed and didn't have a badge, he called the Candyman back.

"He's clean Candyman. What do you want me to do?"

"Count his fuck'n money and tell me how much he has."

"He wants me to count your money."

"No fuck'n way. I'll hold the money and count while you watch."

"That's cool dude."

Shem had to control his fermenting anger. He hated addicts. To him, they were like bugs deserving to be squashed under foot. He removed the roll of cash from his jacket pocket and counted out one hundred one hundred dollar bills.

"He's got ten thousand G's Candyman."

"Bring him by and make it quick."

It was nearly a fifteen minute drive to Carol City. Shem found himself merging back onto Interstate 95 south toward downtown Miami. Twelve minutes later, he pulled into the parking lot of a project apartment building in the heart of the slums of Dade County. He allowed Skinny to exit the vehicle first. As the drug dealer was rising from the car, Shem quickly reached under his seat to retrieve the Colt automatic and placed it inside his jacket pocket. The jacket had a thick lining allowing him to conceal the pistol and silencer without creating an obvious bulge.

The seedy, run-down condition of the tenement reminded Shem of his days in his old neighborhood in Chicago. In spite of the hour, there were residents milling about the property, some gathered outside apartments to socialize and get high, others seemingly wandering aimlessly. Garbage and filth were scattered everywhere amongst children's toys and people's worthless personal belongings. A thick, offensive stench permeated through the common areas like dense smog that chose this particular complex to persecute.

Skinny led Shem to an apartment on the second floor where he knocked three times, hesitated then knocked an additional two times. The door was opened by a well muscled, middle-aged, African American male of average height dressed in a wife beater and a pair of basketball shorts. Shem could smell his stinking breath from ten feet away. He gave the tiny one bedroom apartment the once over. The entire residence consisted of a four-hundred square foot space divided into a kitchen, dining room and living room. The sole bedroom was partitioned from the rest of the apartment by strings of multi-colored hanging beads.

Shem noticed a large, clear, plastic bag of a white powdery substance on the dining room table. He was fairly certain there was no one else in the apartment. In the blink of an eye, he withdrew his pistol from his jacket pocket and shot both men between the eyes at point blank range. The two men instantly dropped to the floor as blood and brain matter soiled the carpet and living room wall. Shem's guess that the bedroom was vacant was confirmed when he poked his head through the beads, saw no one then quickly entered and checked under the bed. He grabbed the bag off the table, opened it and sniffed its contents. It was odorless. He sampled the drug by placing a small amount on the inside of his bottom lip. The intensity of the bitterness told him it was a decent quality heroin. He sealed the bag, kicked the body of the skinny drug dealer out of the way of the door and exited the apartment.

* * *

The following Sunday morning, two days after Shem's successful drug deal, the Joy of the Seas was scheduled to dock at Port Everglades, Florida at 6:00. Since it wasn't to set sail until later on that afternoon, he slept in setting his alarm for 10:00am. Instantly awake and alert at the sound of resounding rock music from his radio, he jumped out of bed, took a shower and dressed in his former King Cruise Line security uniform. The previous evening, he refurbished his old credentials that allowed him access to restricted areas of the port and the company cruise ships. He clipped the badges to his shirt pocket, grabbed his bag he packed in the early hours of the morning and walked out the door. Before he left the parking lot, he pasted a falsified Port Everglades parking decal to the windshield of his car.

As a former security guard, Shem was familiar with the embarkation and disembarkation procedures followed by King. He expected that when he arrived at the port, the warehouse where passengers were registered would be buzzing with activity. It was always a chaotic spectacle when the old passengers were exchanged for the new. Crowds of people would be leaving the ship and searching for their luggage while hundreds of other passengers gathered in line to be the first to board for the next cruise. The crew members and port employees in charge of check-in would be running around like chickens with their heads cut off.

When he arrived at the port at 11:00am, he parked his vehicle in the employee parking garage. From there, he proceeded on foot to the terminal where the Joy of the Seas was docked. As he had predicted, the registration area was a madhouse. He was able to make his way through the building without attracting the least bit of attention. Since Customs and Immigration already cleared the ship, the only people manning the warehouse were employees of King Cruise Line and several port security guards. Holding up his credentials, he walked nonchalantly past the security officer guarding the crew member's entrance to the ship. The officer barely took notice of him as he waved him through.

The next phase of his plan was going to be a little bit trickier. The night before, he looked up O'Brien's cabin number on the King Cruise Line employee website. He was relatively certain his former colleague would be working since all security guards were on duty on disembarkation/embarkation day. There was a chance, however slight, that O'Brien was sick or was granted the day off and could be in his cabin. If that was the case, Shem had a back-up plan. He didn't want to have to kill Ken, not that he had a problem putting a bullet in his head. It would be a nuisance to have to take the time and risk to clean up the mess. Even worse, it had the potential of screwing up the whole mission.

The Joy of the Seas was a sister ship to the Diamond meaning their design was identical. Shem easily navigated his way through the area restricted from passengers to O'Brien's room. He knew exactly where each surveillance camera was located in the crew quarters. Not, that it mattered much on these frenetic Sundays, since the monitors weren't scrutinized as closely. Even more convenient for Shem, there were no cameras that provided a feed of O'Brien's door. When he arrived at the cabin, he removed his lock-picking kit from his bag and was able to open the door in the time it would take to use a keycard. The room was vacant. Without wasting a precious second, he pulled a plastic sack containing two-hundred grams of heroin out of his bag and hid it in O'Brien's underwear drawer underneath a stack of t-shirts. He then quickly gathered his belongings and hurried out of the cabin closing the door behind him.

Once he was off the ship, he located the nearest terminal pay phone and called the number for Human Resources at King Cruise Line headquarters in Ft. Lauderdale. He asked for the person in charge and was transferred to the assistant director on duty. Shem explained to the HR representative he was a Joy of the Seas crew member who wanted to remain anonymous, but was very concerned about Security Officer Ken O'Brien. He told her he was sure that if Ken's cabin was searched, they would find a significant amount of heroin that he had seen with his own eyes. The Human Resources Assistant Director thanked him for the information and assured him she would take care of the matter as soon as possible. Later that afternoon, two hundred grams of one of the purest forms of heroin were found in Ken O'Brien's dresser by one of his colleagues on the Joy's security staff. O'Brien was fired on the spot after more than twenty years of loyal service. That was the least of his worries. He was escorted off the ship by five narcotics agents with the Federal Bureau of Investigations, arrested, and officially charged with trafficking heroin, a felony that carried a minimum mandatory sentence of fifteen years in prison.

* * *

Exactly one week after Ken O'Brien was fired and arrested, the morning after Daniel's geographical profiling coup and the day of his cruise, Daniel was up bright and early. It was a bit discouraging he was finding it an effort to get in the appropriate mindset for his vacation. His heart was with the new discovery and joining his colleagues in pursuit of the lead. He was fighting for his marriage and his family, yet he wished he was getting ready for the office rather than seven days in paradise with his wife. The idea didn't sit well with him. If Deborah knew how he felt, she probably wouldn't ever consider taking him back. His old friend, guilt was bracing itself to pay him one of its uninvited visits, though Daniel was starting to believe the FBI psychologist was right when she said it was his comfort zone. It was without question an emotion that often drove him and determined his behavior. This time, he chided himself for his lack of consideration to the mother of his children who was loving, compassionate and generous enough to try to forgive his transgressions and give him a second chance. Giving his all to her and their struggle to save their marriage was the least he could do.

Disgusted, he threw his personal file of the serial murder case which he had been holding in his hand into his briefcase. He hadn't even packed yet. Deborah and her parents wanted to be sure they were at the port and prepared to board at the earliest possible moment, twelve noon. He shut out all thoughts of work and started to pull shorts and t-shirts from a plastic bag he stored under his bed. An hour and a half later, he had packed one medium-sized suitcase and a duffle bag and it was time to pick up the boys then drop them off at his brother, Dominick's house in Hollywood. They would be spending the week with him. A talk with the agents assigned to their protection was also on his agenda. The fact that a twenty-four hour a day undercover unit was assigned for the continued surveillance of the boys was instrumental in getting Deborah to feel comfortable leaving them behind. He wanted to personally hand them his cell phone number and the ship information and to instruct them to contact him at the slightest indication of suspicious behavior.

Once all his chores were done, he made his way back to the condo where Deborah was waiting for him. It was still early, but knowing her, she could probably use a little assistance getting ready so they could make it to her parents' place on time. They were having a limousine service pick them up there at 11:15. He was surprised to find she was nearly ready when he walked in the front door. All of her luggage was aligned in a neat row in the living room. Recognizing her sincere enthusiasm and excitement to begin their endeavor, the guilt resurfaced in all its fervor. The anticipation of the vacation was always a big part of the fun for Deborah and it was showing in spades. Deborah had a pot of coffee going and they sat down to have a quick cup before they left for the Tylers. Daniel's inner battle continued as he tried in vain to ignore it and absorb some of Deborah's oozing passion. He could only hope that the stress and torment weren't showing on the outside.

* * *

The Falcone and Tyler families couldn't have been more pleased with their accommodations on the cruise ship. They were both upgraded to deluxe owner's suites. The cabins had their own private bedrooms, a separate living and dining area, two balconies, a private courtyard with a pool, hot tub, steam room, gym equipment and sun deck. Daniel and Deborah walked through the door of their suite to find a bottle of Dom Perignon champagne and a huge basket of fresh fruit waiting for them on the living room coffee table. There was a vase of purple, red and yellow lilies on the kitchen counter and a centerpiece of assorted flowers on the dining room table. Next to the centerpiece, Deborah found a note from Annie asking them to accept her gift of the flowers and champagne and bidding them a wonderful cruise.

Deborah found herself having mixed emotions about the gifts. On the one hand, it was nice to be treated like royalty. It was a stretch to think she was ready to completely forgive Annie. Hypocritical or not, there was still plenty of work to be done before she would be able to control the negative feelings she experienced at the mention of Annie's name. She commented, "Do you think Annie might have gone a little bit overboard, no pun intended?"

"I'm not gonna complain. This is amazing. I could live like this." Daniel made a beeline to the bottle of champagne. "Perhaps a toast is in order," he suggested.

"Daniel, really? Do you have to start drinking right away?"

"Sorry, I just thought it would be nice to toast the beginning of our cruise."

"Why don't we wait for Mom and Dad? Or better yet, why don't we have it with the first formal dinner?"

"Sure, honey, whatever you think."

Desperately wanting to change the subject, Daniel inquired, "So honey, what you think of the one king size bed?"

"Hmm, I wonder if Annie planned for that, too."

"If she did, I like her thinking."

"Don't get ahead of yourself, buster. We'll see about that," said Deborah, half-kidding. "For now, let's think about getting these suitcases unpacked."

"I'll join you in a sec, honey. I just want to give the office a call real quick."

"Tell me you're not serious, Daniel."

"No, you don't understand, babe. We had a huge...."

Deborah cut him off in mid-sentence. "I don't even want to hear it. Are you kiddin' me? We are here to make a decision about our lives together," she said emphasizing each and every word. "You tell me you can't live without me. You know my issues with work. I don't want to come in second on this cruise, Daniel. It's the least you could do for me...Unbelievable. Practically the first thing you think of." Deborah's eyes welled up with tears. "Just seven days. It's not asking a lot. You don't think they can get along without you? This is not a good start."

"I'm sorry, honey. You're right. I'm a fuck'n idiot. I know, it's no excuse, but we might have identified the serial killer. But, that's the last I'll talk about it. I promise. This cruise is about us."

"Don't promise me, promise yourself. I tell you what. If you're serious, give me your cell phone. I'll keep it. That way you don't have any temptation and I won't have to wonder whether you're sneaking off to call the office. I know you. You know what I mean. You won't forget about this. If you give me your phone it'll at least show me you're making an effort. Otherwise, I'll just get off this ship right now, before we even leave Ft. Lauderdale."

Displeased with himself, Daniel saw no way out of the situation. He hoped he hadn't already blown it. She was right. He would obsess about the case the entire cruise, eventually break and call Leland. It wasn't fair to her. She deserved his undivided attention. The task force was more than competent to manage the case for the short week he would be gone. If anyone needed to contact them about the boys, Deborah had her phone and an agent could easily contact the ship. He handed his cell phone to Deborah. She shut if off then locked it in the digital safe along with a few other precious items sending Daniel out of the room before she set the password.

* * *

Approximately nine hours earlier, in the wee hours of the morning, Shem Chassar woke to the sound of his alarm. Normally, he was just winding up his night at that time, especially since he stopped following Annie to work due to constant FBI surveillance. This morning, the Joy of the Seas would be arriving at 6:00am in Port Everglades for the first day of the agent's cruise. It was an absolute necessity that Shem be extremely sharp and alert for most of the early part of the day. He had gone to bed and taken a pill to assure sleep at 8:00 the night before. He had already stowed all essential provisions needed to execute his plan in a small suitcase/briefcase similar to the kind used by trial attorneys carrying large files. His clothing and other personal items were packed in a larger bag marked with passenger tags provided by the cruise line indicating the cabin number he reserved under the name Isaac Jefferson.

Despite his aversion to out of shape people, Shem had spent the last several months deliberately putting on twenty- five pounds. Since the age of 21, his typical daily routine included two workouts a day. He hadn't been to the gym once since he began his undertaking to gain weight. The extra pounds were a hindrance to his agility and prowess, but he didn't allow it to concern him. Disguise was a much more vital matter. He was confident that after the cruise when he moved out of the state of Florida, he would be back in shape in no time.

Once the morning cobwebs cleared, he got up from his bed and went directly to the bathroom. Originally, he planned to wear a wig on the Joy of the Seas until last night when an alternative idea came to mind. After digitally altering a photo of himself stored in his computer to test several different looks, he decided to shave his head bald. It completely changed his appearance. When the actual deed was done, he was more than satisfied with the results. There wasn't a chance in hell he would be recognized. In fact, just like the Cherie Tucker look-alike, by the time their vacation was over, he would have the agent and his family eating out of his hands.

After his shower, he donned a United States Immigration Officer's uniform he had ordered through Uniformswarehouse.com several weeks prior. Not only was he able to purchase an outfit identical to those worn by immigration officers, an official badge was also available. It never ceased to amaze Shem what you could acquire these days through the Internet.

The previous Sunday, the same day he framed Ken O'Brien for drug possession, he went to the Broward County Animal Shelter in search for a full grown German shepherd. There were three pure breed adults available. After careful observation of their demeanor and willingness to obey commands, he chose the youngest and what he thought to be most trainable of the three. For the past week, he had put the dog through an intense training program teaching him to follow simple and complex instructions.

At 5:30am, he placed the provisions bag in the back of the Ford Expedition and ordered the dog into the backseat. The German shepherd happily leaped into the car and obediently laid down behind the front passenger's seat. Before Shem got into the car, he admired the United States Immigration logo he had stenciled onto both sides of the vehicle.

It would take approximately fifteen minutes at this time of the morning to drive to Port Everglades from his apartment. He planned to wait in the employee parking lot until the Joy of the Seas was safely moored to the dock. As he approached the entrance to the port in his sports utility vehicle, he was excited to have his disguise tested for the first time. Port Authority officials verified the identification of each individual entering the property at their various checkpoints. He held up his badge and falsified immigration officer photo ID to the port agent seated in her booth. She instantly noticed the dog in the backseat and commented, "That's a beautiful animal you have there, Officer. Anything going on at the port I'm not aware of?"

"Well Ma'am, you might have heard last week an employee of one of the cruise lines was arrested for possession of heroin. We're concerned the cruise ships are being used for drug trafficking. This here's my best friend Lucy. She's gonna do some sniffing around this morning."

"As a matter of fact, I did hear about that. The DEA has been swarming around the port all week. And it's a good thing. There's no place in this world for drugs in my opinion."

"I agree Ma'am. Things are gettin' way outta hand. I'm trying to do my part."

"Thank you for that, Officer. You have a great day. You can go on through."

* * *

A handful of passengers, especially those staying in the higher end cabins and suites, sent their baggage to the ship in advance of the cruise date through a company known as Luggageforward. To get a head start on things, King Cruise Line's baggage handlers ran these bags through the X-ray scanner in the early morning shortly after the ship arrived on the first day of the cruise. Once they passed inspection, they were stacked outside the luggage cargo hold where later all bags were loaded onto the ship. Being quite familiar with these procedures, Shem expected this process would be completed by six thirty or shortly thereafter.

He was patiently waiting in the Port Authority employee garage for the appropriate moment to make his way to the pier. As the King Cruise Line website reported that morning, the Joy of the Seas was right on time. The ship had been docked for the past hour and forty minutes. He figured by the time he walked to the terminal with the dog then to the pier, the Luggageforward bags would already be X-rayed and arranged next to the cargo hold.

When he entered the registration warehouse, he was greeted by a member of the King Purser's staff. He held up his badge for her then said, "Good morning Ma'am. I'm Officer Steven Adams with the United States Immigration Department. Due to recent problems with drugs we've had here at the port, my K9 and I are going to do some looking around. I might have to board the ship."

"You guys are in charge here. Be my guest. If you do need to board the ship, there are security guards posted at the gangway. I'm sure you know the drill."

"Yes Ma'am. Thank you. Have a nice day." Shem had no intention of getting on the ship if everything went according to plan. It would only become necessary if his calculations were off regarding the Luggageforward bags. In that case, things could get complicated. There were times when bags were received more than a week in advance and stored in a special location in the cargo hold. He didn't want to have to make his way there from the inside.

After the sun rose, a light mist formed along the Intracoastal Waterway. Though visibility was somewhat inhibited, when Shem exited the building onto the dock, he was able to see that several hand carts of luggage were already situated in rows at the entrance to the cargo hold. The pier was essentially deserted, except for a few port employees who were performing some maintenance work on the dock. Shem ordered the dog to heal and headed in the direction of the baggage. The German shepherd obediently complied with every command barked by his new master without hesitation.

Arriving at the open hatch of the cargo hold, he found an area between hand carts where he would be out of sight of any potential onlookers. He checked the tags attached to the luggage on the carts to verify they were, in fact, being loaded for the upcoming cruise. Satisfied that these were the correct Luggageforward bags, he placed his suitcase/briefcase securely between two large bags then pulled a luggage ID tag from his pocket with his cabin information and tied it to the handle. He knew there was absolutely no chance the luggage handlers would open his bag. Not only was it securely locked, but to rummage through the personal property of a paying passenger was a firing offense. He was sure that when he entered his cabin as Isaac Jefferson, his suitcase would be waiting for him, untouched, on the luggage stand.

Certain no one saw him engaged in his clandestine act, he emerged from behind the hand carts and allowed the dog to sniff the immediate area. He didn't want to linger too long and chance a meeting with a true immigration officer. Normally, it took a maximum of an hour and a half to clear customs and immigration from the time the ship docked. There were times, however, when it took longer or an immigration officer would stay behind to socialize with crew members. It was now just past 7:00am. There was little chance he would run into an officer, but there was no reason to risk it. The maintenance workers had either finished their job or were taking a break, leaving the dock deserted of any pedestrian traffic. Shem saw it as his opportunity to pick up his pace walking quickly up the dock toward the entrance to the building.

After passing through the doors into the terminal, he slowed to a normal speed as he turned toward the exit to the parking lot. Having successfully completed his morning errands, he decided to treat himself to breakfast in Ft. Lauderdale. Eventually, he would return to his apartment to change into more appropriate clothes for cruising and grab his larger suitcase. A smug and sinister smile distorted his face as he pulled into the Denny's restaurant on Federal Highway just a mile or so from the port. He was excited to begin what he hoped would turn out to be a once in a lifetime vacation.

Chapter 17

The mood in the conference room of the FBI's Miami field office was almost celebratory. Robert Leland was leading an impromptu meeting he arranged late that morning. Most of the members of the special task force assigned to the unknown serial murderer were attending. The New York agents were participating via teleconferencing. The room was buzzing with the new information Agent Leland was sharing with the group.

Earlier in the morning, in preparation for the task force conference, Leland called Annie Bryan to schedule a meeting at her office for the purpose of reviewing Damien Drysdale's personnel file. The files of former employees were kept in a warehouse in western Broward County, in the city of Plantation. When Annie received the call from Leland briefly explaining Daniel's new theory, she immediately sent a courier to the storage facility to locate the file and take it to her office. Leland wasn't thrilled about sharing the information with her, but she was the only witness who could potentially identify Damien Drysdale as the suspect in the Hannah Richards surveillance tapes. He warned Annie that if she revealed the information to a soul, he wouldn't hesitate to arrest her for obstruction of justice. She would have liked to have gone over the file before she met with him, but it had not yet arrived. Normally, she would inspect it thoroughly before turning it over to a law enforcement agency. In this instance, she decided to share the contents of the file with Leland right away. She wasn't so concerned by his threat. King's lawyers would protect her from Leland. In any case, she had no intentions of revealing the information to anyone. She wanted him caught just as badly as Leland and his team and time was of the essence. The murderer could strike again at any moment. This was not an opportunity to play corporate games. If there was any information that could help catch the suspect, it needed to be turned over to the authorities immediately. Lives could potentially be at stake. She didn't want the next death on her conscience nor did she want to expose her company to any future liability.

Thinking back, Annie was able to call up a clear memory of Damien Drysdale. She remembered meeting him on several occasions on the Diamond. Though she thought nothing of it at the time, she had caught him staring at her quite often. She recalled getting the impression there was something odd about him, perhaps even creepy. Ultimately, she just dismissed his reticence and caginess as shyness. It wasn't an unusual occurrence for men to take notice of her. Examining the photograph of him in the employee file, a shiver ran down her spine. She was reminded of how attractive she found him the first time she saw him.

Leland brought the airport surveillance tapes to the meeting as Daniel suggested. Aware Leland was intending to show them to her, Annie arranged for a television and VCR to be set up in the conference room. This time, she instantly recognized the man dressed as a rabbi to be Damien Drysdale. What confirmed her identification was something that had been trying to break out of the prison of her subconscious since the first examination of the tapes. Armed with the knowledge of Daniel's new discovery, the second viewing jogged her memory that Drysdale had a habit of repeatedly clenching his right hand into a fist as did the suspect in the tapes. In her rush to a judgment that would benefit her company, she never really seriously considered Damien Drysdale was responsible for Paul Anderson's disappearance. Perhaps if she had, she could have made the connection much sooner. While everyone else would ultimately be celebrating her identification, Annie felt like crawling into a hole. She was horrified that her carelessness, along with the delay caused by her memory lapse could have already resulted in serious consequences.

Leland, on the other hand, was reveling in the affirmation of his original suspicions. There were some high fives in the room when he relayed the details of his meeting with Annie to the task force. He spouted off a series of commands, warning everyone there was still plenty of work to be done, though he was beaming with self pride. They were currently waiting for the VICAP and photo comparison results. Leland was hoping to get his true identity and address from either a passport or driver's license match. They also knew the suspect was quite proficient at falsifying identifications and in all probability it would take excellent detective work to locate him. Mancini didn't hesitate to remind the group they still didn't even know whether or not he was a citizen of the United States.

In search of clues about Drysdale's nationality, Leland asked Annie at their earlier meeting if the man spoke with an authentic South African accent. To the best of her recollection, she never got the impression it wasn't genuine. That certainly would have been something she would remember. If he was truly from South Africa, Leland's previous exhaustive research of their government's census records bore no fruit. He was able to find several name matches, though none of them fit the description of the suspect. Now that Annie was no longer willing to hide behind the work product privilege, she was more than happy to turn over his employee file and King's entire investigative report regarding Paul Anderson's disappearance.

Two agents on the task force had the exclusive responsibility of organizing and collating paperwork generated by the investigation. Leland handed them the King files and the tedious chore to ferret through them for any other helpful information. He assigned James Mancini to work at getting the South African police involved to make a real, concerted effort to locate Damien Drysdale. A more intense undertaking to determine if this identity was false was now absolutely necessary.

The last update Leland shared with the task force was information Annie provided to him later in the day when she had a chance to review their files and reflect more on the subject. She recalled that three other teenagers were lost overboard during the two years that Drysdale was on the Diamond. She indicated she would be faxing the investigative files for each of those disappearances later that afternoon. Leland was planning to review those reports, himself.

After the meeting dispersed and Leland returned to his office, he realized he forgot to call Daniel to advise him of the results of his meeting with Annie. He picked up his phone and dialed Daniel's cell phone number. The call went straight to voicemail. Leland left a detailed message figuring his cruise ship must have already set sail. He then forwarded a text message to Daniel with a copy of the picture of Damien Drysdale previously scanned and downloaded onto his computer.

* * *

The first full day of the cruise was a sea day. The Falcones and Tylers decided to have breakfast in the main dining room that morning rather than eat at the buffet. The women were already beginning to worry about their waistlines and were hoping to keep the buffet trips to a minimum. It was going to be hard work since it was open eighteen hours a day and food was available around the clock.

The men had plans after breakfast to take advantage of a promotional event at the ship's Sportsplex. A free, welcome aboard golf driving practice session was being offered by the cruise line and sign up was open for a competition later in the day. Deborah and her Mom had appointments for their complimentary spa treatments which were scheduled to last for a couple of hours. Daniel planned to check out the gym after he was through at the golf range. That would give Jack, who fancied himself as an amateur painter, a chance to check out the art auction that was supposed to take place at ten.

When they were through with breakfast, the girls headed back to their respective cabins to change for their appointment. The men went directly up to Deck 17 to put their names on the golf range waiting list and register for the afternoon event. Arriving at the Sportsplex, Jack and Daniel were surprised to see there were only two people in line ahead of them. Daniel recognized the man directly in front of him. He had been sitting alone, eating breakfast in the main dining room that morning. As they stood waiting their turn, the man introduced himself to Daniel and his father-in-law.

"Hi, I'm Isaac. Where you guys from?"

Daniel answered, "Nice to meet you, Isaac. I'm Daniel. This is my father-in-law, Jack." They shook hands. Isaac had to exercise some restraint to refrain from wincing in repulsion as he touched their sweaty palms. "We live in the area. How 'bout you? Where are you from?"

"Nice to meet you guys, too. I'm from Detroit… glad to be away from that mess. There's about a foot of snow piled up in my driveway as we speak. This is paradise. I wouldn't be hitting golf balls at home, that's for damn sure."

"I saw you in the dining room this morning," said Daniel. "You were alone. Are you here with anyone?"

Isaac was hoping to get to tell his story this morning. The agent was definitely observant. Isaac didn't expect anything less. Since they asked, Isaac figured he might as well take advantage. He responded, "Actually, I'm travelling by myself. Believe it or not, this was supposed to be my honeymoon. It's a little bit embarrassing. My fiancée left me at the altar."

Feeling a little uncomfortable and not knowing what to say, Daniel mumbled, "That's rough. Sorry to hear that."

"Yeah, it wasn't fun. I was seriously considering just stayin' home and feelin' sorry for myself. Then I thought, what the hell. Why waste a perfectly good cruise and the beautiful weather? So, here I am."

"That's the spirit, young man," said Jack. "The right woman is out there for you somewhere. You never know. Maybe right here on this cruise."

"I don't think I'm interested in starting a new relationship any time soon. I suppose this'll give me a chance to escape for a while, do a lot of thinking…just get my shit together."

"Good thinking," Jack replied. "I guess that was a stupid thing for me to say."

"Don't worry about it. It doesn't mean I'm not interested in checking out the women."

Jack asked, "What do you do for a living?"

"I'm a firefighter. I work for the Detroit Fire Department. You probably wouldn't know from looking at me. I'm planning to hit the gym while I'm on the ship. Really, I've always wanted to work in law enforcement. So, I need to get back in shape."

"That's cool. Good luck with that," said Daniel. Daniel intentionally left out that he was an FBI agent. It wasn't something he liked to share with strangers. "Maybe, I'll see you at the gym," he continued.

Just then, the crew member in charge of the driving range called for the next person in line. "It looks like I'm up," said Isaac. "It was great chatting with you guys. By the way, I'm on Deck, 9, Cabin 476. The last name's Jefferson. Feel free to give me a call when you're going to the gym. I wouldn't mind joining you."

"Sure thing. It was great meeting you," Daniel repeated though he was anything but sure he would be calling. "I'm holding you up. Have fun."

After his driving session with Jack and his workout, Daniel spent the remainder of the morning and afternoon at Deborah's side. They decided to sunbathe and observe the King sponsored games hosted by the Assistant Cruise Director at poolside. Daniel even participated in a trivia game that won him a cheap bottle of champagne. Once the games were over, they enjoyed the tunes of a steel drum band and drank Pina coladas. Then Deborah cheered him on at the driving competition. Despite his promise to not think about work, Daniel couldn't help wondering throughout the day about how things were going with the investigation. It was a good thing he didn't know the combination to the safe. He probably would have gotten himself in trouble attempting to sneak a peek at his messages.

* * *

Since his meeting with the agent, Shem, now assuming the name Isaac Jefferson spent most of the remainder of the day and evening in his cabin. The only time he left until recently was to avoid being seen by his housekeeping steward who visited the room twice a day. He had been sitting at a table for one at the Seafarer's Lounge for the past twenty minutes. The bar was packed to the gills for karaoke night. Shem never understood why anyone would think there was any entertainment value in such nonsense. At the moment, a middle-aged, overweight Asian woman was screeching "My Heart Will Go On," by Celine Dion. If he wasn't watching it with his own eyes, he would have thought it was a fucking goat bleating. The sound was grinding at his nerves so badly he would have gone up to the stage and torn her vocal chords out with his bare hands, if he could get away with it.

He elected to endure the insufferable show because he overheard the agent's wife saying they would be attending. He wasn't happy with his first encounter with the agent. Falcone didn't seem to take to him as well as he would have liked. He planned to try to meet the entire family here in hope of having more success getting on the women's good side. They were much more likely to have sympathy for Isaac Jefferson's story. As if the irritation of the show wasn't frustrating enough, the risk of bungling his mission was getting greater by the second. Still no one from the family had shown up.

Deciding he couldn't stand the revolting, off-key singing for another second when a fourteen-year-old, snot-nosed girl got up on stage to howl a Madonna song, he left the bar. Hindsight was always twenty-twenty but the more he thought about this effort, the clearer it became that parading through the ship's common areas was probably a risk he shouldn't have taken. He needed to keep his public appearances to a minimum. His best bet was to find a way to cross paths with the agent while visiting a port city. Tomorrow, they would be docked in Ocho Rios, Jamaica. A check of the King website revealed the agent and his family didn't schedule any of the official tours offered by the cruise line. He would make sure they ran into Isaac on the pier before they set off on a private land excursion.

* * *

The Joy of the Seas arrived in Ocho Rios at 6:00 sharp the following morning. By the time they cleared Customs and Immigration, it was just after seven. The temperature on the northeastern coast of Jamaica had already reached a sweltering eighty degrees, the humidity climbing over ninety percent. Large, billowy, snow white cumulus clouds seemed to soar into the stratosphere. The weatherman predicted a high in the mid-nineties by late afternoon. At 7:15 am, Isaac was sitting on a bench at the end of the pier eating an apple he had packed in his suitcase along with other energy and protein-packed perishables necessary for his nourishment for the week. He would sit on the bench as long as it took for the Falcones to pass.

Approximately an hour later, Isaac saw the agent and his family strolling down the pier dressed in shorts and matching King Cruise Line tank tops. Sitting in the hot sun, perspiration had already soaked through Isaac's t-shirt. He changed into a fresh tank top from his back pack then began to flip through several brochures he collected earlier in the morning. His goal was to appear as though he was planning his day in Ocho Rios. Daniel noticed him fumbling with his reading materials and considered ignoring him when Jack called out, "Hey there, Isaac. How you doin' this morning? I don't think you've met my wife Kate and my daughter, Deborah."

Isaac reluctantly extended his hand and said, "Pleased to meet you ladies. I'm hangin' in there. I'm tryin' to decide what I'm gonna do today. I originally had a bunch of excursions reserved for me and Brynn. That was my fiancée's name. I went ahead and cancelled them. Then I figured why sit on the ship and mope. So, now, I'm just winging it."

As Isaac had hoped, Deborah was touched by his alleged misfortune having heard the story from her father. She was happy to extend Isaac an invitation. "You know, we're gonna take a taxi up to the Dunn's River Falls and climb the rocks," she said. "We'd love it if you'd join us."

Daniel tried not to show his disapproval. It wasn't that he didn't like the guy. There was just something about him that made him feel uneasy. Isaac replied, "That's nice of you to offer. I couldn't impose."

Daniel was about to let the man have his way, but was foiled once again when his father-in-law beat him to the punch. "Nonsense," Jack said. "You're more than welcome to come with us."

Deborah and Kate shook their heads in agreement. Deborah added, "We're not gonna take no for an answer."

"Well, if that's the case, I guess I have no choice. Actually, I've always wanted to go there. I was just worried I wasn't gonna be able to get my fat ass up those rocks."

"You're exaggerating young man," argued Kate. "If this old lady can do it, so can you."

"Part of the problem is I injured my knee at the gym yesterday. Sorry, Daniel, I don't think I'm gonna be able to work out for the rest of the cruise. Anyway, thanks for the invitation to the falls. I wasn't really looking forward to spending the day alone."

"And there's no reason why you should," said Daniel finally deciding to concede he was outnumbered and join in on the invitation. "No worries about the gym. Take care of that knee. You'll need it. You sure you'll be alright climbing the rocks?"

"It shouldn't be a problem so long as I take it slowly."

"Great, then let's get our asses moving and see about hiring one of those passenger vans."

Jack chimed in, "Now you gotta negotiate with those guys. Don't accept the first price they offer you. Let me do the talking."

"You're the business man, Jack. Be my guest," Daniel replied.

The group of five walked over to the Port Authority welcoming facility. A boisterous and chaotic mob of taxi drivers were gathered vying for the business of the multitudes of passengers disembarking from the various cruise ships. Daniel was assaulted by a group of five drivers when a woman in a uniform came up to advise them she was the official negotiator. Jack was able to settle on a price of eight dollars apiece for a round trip ticket to their destination.

The mouth of the river leading up to the falls turned out to be just a ten minute drive from the port. The van driver dropped them off in a large parking lot crowded with buses, vans, taxis, and swarms of tourists from around the world. It was just a short walk to the park entrance where Isaac pretended to be flustered by a large sign forbidding guests to climb the rocks without a pair of sneakers or special slip-free shoes which could be rented or purchased at the souvenir store. He was well aware of the regulations having visited this island many times on the Diamond. The Falcones and Tylers were well-prepared. They had worn tennis shoes in anticipation of the climb. Isaac, on the other hand, was forced to buy a pair of treaded, rubberized slippers, having worn flip flops. After he made his purchase, together, the group descended the more than one hundred steps to the base of the falls. Jack and Kate, acknowledging that Deborah and Daniel were much more agile and athletic than the rest of the group, suggested they go ahead. After the couple's polite rejection, Isaac, trying to score brownie points, convinced them to comply with their parent's recommendation. He promised he would do his best to take care of Kate and Jack.

Once again fate flexed its bulging Hulk-size bicep and chose the side of evil. For, if Deborah and Daniel had stayed with the group, Shem Chassar would be the one waiting in a death row cell for a lethal injection to end his life and Deborah and her parents would still be alive today. Daniel and Deborah started up the rocks holding the hands of the people in front of and behind them as was the tradition for climbing Dunn's River Falls. Within minutes, they were twenty to thirty yards ahead of Isaac and their parents. As Isaac was about to take his first step up the Falls, he heard a voice vigorously calling from behind.

"Damien. Damien Drysdale, is that you?"

He froze in his tracks. He did his best to ignore the person calling out his former alias, but she persisted. She continued to shout out the name at what felt to him at the volume of a loud speaker. King Cruise Line security officer Terry Smithson then ran up behind him and tapped him on the shoulder, forcing him to turn around.

"Damien, why are you ignoring me? It's me Terry, from the Diamond. What are you doing here? Do you work for one of the other cruise lines now?"

"Excuse me, but I'm not the person you're looking for. I'm not Damien. My name is Isaac."

"Oh come on. Don't bullshit me. You jokin' or what?"

"No, I'm very serious. You made a mistake."

Confused, Terry hesitated a moment and studied Isaac's face. There wasn't much of a doubt this guy could pass for Damien Drysdale's twin. There were some obvious differences including his weight, however, there was no mistaking his face and especially those eyes. Embarrassed, though still unsure, she continued, "I'm sorry, but you're the spitting image of a guy I used to work with on a cruise ship in Europe. He was from South Africa, though." Terry was beginning to doubt herself more, especially because of the degree the guy was out of shape. She remembered Drysdale was obsessive when it came to taking care of his body.

"I'm American. And my name's not Damien. I've never even been to South Africa."

"Yeah, come to think of it, Damien had hair, too. I'm sorry to bother you."

"Don't worry about it. It was an honest mistake." Terry finally admitted defeat and walked off onto the beach to join the other Joy of the Seas crew members who were climbing the falls with her. Isaac was furious. He couldn't believe she saw through his disguise. In a state of bewilderment as to how he could have possibly missed her name on the employee roster, he considered fleeing. Then suddenly, he realized the agent might have overheard her calling his former alias. He looked up to see that the couple was now more than fifty yards ahead and hadn't slowed in their ascent. It was obvious they were too far away to hear Terry Smithson especially considering the bluster of the falls. He wasn't even sure whether the agent was familiar with his alias, but it had to be a part of the FBI's Anderson file. The fact that the agent didn't turn back gave Isaac confidence that the name Drysdale was neither heard nor recognized.

Shem's thoughts and analysis of the situation continued in overdrive. He considered the possibility that the in-laws could repeat the story to the agent. He was hoping if they were so inclined, perhaps they would forget the name. He couldn't rely on that, but wasn't willing to give up on his mission so easily, either. The instinct to run was more present than he would have preferred. Normally, he trusted his feelings. A conversation with the parents was in order.

"That was bizarre," commented Isaac. "I guess it can happen though. I've been told that I have a familiar face."

"Yeah, it's happened to me before, too," said Jack. "They say we all have someone who could be our twin somewhere in the world. I guess that guy was yours."

Isaac settled a bit thinking Jack's failure to mention the name was a good sign. He would stick with the mission for the moment. He replied, "I guess. What do you say we try to conquer these rocks?"

"After you, sir," said Kate.

Isaac did his best to squelch his fury and anxiety. He continued to evaluate his options rationalizing there would be no reason for the old folks to repeat the story. It wasn't that interesting. Though he wasn't a gambling man, especially when the stakes were so high, he reaffirmed his decision to play the odds and began his ascent up the falls.

Regardless of his efforts, his mind continued to work unrelentingly. If Terry was on the Joy of the Seas, he would have to make sure he didn't run into her again. His plan to stay away from public places on the ship was now, more than ever, absolutely critical. Yet, the more he thought about it, his good sense prevailed warning him it might not be enough. He would have to give the matter more thought. When he got back to his cabin, he would figure a way out of this mess.

* * *

Isaac was almost convinced his beliefs concerning fate were wrong. He was feeling truly favored by the Gods as he surfed the Internet on his laptop computer. The parents never said a word about the incident that occurred at the bottom of the falls. It had to be more than pure-luck that his ex-colleague didn't call his former alias out just five minutes earlier. If that had been the case, there was the distinct chance he would have been forced to run for his life. In the shape he was in, he didn't think he would have made it very far. Instead of his plan going up in smoke, things were progressing as smoothly as ever.

After the excursion at the falls, the agent and his family invited him to lunch with them in Ocho Rios. During the meal, they insisted he come to their cabin after dinner to play a game of dominoes. He ended up spending the entire evening at their suite. It was more than probable he was working his way in. It wasn't easy for him to be in the company of people for extended periods of time, nor was he used to it. His feelings would have to take a backseat, especially in light of the fact he couldn't have hoped for a better result. The women seemed to be treating him like a part of the family.

Finally returning to his cabin after midnight, he took the opportunity to do some serious thinking about his ex-colleague, anything that would help formulate an airtight plan to rid of the nuisance. He remembered she had an obsession with cave diving. She used to go on obnoxiously incessant about it. He had made the mistake of telling her he was a certified cave diver. Subsequently, every time the Diamond sailed the Western Caribbean, she would ask him to accompany her to the underwater caves of Atkun Chen. He wasn't aware of a time when she missed an opportunity to visit the sub-aquatic world of the Mexican caverns.

The first order of business after he returned to his cabin was to determine how he failed to notice her name on the employee roster. The explanation became clear once he hacked his way onto the King website. He discovered this was her first week on the Joy of the Seas, having been transferred from the Diamond the previous Sunday. His digging further revealed that the Diamond was currently sailing the Eastern Caribbean. It had just repositioned from Europe. After searching through her contract history, he calculated she had not been assigned to a ship that stopped in Cozumel or Cancun for at least a year and a half. It was a sure bet she would be visiting Atkun Chen the very next day. The Joy of the Seas would be in port for more than twelve hours and her computer schedule reflected she had the day off.

Isaac was so confident in his prediction that as soon as the ship was cleared for disembarkation at Cozumel the following morning, he headed down to the port and hailed a water taxi to the mainland. He was dropped off at Playa del Carmen where he was swamped by a flock of taxi drivers. He negotiated a fare for the forty five kilometer trip to Atkun Chen with a young driver willing to charge a forty dollar fee to lease his services for the day. Before leaving Playa del Carmen, he had the driver wait for him while he purchased some provisions at the local shopping center.

Atkun Chen was actually the name of an underground river located just sixteen kilometers north of the ruins of Tulum, on the east coast of the Yucatan Peninsula. The caves and river were part of Atkun Chen National Park which covered almost one thousand acres of unexplored rainforest. The fee for entering the park was twenty two dollars with an additional ninety nine dollar charge for the rental of diving equipment. He arrived at the park at 9:00am, paid for his entrance tickets and scuba gear rental, sat at a café twenty yards inside the park entrance and waited.

Three hours later, when she still hadn't shown up, doubt began to creep in. The ship was scheduled to set sail at 7:00pm which meant the passengers and crew were required to be onboard no later than 6:30. The taxi ride back to Playa del Carmen and ferry ride to Cozumel would take a minimum of an hour and a half. Doing the math, he would have to leave the park no later than five o'clock in order to be back at the ship in time. Even that would be cutting it close. To truly take advantage of the stunning scenery of the three caverns and underground rivers, a diver would need a minimum of three hours. If she didn't arrive within the next couple of hours, he would have to consider not returning to the ship.

Almost willing it to happen, refusing to believe he would have to abandon his mission, all of his fears and tension were resolved when, at 12:30, Terry Smithson came rushing from the parking lot to the ticket booth to pay her admission fee. Isaac quickly gathered his scuba equipment and provisions bag and followed the signs to the diving area. The path led down a steep, rocky descent into a dense wooded area. At the foot of the precipice, a spectacular crystalline, blue-green, fresh water sinkhole known as a cenote flowed into a six-hundred meter grotto. As sure-footed and balanced as a mountain goat, he approached the cavern where a tour group of divers gathered at its entrance. They were receiving instructions from the tour guide.

Isaac ducked behind the trunk of a tall, Florida Strangler Fig tree and slipped into his diving suit. He removed a large, jagged-edged fishing knife and sheath from his provisions bag and attached it to his belt. Once his scuba tank was firmly secured on his back, he placed his mask and flippers under his arm and walked toward the tour group. The ticket he purchased included the guided tour allowing him to take his place amongst the divers. Within minutes, his former colleague arrived at the entrance of the cavern, carrying the heavy equipment, out of breath from having run the entire distance from the ticket booth. She apologized for being late and handed the tour guide her admission stub. Isaac slipped his mask over his head and onto his face so that she wouldn't recognize him.

The group was forced to wait while Terry got into her suit and adjusted her scuba equipment. As she put on the last pieces of the ensemble, the guide addressed the group.

"Good afternoon, everyone. My name is Fernando. I will be your tour guide for this cave dive. Before we begin, I want to go over a few safety rules. First, and foremost, you must never venture away from the group. Nunca. I will be leading you to the most incredible underwater sights in the cavern. You will not find anything more interesting than what I will show you.

Second, the underwater currents can be quite strong and therefore very dangerous, muy peligroso. Do not swim below the level of the rest of the group. I am very familiar with the currents and will be sure never to dive below a safe depth.

I know you are all experienced divers, pero por favor, be careful to ascend slowly when we return from the more significant depths. We don't want any cases of the bends. Es muy doloroso, very painful. Do not be concerned about any dangerous fish. All the fish you will encounter in the crystal clear waters of Atkun Chen will be friendly and safe, seguro.

It can be quite dark in many of the areas that you will be visiting, so please keep your flashlights handy. I will have a large fluorescent green flashlight attached to my belt so you will know where I am at all times. There will be a time when I have everyone shut off their flashlights to demonstrate how blinding the blackness of the cenote can be. Ten cuidado, es muy oscuro. Be very careful, you will not be able to see. It will only be for twenty or thirty seconds, so please do not be frightened. If you have a problem with this portion of the tour, please let me know before we dive. If anyone has any questions, now is the time to speak. Have a great dive and be careful. Gracias. Vamos."

Everyone was anxious to get the dive started. No one had any questions. Fernando led them downward hundreds of feet below the surface then through the entrance of a breathtaking limestone cavern. Thousands of stalagmites and stalactites of all sizes, shapes and colors jutted from the ground and ceiling. Roots from the trees above broke through the roof of the cave creating a dramatic scene that resembled an endless curtain of elongated Tarzan swinging vines.

Fernando continued to the edge of the cenote and described the formation in which the divers would swim. He would take the lead followed by the divers in two rows of three abreast with one person bringing up the rear. Isaac volunteered to take the aft position. Fernando assigned the rest of the group their places in the formation. The divers then jumped into the sinkhole in the order designated.

For the first half hour of the dive, even Isaac enjoyed the unparalleled beauty of the underground river. The previous night, he did some research about Atkun Chen and the other cenotes of the Mayan Riviera. He discovered that the ancient Mayans thought of these sinkholes as sacred, being their only source of fresh water. They used them as a medium to communicate with their Gods who lived in the Underworld. It was even said they would make human sacrifices to appease their Deity of the Water during a period of drought.

An hour into the tour, Fernando led the divers to an area deep under the water's surface where the rock formed a small open-ended chamber. It was in this area the tour guide planned to demonstrate the stark obscurity of the water. Isaac maneuvered himself so that he would be next to his former colleague. Fernando motioned to the group with his flashlight that he would now be turning it off and they should do the same. For the next thirty seconds, the group was immersed in a black vacuum of nothingness.

Isaac's moment had arrived. He grabbed Terry Smithson around her arms and chest and pulled her with great force out of the chamber down to a depth of which Fernando would not have approved. A shocked and horrified Terry tried with all the strength she could muster to break her attacker's grip to no avail. When he felt he had reached a distance that would be outside the range of the tour guide's flashlight, in his trademark, lightning quick motion, he released the grip of one hand, pulled the knife out of its sheath and slit her throat. Within seconds, Terry Smithson's body went limp. He kept his grip with the one arm and swam as fast as his legs would allow away from the tour group and back in the direction of the original dive site. He continued to swim until he felt it was safe to turn his flashlight back on. By the time Fernando completed the darkness exhibition, Isaac and the half-dead Terry Smithson were well out of view.

The current was flowing in such a direction that Fernando and his group never witnessed the blood cascading out of Terry Smithson's slashed carotid artery. When the tour guide realized two of his charges were missing, he began to search the immediate vicinity for the next five minutes. They were nowhere to be found. Agitated they would have violated the most important rule and knowing he still had five other divers to worry about, he decided to continue the tour and let the cabrones fend for themselves.

In the meantime, Isaac continued to dive as deep as he dared until he was sure the woman was dead. Since he removed her mouthpiece more than five minutes before, he figured if she hadn't already bled to death, she had surely drowned. He released the body and closed off her tank so that no more oxygen would be discharged and the apparatus would maintain its weight. The body slowly sank deeper into the black water. He laughed to himself as he wondered if the Mayan God of water would be satisfied with his offering.

Chapter 18

Chief security officer Ted Hauser was having one of the worst weeks of his professional career. It all started when one of his best security officers was fired for possession of narcotics. He knew Ken O'Brien for many years and never would have taken him for a junkie. But, Ted had lived long enough to know that people had plenty of skeletons in their closet. He hoped everything worked out for Ken, though he figured he was going to be spending a long time behind bars.

To make matters worse, at the beginning of the next cruise, the entire surveillance system on the Joy of the Seas went haywire. They weren't able to get their cameras and monitors to work since the first Sunday of the cruise. He wasn't getting much cooperation from headquarters in Ft. Lauderdale, either. The head honchos weren't responding very quickly to his many requests to resolve the situation.

The final straw was the disappearance of the security officer who replaced Ken O'Brien. No one had seen her since she got off the ship in Cozumel. He was most concerned about this issue. From everything Hauser had heard about Smithson, she was a very loyal and responsible employee. Certainly, it wasn't an unheard of occurrence for crew members to quit without warning. Still, he couldn't imagine Terry taking that route. Just the other day, she was raving about how happy she was to be working on the Joy of the Seas because some of her best friends were on the ship. He called her mother in Sydney, Australia to determine if she had any contact with her daughter. All he managed to do was cause her to agonize. The authorities in Cozumel were also contacted about Terry's disappearance. They were no help since it was too early to start a missing person's investigation.

If she didn't turn up by the end of the week, he would have King Cruise Line initiate an internal investigation. The circumstances surrounding her disappearance were just too suspicious. He considered calling Annie Bryan about the problem then thought better of it. If Smithson did end up missing for more than twenty-four hours, it would be best not to stir the pot until after the Mexican police conducted at least a rudimentary search of the hospitals.

Now, if he could just figure out what was going on with the damn surveillance system. His maintenance people were telling him there was some type of computer glitch or virus causing the problem. No one on the ship had the skill or knowledge necessary to repair the malfunction. Ted asked his supervisor to fly someone from Information Technology to one of the Joy of the Sea's next ports to try to take care of the problem. Not surprisingly, headquarters didn't want to spend the money. His boss's idea of a resolution was to wait until they were back in port in Ft. Lauderdale.

Ted supposed it was rare for crimes to be committed onboard and most likely delaying the repairs wouldn't have any grave consequences. However, the surveillance system was also used just as much to keep an eye on the crew as it was the passengers. If headquarters was willing to wait until Sunday, he decided he shouldn't worry himself into an ulcer about it. He did his part. If anything went wrong, his ass was covered.

* * *

It was approaching the end of the cruise and although Deborah and Daniel missed their children, they had gotten used to being in exotic paradises and treated like royalty. Seven days seemed short even to Daniel. They both wished they had a few more days before they had to rejoin the rat race. By the middle of the week, Daniel had surprised himself that he had actually done a decent job finally putting the investigation out of his head. A break from work had not been so bad after all. The fifth day of the cruise provided that much more incentive for delaying their return.

That Friday night, after an incredible meal he and Deborah shared alone at one of the specialty restaurants on the ship, they returned to their suite to retire for the evening. Daniel was beginning to doubt Deborah was going to ask him to move back into the condo. The truth of the matter was she had been quite distant and hesitant from a physical standpoint. He hoped he hadn't blown it with his idiot move to make a call to the office. As he prepared for bed, he was thinking hope was all but lost. There were only two nights left before he had to go back to his depressing studio apartment. Just when he thought this night was just about over; Deborah called out from the bathroom.

"What an amazing cruise it's been," she said as she slipped into a sexy, black negligee without revealing herself to Daniel.

"It's not over, yet," he protested. "Don't rush things. I'm not ready..." Daniel stopped speaking midsentence. His wife was approaching him in a see-through teddy that gave him an instant erection. It had been quite a while since he was in the same room with a half-naked woman. Deborah inquired, "Cat got your tongue?"

"You look amazing, honey. I lost concentration." He began to move toward her but she raised her index finger and waved it back and forth signaling him to stop.

"Before we get to that, I have something to say... Here goes. It's been months since we were separated. For most of that time, I was a mess. No doubt, the worst time of my life. I don't mean to put a damper on the amazing time we've had, but I was very close to hiring a lawyer to file for divorce. Luckily, I didn't rush into anything. I can honestly say it would've been a big mistake. We're all human. We all make mistakes. Granted, yours was a huge one. But, I love you, Daniel. Over the past few months you've made me realize you really do love me too. Sometimes you have a strange way of showing it. But, I know I mean a lot to you. Believe it or not, I just made this decision today. I've been on the fence about it. I think we're worth another try. I want you to come home when the cruise is over."

This time, instead of motioning with her index finger to stop, she used it to gesture for him to come to her. He swept her up off her feet and gently laid her on the bed. In a matter of seconds, he stripped them both naked. For the next three hours they made intense, passionate love like never before. In the first years of their relationship, their sex was always above average. For both of them, it felt like the first time again. After an hour and a half and an intense orgasm, Daniel rolled over on his back in total exhaustion only to find that Deborah wasn't finished. She climbed on top of him and they made love for a second and final time.

* * *

The following morning, Daniel was woken by the intercom public address announcement of a training drill for crew members. He looked at his watch and saw they had slept in on the last full day of the cruise. The memories of the reason why they were still in bed quashed any ill feeling he may have developed by missing the morning's festivities. Both the Falcones and the Tylers decided they would relax this final day away. After they finished a late breakfast, Daniel and Deborah decided to lounge at the public pool on the Lido deck rather than take advantage of the suite's private pool. They made a quick run to their cabin to change into their bathing suits, grab some towels and the books they were reading then made their way to the elevators. While waiting for the next one to arrive, they ran into Isaac who was descending the stairs with a plate of food apparently from the buffet. In fact, it was a couple of pieces of fruit he had brought along with him in his suitcase. His appearance wasn't accidental.

Daniel said, "Hey Isaac. Where have you been? We haven't seen you in a few days."

"Yeah, sorry about that. I haven't been feeling that great. Not that I'm sick or anything. I've been thinking a lot about Brynn."

"I'm so sorry, Isaac," said Deborah. "One of the worse things you can possibly do is be alone when you're feeling that way. Why don't you join us at the pool? We're just gonna relax, read and people watch."

"I don't think I feel up to being around that many people. I'm gonna pass."

"Are you sure? This is the last day of the cruise, Isaac."

"I can't handle it, really. I'm not gonna just stay in my cabin though. I'm thinking about going to the library and reading a book. It'll be nice and quiet and it'll take my mind off things."

"Well I have a great idea," Deborah replied.

"Tonight, we're having our final championship game of dominoes in our suite. Daniel's been winning way too many games. We want to take him down tonight. It's just the four of us. You should come. Maybe you can help us knock him down a notch or two."

"I feel like I'm imposing. I don't want to be a burden."

"Don't be silly. We'd love to have you. The more the merrier when it comes to dominoes. Right, Daniel?"

"Yeah, right. It would be great to have you. You should definitely join us," said Daniel in a much less convincing manner than his wife as far as Isaac was concerned. Not that it mattered. He was definitely going to accept their invitation.

"Well, if you're sure. I guess I shouldn't be alone on the last night of the cruise. Thanks again for how good you guys have been to me. I really appreciate it. What time is the game?"

"We're gonna have dinner then see the early farewell show at the theatre. We should be back at the suite a little bit after nine. Why don't you come by at 9:15," said Deborah.

"Sounds like a plan. I'll be there. Get ready to be crushed, Daniel."

"Them's fightin' words, Isaac. Bring it on."

* * *

In the miniature shower stall of his cabin, Isaac shaved his body from head to toe, making sure every last trace of hair was flushed down the drain. He had been going through this process at least twice a day, every day for the past two weeks, so that any hair that he removed from his body would be too small to collect. Each time afterwards, he would inspect the floors and walls of the shower and bathroom with a magnifying glass to be absolutely certain he didn't miss a stray hair. That was a mistake he never intended to make again.

Just before he left the cabin for the game of dominoes, he took his third long, hot shower of the evening. He dressed in a pair of jeans and an NYPD T-shirt then checked and double-checked his bag of provisions. Satisfied he didn't forget anything, he pulled out his laptop computer to confirm the virus he planted in the ship's video surveillance program was still doing its job. He was sure the dumbasses on the ship would never be able to figure out how to repair the problem, but it didn't hurt to verify it every time he left the cabin. Noting the system was still down; he snatched his bag from the floor of the closet, exited the cabin and made his way to the agent's suite.

Deborah answered the door when he arrived. "Hey there, Isaac. How was your day? I hope you're feeling better."

"Much better, actually. I've really been looking forward to the game tonight."

"You brought something with you. What's the bag for?"

"Every game of dominoes so far, I've come empty-handed. They delivered the alcohol I ordered last week, so I thought I'd make you guys my specialty tropical drink. I thought it was the least I could do."

"You know it wasn't necessary. All the alcohol is free in this suite. Why don't you save it for yourself? I'll put it in the kitchen for you and you can just take it back later."

"I'd really like to do something for you guys. It's a one of a kind drink. It's an old family recipe passed down from generation to generation. Once you try it, you'll never forget it. I insist."

"Alright, if you insist. That's very sweet of you. It sounds delicious. Let me take it. Does it need to stay cold?"

"No, it'll be fine at room temperature. But, it's kinda heavy. I'll carry it. Just show me where to put it."

"Ok, follow me. You can put it in the pantry. Everyone's anxious to get the game started."

He placed his bag on the floor of the pantry then he and Deborah joined the others on the courtyard balcony. A card table was set up with five folding chairs surrounding it. Daniel and his in-laws greeted him as Isaac took his place between Deborah and Kate. The warm, heavy, humid sea air immediately struck Isaac when he passed through the sliding glass doors. As he took his seat, he thought it was a good thing perspiration couldn't be collected for DNA evidence. It was going to be a hot night and he had a lot of work to do.

The game of Mexican Train dominoes had the potential to last for several hours. For the first hour, Isaac played along with the farce. The group of five engaged in some trash talk and munched on snacks they ordered from room service. Isaac's keen sense of smell allowed him to detect the distinct body odor of each person permeating the air around him. The smell of perspiration invariably reminded him of his countless sweaty sexual encounters with his mother's johns and had the effect of heightening his animalistic sense of aggression. As the banter continued between the Falcones and Tylers and the game wore on, Isaac had to make a conscious effort to bide his time.

At the half-way point, Daniel had a substantial lead. Deborah was so disgusted with her husband's good fortune, she complained, "How the hell are you so lucky every single time, Daniel?"

"It's not luck, it's skill."

"Oh, bullshit," said Jack. "You've been getting the perfect dominoes every round. There's no strategy to this game."

"See, that's exactly why you never win. There is a method to my madness."

"Alright, alright people," Kate interjected. "I think now would be a great time to take a break."

"That's a great idea," Deborah responded. "Isaac, why don't you make those special drinks of yours? I could use one just about now."

"Sure thing. You guys sit and enjoy the beautiful night. I'll go fix them. I'll be right back."

"The glasses are in the cupboard to the right of the sink. You sure you don't need any help?" asked Deborah.

"I'll be fine. I want to do this for you guys. It'll just take a few minutes."

Isaac entered the suite through the sliding glass doors. The cool of the cabin's air conditioning was an instant relief. He made his way to the kitchen, carefully listening to be sure no one followed him inside. Hearing the constant, animated repartee on the courtyard, he went directly to the pantry and zipped open his provisions bag. Inside were a bottle of Cruzan Coconut rum, a tropical mixer he had laced with a strong tranquilizer, a .357 Magnum with silencer, a butcher's cleaver, a surgeon's saw, a scalpel, two syringes, several pairs of rubber gloves, a cigarette lighter, and the remaining fifty grams of heroin.

He removed the bottle of alcohol and the plastic jug containing the mixer and placed them on the kitchen counter. The excitement he derived from the execution of the final stages of a plan was at the point of escalating. He had to remind himself the job was far from over, that he must keep cool, calm and collected. His mind had to be razor-sharp dealing with a highly-trained law enforcement agent. He reached up into the cabinet, pulled out four high-ball glasses and placed them next to the alcohol and mixer. He poured a generous portion of the drugged mixer into each glass then added a shot of Cruzan Coconut rum. The date-rape type tranquilizer he chose quickly metabolized and seldom showed up in blood testing after twelve hours. If everything went according to plan, their blood wouldn't be drawn until sometime late the following afternoon at the earliest, when they were turned over to the medical examiner.

When each of the drinks was properly mixed, he placed them on a tray and carried them out onto the courtyard. The family was still engaged in a playful exchange of insults. As he placed the drinks on the table, he said, "I hope you enjoy."

"I'm sure it'll be delicious. Tropical drinks are our favorite," commented Kate. "But where's yours?"

"I can't drink. I'm a diabetic. I bought the alcohol to say thanks to you guys and to bring a couple of bottles home for some friends."

"That's so sweet of you, Isaac. It's a shame you can't enjoy it with us. I know alcohol is an absolute no-no for diabetics," said Deborah.

"Don't worry about me. You guys enjoy. Drink up."

The Falcones and Tylers raised their glasses and toasted to better times for Isaac. They took their first sip from the glass and politely complimented him for his delicious family recipe despite the noticeable bitter under-taste. They chatted about the great times they had on the cruise while they downed their drinks. Isaac estimated it would take about fifteen minutes for the tranquilizer to take effect after drinking a minimum of half of the glass. By the time the game resumed, they were beginning to show signs of sedation. Their speech was slowed and slurred and Kate was having difficulty keeping her eyes open. They joked with Isaac that his recipe must have called for a heavy hand with the liquor.

Before the next round of dominoes was complete, Deborah and Kate had slumped over the table. Jack was barely conscious, but Daniel, being the biggest and heaviest of the group, was aware and alert enough to see his wife and mother-in-law had passed out. In his concern for them, he attempted to stand up to render assistance, stumbled, lost his balance and fell to the ground in a semi-conscious state. Shem had to control himself to keep from kicking the agent in the face.

Apparent they weren't going anywhere any time soon, he went to the kitchen to retrieve his provisions bag. He removed the syringe and bag of heroin and measured out what he estimated to be one-hundred-fifty milligrams. After mixing the drug with water in a tablespoon, he heated it from underneath with the cigarette lighter. The drug melted into liquid form in a matter of seconds. He filled the syringe, went back out to the courtyard, tied Daniel's upper arm with the sleeve of a shirt he found in the bedroom and injected the heroin into his radial vein. He hummed Cool and the Gang's "Celebration" as he went back to the kitchen to retrieve the cleaver, gun and surgeon's saw.

The order of the killings was decided weeks ago. The least satisfying would be the bullet to the father-in-law's head, so he would be first. The mother-in-law would be next and he would save the wife for last. He pulled the bodies one by one into the suite starting with the agent. Once everyone was inside and exactly where he wanted them, he stripped Daniel of his clothing. Shem then removed his own shirt, slacks and shoes, set them aside in the bedroom and put on Daniel's clothes.

Before grabbing the .357 Magnum with the silencer already attached from the bag, he slipped on a pair of rubber gloves. He picked up the gun, pointed it at the father-in-law who was lying on his back closest to the sliding glass doors, placed the end of the barrel of the silencer just five inches from the center of his forehead and fired three times in rapid succession. Jack's body jolted spasmodically as the bullets penetrated his cerebellum. Bits of brain matter and blood splashed in all directions covering the sliding glass doors, the wall, Daniel's pants at shin level, his shoes and the carpet underneath the old man's head. Holding the fingers of Daniel's left hand, he molded them around the pistol's handle and trigger and fired the gun out the open sliding glass doors a fourth and final time.

The butcher's cleaver he chose for the mother-in-law was of the highest quality. To maintain the edge, he had honed it every day since he purchased it. He carefully pulled it out of its protective sheath. The mother-in-law was lying right next to her husband in a supine position. Shem stepped over the corpse and knelt over the unconscious woman. With his left hand, he grabbed her hair and pulled the head up and back to expose her neck. He raised his right hand, which was holding the cleaver, as high as he could reach and with brute force swung down across her throat cutting through the flesh all the way to the spine. Blood spurted across the room dousing the far wall with spatters of red gore. He stood over her, in front of the fountain of blood, so it would drench Daniel's shirt and slacks. The sensation of warm blood against his skin sent a bolt of pure ecstasy through his body. When the bleeding slowed, he returned to Daniel and placed the cleaver in his right hand.

Shem intended to take his time to sculpt his next piece of artwork. He wanted it to last as long as possible, though the first step of the process would be extremely unpleasant. When he first devised this part of the plan, he wasn't sure he could go through with it. In the end, he decided it would be an essential factor in determining guilt in the agent's trial and couldn't pass up on at least giving it a shot.

Heroin was a well known enhancer of sexual performance. It was one of the several reasons why he chose to inject the agent with the drug. He wasn't one hundred percent sure it was going to work, but his research on the Internet led him to conclude it was certainly possible. As he prepared to perform the act, he took a few deep breaths to control the sickness in his stomach. It would destroy everything for him to vomit and leave evidence of his DNA on the scene. He walked over to the agent who was lying on his back then put his hand around the agent's penis and began to slowly masturbate it. Sour bile rose into his throat, though he was able to stifle his gag reflex. To his pleasant, yet at the same time, repulsed surprise, it began to stiffen. He increased the speed of the stroking and within seconds, the agent's penis was fully erect. In spite of his tiring arm, he continued the motion for several more minutes when finally he was gifted the fruit of his labors.

He was both pleased and infuriated at the amount of semen produced. It was too much of a reminder of his own sexual inadequacies and inability to ejaculate. Petulance seethed from deep within threatening to burst to the surface at the recollection of the mocking he endured as an adolescent and young adult. The shame came flooding back as if it were just yesterday he suffered the embarrassment caused when his mother, her johns and prostitutes he hired laughed in his face at his inability to produce a drop of semen. At that moment, he wanted the agent dead. If a cooler head had not prevailed, he would have castrated him. He took a few minutes to calm down, convincing himself the agent was going to suffer a fate much worse than death.

Shem's next task wouldn't be any more pleasant. He removed the second syringe from the bag and filled it with the agent's ejaculate. The agent's wife was lying in a prone position in a pool of blood beside her dead mother. He turned Deborah over, ignoring the blood that covered the entire front of her body, unzipped her pants and pulled them and her panties down below her knees. After injecting most of the syringe full of semen into her vagina, he splashed a few drops on the surface of her labia.

At that point, he was ready for what he expected to be the most exhilarating part of the evening. He would have preferred to wait for the wife to wake up to mutilate her, but time was an issue and there was still much to accomplish. The toughest decision he had to make was whether to slice her from navel to sternum first or cut off her hideous head. He chose the former. He hoped the intense pain from the incision would wake her from her unconscious stupor if he was sure not to puncture any vital organs. He reached into his bag and pulled out the scalpel. He removed the wife's blouse and bra and threw them to the side. With the steady hand of a trained surgeon, he placed the sharp end of the scalpel a millimeter above the navel and applied just enough pressure to cut through the skin, thin layer of fat and underlying abdominal muscles. Upon reaching what he estimated to be a safe depth, he tore upward through the stomach area continuing in a straight line to the sternum. Blood poured in streamlets from the wound over both sides of the body. Gripping the torn flesh on either side of the incision, he pulled the skin, underlying tissue and ribs apart to expose her innards. He was disappointed she never woke up; having to settle for the fact she was still alive. He wanted her heart to be beating when he sliced through her throat.

Blood and gore was saturating the carpet and spreading through the room up to the linoleum floor of the kitchen. The smell of death was beginning to imbue the air. Still, the bloodbath was not complete. Shem removed his final piece of equipment from his provisions bag. The surgeon's saw was not easy to come by. He originally tried to order one from a medical supply store. They wouldn't issue it to him unless he submitted his physician's license number or proved he was ordering it on behalf of a hospital or doctor. He ended up stealing one from Broward General Hospital. Despite its near perfect condition, he used his sharpening stone to give it a clean, razor-sharp edge. By the time he was done tapering the blade, it could split a human hair.

He knelt on one knee next to the agent's wife and placed the edge of the saw on her throat. Just the slightest touch to her skin immediately drew blood. He began to saw in a slow, easy motion, cutting through the flesh as though it were a loaf of bread. Blood gushed in pulsating rills drenching his face, neck and shirt. He averted it splashing into his eyes while he continued to saw until he reached the spine. The saw was so sharp it only took ten additional strokes to cut through the spinal canal and vertebra to completely detach the head from the body. As it rolled away from the neck, Shem achieved the most intense orgasm of his life. The sensation lasted for more than a minute, causing his body to spasm convulsively with exquisite pleasure.

When he was able to regain his composure, he took several minutes to admire his work. He considered masturbating to reach orgasm again, but there was no time to waste. The meticulous and thorough clean up he had planned would take a great deal longer than the actual murders. By the time he was done, he expected the most minute trace evidence of his presence to be gone. He decided he wouldn't leave the surgeon's saw or the scalpel at the scene. He wanted the investigators to figure out for themselves how Daniel accomplished the decapitation. There was also the possibility the defense might be able to identify the two pieces of medical equipment and use the information to create a reasonable doubt at trial.

The plastic jug of mixer and the Cruzan Coconut rum were still in the kitchen. Moving with purpose again, he retrieved both items, replaced them in the bag, pulled out the cigarette lighter and liquefied an additional twenty-five milligrams of heroin then injected it into Daniel's arm. With the drug syringe already in hand, he collected the semen syringe and the cigarette lighter and threw them overboard with the towel he used to clean up the remainder of the agent's ejaculate. When he returned indoors, Shem stripped of the soiled clothing and put them back on the agent as he lay unconscious. After tying Daniel's final shoelace, it was time to clean the remnants of the murders from his own skin. He made his way to the bathroom where it took him thirty minutes to scrub the blood, gore and brain matter off of his face and hands. The washing served two objectives. In the unlikely event someone saw him as he returned to his room, it wouldn't do to be covered in blood. Secondly, since much of Daniel's face and hands would be free of any bodily fluids, Shem wanted the authorities to believe it was the agent who used the sink to wash himself.

After dressing in his original clothes, Shem grabbed a towel from the bathroom and took to the task of wiping down every surface he had touched in the suite. He had made a point of making finger contact with items as little as possible before he put on the gloves. Since he had only been inside the suite for a limited amount of time, he made quick work of wiping away any fingerprints he might have left behind in the living room and bedroom. Next, he slipped on a new set of rubber gloves and fastidiously rubbed the fingerprints off of all ninety dominoes. That job complete, he returned to the kitchen to wet a clean dish rag. Back in the living area, he temporarily removed the butcher's knife from the agent's hand and proceeded to wash Falcone's fingertips and those of the three corpses. For a solid hour thereafter, he set himself to the chore of pressing their fingertips against the front and back of each and every domino. In order to conceal the fact the corpse's fingers had been washed, he placed their hands back in the puddles of the blood-soaked carpet and applied pressure then replaced the cleaver in Daniel's right hand.

Continuing with the tedious task of erasing his presence, Shem scrubbed the courtyard table top and repositioned four of the chairs so they were equidistant from each other. He gathered the high-ball glasses, washed them thoroughly in the kitchen sink and wiped down all surfaces in the room including the refrigerator and freezer doors. When he was certain he had eliminated all of his fingerprints, he grabbed the chair he was sitting on for the game of dominoes and put it in its original place in the living room. Finally, he fetched the towels he used to clean the hands and fingerprints and tossed them overboard.

Before leaving the suite, he took one last, long look at his masterful work. The agent would wake up in a few hours in a drug-induced trance. Shem would like to be there for that, but it was time to make himself scarce. He opened the door and peeked out into the hallway. Seeing no one, he exited the suite, closed the door behind him, and strolled back to his cabin experiencing an unrivaled and unprecedented high.

* * *

Three hours after Shem Chassar left the Falcone suite, Daniel began to stir into a state of semi-consciousness. A thunder and lightning storm raged inside his head making it impossible to formulate even the most simple of ideas. If he had been required to identify himself, he would have drawn a blank. He couldn't recall where he was nor would he have known the day of the week, if asked. He tried to open his eyes. The effort sent bursts of searing pain radiating through his forehead to the base of his skull. An attempt to move his limbs was pitifully unsuccessful and only served to exacerbate his suffering.

After twenty minutes of lying motionless on the floor, finally, he was able to raise himself up on his hands and knees. He wasn't conscious that he was holding a meat cleaver in his right hand. When he applied pressure against his arms to lift himself to his feet, the blade of the knife cut across his arm causing a deep laceration that just missed severing a major artery. Due only to Shem's concern the agent could accidentally kill himself, the .357 Magnum in his other hand was on safety or Daniel would have shot off his foot. He did his best to try to get his bearings. His vision was significantly blurred and he couldn't see more than six inches in front of his face. He stood in place for a minute waiting for the intense pain in his head to subside while trying to maintain his balance. Several minutes passed before he was able to see clearly enough to notice there was a door directly in front of him. He walked toward it, every step causing an explosion of throbbing agony between his ears. Absent-mindedly, he reached for the knob, but something in his right hand was preventing him from getting a firm grip. Daniel placed the object under his left arm, opened the door and exited the cabin. As he walked down the hallway, he felt a stabbing pain in his arm pit. Instinctually, he removed the object and placed it back in his right hand.

His clothes covered in blood and gore, the butcher's cleaver in one hand and the pistol in the other, Daniel aimlessly wandered the halls of the Lido Deck. At the same time, Chief Cabin Steward, Co Chi Cuyengkeng was taking his nightly stroll, a part of his routine to tire himself to the point of collapse. He would have liked nothing more than to pass out on the spot. For the previous three nights, he had gotten a total of four hours sleep. Co Chi was an insomniac since he was a young child and didn't usually get more than a few short hours of precious sleep per night. This particular night, he wouldn't sleep at all.

He was the supervisor of the cabin stewards who worked on the Lido Deck. Part of his nightly ritual was to patrol its corridors to be sure all common areas were neat and in order. Rarely, but at times, this work was monotonous enough that upon his return to his quarters, he would be rewarded with an hour or two of uninterrupted sleep. As he exited the elevator at Deck 14, and turned the corner to inspect the hallway leading to the owner's suites, at first, he thought he was hallucinating from sleep deprivation. A tall, muscular man covered from the top of his shirt to the toe of his shoes in blood, bits of flesh and brain matter was approaching him carrying a gun and what seemed like a Michael Myers butcher's knife from the Halloween movies. Frightened out of his wits, Co Chi ran back to the elevator area where there was a public phone attached to the wall. He dialed the number for security and reported what he saw to Security Officer Brett Gerhardt. Gerhardt asked Co Chi if he could keep an eye on the passenger but to be sure to maintain a safe distance from him. He promised to be there in less than 5 minutes.

As Gerhardt rushed to the elevators from his office on Deck 5, he called Chief of Security, Ted Hauser, on his mobile phone. Hauser instructed him to notify the bridge of what had occurred and promised to join him on the Lido deck as soon as he could get there. When Hauser arrived at the scene, Gerhardt was trying to coax the passenger to hand him his weapons. Both men were making a concerted effort not to vomit. The nauseating stink of decomposing flesh and stagnating blood was diffusing throughout the hallway. Initially, Hauser wondered if the psycho didn't understand English due to the blank look on his face in response to Gerhardt's pleas. As he got closer, he realized the guy was as high as a kite. Daniel's pupils were fully dilated, almost covering the iris to the point it was not possible to distinguish the color of his eyes. Standing motionless, spouting out incomprehensible gibberish was another pretty good indication he was under the influence of some type of major drug.

Within minutes, the Captain of the ship, Lars Bjornson, arrived with one of his Lieutenants who was armed with a pistol. The passenger didn't make any aggressive moves nor did he seem to have any plans to harm anyone at the moment. The Lieutenant took it upon himself to approach Daniel slowly with the goal of disarming him. Since Daniel made no move to threaten him, the Lieutenant gently removed the gun and cleaver from his possession giving it his best effort to touch as little of the surface of the weapons as possible. He requested that Co Chi run to the housekeeping supply room to fetch a plastic bag to preserve the evidence while he held the two weapons in a pinch-grip between his index finger and thumb of each hand. Captain Bjornson, who was carrying a pair of handcuffs, locked them on Daniel's wrists. There was not the slightest attempt to resist, Daniel frozen in place in an apparent catatonic state. The Captain instructed Chief of Security Hauser and Gerhardt to escort the detainee to the brig located on Deck 4 while he and the Lieutenant attempted to determine what had occurred.

Heading back in the direction from which Daniel had come according to Co Chi's account, they happened upon the open door of Daniel's suite minutes later. The stench penetrating the hallway just outside the cabin was more than both men's stomachs could handle. They sprinted for the nearest bathroom, barely making it ten feet down the hall before they retched up that night's dinner. Once they regained their composure, neither man was anxious to investigate what was causing the putrid stink. The Captain was not one to shirk his responsibilities. If someone was still alive in that suite, they could be in desperate need of immediate medical attention. He instructed the Lieutenant to call the physician on duty while he returned to the scene.

It took every ounce of his mental fortitude and concentration not to pass out when he entered the suite. Unable to control his sick stomach, he turned quickly and vomited a second time in the door's threshold. He continued to retch to the point of dry heaves, mule-like in his refusal to lose consciousness. He waited several minutes for his stomach to settle then reentered the cabin. Looking into the living room, he witnessed the aftermath of a horrific massacre that would forever be implanted in his darkest memories. It was obvious there were no survivors. He saw that one woman had been completely decapitated while the other's head was hanging by a thread. The third individual, whose sex he couldn't positively identify, had three quarters of his or her head blown off. Realizing the situation was way beyond his proficiency, he decided to leave the scene for the experts. He thought that if he explored any further, he could very possibly end up contaminating essential evidence. Before he left, he quickly searched each room and the courtyard to be sure there were no other victims. When he stepped back into the hallway, he called Ted Hauser on his mobile phone.

"Ted, it's Captain Bjornson. I need you to send someone up immediately to seal suite 124 on the Lido deck. Absolutely no one is to enter that room without my permission, understood?"

"Yes, sir."

"Good. I also want you to contact the federal authorities. There's been a triple homicide on my ship, under my watch." Bjornson could hear an audible gasp on the other side of the line. He continued, "I want this handled according to the book, no slip ups. We should be at Port Everglades by 6:00am. Please request they have their team on this ship as soon as possible. We don't want to lose any evidence. At this point, we seem to have a pretty clear suspect.

Tomorrow morning, I'll be making an announcement to all passengers and crew that no one is to leave the ship until further notice. When we arrive at the port, we'll need all gangways manned around the clock or until the ship's cleared for disembarkation. I don't want anyone slipping through the cracks. You'll want to notify headquarters what's happened and let them know, at least at this point, next week's cruise is cancelled. They might want to bring in a new ship. I'm sure you don't need me to tell you but protocol dictates Annie Bryan must be notified of the murders immediately."

"Have you identified the suspect yet and can you look up the names of the passengers staying in Suite 14-124?"

"No, sir, we haven't identified him yet. He's still not making any sense. There's no doubt he's on some type of hardcore drug. What I'd like to know is how he got it onboard along with the knife and gun. This was a major breach of security. Hold on a sec. I'll check the suite number…. Holy Shit!"

"What's wrong, Ted?"

"Sir, the passengers staying in that suite were guests of Annie Bryan. Their names are Daniel and Deborah Falcone."

Chapter 19

Consecutive flashes of lightning created a strobe-like, eerie glow over the horizon of the Atlantic Ocean. The flickering light effect and winds gusting at near gale-force strength caused the ghostly coconut palms along Ft. Lauderdale Beach to bend over as if they were looking for seashells in the sand. As Annie looked out the picture window of her bedroom, she could barely see the search of the palm trees or the bolts of electric charge in the sky. A torrential downpour formed a solid curtain of water that nearly blinded her view of anything beyond the window ledge. She woke from a deep sleep a half hour before to a loud crash of thunder that seemed to rock the very foundation of her 10 story building. She hadn't been able to sleep since.

She poured herself a glass of warm milk, her mother's tried and tested remedy for insomnia. It wasn't going to work its magic this time. On the way to the kitchen, the telephone began to ring. Annie immediately knew nothing good was going to come of a phone call at two o'clock in the morning unless it was a wrong number. Her instinctual thoughts were for her mother. Annie prayed she was alright. When she looked at the caller ID, she saw it was coming from an unknown source. That usually meant she was getting an emergency call from one of King's ships. For the moment, she relaxed erroneously assuming at least, the crisis didn't involve any loved ones. She picked up the extension in the kitchen.

"Hello, Annie Bryan."

"Good morning, Ms. Bryan. It's Ted Hauser from the Joy of the Seas. I'm sorry to bother you at this hour but something tragic has happened. Three passengers were brutally murdered. You may want to sit down for the next part."

Making the connection that Daniel and Deborah were on the Joy of the Seas, Annie panicked.

"Just tell me what happened, Ted, please."

"The three victims were members of the family you invited on the cruise."

Annie's heart took a precipitous plunge into her stomach. Terrified, she managed to ask, "Oh my God, is Daniel dead?"

"Actually, no, Ma'am. We found him wandering the halls covered head to toe in blood carrying the murder weapons. The victims were his wife and her parents."

Annie couldn't believe her ears. Reflexively, she rejected Ted Hauser's news, but instantly realized this couldn't be some horrible and tasteless joke. She felt a constriction in her chest making it difficult to breathe. That was followed by a sensation of vertigo and lightheadedness which threatened a loss of consciousness. She finally took Ted's advice and sat down at the kitchen, breakfast nook table. Tears poured down her face as violently as the deluge assaulting Ft. Lauderdale Beach.

Ted Hauser said, "Are you alright, Ms. Bryan? I can call back in a few minutes, if you'd like."

Placing her head between her knees to catch her breath, Annie used those few seconds to compose herself. Her analytical mind miraculously switched into high gear. Immediately, she started to develop a plan of action. Thoughts of the serial murderer almost sent her into another tailspin. Finally, she replied, "No, I want to discuss this now. What are the ship's coordinates?"

"I can't tell you the exact coordinates, but we're about sixty nautical miles from Port Everglades. I can get them for you. We're scheduled to arrive at 6:00am, but the Captain is trying to speed things up. He's hoping to be there before five."

"It's absolutely essential no one is permitted to leave that ship. I assume the Captain's already made that decision?"

"Yes, Ma'am."

"Ted, Daniel is a special agent with the FBI. He's been investigating a series of murders that seem to have some connection to me. We don't have a name, but we have photos of the suspect. I'll have a copy faxed to the ship ASAP. He was a former employee of King, using the false name Damien Drysdale. He's thirty-five-years-old 6'2" tall, blond, blue eyes, supremely fit and extremely dangerous. He's been linked to at least 2 horrendous murders, both of them involving mutilation." Annie, not privy to the FBI's investigation, was unaware of the other murders attributed to the same suspect.

She didn't know she really wanted to hear the answer to her next question. "How were the victims killed?"

By that time, Captain Bjornson had decided it was imperative they identify the victims, if possible. He allowed his lieutenant to enter the room for a quick search for any item that might shed light on the issue. A wallet was found in Jack Tyler's pocket with his identification and photographs of him, his wife and daughter. Deborah was also wearing a locket necklace with a picture of her, Daniel and the children.

Ted Hauser responded, "It was incredibly gruesome, Ms. Bryan. Mrs. Falcone was decapitated. Her mother's throat was sliced through to the spine. Mr. Tyler was shot in the head as far as the Captain and Lieutenant could tell."

"Unbelievable. It's got to be him. Where is Daniel now? I want to talk to him."

"I don't think that's gonna be possible. He's pretty much out of it. Definitely on some type of mind-altering drug. We can't get him to respond to us. At least not anything that's understandable. When he talks, it's just nonsense."

"Daniel doesn't take drugs. He's totally against them. He's never even smoked marijuana."

"Well, he did tonight."

"No way. It had to be Damien. He probably drugged him somehow. You guys need to search the ship from top to bottom and find that maniac. I'll call the agent in charge of the investigation. He's out of Miami. I'm sure he'll want to be there at the port when the ship arrives, if not sooner. They may want to helicopter in. I assume you already contacted the authorities?"

"Yes. I spoke with the agent on night duty. He told me he'd contact the agent in charge."

"Actually, Daniel is the Special Agent in Charge. But, someone must've taken his place while he was on vacation. I assume it's the Assistant Special Agent in Charge. Anyway, there's no need for me to catch a helicopter out to the ship at this point. You guys are just a few hours out. By the time I get to the airport and hire a pilot, you'll be here. I'll just meet you guys at the port. Please tell the Captain about Damien Drysdale and be extremely careful."

"Sure thing, Ms. Bryan. I'll keep you posted."

When the call was disconnected, she stood to hang up the phone, collapsed on the hard, marble floor, then sat with her back against the refrigerator and wept. She wondered what she did to deserve such heartache. The maniac struck again and was destroying the people she loved one by one. She cringed at the thought of who could be next, fearing for her mother and Daniel. There was only one way to be sure they were safe. The bastard must be caught and she would do everything in her power to make sure that happened. She picked herself up off the floor and made her way quickly to the bedroom to dress. There would be no one working at the office at this hour. She needed to get there as soon as possible to fax a picture of the monster to the Joy of the Seas.

* * *

The rumors were flying the next morning when Captain Bjornson announced the ship was under quarantine and no one was permitted to disembark. At the buffet, people were reluctant to eat as one passenger heard the food was contaminated with the legionnaire's disease virus. Others were saying a major South American drug kingpin had been on the cruise all week and a sting operation was in progress to arrest him. In the piazza, where many people were gathering in hopes of collecting some information, a rumor was being spread that the ship was taken over by terrorists. When the Captain addressed the passengers, he assured everyone with the white lie that there was no need to be frightened and no one was in danger. Evidently, it wasn't enough to stop the gossip mongers from converting conjecture into fact.

Special Agent Robert Leland arrived at the port with Special Agent Christopher Frye, the North Miami field office co-lead on the serial murder investigation, a half hour before the ship had docked. Leland received the call about the murders from the field office after two in the morning. Initially, he planned to have a helicopter fly him out to the ship. When Leland talked to the ship's First Lieutenant, he learned the Captain had increased the speed full throttle and planned to be at the port two hours ahead of schedule. Going through the same thought processes as Annie concerning the time it would take to get a pilot, he decided to be at the port waiting for the ship.

Procedure dictated that Homeland Security be notified any time a violent crime was committed on a cruise ship bound for an American port. It was their responsibility to ensure no terrorists or dangerous criminals entered United States' territory. They would help man the gangways after the ship docked to guarantee no one disembarked before they were authorized to do so. Together with Leland and his team, the agents from Homeland Security boarded the ship at exactly 4:14am.

Captain Bjornson was waiting for Agent Leland at the main entrance to the cruise liner's gangway. After Leland introduced himself as the FBI investigator in charge, he asked to be taken directly to the crime scene. The Captain and a group of ship officers led Leland, Frye and their team of crime scene analysts to the center of the ship where they crammed into both glass elevators to ascend to the Lido deck. Looking out into the throng gathered in the ship's atrium was a glaring confirmation of the work Leland and his team had cut out for them.

When they exited at Deck 14, Leland's senses were assaulted with the familiar stench of death. The stomach-twisting stink intensified with each step he advanced toward the Falcone suite. Before he entered the cabin, he instructed the ERT to wait outside while he and Frye conducted the initial inspection of the crime scene. Covering their noses and mouths with handkerchiefs, they passed through the threshold.

The death odor in the hallway didn't prepare the two FBI agents for the chamber of horrors the Falcone suite had become. Leland prided himself for never getting sick at a murder scene. Christopher Frye, who was almost as experienced as Leland, hadn't vomited at the sight of murdered corpses since he was a rookie. After they moved into the living area of the suite, both men made a mad dash for the hallway to extricate whatever half digested food was left from the previous night's meal. When there was nothing left in their stomachs to throw up, they covered their noses with towels provided by a steward and re-entered the cabin. It hardly gave a scintilla of relief without totally plugging their nasal passages.

Typically, a crime scene investigator would do their absolute best to avoid stepping in any bodily fluids to prevent evidence contamination. In this instance, it would be impossible. Just about every square inch of the living room carpet was saturated with razed flesh, blood, and or brain matter. The men hiked up their pants and placed plastic booties provided by the ERT over their shoes. With each cautious step they took further into the cabin, they heard the squishing sounds of the blood as it soaked into the slippers. Trying his best to ignore the unpleasant conditions, Leland carefully inspected each of the bodies and the surrounding area, keeping the number of steps he took to a minimum. Besides the obvious ravage to her body, he noticed Deborah was naked and made a note to himself to instruct the ERT to test for a semen sample. They studied and photographed the position of the bodies and their relationship to each other. Leland carefully examined the walls and floors for any blood or tissue spray patterns and took pictures when necessary. When he saw the remains of Jack Tyler, he immediately knew from the proportions of the damaged flesh he was shot with a high powered automatic pistol at point blank range. The two men scoured the room visually for bullet holes in the walls or ceiling. To minimize disrupting the scene, Leland ultimately decided to let the ERT continue the search for cartridges after the team was through with their analysis.

When they had completed their inspection of the room where the bodies were located, they searched the remainder of the suite for any potential clues. On the courtyard, Leland found the table set up for a game of dominoes. The ERT would have to dust each individual piece for fingerprints then later bag them for storage. He took photographs of the scene making a mental note there were four folding chairs arranged around the game table. There was nothing found of any particular interest in either the kitchen or the bedroom.

Once Leland and Frye had done as much as they could under the circumstances, they sent the ERT in to do their thing. Leland expected they would be spending a good part of the day combing the cabin for evidence both large and small. They would be particularly interested in items such as hair, carpet fibers, fingerprints, bullet cartridges, blood, rags, cigarette butts, clothing fibers, plant debris, pollen, metal filings, cosmetics, paint specks and any other trace evidence that could possibly be connected to the suspect's world. Special Agent Jonathan Frazier was on his way from Quantico. The profiler would be the last to analyze the crime scene after all the evidence was collected, but before the bodies were removed to be transported to the M.E's office.

The Captain was waiting for Leland and Frye in the hallway just outside the suite. Interviewing Daniel was next on Leland's list of things to do. He asked Bjornson to be taken to the brig. Complying with the request himself, Bjornson escorted the agents to the bowels of the ship where the rare passenger suspected of a crime was detained. When the men entered the office adjoining the brig's lone cell, the all too familiar stench of stagnated blood and decaying brain matter assaulted their senses. The security officers manning the jail had neglected to clean Daniel for fear of destroying evidence. The Captain introduced Leland to Ted Hauser. Directing his inquiry to the lead security officer, Leland asked, "Has he made any statements?"

"That would be difficult. He's been unconscious or sleeping, I don't know which, for the past two hours. I tried to get him up several times...no luck."

"Where's the doctor? Agent Falcone lost a decent amount of blood, he's most likely heavily under the influence of some drug and you just let him sleep for two hours?"

Feeling the need to step in, Captain Bjornson responded, "Our doctors on this ship are extremely qualified and well-trained. He's been thoroughly examined by Dr. Kriek. The doctor tells me he's in stable condition."

"I don't know. He doesn't look stable to me," said Leland. He attempted to wake Daniel to no avail then directed his attention to Daniel's chest and abdominal area to ascertain whether he was still breathing. His respiration was definitely somewhat shallow and sluggish, the rising and falling of his diaphragm just barely perceptible.

"I don't like the way he's breathing," Leland continued. "I've seen a lot of drug-induced comas over the years. I wouldn't be surprised if that's the case here. Let's get him back up to the infirmary. I want him re-examined by Kriek. I wanna know if we need to get him to a hospital."

"Not a problem…Hauser, get him up to the infirmary," ordered Captain Bjornson.

"Hold on. Before we move him, I just want to get a few pictures." Leland had Frye take several quick photographs of Daniel from all angles, front and back then released him for transport to the infirmary.

Leland's next order of business was to set up a command center. He asked Bjornson if there was a space available large enough to accommodate at least fifty agents and their equipment. Time was ticking and innocent passengers would soon be getting restless, not to mention a killer could be on the loose. An efficient plan to interview each and every individual on the ship, including crew members was essential. Captain Bjornson suggested the theatre which had more than enough space to comply with Leland's request.

Dealing with angry, impatient crowds was the last thing Leland needed. He had enough on his plate. An orderly process to capture the murderer and interview passengers now being his number one priority, he was reminded that Annie hadn't shown up yet. Her knowledge of the ship and its facilities and protocols for security could be helpful for organization and implementation of the operation. He pulled his cell phone from its case attached to his belt and called her.

"Hello Agent Leland. I'm sorry I'm running late. I've really had a rough time getting myself together this morning. I promise I'll be there soon. I'm on the road now. I shouldn't be more than ten minutes. How's Daniel?"

"He's been sleeping or unconscious for the past two hours. He's not breathing great. He's been transported from the brig to the ship's infirmary. The doctor's examining him now to make sure he's not in a drug-induced coma. I'm expecting he's gonna send him to the hospital."

"Maybe we shouldn't wait. I can get an ambulance there right away."

"I'm sure he'll be ok if your doctor knows what he's doing. The Captain assures me Kriek's gonna keep an eye on him. We'll get him the care he needs. I have no doubt we'll be calling that ambulance in the next few minutes."

"Ok well, I assume no one's located Damien Drysdale?"

"We haven't started a coordinated search or the interviews, yet. We need to come up with an organized and effective plan. I'm getting some reinforcements in here and believe me, we'll scour the ship from top to bottom. The Ft. Lauderdale Police Department and Broward Sheriff's Office are sending as many men as they can spare over here. Our S.W.A.T. team is on its way, too. I'm not gonna assume anything at this point. I don't know for a fact this was Drysdale. He's a top suspect for sure, but we've just started the investigation."

"You've got to be kidding me." Annie was thinking this guy had to be a total moron. She continued, "I think it's obvious what happened here. We can't let this guy slip through our fingers."

"Relax. I'm not saying it wasn't him. Believe me, if the asshole is on this ship, he's not gettin' past me. I'm just sayin… there's a lot to consider here and we're about an hour into the investigation. I don't jump to conclusions. It's come back to bite me in the ass too many times. Don't worry, finding Drysdale will be our number one focus. I can promise you that. And I'd like to get started."

"Sorry, I'm not myself. This has been the worst nightmare I could possibly imagine. I just want that maniac caught."

"No worries. Our goals are exactly the same."

"Alright, well, if you're ok with it, you can use the port terminal building to take statements. That way the disembarkation process can run more efficiently. We can let the passengers off in groups, interview them then let the ones who clearly have nothing to do with the murders be on their way."

"Excellent plan. I'm gonna need cooperation from your people to get the terminal building set up. Who should I talk to here, the Captain?"

"I should be there in a minute. Where are you on the ship?"

"I'm in the theatre."

"Ok, I'll meet you there. See you in a few."

* * *

Shem was unable to get any sleep during the night. The thrill from the murders had been sending an uninterrupted supply of adrenaline coursing through his veins. He was incapable of sitting still, much less falling asleep. At least, he would have more than a sufficient amount of energy to bring this night to a successful conclusion. When he arrived at the cabin after finishing the job at the suite, he immediately pulled out his laptop from its hiding place under the bed and booted up. Once online, he hacked into the Joy of the Seas' current passenger list and erased all traces of Isaac Jefferson from their database.

For the entire seven days of the cruise, he did his best to avoid being seen entering and exiting the room. The most difficult challenge was evading the stewards who were constantly in the hallways and servicing his cabin. The first two days, he carefully and covertly observed the behavior patterns of the housekeeper assigned to his cabin. Based on the information he collected, he chose the best times for ingress and egress. In order to avoid being heard by neighbors, he only used the bathroom well after midnight and never left or entered the room without being sure not a sole was present. Whenever he was inside the cabin, the first order of business was to don a pair of gloves. Upon exiting, he wiped down both sides of the door handle with a handkerchief. He slept on the floor every night and each time he left the cabin, he hid his bags under the bed beneath the extra blankets and life preservers that were stored there.

Every steward was required to keep a list of their passengers in the maintenance office located on the floor they serviced. Shem printed out a copy of a new falsified passenger list after deleting Isaac Jefferson, dated it the first Sunday of the cruise then headed for his steward's station at the end of the hallway. The previous

Monday, he searched that same office, his specific task to find where the list was kept. He located it in a file on a shelf directly above the steward's desk.

Aware the door to the maintenance room was typically locked, Shem took his lock picking kit with him on that last morning of the cruise. He broke in with relative ease, found the file exactly where it was on his prior visit, replaced it with the new list and returned to his quarters.

Shem had intentionally reserved a cabin that would be facing the terminal building when the ship returned to Port Everglades. As soon as it pulled into its mooring that morning, he kept a look out on the dock from his balcony for the boarding of immigration officers. There were at least twenty-five of them milling about waiting to embark. He waited a good forty-five minutes after they boarded to decide to make his final move. Earlier, he dressed in his immigration uniform he purchased from Uniformswarehouse.com. During the night, he threw his clothing suitcase overboard leaving only the suitcase/briefcase which contained some articles he didn't want to leave behind.

He grabbed the case, opened the door to the cabin and peeked out. Seeing no one, he left the room and made his way to the stairway. Descending the steps two at a time, he wasn't too concerned he would run into any immigration officers. He was pretty sure they would still be meeting with ship officials to devise a plan for getting passengers off the ship. He couldn't believe his good luck when he arrived at the gangway on Deck 4. The purser who greeted him with his German shepherd at the port building the previous week and a Homeland Security officer were manning the exit. He approached the duo and said, "Good morning. How's it goin? It's been quite a week, hasn't it? We usually don't have this much drama at the port over an entire year."

"Good morning, Officer," the purser responded. "Nice to see you again. It's been one thing after another. This ship can't seem to catch a break. I'm wondering if they're making a big drug bust or something. Where's your dog?"

"She hasn't been requested. The FBI has their own K9's. They don't need me here anyway. Everyone at our office was so anxious to check out what was happening on the ship, we left no one back at the office to take calls. I was the lucky one elected to go back. I can't say I'm not happy to get out of this mess. It could take a while."

The Homeland Security officer commented, "We may not be able to get everyone off the ship until late tonight or maybe even tomorrow. You're a lucky man. Unfortunately, they're not telling us much. You wouldn't happen to know what's going on, would you?"

"I could tell you but then I'd have to kill you."

The officer and purser chuckled at what they thought was a joke. After a few more minutes of small talk, Shem was permitted to disembark. As he made his way to his vehicle parked in the employee parking garage, he whistled the tune, "Happy Days Are Here Again."

* * *

Shortly after Daniel's examination by Dr. Kriek, he and Agent Leland made the decision to transfer the patient to Broward General Hospital. The emergency room physician on duty ordered a host of blood tests upon Daniel's arrival. Based on the concentration of six-monoacetylmorphine found in his system and the amount of time that had elapsed since the ingestion of the drug, the doctor diagnosed a near heroin overdose. He ordered the immediate intravenous administration of naloxone, a medication commonly used to counteract dangerous levels of opiates in the blood. Only when he was certain his patient's condition had stabilized, he phoned Leland and advised him Daniel could remain unconscious for as much as an additional twenty-four hours. At that point, Leland's only option was to focus on conducting the ship interviews and finding Drysdale, if, in fact, he was responsible for the murders. He asked the purser's desk for a list of adult male passengers who were travelling alone. It was uncommon for people to cruise without friends or family, making the list short. Four men were identified and called over the public address system for immediate questioning. It was obvious that none of them were Damien Drysdale since the youngest of the group was fifty five years old.

By mid-afternoon, a team of twenty-five men and women from four different law enforcement agencies were able to examine and release five hundred passengers. The FBI's S.W.A.T. team, equipped with King's employee photograph of Damien Drysdale, was searching every cabin and common area on the ship. If they didn't locate him by the time all passengers were deposed, it was Leland's plan to use K9s to search every inch of the luxury cruise liner.

As far as the lead investigator was concerned, there was absolutely no way Drysdale could have gotten off the ship without being seen. Every exit to the dock was guarded by at least one King employee and either a Ft. Lauderdale police officer, Broward County Sheriff's Office deputy or an officer of the ship. Photographs of Damien Drysdale were posted in all common areas and gangways. If Drysdale was on the ship, they would catch him.

Leland along with Frye, other task force members, Captain Bjornson, those cruise officers in charge of navigation and ship security had already considered the question whether Drysdale could have jumped ship anywhere in close proximity to the port or anywhere else for that matter. The first call Leland made after receiving notice of the murders was to the United States Coast Guard. He requested they send a fleet of boats and helicopters to usher the Joy of the Seas to port. The Coast Guard rendezvoused with the cruise line in the Atlantic Ocean, eighty five miles from the coast. Six boats flanked the Joy while two helicopters shined floodlights on the stern, bow, starboard and port sides until it was securely tied to the dock. During the entire escort mission, they were keeping a close eye to be certain no one attempted to escape overboard. If the murderer jumped ship more than 85 miles out to sea, there was no way he could have survived. It was also highly unlikely that Drysdale had an accomplice waiting with an escape boat. No other craft were detected through the ship's navigation and radar systems for hours before the estimated time of the murders until the formal escort arrived. That type of thing would have been recorded in the log. Further confirmation was provided by eyewitness accounts of those officers responsible for sighting other vessels and the like with the naked eye.

The forensics team had been diligently collecting evidence at the scene for many hours. By that afternoon, they determined there were four sets of fingerprints on the dominoes. Throughout the remainder of the suite, there were countless distinct prints found on the walls and various surfaces. They would be run through AFIS, an electronic databank that compared unidentified latent and patent fingerprints to the known fingerprint file. The team was also able to conclude there were only two sets of fingerprints on the murder weapons. One of the sets belonged to Daniel. The others were already identified as those of the Lieutenant who disarmed him.

The medical examiner that inspected the bodies came to the conclusion that Deborah engaged in some form of sexual relations just before or after the time of the murder. She was able to identify dried semen along the exterior walls and on the labia of Deborah's vagina. Those samples were stored for later DNA testing. Around four o'clock in the afternoon, the ERT completed their examination of the crime scene and the bodies were being prepared for transport to the County Coroner's Office. Leland was hoping to have complete autopsy reports by the following morning. He already contacted the Chief Medical Examiner of Broward County who promised he and his team would work tirelessly throughout the night.

The ship roster reflected there were 2,534 passengers and 1,209 crew members. At 6:00pm, ten hours after the interviews began, 1,800 passengers were questioned and released. Every interviewee was first compared to the photograph of Damien Drysdale then given an opportunity to examine it to ascertain if they had seen him at any time during the cruise. As of yet, no one had recognized him. Leland was beginning to wonder whether Drysdale was actually on the ship. Certainly, by now, someone would have been able to identify the picture.

Perhaps it was time to change tack. Leland decided to shift his focus to the crew, especially the cabin stewards whose responsibility it was to cater to the passengers and clean their rooms. His team had done a reasonable job moving the passengers quickly through the exercise. He could now afford to assign a good number of the interviewers to the ship's service providers. He called Agent Frye who was overseeing operations at the security office and ordered him to get the process started. He barely had time to end the call when his dog bark ringtone echoed against the walls of the theatre.

"Sir, it's Howard Klein." Leland had assigned Special Agent Klein to stand watch outside Daniel's hospital room. "Agent Falcone regained consciousness about five minutes ago. He's been asking a lot of questions. He wants to know what's going on."

"He has no idea his wife and in-laws were murdered?"

"He doesn't seem to be aware, sir."

"Don't say a word. Stall him for now. Try to distract him and keep him calm. I'm on my way."

Robert called Annie to notify her Daniel was awake. Having a moment of rare compassion, he thought it might help to have a close friend present when they told Daniel his wife was murdered. Annie didn't hesitate to accept his invitation. Broward General was less than a ten minute drive from Port Everglades.

Dropped off by one of his men directly in front of the main entrance to the hospital, Leland held up his badge as he bolted past the security guard on the way to the elevators with Annie in-tow.

Daniel was in a private room on the third floor. Agent Leland and Annie could see that Agent Klein and the attending physician were standing outside Daniel's room as they darted out of the elevator. After making their way up the hallway, Leland addressed the physician, Dr. Fred Clauson.

"I'm Agent Robert Leland. I'm in charge of a criminal investigation involving your patient. This is Annie Bryan. How is Daniel doing?"

"Physically, he's doing fine now, although his body's been through a great deal of trauma. The amount of heroin found in his system approached levels significant enough to cause overdose and death. All his vital signs are currently back to normal. Psychologically, he's very agitated and obviously distressed. He wants to know where his wife and in-laws are and how he ended up in the hospital. He had no recollection of what happened. Agent Klein told me it's your preference to notify the patient of their deaths. So far, we've been able to avoid telling him, but I'm glad you're here now. I know this is going to be devastating news for him, but I don't think telling him will have any adverse effects on his health at this point."

"Well, I guess we better get to it, then. Agent Klein, you wait out here. Unless you feel the need to be in the room when we talk to him, Doctor, I'd prefer Annie and I do this alone."

"That's fine. I'll be at the nurse's station if you need me."

Annie and Robert entered the room. Daniel instantly lurched upright into a seated position and almost screamed, "Annie, Robert, thank God you're here. What the hell is going on? Where's Deborah? Is she alright? No one wants to give me any information around this place. What the fuck am I even doing here?"

Leland said, "Daniel, try to settle down. It's not doing you any good to be so agitated. Why don't you sit back and take a deep breath."

"I don't want to take a deep breath. I want to know what's going on. I have a right to know. I'm sick of people telling me I need to relax."

"Alright, Daniel. You're right. You do have a right to know... I've got really bad news. There's no easy way to do this so

I'll just come right out and say it. I'm very sorry. Your wife and in-laws were murdered last night on the cruise ship."

Daniel cried out, "What? That's impossible. No, no way. How could you say something like that, Robert? Annie, what's going on?"

With tears flowing down her face in narrow, crooked lines of black mascara, Annie responded, "I'm so sorry, Daniel, it's true. Robert wouldn't joke about something like that."

Daniel collapsed in his bed. He released an agonized howl that could be heard at the nurse's station at the opposite end of the hall. The emotional pain caused by the realization that unexpected tragic news was true pierced his heart like a poisoned spear. He frantically tore at the intravenous needle in his arm in an attempt to tear it out. It took Robert, Annie and two orderlies to restrain him. When they were finally able to calm him to the point of concession, Daniel said, "I need to get out of here. I want to be with Deborah."

"There's nothing you can do for her right now, Daniel. You need to concentrate on getting yourself better," said Robert.

"I don't give a fuck. I want to see her. Physically, I feel fine," he lied, his head pounding like it had been hit with a sledge hammer. "Who did this to them, Robert? How were they killed? Is the murderer in custody?"

"Daniel, we think it was Damien Drysdale. It wasn't pretty. You don't want to know the details. They haven't found him yet," said Annie.

Daniel buried his face in his hands. Annie was right. Knowing the particulars of Drysdale's previous murders, he didn't even want to imagine what might have happened to his wife. He asked, "How's it possible? He was on the cruise ship? Was he a crew member?"

"We don't know, yet," said Robert. "We've been searching the ship, turning it upside down. We've been showing his employee photograph to every passenger before we let them off the ship. Three quarters of them have already been interviewed and not one indicated they recognized him. I have the team going through the crew members as we speak. If he's on the ship, he's found a great hiding place."

"This is my fuck'n fault. I'm a trained law enforcement officer, for Christ's sake. I should've seen something. Maybe, if I was more alert. Oh God, this can't be happening. I've got to get to that ship. I'm not gonna sit here and do nothing while that fuck'n psychopath is on the loose. Call the doctor so I can get these needles out of me." Daniel rummaged around the bed and under the sheets for his call button. Before he was able to grab it, Leland pulled it out of reach.

"Daniel, we have everything under control. The first order of business is to get yourself healthy. You can worry about helping with the investigation when you get out of here."

"Don't tell me what I can and can't do, Robert. I'm the Special Agent in Charge. It was my family that was murdered. I need to be there. I'm checking out of here right now."

"I'm sorry, but, no you're not. Sit back and I'll tell you why."

"You're not gonna tell me what to do. I'm not gonna sit here and twiddle my thumbs. Now, either call the doctor or give me that damn call button, now, Robert. I'm not gonna ask again."

Robert raised his voice in an attempt to get control of the situation. "Daniel, listen! After the murders occurred, you were found wandering the halls holding both murder weapons. You were covered in blood. We have a lot to talk about. I understand you're in a lot of pain right now, but we need to get some information from you and fast."

Daniel took a couple of minutes to digest what Leland had said. It was all beginning to feel like some kind of surreal nightmare. Nothing was making sense. One thing he knew for sure. He didn't like the way Leland was looking at him. After a long period of uncomfortable silence, Daniel responded, "You're not suggesting I had anything to do with this, are you? You're out of your fuck'n mind if you think I'm gonna put up with this shit. Annie, please go get the doctor."

"Daniel, calm down," implored Robert. "No one is saying you murdered your wife. This is a very complicated situation and you're way too personally involved. That's all I'm saying. I can't begin to understand what you're going through and I'm very sorry. But you've got to back off and let us handle this. Now, I'd like to give you a few minutes to settle down and then we need to go over what you remember. I'm gonna step out for a few minutes. I don't mind if Annie stays while I'm gone. It's up to you. But, when I get back, I'm gonna have to ask her to give us some privacy."

No matter how much it was repugnant and perverse to every fiber of Daniel's character to sit back rather than act, he realized Leland was not being unreasonable. Coming to that understanding caused the reality of the situation to come crashing down on him. In that moment, he lost all control of his emotions and began to weep silently. The piercing pain slashed at his heart leaving him unable to speak. Annie sat on the edge of the bed and put her arms around him. Together, they cried and tried to comfort each other, though there was no possibility of peace for either of them. Leland left the room to give them time.

* * *

Daniel felt as though a twenty pound boulder was lodged in the pit of his stomach. The thought of telling his children their mother and grandparents were dead was more than he could bear. He considered himself a complete failure. He was a highly trained FBI agent who dedicated his entire being to protecting the public, yet he couldn't even save his own family. There was no denying it. It was a theme, a curse he couldn't escape. The same shame that crushed him after his brother's death was threatening to squeeze the life out of him now. The disgrace of it all combined with his grief over Deborah and his in-law's death was a heady cocktail. Rallying every ounce of discipline available in his weakened mental and physical state, he sat with Leland and tried to relate his recollections of the last night on the ship before he lost consciousness.

"Robert, I can't remember anything that happened after we decided to take a break from a game of dominoes we were playing. I definitely don't remember walking down the hall with a knife and .357 Magnum. That's just crazy."

"Why don't we start with what you do remember? The coroner estimated the time of death anywhere between ten p.m. and midnight. Do you remember what you did for dinner?"

"Yes, we ate at the main dining room."

"Who's we?"

"Deborah, Jack, Kate and I."

"What time did you get there?"

"Deborah and I spent most of the day relaxing at the pool. We went back to the room about 4:30 to get ready for dinner. We both took showers. By the time we dressed and were ready to go, it was about 5:30. We called Jack and Kate. They said they needed a little extra time, so we agreed to meet them down at the dining room at six."

"Why don't you just take me through the rest of the evening? Up to the time you have no memory."

"Ok, the women wanted to go to the early farewell show. It started at eight. I would say we were done with dinner at about 7:30 then headed straight for the theatre. When it was over, we all went back to our cabin, Deborah's and mine. Deborah's parents are really into dominoes. We played just about every night of the cruise. Deborah invited this guy we met one of the first days of the cruise. He played once or twice with us."

"How many people played the game that night?"

"The five of us."

"There were only four chairs around the table."

"No, there were five."

"I'm telling you there were only four chairs around the table. Who was this guy you invited to the game?"

"I didn't invite him, Deborah did. His name was Isaac Jefferson. He was kind of a pathetic guy. Deborah felt sorry for him. His wife left him at the altar and the cruise was supposed to be their honeymoon. We hung out with him a few times. He climbed Dunn's River Falls with us. But, there definitely were five chairs around that table."

"If that's the case, then someone took one away before we inspected the room. Before we get to that though, I want you to take me through the rest of the evening. What time did you guys get back to your cabin?"

"Just after nine. Isaac probably showed up five minutes later. We started the game almost immediately after he got there. We played for an hour or so. Then, we decided to take a break. Isaac fixed us some drinks and that's about all I remember. The next thing I knew, I woke up in the hospital."

"Can you describe this guy, Isaac, for me?"

"He's about my age, about the same height, 6'2. Probably weighs around two-forty, definitely overweight. He was completely bald. Had blue eyes. He was from Detroit, a firefighter. He was travelling alone. Like I said, the cruise was supposed to be his honeymoon."

"Was he naturally bald or was it shaved?"

"I couldn't be absolutely positive. Probably shaved. It was pretty clean."

Up to that point, Daniel had been so distraught he didn't have the opportunity to analyze the events leading to his memory loss. Relaying them to Leland, the light bulb in his head suddenly and terrifyingly switched on. He asked, "You don't think he was Drysdale, do you?"

"I don't know, Daniel. It's possible. Other than you, he would have been the last one to see Deborah and her parents alive. There's a way to find out. I have a picture of him."

Leland picked up his briefcase, opened it, pulled out the photograph of Damien Drysdale and handed it to Daniel. In an instant, Daniel recognized the eyes that initially gave him an uneasy sensation. A lump that felt like the size of a grapefruit developed in his throat as he gradually realized his fatal mistake. He was so concentrated on his reconciliation with Deborah and governed by his guilt over her disapproval of his inability to forget work, he totally let down his guard. The more he thought about it, the more obvious it became. Isaac always seemed to show up at the most opportune times. He weaseled his way into spending time with the family with his pathetic story, a form of manipulation Daniel should have surely identified. Other than the occasions when they were with Isaac, Daniel never saw him anywhere on the ship. The few times Daniel knocked on his door, he wasn't there. How he could have ignored his first instinct was moronic and unacceptable. It was a skill he had honed over many years of investigating crimes and the criminal mind. Never, would he be able to forgive himself. Once again, he lost complete control of his emotions. If he had a weapon in his possession, he would have seriously considered putting an end to his life. After several minutes passed, he finally regained his composure enough to speak. By then, Leland had already guessed what his answer would be.

"It's him, Robert. He must have gained weight to disguise himself. He was a good twenty to twenty five pounds heavier than what I saw in the airport surveillance tapes. And, obviously, he shaved his head bald. How could I be so stupid? I should've insisted that I get in touch with you when I wanted to. Deborah talked me out of it. None of this would've happened. The motherfucker would be behind bars. Deborah and her parents are dead and it's all my fault. I was so concentrated on our reconciliation, I lost all focus. Now, instead of having my wife back, she's gone forever. My children have no mother."

Daniel turned away from Leland to weep privately. Though he thought he had already depleted his inventory of tears, it was going to be a while before he was able to collect himself. Sensing

Daniel wanted to be alone, Leland took the opportunity to leave the room to call Agent Frye. He described his conversation with Daniel and gave him an updated, detailed description of Damien Drysdale. He asked him to have Ted Hauser look up Isaac Jefferson's cabin number and try to locate him as soon as possible. Doubting the suspect would respond to a public address summons, he asked Frye to have the ship searched again and once found, take him into custody without delay. For at least the moment, he decided not to inquire about what happened to the picture of Drysdale he had sent to Daniel via text message on the first day of the cruise.

* * *

Agent Frye ended his interview abruptly with a middle-aged man from Venezuela and allowed him and his wife to leave the ship. He walked briskly to the security office to find Hauser wasn't there. Emphasizing the urgency of the issue, he asked the security staff secretary to contact her boss and have him come back right away. When Hauser arrived moments later, Agent Frye updated him on the latest information obtained from Daniel. Hauser sat behind his desk and punched in the name Isaac Jefferson using the search engine of the computer software for locating passenger information. The window that popped up surprised both men. It read, "Passenger not found." Hauser repeated the process with no change in the result.

"What does that mean?" Frye asked.

"It means no one by that name was on the cruise."

"No way, you sure?"

"I'm positive. That's exactly what comes up if the passenger wasn't on the cruise you're looking at." Confused, Agent Frye called Leland to report their findings.

"Yes, Chris, make my day and tell me you have Jefferson already in custody."

"No such luck. Far from it. The guy's not even on the passenger list. Now, Hauser's telling me King has never had a passenger by that name."

"It doesn't totally surprise me. If it was Drysdale, he could've given the Falcones one name and the cruise line another. Hold on. Let me ask Daniel if he knows his cabin number." Leland turned to Daniel and said, "Daniel, they didn't find him on the passenger list."

"That's impossible. I saw his keycard with his name. I also went to his cabin."

"I'm sure the name had to be false. And he probably fabricated the card. The son of a bitch is clever. Do you remember his cabin number?"

"Yes, it was Deck 9, Cabin 476. But Robert, it would've taken huge balls to give us a different name than the one he used to reserve the cabin. What if I had checked on him at the purser's desk? He's not that sloppy. It doesn't make sense to me."

"We'll sort that out later. Right now, we need to find the son of a bitch."

Daniel agreed with Leland, but was totally baffled by the results of the computer search. Some hard thinking would be necessary. Leland had already moved on relaying the cabin number to Agent Frye.

"You need to get to that cabin right away, Chris. Take a few agents and the S.W.A.T. team with you. Is the ERT still there?"

"No, they left just after you did."

"Give them a call and have them come back ASAP. We'll need them to go over the cabin from top to bottom whether you find him there or not. Call me as soon as you have something. I should be on my way back in a few minutes."

Agent Frye recruited two other FBI agents and radioed the S.W.A.T. team to meet him at the security office to devise a plan of attack. It was decided the two agents would guard the door outside Jefferson's cabin, while three members of the S.W.A.T. team entered. Once everyone agreed on the procedure, they climbed the four flights of steps to Deck 9 then made their way to number 476. The two agents posted themselves on either side of the door with guns drawn. On the count of three, Frye unlocked the door, opened it and stepped aside. The S.W.A.T. team member responsible for securing the balcony entered first, gun held in a two-fisted grip out in front of him. He checked quickly to his left where the closet and bathroom were located. Seeing no one, he continued into the bedroom and onto the balcony. The second member entered next followed by the third and final agent. It became obvious rather quickly that the cabin was vacant. To be absolutely sure, one agent checked under the bed while the other inspected the bathroom and shower. If this was Jefferson's room, he was already gone.

Disappointed, Frye pulled his cell phone out of his pocket and called Agent Leland.

"What do you have for me, Chris?"

"Not a whole hell of a lot. There was no one in the cabin. If Damien Drysdale or Isaac Jefferson or whoever the hell he is, is on this ship, he's somewhere amongst the remaining passengers or crew. I can't believe we let three quarters of the passengers disembark and we were showing them an out-dated picture of the suspect. I hope to God we didn't let him off the ship. If we don't find him, we're gonna have to locate all the passengers again and show them an updated composite drawing. This fuck'n asshole is causing us all kinds of headaches."

Leland, who had a different take on the situation responded, "I can't imagine we let him get away. Even if he put on some weight, every officer conducting interviews had a photograph of Drysdale's face and was purposefully scrutinizing the features of every male close to his age. I don't think a trained FBI agent or police officer would fail to recognize him. Daniel didn't. We've already called a police artist who's on his way to the hospital right now. I'm hoping to have a new rendition within an hour."

"I hope you're right about this, Robert. I have to say, I agree with you now that you put it that way."

"I'd be willing to bet a month's paycheck he wouldn't get by our men, and I'm not a gambling man. If he's on the ship, we'll find him. So, we better get busy. Let's double our efforts and get through the rest of the passengers. Then we'll be able to concentrate exclusively on the crew. In the meantime, will you have Ted Hauser find out who was staying in that cabin?"

"Sure thing, Robert. See you when you get here."

Agent Frye returned to the security office where Hauser was waiting for him.

"How did it go?" Hauser inquired.

"Fucker wasn't in the cabin. Would you mind looking up the name of the passenger who was staying there?"

"I already did. It wasn't occupied."

"What? What do you mean?"

"Just what I said. No one was staying in that cabin."

"For the entire week?"

"Exactly."

"No one made reservations or did the guest not show up?"

"From what I can tell, it was never reserved. It was one of four cabins on the ship that was vacant for this cruise."

"Holy Shit, I wasn't expecting that. This is getting stranger by the second. Well, if Damien Drysdale was staying in that cabin, our forensics team will find evidence to prove it. The prick is smart, but he's been sloppy before. He left something for us at just about every murder site. The ERT should be here any minute. For now, we need to keep plugging away. I was hoping we'd catch the bastard by now. I should have known it wasn't gonna be that easy."

Chapter 20

The frenzied activity in the press room at the offices of the Miami Herald was winding down, most reporters and staff having left for the day. Clifton Harris, senior journalist in the crimes division was also considering packing it in for the night. For the past half hour, he had been checking out the AP press releases in hopes that a worthwhile story would come up for his feature column. Good stories were hard to come by for the past couple of weeks and that afternoon wasn't proving to be any different. Just as he was about to give up and close down his cubicle, his cell phone rang. He looked down at the telephone's monitor screen to check caller ID and recognized the number of his source from the FBI. He didn't hesitate to answer. For the next forty minutes, he listened carefully to the information being provided, rapidly taking notes when necessary. By the time the conversation was over, his writing hand was cramping, his wrist pulsating from fatigue. More thrilled by this lead than any other in recent memory, the pain was easy to bear. He picked up the phone with his good hand and dialed his editor's extension to request a hold for the front page and explained the story he was writing. He would have to type fast. The deadline was quickly approaching.

Harris had been working the crime beat since Daniel Falcone was a rookie special agent at the FBI North Miami field office. From the first time the reporter met Falcone, he didn't like him. It seemed obvious to Harris that FBI prodigy was one of those obnoxious law enforcement agents who despised the press. When Falcone first made national headlines, Harris had plans to do a feature article about him. He hoped to develop a better relationship with the man who seemed to be growing in stature at the Bureau in leaps and bounds. Despite Harris' efforts to interview him, Falcone thwarted the journalist at every turn. The drop that spilled the cup was when Harris was embarrassed in front of all his peers and colleagues at a Falcone press conference. Harris asked him a question about how a high profile murder victim's family had reacted to the news of their daughter's brutal slaying. Falcone told him to sit down and shut the fuck up. Harris did his best to have Falcone reprimanded for his behavior and even considered suing him. The "Golden Boy" had too many friends in high places and Harris' efforts went by the wayside. It was even more frustrating when Harris wasn't able to bring Falcone down with the article accusing the agent of taking gang bribes. Harris almost got himself fired as a result of that one. If it hadn't been for his source at the FBI, he could have found himself writing stories about polar bears in Alaska.

His most recent run-in with Falcone was just several months ago when the reporter wrote the article revealing there was a serial killer loose in South Florida. Falcone was furious. He showed up at the offices of the Miami Herald insisting that Harris reveal his source. The Special Agent in Charge was normally pretty even-keeled when he ripped Harris a new one, especially since he took over that position. Falcone's stake in the resolution of this case was much more personal. He was in Harris' face, making a scene in front of the entire press room. Harris was enjoying every second of the tirade. He knew in the end, he wouldn't have to give one iota of information to the prick. Harris' editor joined in the melee then the paper's in-house lawyers were called down from their offices upstairs to tell Falcone how things were going to do down. Daniel argued that the source was obviously an FBI agent and they weren't protected under the first amendment. The lawyers set him straight, filing an injunction to prevent Daniel from getting a name and showing up at the Herald again to make such demands in the future. An emergency hearing was held that evening, the judge granting the newspaper's motion. There was even a cherry for the top of the cake. It made for a great story in the next morning's paper.

Harris could barely contain his excitement. As his fingers typed furiously across the computer keyboard, he thought about what the world would think about the FBI's "Golden Boy" now.

* * *

By the following afternoon, the media frenzy was in full flight. Clifton Harris had broken the story of the month. His article was heavily slanted toward Daniel's probable involvement in the murder and the rest of the media ran with it. CNN was broadcasting updates from the King Joy of the Seas. CNBC, Fox Network News and MSNBC were giving the story twenty-four hour coverage. Annie could no longer stand watching the reports. She couldn't imagine what Daniel could possibly be going through seeing his name disparaged all over the air waves. Already, he was suffering from the death of his wife, and his children would be dealing with the loss of their mother and grandparents. Now he was being implicated in the tragic murders. She shut off the TV in her office and threw the remote halfway across the room shattering it into several pieces when it hit the ceramic tile floor.

Clifton Harris' article revealed information he could only have gotten from an inside source. Already, the networks were referring to Daniel as the "Blood Boat Butcher" as he was described by the Miami Herald senior journalist in his front page article. Annie knew Leland and his team were specifically admonished to refrain from sharing any information about the murders with the press or anyone outside the task force. A similar directive was given to all King employees, especially the security staff. Most of the important elements of the murder were supposed to be held back in order to weed out the multitude of nutcases who would be calling in confessing to the murders. Just about every component of the horrific method in which the Tyler's and their daughter were slain was included in Harris' article. It was also reported that Daniel was found shortly before the bodies were discovered draped in blood and in possession of both murder weapons. Annie was even more shocked by the revelation of her and Daniel's illicit affair. There wasn't a doubt in her mind someone very close to the investigation was releasing information in violation of the task force gag order and the bastard had it in for Daniel.

Earlier that morning, after Annie read Harris' article, she immediately phoned Leland on his cell phone to ask if he had read it yet. She wasn't able to reach him, but left an explicit message hoping some heads would be rolling. There was someone on the task force that had no business being a part of it. She also tried to call Daniel at the hospital to find out what he knew only to be refused the connection. He wasn't allowed to receive any calls. She was hoping to visit him after work. Whether she would be able to get in didn't seem to be likely. So far, Leland hadn't returned any of her phone calls. She was planning to ask him if he would, at least, be able to get her in to see Daniel.

Annie hit more stumbling blocks when she tried to contact anyone who would talk to her at the Miami Field office. Supposedly, no one was available. Even if they had rejected her request for information about Daniel, it would have been nice to get an update on the investigation. By midnight the previous day, all passengers were released from the Joy of the Seas. The FBI was still conducting some interviews of crew members. They were hoping to have that wrapped up by the end of the evening. Leland thanked Annie for her help yesterday then told her she was no longer needed. The last she knew was that Drysdale was still at large. If Leland didn't return her call sometime soon, she was seriously considering taking a trip to the port to meet with him personally.

As the hours passed, Annie was becoming increasingly less optimistic they would find the murderer. If he slipped off the ship, she couldn't figure for the life of her how. As far as she knew, it had been sealed as tight as a drum. A tense and worried feeling was beginning to invade her already distraught frame of mind. If they didn't find Drysdale, it wasn't going to look good for Daniel. Either way, she couldn't imagine he would ever be charged with the crimes. With all the forensic work done at the scene, something had to turn up to exonerate him. She was absolutely sure of it.

* * *

Before returning to the ship after his meeting with Daniel at the hospital, Leland made a telephone call to one of the few men in the world he held in high regard. Whether Chief Federal prosecutor Norman Dallas's feelings were mutual was debatable. Either way, he was the only person with whom Leland was willing to share his theory of what happened on the Joy of the Seas.

"Good afternoon, sir. I'm glad you took my call."

"Get on with it Leland, I don't have all day."

"Well, sir, I have a legal question." Leland described the horrific murders on the cruise ship. As soon as he mentioned Daniel Falcone's involvement, he had Dallas' full attention. Leland went on to explain his interview with Daniel and some of the details of the investigation of the serial murderer, specifics not included in media reports.

"The problem I have sir, is I'm not so sure Falcone is being totally upfront with us. I haven't mentioned any of this to anyone, yet. The day we identified Damien Drysdale as the serial murderer…which happened to be the first day of Falcone's cruise, I sent him a text message with a photo of Drysdale. I still have it here on my phone. Falcone is trying to tell me he had no idea this Isaac Jefferson character was Drysdale. I don't buy it. I didn't say a word to him about it at the interview. My question is, do we confront him?"

"No fuck'n way. That was smart on your part. Don't tell a soul, not even your buddies at the Bureau. He's got a lot of friends there. Do you have his cell phone?"

"They have it on the ship with the rest of Falcone's personal belongings."

"Get that phone right away. Keep it somewhere safe. And call me when you confirm the text was received. Highly suspicious."

As soon as Leland returned to the ship, he made his way to the security office where all evidence collected was being kept until it was transported to the FBI lab or storage facility. He found Daniel's tagged bag of personal items next to his bloody clothing on a table set up by the security staff. After taking possession of the cell phone, he sought out an abandoned office where he could be alone, turned it on, checked Daniel's text messages and saw it was received while the ship was still in port in Ft. Lauderdale. Next, he called Frye to question him about where it was found.

"It was in the safe in the suite with a few other things. We had to get security to open it up for us since we obviously didn't know the pass code. Why do you ask?"

"That's not for you to worry about right now. Were you there when they got it open?"

"Yeah. What gives? I am your partner in this investigation. What's with the fuck'n secrets?"

"Never mind. I can't share it with you. I better not hear later you were asking around either. I don't want anybody knowing about this conversation. I'm dead serious. Was the phone on?"

"It was just like it is in the bag now. Off."

* * *

Three weeks after the murders, a small group of highly placed officials with the FBI, including Assistant Director Howard Evans, met with Robert Leland and a few specified members of the task force. Overseeing the gathering was Chief Federal prosecuting attorney, Norman Dallas. Damien Drysdale was never located. All forensic testing for the Joy of the Seas murders was completed and the results had come back. The preliminary DNA analysis for the semen collected at the crime scene identified it as belonging to Daniel Falcone. The cabin supposedly occupied by Isaac Jefferson was thoroughly searched and all fingerprints found were run through AFIS without any useful matches. Not a trace of evidence was found to substantiate Daniel's claim that Damien Drysdale was on the ship. No crew member or passenger was able to recognize either the employee picture of Damien Drysdale or the sketch prepared after Daniel's updated description. By the time the meeting was adjourned, it was a unanimous consensus that Special Agent in Charge Daniel Falcone would be officially charged with the triple homicide of Deborah Falcone and Jack and Kate Tyler.

* * *

For the first few days after the murders, Daniel was held for observation against his will at Broward General Hospital. When he was ready for discharge, the task force had already given up hope of finding Damien Drysdale. Daniel was kept apprised of the manhunt and that ultimately, not one scintilla of evidence was found to confirm his claim that Drysdale had stayed on the ship. He was permitted to leave the hospital to attend the funeral of his wife and in-laws. He was stunned, however, when Leland felt the need to instruct him he shouldn't think about leaving the county until further notice. Daniel was well aware of the attention he was getting from the media. He never once imagined his colleagues would believe he was responsible for the murders.

One week after the funeral, Daniel knew he was more than just a suspect. He was called into the office by Assistant Director Howard Evans who ordered him to turn in his weapons and FBI identification and take an extra couple of weeks off. Daniel's initial reaction was anger and outrage. He fully intended to take advantage of his sabbatical to throw himself into his own personal investigation of the murders. His determination was short-lived. That evening, he had his mother take the boys and for the remainder of his days as a free man, he barely left his bedroom, sleeping most of his days away, drinking himself into a stupor late into the night. He ignored the phone that rang off the hook until he disconnected it.

He couldn't find the motivation or energy to hate the man who murdered his wife. Any fire for revenge that may have temporarily burned brightly was drowned out in a flood of self-pity. Why bother when there was the distinct possibility he might have to orchestrate his mission from behind bars? Even his normally unflinching confidence in the American justice system was lost. The truth meant nothing. The day Robert Leland and Christopher Frye showed up at his house to place him under arrest they found him drunk and passed out on the cold tile floor of the upstairs bathroom. When he regained consciousness to find himself in the bunk of his jailhouse cell, he turned over and went back to sleep.

* * *

There was no blanket of pristine, shimmering snow covering the flat, dull landscape. The nearest icicle was more than eight hundred miles away. The only sleigh bells anyone would have the pleasure of hearing could only come from the speaker of a stereo playing Yuletide music. Outdoors, the grass was as green as a Saint Patrick's Day shamrock. The trees and shrubbery maintained most of their leaves while the foliage continued to bloom flowers. It wasn't the typical picture for a greeting card for the month of December, but it was the holiday season in sunny Miami, Florida. Normally, this was a slow time of year for Chief Federal Prosecutor Norman Dallas. It certainly wasn't a time to expect his staff to be overly productive, unless, of course, the case of a lifetime had miraculously landed in his lap. Norman Dallas' idea of celebrating this Christmas was by cracking his whip, requiring his people to work overtime in preparation for the trial he considered his long, overdue opportunity.

It wasn't often the Chief Federal Prosecutor tried a case from start to finish. On the average, he didn't step foot inside a courtroom more than two or three times a year. That digging in the trenches type of labor was left for his Assistant Federal Attorneys. It wasn't that he didn't enjoy litigation. He was born to argue in front of a jury. Anyone who had observed him performing in a court of law would agree he was a master. It was his time to shine. He had tried more cases as a young attorney than most trial lawyers handle in an entire career. At this stage in his life, it was a time to be selective. He was a man with ambitious political aspirations. His ultimate goal was to be a Justice of the United States Supreme Court. The first order of business on his agenda was to be appointed to the Federal Court of Appeals for the Southeastern District of the United States in Atlanta. It was a necessary stepping stone on his way to the highest court in the land. One of the Justices had already announced his intention to retire. There was a lot of talk that a second Justice was considering leaving shortly thereafter. Dallas planned to have one of those seats. The way he would get there was by choosing to try only those cases that would give him media attention and national exposure. To have the Falcone case come his way at just the right time was a Christmas gift from heaven.

Norman Dallas was a tall, slender man with a full shock of cotton-white hair, bright green eyes and a wise, handsome face. When he walked into a room, he commanded it. If he spoke, people had a tendency to listen. He met Daniel Falcone for the first time more than five years ago. At the time, Daniel was just a rookie agent, wet behind the ears. Dallas wasn't fooled by his inexperience. Falcone was going places. He helped round up and then prosecute to conviction a band of organized crime leaders in the Greater Miami area. When the story began to get national attention, Dallas pulled the file from his Assistant United States Attorney and tried the case himself. Both Dallas and Falcone were congratulated in person by the President of the United States for their work in the case. Just this year, Daniel was responsible for the downfall of a powerful South American drug cartel for which he'd received a Presidential award. Heroin, cocaine and marijuana valued at a total of three hundred million dollars had been confiscated. Eight crime lords who had been avoiding arrest for decades were now behind bars. Dallas didn't hesitate to get a piece of the action, trying the case to conviction and also receiving national acclaim.

There weren't too many federal agents who impressed Norman Dallas more than Daniel Falcone. That didn't mean the Special Agent in Charge was above being used as an instrument for Dallas' climb to the top. The U.S. Attorney for the Southern District of Florida was sure he would be making headlines with the talented agent again. This time, Falcone would be a means to an end. It was just yesterday Dallas was told the President would soon be disclosing to the media his short list of candidates to replace the retiring Justice and Dallas was on it. If he could get a conviction in the cruise ship triple homicide case, it could seal the deal.

Falcone had maintained his innocence from the very beginning. As far as Dallas could tell at these early stages of his preparation, Daniel's primary defense was that a known serial killer had framed him. There were several major holes in this theory. Besides the fact that there was no physical evidence found to prove Isaac Jefferson was on the Joy of the Seas, Lee Andicoy, who was the steward responsible for cabin 9-476, controverted Daniel's allegations it was occupied the week of the murders. In Andicoy's deposition taken just two weeks ago, he testified that every day of the cruise, he entered this one of fifteen rooms assigned to him to perform his housekeeping duties. Each day, he found it untouched and in perfect order. There were no clothes hanging in the closet. Once, he peaked under both beds to check if there was any luggage and saw none. He wondered several times during the week whether there was actually someone staying there, but didn't think it important enough to check the passenger list. He didn't actually verify it until asked by the FBI agent investigating the murders. It was at that point he discovered the cabin had been vacant for the entire week.

The forensics team did a complete and thorough sweep of 9-476, including the balcony. When all the analyses were interpreted and DNA results were in, there was not one shred of proof that Isaac Jefferson or Damien Drysdale ever stepped foot in that cabin. The cherry on the cake was the text message sent to Falcone by Special Agent Robert Leland with the picture of Drysdale attached. It would probably be one of the more powerful proffers of evidence. As far as Norman Dallas was concerned, Jefferson was a creation of Daniel Falcone's imagination. It was his obvious plan to murder his family deliberately replicating the style of the serial killer.

Demonstrating motive and state of mind was often one of the more difficult elements of proof in a murder trial. Falcone might as well have handed Dallas his evidence on a silver platter. The Chief Federal Prosecutor had several different forms of evidence at his disposal that would illustrate the defendant's marital woes. While searching the wife's house, the investigators found photographs of Daniel having sex with Annie Bryan. He knew from the defendant's own admission and statements of his colleagues that the Falcone couple was separated for months before the cruise. Dallas couldn't have written the script any better. It was one of the oldest motives in the book. Get rid of the wife to be with the mistress. There was no better way than proof of infidelity to rile up a jury, especially the women.

In addition to the pictures, the investigators located a videotape of a heated argument between Daniel and his father-in-law at the Tyler home. Dallas assumed one of their neighbors recorded the incident and gave the Tyler's a copy. No one from the neighborhood who claimed to have witnessed the incident would take credit for the tape. Dallas figured it was most likely a matter of not wanting to get involved. He would do everything in his power to get the video-maker to come forward. One way or another he would get it admitted into evidence. It would be very useful to establish a strained relationship between the defendant and his father-in-law.

The most damning DNA evidence of all, in Dallas's opinion, was the discovery of Falcone's semen, proving he had sex with his wife at or after the time of the murder. Even his closest colleagues at the Miami field office were stunned by the news. They were fully expecting the results would match those found at the Damien Drysdale murder sites. Of course, it didn't hurt that Falcone was found covered in the victims' blood holding both murder weapons. Lab tests revealed the gun was discharged four times. A member of the ERT was able to collect gunshot residue from Daniel's hand while he was still unconscious in the ship's brig. The results confirmed that the gun in his possession was, in fact, the murder weapon. The fourth cartridge was never found. That didn't concern Dallas. He didn't think it was enough to create a reasonable doubt in the minds of the jurors. If the balcony doors were open, a miss could clearly have ended up in the ocean. Bad aim was certainly not out of the realm of possibilities considering that Falcone was using heroin that night.

There were two potential stumbling blocks that Dallas felt could conceivably cause a jury to acquit Falcone. First was the drug issue. Dallas had his support staff conduct a thorough investigation into Falcone's past. The defendant's relatives, close friends, college buddies and even some enemies were interviewed during the process. No evidence surfaced proving the defendant ever used or abused any type of narcotic ever in his life, not even marijuana. He was squeaky clean when it came to drugs. The investigators' discovery of almost fifty grams of heroin hidden under the mattress of Falcone's bed at his studio apartment was big. At the very least, it opened up the door to making the argument Falcone turned to drugs due to his marital problems. All of his colleagues agreed he was distraught and depressed over his separation with his wife. When all was said and done, Dallas was confident enough in his skills of persuasion to prevent this issue from having a significant impact on the jury's verdict.

The second problem was the Terry Smithson disappearance and the possibility it could lend credence to the defendant's contention a serial killer was on board. The absence of the security officer's body would not help the defense. Even though, by most accounts, she was a responsible employee, it was a frequent enough practice for cruise ship employees to disappear at a given port and never return to the ship. With the lack of a corpus delecti, the prosecutor could reasonably argue that any testimony concerning the Smithson woman had no probative value whatsoever.

All things considered, Norman Dallas was feeling quite secure about his chances. He would put his talents up against the best defense attorneys in the country even under more dubitable circumstances. The mountain of evidence still building against Falcone would surely bring victory. Best of all, Dallas' performance would have an international audience. According to his sources, the trial would be broadcast in over one-hundred and fifty countries around the world.

* * *

The television blared in the background with Kiran Chetry anchoring the morning's headline news on CNN. Shem Chassar was scrambling eggs for breakfast as he listened carefully for updates on the "Blood Boat Butcher" story. Chetry was reporting that the attorneys would begin jury selection the following Monday then segued to a clip of an interview with the agent's lawyer. He was estimating jury selection alone could last up to two months. Shem was fine with it. The longer the process lasted, the better. It would give the agent more time to fester in his cell and suffer the torturous pain of knowing his cheating ways caused the death of his beloved wife leaving his children motherless.

His plan had truly worked to perfection. The tranquilizer he chose to spike the drinks worked as he had expected. By the time the investigators drew blood from the victims, it had completely metabolized. The toxicology reports were released to the press and there was no mention that any of the victims were drugged before they were murdered. Even if this was a piece of evidence the FBI was holding back, it didn't worry him. A prosecutor worth half his salt should be able to convince a jury it was the agent who drugged the family. The important thing was that they found no sedative in Daniel's test results.

Shem was very pleased with the United States attorney who was prosecuting the case. He researched his background online and discovered that Dallas had never lost a murder trial. The man was obviously a mover of mountains with very impressive credentials. With the help Shem provided, he was certain the prosecutor would have no trouble securing a conviction. He handed the investigators a few gifts to assist them in building a rock solid case against the agent. While the authorities were busy concentrating on analyzing the crime scene and searching the ship for him, Shem broke into the in-laws house and the agent's studio apartment. At the Tyler home, he slipped the DVD of the argument between the agent and his father-in-law into their DVD library. He placed the left-over heroin under the agent's motel mattress.

Before twenty four hours had elapsed from the time of the last murder, Shem's bags were packed and he was on his way to Memphis. Being a fan of the King of Rock and Roll, it was a city that always fascinated him. It was where he chose to bide his time while the tortoise-paced American justice system plodded through completing his masterpiece. He knew it wouldn't be long now before his Job-like patience would render its just rewards. He sat in his favorite recliner in front of the TV and kept his attention pealed on the screen as the clip of Norman Dallas announcing he would be vigorously seeking the death penalty was replayed for the fifth time in the last hour.

Chapter 21

The Federal Detention Center in Miami was located east of the downtown area in a high-rise building that housed over seven-hundred cells. The weekly population of inmates could vary from as low as a thousand to as many as fifteen hundred. The cells were exclusively reserved for prisoners who were sentenced to less than a year in custody or those awaiting trial for various federal offenses, including defendants accused of capital crimes. Fearing for his safety as an FBI agent, the warden granted Daniel a private cell on the tenth floor. Jails and prisons didn't exist in a vacuum. The inmates were well aware of Daniel's story. Although the detention center was a minimum security facility, there were several prisoners who were previously convicted of serious felonies. In fact, there were over fifteen residents of this jail that Daniel had a hand in arresting.

For the first few weeks after his arrest, Daniel was in a state of total despair. The depression over his wife's death combined with the idea that his children might believe he was a murderer was almost impossible to overcome. He blamed himself entirely for Deborah's and her parent's murder and felt it was only justified he should pay the price. His life was over anyway. If one were to add all the deaths of family members he had a hand in, he could compete with some of the most infamous murderers in history. He had spent his entire life trying to regain the love and respect of his father after his brother's demise. The only thing he managed to accomplish was to confirm he deserved the label his father placed on him so many years ago. He was a murderer. His failure to prevent the massacres on the ship was inexcusable. He might as well have been the one who wielded the knife that slaughtered Deborah and her mother and fired the gun that blew Jack's brains out.

Rick Suarez, his brothers, his mother and Annie seemed to be the only people who believed him. It took Annie to convince him he was worth the effort of defending himself. She reminded him he still had two beautiful boys to think about. They already lost their mother. They didn't need to lose him on top of it all and live the rest of their lives with the unthinkable burden of wondering whether their father murdered their mother and grandparents. Only a coward would concede defeat and leave his children to wallow in the aftermath with no support.

Annie's words could never convert Daniel's sense of hopelessness to one of promise for the future. But, he was no coward and had never sloughed his responsibilities off on anyone else. It was just enough to give him the kick in the butt he needed to at least do the bare minimum and find himself representation. With Annie's help, he hired one of the best criminal lawyers in the country. Alan Shipman was glad to take his case despite Daniel's inability to afford his exorbitant fees. The publicity the attorney would get from the international coverage was payment enough. Over the ensuing weeks, Annie together with his new lawyer were able to light a small flame in Daniel's heart, nothing more than the beginnings of a desire to avenge his wife's murder, not only on his own behalf, but more so for his children. Things would never be the same. At that point in his life, Daniel saw no peace of mind for himself. That didn't mean he was absolved of fighting for his boys' happiness. Even if he was convicted of the murders, he decided he would work from inside the prison to pursue his revenge.

He knew he would always have an ally in Annie. She felt just as bad, if not worse than he did about the death of Deborah and her parents. She took it very hard coming close to resigning her position with King Cruise Line. For an entire month after the incident, she didn't leave her apartment. With time, her depression turned to anger and now her new purpose in life was to make sure the monster was punished. She offered to assist Daniel with attorney's fees and costs, but that turned out to be unnecessary. She devoted her time instead, working closely with Alan Shipman in preparing his defense. After the murders, she hired a private investigator, at her own expense, to try to identify and locate Damien Drysdale. To date, he was no more successful uncovering any significant information than the FBI.

Daniel had never encountered anyone in his law enforcement career that was as illusive, obscure and unidentifiable as this evil demon that was making his life a living hell. The murderer was always at least two or three steps ahead of everyone else. There was no uncertainty in Daniel's mind it was going to take an intellectually herculean effort on their part to trap him. For the boys, he would begin to do his part.

* * *

Daniel tried to shut out the echoed shouts of prison guards spouting off instructions to the newest group of inmates being processed for admission to the federal jailhouse. He was in his cell studying his notes in preparation for a meeting with his attorney, Alan Shipman scheduled for later that afternoon. It didn't seem to matter a whole hell of a lot that he was having problems concentrating. The trial was coming up in just a few days and the prognosis couldn't possibly look more bleak. Feeling sorry for himself wasn't going to get much accomplished, but maintaining any semblance of his newfound willingness to put up a fight was going to take a real effort considering all the evidence overwhelmingly pointing to his guilt. His lawyer was telling him his best chance of being acquitted would likely depend on his own performance on the stand. How he was going to get a group of twelve strangers to believe him when his own colleagues and friends doubted his veracity was a disturbing proposition to say the least.

At times, Daniel even wondered if Isaac Jefferson were a figment of his imagination. It was beyond comprehension how a person could spend a whole week on a cruise ship, slaughter three human beings and not leave a single trace of his presence behind. The past weeks had certainly threatened his sanity, but Daniel was of sound enough mind to realize those moments of doubting Jefferson's existence were not logical. He couldn't be more certain the monster murdered his wife and in-laws. The problem was getting twelve jurors to believe it when neither the authorities nor his lawyer had uncovered any evidence that would corroborate his testimony that Drysdale was on the ship.

Special interviews of the passengers staying on the same deck as Isaac Jefferson were conducted by both the defense and prosecution during the discovery phase of the upcoming trial. The next door neighbors on either side couldn't say with any certainty they ever heard voices or sounds coming from that cabin. Like everyone else on the ship, crew and passengers alike, not one resident on the entire deck recognized any photos or artist's renditions of the serial murderer. Under the circumstances, Daniel's job on the witness stand seemed more daunting than any he had ever undertaken in his life.

As if that wasn't enough of a challenge, his credibility would be that much more critical regarding the issue of the text message and picture of Damien Drysdale sent to him by Leland on the first day of the cruise. The Federal Rules of Criminal Procedure required that the prosecutor provide the defense with a list of the items the United States intended to introduce into evidence during the trial. Daniel couldn't believe his atrocious luck when his attorney first notified him that his cell phone had received the message. He truly felt like either the heavens or some evil force was working against him to make his life an unimaginable nightmare. He worried that not even his lawyer, family and friends would believe his lame excuse that Deborah had confiscated his cell phone. Thoughts of despair threatened to resurface. It required a search of the depths of his soul to find the strength to continue to fight, calling to mind Annie's words about his children. Shipman and the rest of the world would have to accept the truth. Daniel's only option was to have confidence in its power. He might as well plead guilty if he couldn't make himself believe his testimony would create the reasonable doubt necessary to acquit him.

The disappearance of Terry Smithson was the one issue the defense originally thought might work in their favor. With Annie's help, it was discovered Smithson was a former colleague of Damien Drysdale. At trial, the defense would take the position that the missing security guard was evidence of the serial killer's presence on the ship. It would take some creative persuasion, but Shipman felt he could convince the judge to allow him to argue to the jury she was a threat to Drysdale with the potential to expose him. After many weeks of investigation, the optimism quotient for Shipman and his team took a significant hit. Due to a rash of kidnappings of American citizens in Mexico, the Mexican police were overwhelmed with work and pressure from the American government and victims' families. Terry Smithson was one of dozens of cases they were attempting to resolve with minimal staff and less than adequate facilities and technology. Not a lot was being done to determine what happened to Terry Smithson. Alan Shipman was forced to hire a private detective to travel to the Yucatan Peninsula to conduct a thorough investigation. It proved to be no more fruitful than any other line of defense Shipman hoped to establish. The detective's efforts turned out to be a bust.

Several of Smithson's colleagues and friends on the ship were aware she had gone to Atkun Chen alone on the day of her disappearance. The detective had also checked Smithson's credit card purchases and learned she had rented diving equipment that day for the underwater caves. After slipping the park's manager a few pesos, he was permitted to search through their records to find

Fernando Ramirez, the tour guide who led Smithson's group. The detective showed Ramirez a picture of both Terry Smithson and Damien Drysdale and an artist's rendition of Daniel's description of Isaac Jefferson. Fernando, who directed several tours a day consisting of dozens of people in wetsuits and masks didn't recognize them. He never even told the detective the story of the two members of his group who decided to ditch him halfway through the tour. The interview was months later and his memory wasn't sharp enough to link that event with the date the detective provided. Alan Shipman had spent thousands of dollars out of his own pocket only to come up with nada.

* * *

The media circus had commenced their invasion of the Wilkie D. Ferguson United States Federal Courthouse in downtown Miami. The main attraction was the trial of the "Blood Boat Butcher." Under the big tent, CNN set up live twenty-four hour television coverage. The set was situated beneath an eight story curved glass form resembling the hull of an enormous ship resting between the twin glazed towers of the Federal Building. The side shows boasted thousands of reporters from around the world transmitting live broadcasts of updates of the event touted the trial of the new millennium. News vans crowded the parking lot in a hodgepodge of satellites, tripods, cables, cameramen and spectators.

An aberrant entrepreneur set up a stand to sell t-shirts with a print of Daniel Falcone holding a cleaver dripping with blood. Onlookers held up posters calling for Daniel's decapitation. The pacifist groupies took the opportunity to picket and protest capital punishment. Hundreds of police were assigned to provide security for the building and its surrounding areas. They were dressed in full combat gear and equipped with the latest non-lethal mob control weapons.

The judge had not yet rendered his verdict whether he would allow the live television and/or radio coverage of opening statements and the remainder of the trial. He forbade the presence of cameras in the courtroom during jury selection. The decision didn't mar the excitement of this big day for the hordes of journalists assigned to reporting the event. Before he commenced jury selection, Judge Jackson was going to announce his ruling today on the broadcast issue for the rest of the proceedings. Alan Shipman vehemently argued against live media coverage. He alleged that allowing the transmission of the trial to the public had the potential to irreparably prejudice his client and threaten the sanctity of the jury. He also expressed concern for witness safety and maintained it would taint the dignity of the courtroom and judicial process.

It wasn't a big surprise Norman Dallas was in favor of television coverage and contended that the public had the right to access to the courts. He argued that the constitutional right was one to observe, not exclude and the public was now used to the television broadcast of courtroom proceedings. It was no longer a sensational event. The rules banning cameras from the federal courtroom were outdated and unconstitutional, violating the first amendment right to freedom of the press.

In the courtroom, one hundred prospective jurors were being marched into the gallery area and jury box. Daniel was seated at the defense table in a dark blue, tailored suit with a white shirt and red tie. In the chair next to him, Alan Shipman was flipping through a list of names of the potential jurors. He was sporting a Kiton gray suit with a pinstriped white shirt and light purple checkered tie. The entire ensemble had a price tag upwards of seven-thousand dollars. Alan concentrated on the list memorizing the names of the first jurors to be questioned. They would be interviewed in groups of twenty. When conducting his examination, he preferred to use the individual's name without having to refer to his notes. The jurors were usually very impressed with this typical attorney trick. Not every lawyer was capable of remembering so many names at one time. He didn't doubt that at this moment, Norman Dallas would be busy himself committing the names to memory.

Dallas, whose wallet was not quite as deep as Shipman's was wearing a charcoal gray suit, light blue shirt and blue and gray striped tie that he purchased on Italsuit.com. The fact that he wasn't wearing as expensive a suit as his adversary took nothing from his ability to exercise mastery over his environment. Just before the judge entered the courtroom, he glided to his position at the prosecutorial table with a distinct, but not off-putting sense of confidence.

"All rise. The United States District Court, Southern District of Florida is now in session, Judge Clarence Jackson presiding." Judge Jackson slid into the courtroom from a side door behind the witness stand. He requested that everyone be seated then settled into his large chair behind the bench. Addressing the courtroom as a whole through the microphone placed on his desk, he said, "Good morning counsel, members of the prospective jury and spectators. We're here today for jury selection in the case of the United States vs. Daniel Falcone. However, before we begin the selection process, I would like to announce my ruling concerning the television coverage of the trial.

I'm well aware there's a Federal Rule of Civil Procedure in the Southern District of Florida banning television cameras from Federal Courtrooms. However, the recent trend across the country has been to slowly allow more and more access to the visual media. The 1996 Judicial Conference Report allowed each Federal Court of Appeals to decide on a case by case basis. Although the report discouraged courts from allowing cameras into federal courtrooms, in that very same year, the Ninth District Court of Appeals announced it would allow electronic media coverage of most of its proceedings.

In 2006, the United States House of Representatives voted 375-45 to allow Federal Appellate Court and District Court Justices discretion to authorize television and radio coverage in their courtrooms. This was the third time such a bill passed one branch of Congress. Attitudes toward this issue are without a doubt changing. It's my opinion television coverage would not only provide a very important public service but can also aid the judiciary. For these reasons, I am going to allow both television and radio coverage of this trial beginning at opening statements. My Judicial Assistant will prepare a detailed list of rules that must be adhered to at the risk of being held in contempt of court."

Alan Shipman stood up and asked the judge to note his objection for the record. Being just a formality necessary for the purposes of a future appeal, the judge allowed the motion to be heard then overruled it. He turned to the prosecutor and said, "Now Counsel, let's get started with Voir Dire. Mr. Dallas, you're up."

* * *

Shem wasn't one to get giddy over good news, but what he read on the headlines banner running across the bottom of his television screen made him want to rejoice. He was going to have the opportunity to be present for the trial and didn't have to leave the comfort of his own living room. CNN would be providing all day coverage of every stage of the process starting with the opening statements. Already, the defense had been struck down on a significant issue. The agent's attorney fought tooth and nail to forbid cameras in the courtroom. From what Shem read, the defense attorney usually had judges eating out of his hands.

His next undertaking was going to be key to his ultimate success. He couldn't afford to screw this one up or the consequences could be disastrous. Much deliberation and reflection would be necessary. He already conducted a search on real estate websites for his next home. He wanted it to be secluded, out of sight of the public eye. It would be his private fortress. A cabin in the mountains of Georgia or North Carolina on an exceptionally large plot could fit the bill.

According to the agent's lawyer, Shem still had two months before the evidentiary portion of the trial commenced. He needed to take advantage of the delay to get some vital work done. It was time to take to the road. He could actually kill two birds with one stone. It was the perfect opportunity to real estate shop and it had been more than a month since the murders on the ship. The compulsion to kill was growing too strong to ignore. He was doing his best to control his impulses in order to keep a low profile. Damien Drysdale was still the prime suspect for the Hannah Richards and European murders and the FBI made him number one on their most wanted list. This time, he would have to completely change his modus operandi. It may not be as pleasurable without slashing a throat or performing a decapitation. He could only hope his chosen method would satisfy the killing itch.

During his travels to the Southern Appalachian Mountains, he would take a day or two from his schedule to try his hand at something new. It was probably going to take a bit more creativity to derive as much pleasure from the experience as he normally would. He enjoyed gurgling noises and the bulging terror-filled eyes while strangling his victim. Then again, it could never compare with the blood saturated spectacle of the transection of a carotid artery or the removal of a head. There had to be a more innovative and satisfying method of killing than strangulation without decapitation. He would think on it.

Two months should give him sufficient time to satisfy his craving and find a stronghold on which to place a down payment. This was going to be the first time he ever owned a home. He had always avoided owning real estate property in the past. It involved too much documentation and even worse, traceability. He was proud of the fact he had never paid a penny in taxes. Even though he was never given an official name or social security number, it took a significant amount of ingenuity to avoid Uncle Sam. In order to invest his money and open up new accounts, he created fictitious characters. Never once did he file an income tax return under any of his false names. If there was a loophole in the tax laws of a given country, he was aware of it. There wasn't a tax attorney who knew the United States Tax Code better than he. He was confident he would be able to find a similar escape clause in the registration laws of real estate to help obstruct the government's ability to locate him.

Tonight, he would pack his bags to get an early start for his trip the following morning. After the sun set, he went for his nightly five mile jog. He was so repulsed by the extra weight he gained for the Joy of the Seas, immediately after moving to Memphis, he got himself into the best shape of his life. As he ran through the streets of the city, he thought about the upcoming trial. He would be sure to record the proceedings for posterity's sake. He couldn't wait to see the look on the agent's face when the jury announced their guilty verdict.

* * *

After shopping for real estate for several days on his cherished Internet, Shem's final choice was a secluded, two story waterfront cabin abutting the Nantahala National Forest in the Blue Ridge Mountains of Western North Carolina. It took him a total of eight and a half hours to drive from Memphis straight through to his new mountain hideaway. Pulling into the driveway, the first sight that attracted his attention was a whitewater stream flowing on the property parallel to the access road. He had seen it in pictures on his computer and was impressed by its beauty. Taking it in with his own eyes, he was amazed by its sheer force. The river raged just fifteen feet from the front porch that stretched the length of the cabin's façade. It would serve as an adequate moat to prevent the invasion of any unwanted visitors for the main residence.

The deck was bordered by a cypress, colonial picketed railing, and was furnished with a classic cedar hanging swing and two acacia wood rocking chairs. On the west side of the residence, there was a spectacular waterfall that cascaded thirty feet downward over a staircase of boulders into the racing torrent. The nearest neighbor was miles away. The entire city had a population of less than one hundred people.

He contacted the real estate agent immediately and scheduled an appointment to view the inside. With a little bit of coaxing and a great deal of insistence, he was able to convince her to meet him at the home an hour later. Stepping through the threshold, Shem knew the interior was going to need some work to make it more functional. The floors were polished golden oak. The vaulted ceilings were of the rustic style with thick, exposed birch wood beams. The living room extended into a kitchen adding at least another five hundred square feet to the already large and open space. It wasn't ideal for security purposes. The problem was exacerbated by a fifteen- by- fifteen foot picture window overlooking the rapids and forest beyond. It allowed for an unobstructed view of most of the living space inside the home. There were two bedrooms, the master bedroom having a dramatic view of both the front of the property and the waterfall. Both rooms had windows on all sides purposefully offering a panoramic view of the surrounding area. Shem needed to be able to keep a close eye on the property from inside the cabin, but most of these windows had to go.

He made a cash offer on the spot to the real estate agent. Despite the issues with the interior, it was the perfect location and other characteristics of the property made it a worthwhile investment. The agent told him she would relay the bid to the owners, but Shem couldn't help noticing she was taken aback by his choice of payment. In an attempt to offer what she mistakenly thought would be helpful counsel, she suggested he apply for a mortgage explaining that the great majority of home buyers took that route. She pointed out that depending on the interest rate he could negotiate, that large sum of cash could earn more money than he would pay in interest over the thirty year life of the loan. He didn't appreciate the woman meddling in his affairs and was furious she had the unmitigated gall to give him financial advice. There was no doubt he could buy out her real estate business and every piece of property she had for sale. If he wanted to pay cash, he had a good reason for it. This woman was treading on thin ice. If he didn't need her for this transaction, she would have been the perfect candidate for what he had planned for the second half of this trip. Flashing his best effort at a smile which was really nothing more than a twitch of his upper lip, he made it clear he wasn't interested in a mortgage.

In this part of the country, most things didn't happen very quickly. The residents had a much more laid-back, relaxed attitude than the city life to which he was accustomed. Even though he was paying cash, the whole process from purchase to closing was estimated to take almost the entire two months needed to pick the jury in the agent's murder trial. The wait worked into his schedule perfectly. It would give him more than enough time to engage in his favorite hobby. After signing the contract of purchase and placing a down payment on the cabin, he hit the road once again.

* * *

Shem had never been to the state of Kentucky, so after he checked out of his hotel in Asheville, North Carolina, he headed north on US19 toward I26. The interstate would take him in the direction of the southeastern part of Kentucky. When he studied the map, he decided that Hazard sounded like a good name for a city to find some poor unsuspecting bitch and bury her alive. After contemplating several different methods to torture his next victim, he decided the thought of interring a living, breathing person could have lasting effects. He might even be able to enjoy it for hours or maybe days later.

Hazard was a small, rustic town covering seven square miles with a total population of two thousand residents. According to Mapquest.com, it would take him approximately three and a half hours to arrive at his destination. Since he had plenty of time, he decided to take the scenic route. He drove his Ford F-150 he purchased when he arrived in Memphis through the mountainous terrain of Southeastern Kentucky. Once he exited the interstate on KY-15 west, the scenery was so awe-inspiring, he pulled off at several vistas to enjoy the view. Though he enjoyed geographical beauty just as much as the next person, he also had the ulterior motive to search for a secluded area that could serve as an appropriate burial ground. It would have to be sufficiently isolated from any populated areas so his victim's screams could not be heard. He wasn't planning on gagging her. It would dull the experience. He wanted an unabridged opportunity to delight in her terror. Once underground, he was sure any sound she made would be muffled and inaudible.

Five hours after his departure from Asheville, he pulled into the parking lot of the Hazard Hampton Inn. He checked in at the registration office then immediately went to work. As soon as he entered the corner room he requested, he removed his laptop computer from its briefcase and took a few minutes to seek out instructions for building a coffin. He jotted some notes on the hotel's stationary and made a list of the equipment he would need to get the job done. Conveniently, Hazard actually had a Lowe's. Surfing their website, he determined that the only wood sturdy enough to support a body underground was available in five inch thick panels of pine that were eighty four inches in length. It might not make for the most elegant burial, but he was sure it would serve its purpose.

It was late evening when all the details were finally sorted out. This wasn't a city where strangers could wander about without being noticed. The risk of being remembered was too great. Not wanting to linger in this pint-size town longer than necessary, he grabbed his keys from his jacket pocket, walked out the door, hopped into his truck and set out on both the paved and dirt roads of Hazard to hunt for a victim. At 10:00 in the evening, the city was a ghost town. Most businesses had long since closed their doors for the night. The only activity he was able to find was at a local bar where there were a total of five cars in the parking lot. The sounds of Garth Brooks playing on the juke box could be heard from the shoulder of the road across the street where he had parked his vehicle.

After about an hour of observation, a pickup truck approached from the north advancing at a high rate of speed. The driver swerved into the gravel parking lot littering the street with a spray of stones and mulch. He came to a screeching halt in front of the entrance to the bar. The truck had barely come to a complete stop when he hopped out, rushed toward the door and entered the bar. It was apparent to Shem the guy was in a high state of agitation.

Three minutes later, he was dragging a blond woman by her collar out into the parking lot. The woman, who Shem could only describe as white trash, was struggling to liberate herself from the man's grip. He was trying to open the passenger door of his truck with one hand and hold the girl with the other. As he opened the door, she succeeded in stripping herself free and ran back toward the bar. A loud and animated argument ensued then the woman started to pummel the redneck's chest with both fists. Finally, he got sick of dealing with her, got in his truck, started it, pulled out of the parking space and crashed his front grill into the front driver's side of a white Chevy Camaro parked two spaces over. He disappeared at the same speed at which he arrived.

The girl was left in the middle of the parking lot crying hysterically. Shem started his engine, drove into the lot beside her and rolled down his window. "Excuse me, Ma'am, can I help you?"

"That fucker of an ex-husband of mine just smashed my car. He's always so fuck'n jealous. I hate that bastard."

"I don't think your car is drivable."

"I think maybe I should call the police. But shit, I just got into an accident last month and already my premiums are through the roof."

"Well why don't you just leave the car here tonight and think about it? You've been through a lot. You shouldn't make any important decisions. I don't mind driving you home."

"The car is a piece-a-shit anyway. It's probably not worth fixing. I should probably try to see if it starts, though. Maybe I can drive it home. Are you from around here? I've never seen you before."

"I just bought a cabin a few miles from here. I'll be moving up this way in a couple of months. Are you sure it'll be safe to drive the car in that condition?"

"It's worth a try. I don't want to leave it here in Billy Bob's parking lot. Besides, I don't live very far from here."

The woman unlocked the door and slipped in behind the wheel. She placed the key in the ignition and turned it to the right to no avail. The engine cranked but wouldn't turn over. After exiting the vehicle, she walked up to the passenger's side of Shem's truck and asked, "You ain't no rapist or anything like that, are you?"

"Now, do I look like a bad guy to you?"

"You sure are a handsome man. I guess it wouldn't hurt if I let you take me home. My whole night turned to shit because of that bastard anyway."

"Hop in. I'm Ted. What's your name?"

"Patty, pleased to meet you. It's awfully nice o' you to do this for me. My apartment is just a few miles from here. Everything's close in Hazard. Head up to the light at the next intersection up yonder and turn right."

Patty opened the passenger door and lifted herself up into the truck. The instant she sat in the passenger's seat, he stuck the syringe he was hiding under his right hand into her left arm and injected fifteen milligrams of liquid morphine. Within seconds, she passed out. As they were leaving the parking lot, her upper body slowly fell over toward him, her head neatly coming to a rest on his shoulder. After he was back on the street and able to straighten the wheel, he violently shoved her back to her side of the vehicle, the right side of her head and ear smashing into the lower frame of the open window. Careful to heed all traffic rules, signs and signals, he drove the two miles back to the hotel taking the parking space directly in front of his room. Before getting out, he scanned the area to be sure no one was around. There was one other car in the parking lot, but it was empty. He quickly jumped out of the vehicle and unlocked the hotel room door. Once it was secure in the open position, he made an about face, returned to the passenger side of the truck and opened its door. He lifted the woman out of the seat, kicked the door closed, carried her into the room, threw her on the king-size bed then shut, locked and chained the hotel room door.

The room smelled of wet carpet and mildew. The faucet in the vanity area was leaking incessantly making a rhythmic and obnoxious plunking noise. Normally, these irritants would affect his ability to concentrate. Excited to embark on a new adventure, he was able to ignore the outside distractions with relative ease. He went about his work unzipping his suitcase and pulling out a roll of twine and a bandana he would use as a gag. He then tied the woman from just below the neck all the way down to her knees, binding her arms tightly to her sides. When he was satisfied she wouldn't be going anywhere, he extracted a pink, rubber handball from his bag, placed it in the woman's mouth and tied the bandana securely around her face and head leaving her eyes exposed. Unwilling to sleep in the same bed with her, he picked her up, carried her into the bathroom and dumped her in the bathtub face down. He closed the door behind him, undressed, and hopped into the bed. Impervious to the maddening sound of the leaky faucet, he was asleep before his head hit the pillow.

* * *

Lowes was scheduled to open at 7:00am. At 6:55 the following morning, Shem parked his pickup truck in a space near the store entrance and waited. Once the doors were unlocked, he purchased the lumber and supplies and loaded them into the truck. He was planning to spend the day in the hotel room until well after sunset, preferring to drive to the burial site under the cover of darkness. He wasn't concerned about leaving the woman in the bathtub since he placed his do not disturb sign on the door. It was doubtful a housekeeper would enter the room unless he or she was a thief or wanted to get fired. That wasn't likely to happen in this town. Besides, housekeeping usually didn't get started until well after 9:00am. He was pretty sure no one else would discover her presence. The woman was making bizarre noises all night long that definitely weren't loud enough to be heard outside the room. As an extra precaution, he injected her with the additional 10mg of morphine he had left. It wouldn't knock her out, but she'd be pretty much out of commission.

When he returned to the hotel and stored the lumber inside his room, he found the woman making a vain and pathetic attempt to call out for help. Although the sounds she made weren't that loud, he knew this would get on his nerves very quickly. He went to his suitcase and pulled out a butcher's knife, opened the door to the bathroom and waved the knife in her face. His threat to cut her tongue out if she made any more noise served its purpose. He availed himself of the silence to take a decent nap as he expected to be up most of the night.

Shem was able to get a long, restful sleep, waking up well into the afternoon. He spent the remainder of the day relaxing and watching T.V. Every so often, he would go into the bathroom to let the woman know he was still there keeping an eye on her. Seeing her horror-stricken face motivated him to visit a few extra times. Finally, just after nine o'clock, he was ready to get started. The first order of business was to check the parking lot for signs of activity. Seeing no one, he took advantage of express check-out via the television then reloaded the lumber and supplies into the bed of the truck. After placing his suitcase in the cab behind the passenger's seat, he left the door ajar. He re-entered the room, headed straight for the bathroom, lifted the woman out of the tub, carried her to the door and checked a final time for onlookers. Assured the parking lot was still vacant, he lugged her to the passenger's side of the truck and stuffed her on the floor in the space underneath the glove box. When he looked into her eyes, it appeared they were going to bulge out of their sockets. As it had already done several times that day, the terrified look on her face caused him to slightly stir between the legs. It gave him hope this night would bring him the fulfillment he was seeking. The drive to the location he selected would take approximately thirty minutes. That would give him a full eight hours before sunrise to build the coffin and dig a hole while she watched the preparations for her ultimate demise with that wild, horror-stricken expression.

As he pulled out of the hotel parking lot and made his way back east on State Road 15, he warned the woman not to attempt to alert anyone on the road. He placed his butcher's knife on the seat beside him for insurance. Twenty minutes later, he was turning northeast on US-119, a two lane winding mountain pass. He drove another seven miles climbing higher into the black wilderness then turned right onto US-421 which led to a series of wildlife and birding paths. Recognizing his landmark, a street sign with the name Pine Mountain Trails, he continued another two-hundred feet then pulled into a dirt parking lot. The area was not normally visited by humans. It was no different that night.

Before he exited the truck, he reiterated his warning to the woman to be silent at the risk of losing a body part. Next, he hopped out of the vehicle and began unloading the lumber from the truck bed. For the better part of an hour, he carried the pine and other tools he purchased at Lowes to the location he had previously chosen to perform his work. He also found an ideal spot to place the woman giving her a front row seat while he built her coffin.

When he returned to the truck, he found her trying to escape though her attempts were pitifully futile. It took him an additional thirty minutes to carry her to the burial site as she struggled to free herself from his grip every step of the way. He wanted to smash her face against the tree he selected as her observation point, but was concerned he might damage one or both of her eyes. Instead, he smacked the side of her head with the back of his hand and forcefully pushed her down into a seated position. The blow caused a severe gash inches over her left ear. The impact with the ground sent a sharp pain from her coccyx that ran all the way up her spine to the base of her brainstem. Instantly, the laceration began to spout copious amounts of blood. Dazed to the edge of losing consciousness, she was tied in a position where she had no choice other than to watch him work. He checked the wound then applied pressure to it with a towel from his equipment bag. When the flow of the blood slowed and she appeared to regain her composure, he turned to the task of assembling her final resting place.

It took him approximately an hour and a half to erect a crude pine box. He overcompensated by using several packages of nails to be sure the coffin didn't break apart once he started pouring dirt into the hole. He wanted the experience to last for her. It would dull his pleasure to know the box could possibly fail and she would die quickly of asphyxiation. Every few minutes he looked over at the woman to use her terrified expression to renew his efforts. Her screams for help amused him knowing there wasn't a soul anywhere within miles. Her pleas for her life only managed to incite him further to continue the work.

When he grabbed a shovel from behind a tree to dig the hole, he wondered whether the stupid bitch just realized for the first time what was going to happen to her. She began to writhe frantically in an attempt to free herself from the tree. Her labors became so violent the twine around her arms tore into her sweater and cut through her skin leaving streaks of bloodstains up and down the sleeves. She screamed as loud as her damaged vocal chords would allow. Shem was beginning to worry she was going to shriek herself into unconsciousness. Nevertheless, he found her actions to be very arousing and let her continue.

It took him several hours to dig the hole to a sufficient depth. Every time her silence gave him the impression she may have passed out, he would approach to examine her. Like the flipping of an electrical switch, she would instantly resume her fitful outburst. By the time he finished the job, she had completely lost her voice. Her features and mouth were contorted like that of a person screaming bloody murder though all she produced was a rush of silent air. The sleeves of the sweater were soaked red and the friction of the twine against the front of the garment had painfully torn the skin of her breasts and stomach. He reached underneath her sleeves with his right hand, but was dissatisfied to find an inadequate amount of his favorite erotic substance. To resolve the problem, he snatched his shovel from the side of the tree and used the tip to reopen the gash on her head. His semi-state of arousal bloomed into a massive erection. To the horrified disbelief of his victim, he reached down his pants and used her blood to masturbate collecting more of the red lubricant as necessary.

After he attained his first orgasm, he advanced toward the woman to let her know he was going to untie her from the tree. Again, his threats to not struggle fell on deaf ears. She fought with all the strength she had remaining to either get away from the monster or anger him enough to do her in with one swift stroke of his hammer. The more she battled for her life, the more he became sexually stimulated. During the struggle, he spontaneously orgasmed for a second time. It took him several minutes thereafter to compose himself then restrain her sufficiently to throw her into the pine box positioned at the bottom of the hole. Although she was free from the tree, her arms were still tightly bound. Once she was settled inside the coffin, he focused on her eyes as he placed the lid on top. The pure and unadulterated panic they expressed sent a bolt of rapture directly to his loins. The adrenaline running through his body wasn't quite as intense as for a decapitation, but it was a close second. It replenished him with the energy necessary to fill the hole.

Forty five minutes later, the grave was complete. If she was making any noise, it was inaudible. Shem removed the garden gloves and tossed them, the shovel, and remainder of his tools into the thick underbrush. As he strolled back to his truck, he thought about how happy he was going to be in his new mountain chalet.

Chapter 22

The murmur of the capacity crowd came to a sudden halt as if the volume in the courtroom could be manipulated by a remote control turned to mute. The silence was broken by the clicking of cameras as Daniel Falcone was escorted to the defense table in handcuffs by two United States Deputy Marshalls. The court deputy warned the row of photographers that picture taking was forbidden when court was in session. Anyone caught snapping a photograph after the judge entered the courtroom would be held in contempt of court. The announcement provoked a doubling of their efforts wanting to get as many shots before the proceedings commenced.

Jury selection went a little bit faster than anticipated. It took a total of five and a half weeks to seat the panel of twelve jurors and three alternates. Once the jury was chosen, Judge Jackson adjourned for a period of one week to give the attorneys and court personnel time to prepare for the evidentiary portion of the trial. The television networks took the opportunity to install the state of the art equipment necessary to transmit the broadcast around the world. The trial would be televised in over one hundred and fifty countries. The networks would need every precious second of the week to set up their machinery. Cameras were positioned in every nook and cranny of the courtroom so that all angles were covered. Any visual aids employed by the attorneys would be captured by two special projectors strategically placed on the witness stand and judge's bench allowing the home viewer to examine the item along with the jury.

Daniel always felt he would be a household name some day. He never imagined it would be in this fashion. As he was seated in his chair beside his attorney, the Deputy Marshall removed his handcuffs. Daniel had a short conversation with Shipman who explained the motions he would be presenting to the court that morning. Shortly afterwards, the Court Deputy made the announcement that court was now in session and Judge Clarence Jackson entered the room through his private door. He greeted the court personnel then made a short announcement concerning courtroom decorum. As the first order of business, the judge would hear pre-trial motions. Opening statements were scheduled to begin later in the morning.

It was the judge's responsibility to make decisions concerning questions of law while the jurors were the finders of fact. As a result, the panel would not be present for the morning's arguments dealing exclusively with legal issues. After taking care of some preliminary matters with the court clerk, Judge Jackson asked the attorneys to make their pretrial motions. Mostly for the benefit of the cameras, Alan Shipman renewed his motion that was previously argued and denied, to have the trial transferred from the State of Florida. He contended his client could not get a fair and impartial trial in this state due to the extensive and slanted media coverage that already tried and convicted him. Once again the judge denied his motion.

For the next hour, the lawyers addressed various, clerical concerns dealing mostly with procedural housekeeping. When the last motion was heard, the judge announced a five minute break after which he would call in the jurors and begin opening statements. The jurors entered the room fifteen minutes later. Daniel attempted to make eye contact with each and every one as his lawyer instructed him. It wouldn't be a good message to send if he avoided their gaze. In the end, not one juror held their look toward him for more than a split second.

Pursuant to the Federal Rules of Civil Procedure, the prosecutor presented his opening statement first. The defense attorney had the option to follow the State immediately or wait until they rested their case. Daniel listened intently as the United States attorney methodically set forth what he purported the evidence would demonstrate. As he skillfully recounted the gruesome story of the triple homicide, the jury hung on his words, leaning forward in their seats, their eyes following every move he made. His articulate and eloquent recitation of each and every item of proof that linked Daniel to the crime combined with the total lack of evidence that Isaac Jefferson was a passenger on the cruise ship was more than compelling. By the time he completed his statement, an eerie hush settled over the courtroom sending a chill up Daniel's spine. It was going to be a hard act to follow.

Alan Shipman decided he would not defer his opening statement until the prosecution rested its case. He couldn't risk allowing the existing mood to prevail. As he began the account of his perspective of what the evidence would show, eight of the twelve jurors and two alternates crossed their arms over their chests. Daniel knew from his vast experience with jury trials this was a typical expression of disapproval and refusal to be open or receptive. He tried to remain optimistic, though already all signs were pointing toward a long and difficult trial. Shipman introduced the defense's theory that a known serial killer was aboard the ship and committed the murders. Unfortunately for the defense, the only evidence he could cite in support of his position was the testimony Daniel would offer when he took the stand.

Shipman hammered on the fact that Daniel was a model citizen from a very young age concentrating on his impressive academic career, his results as a law enforcement officer and his expected rise to the top of the Federal Bureau of Investigations. He emphasized the inconsistency between his client's lack of history with narcotics and the fact he was drugged to the point of incoherency at the time of the murders. The suspicious nature of the Terry Smithson disappearance and the convenient mishap with the ship's surveillance system was described in detail. The final point Shipman stressed was the cabin steward's expected testimony that he was under the impression for most of the duration of the cruise 9-476 was occupied. When he was through with his statement, he succeeded in uncrossing the arms of two jurors. One small step at a time, thought Daniel. Perhaps there was still a chance he could convince these people he was an innocent man.

The opening statements lasted for over two hours. The judge felt it was a perfect time to break for lunch and adjourned the proceedings until 1:30 that afternoon. He admonished the jurors to not talk about the case amongst themselves or anyone else. Normally, he would restrict them from speaking at all with any of the participants of the trial. However, since he already ordered that they be sequestered, the warning was unnecessary. Once the jurors left the room, the judge dismissed the attorneys and remainder of the court staff. Daniel was placed back in handcuffs and lead to a holding cell, where he would enjoy a peanut butter sandwich and a dry unidentifiable cookie for lunch.

* * *

When court resumed, the United States called their first witness to the stand, Special Agent Robert Leland. Daniel watched and listened as one of his closest colleagues for more than five years offered testimony in support of the prosecution's case for the remainder of the afternoon. Through Agent Leland, Norman Dallas introduced into evidence the videotape Leland found at the Tyler home, the photographs of Daniel having sex with Annie taken from the Falcone condominium and the bag of heroin discovered in the defendant's studio apartment. Understanding how prejudicial and harmful they could be to his client's case, Shipman objected vehemently to the introduction of the videotape and photographs. He argued that a legal chain of possession was not established in violation of the longstanding rule of criminal procedure to protect the authenticity of evidence. The prosecution couldn't even produce the individuals who created the images much less provide a clear picture of whose hands they had passed through since. The objections were overruled temporarily, the judge allowing Dallas' request to call an expert witness later in the trial to confirm there was no tampering. If necessary, he was also prepared to have one of the Tyler's neighbors who witnessed the incident testify that the events that took place on the recording were accurate. The judge ruled he would have to wait until those witnesses offered their testimony before he allowed the tape and photographs to be published to the jury.

In a way, Daniel understood Leland was doing his job. What hurt the most was Leland's actual enthusiasm about offering evidence that could send Daniel to the gas chamber. He seemed to be enjoying the experience. Daniel had to restrain himself from jumping out of his seat when Leland commented that just before the murders Daniel was acting bizarre at work to the point Leland wondered if he was using drugs. Daniel was sure that even these 15 strangers on the jury would agree that anyone who had been in his shoes would have behaved the same way. He had committed a major fuck-up and lost his family as a result. He always knew Leland wasn't happy when he was passed over for Assistant Special Agent in Charge and couldn't have been any more pleased when Daniel was appointed to his current position. Evidently, the emotions Leland experienced were deeper than Daniel ever imagined.

Throughout Leland's time on the stand, Daniel did his best to stifle his growing anger and not react to his former friend's testimony. His lawyer advised him that any demonstration of negative emotion could adversely affect the jury's opinion of him and have devastating results. He hoped he was maintaining an even keel and that his true feelings were not showing on the outside. It wasn't easy. Leland's bitterness was obviously influencing his assessment of the case.

Dallas had saved Leland's most impactful testimony for last. It also had the effect of creating the most intense emotions of anger and frustration Daniel had experienced up to that point. Daniel's blackberry along with a blow-up copy of the text message and photograph of Damien Drysdale were admitted into evidence with Leland's obvious seal of approval. As if giving no consideration to the fact he was testifying about a close colleague rather than a dangerous criminal, Leland accused Daniel of fabricating the entire Isaac Jefferson story. At the termination of his testimony, Daniel had to use every ounce of his self-control to refrain from strangling the man as he passed by the defense table on his way out of the courtroom.

Over the next several days, the agents that assisted Leland in the investigation took the witness stand to recount their observations on the cruise ship and interviews with the passengers. Not one of them greeted Daniel with a nod of the head or even looked in his direction. Surely, the jury would notice their attitude toward him. Again, he understood they were just doing their job, but couldn't help feeling wounded by their behavior. These were men he would have trusted with his life. He was especially hurt when the FBI's blood spatter expert, Christopher Frye took the stand.

Of all the people with whom Daniel worked, Frye had to be his favorite and closest friend. Like Daniel, he was one of the hardest workers in the North Miami field office. Many nights, they were the only two agents moonlighting until late into the evening. They shared countless cups of coffee and intimate stories about their lives. The proof Frye offered was devastating to Daniel's case. Frye had studied blood spatter patterns over his career with the FBI and often travelled the country to give seminars about the subject to other law enforcement officers. He offered specific and complex proof based on the position of the bodies and the manner in which they were slaughtered. The blood patterns on Daniel's pants, shirt, socks and shoes were exactly what he would expect to appear on the clothes of the murderer. Despite the disastrous effect his testimony had on Daniel's chances, it was Frye's refusal to look at him that injured him the most.

There wasn't much Daniel's talented defense attorney could do during cross-examination to attack the physical evidence and the expert opinions, the most damaging proof being presented by the FBI agents. Not having much to work with other than Daniel's impeccable reputation, Alan Shipman persuaded each of them to admit Daniel was a model law enforcement officer who typically went above and beyond the call of duty. Through a series of artfully crafted questions, Shipman cornered them into acknowledging that drug use and triple homicide were a complete contradiction to what they would expect from a man of Daniel's character.

When the chief investigating agents completed their testimony, Dallas began the process of building the mountain of scientific evidence under which he expected to bury the defendant and lay him to rest. His only concern was finding a way to make the subject matter interesting enough to keep the jurors awake. It was estimated this portion of the trial would take almost a week to complete. The testimony they offered would be the most tedious of the trial. In order to admit DNA testing into evidence, the Rules of Criminal Procedure required that the prosecution lay a proper foundation. The lab technicians were responsible to provide detailed testimony concerning the step by step process followed in performing a DNA analysis. This usually involved the use of many technical terms that necessitated lengthy, scientific explanations. It was during this phase of the trial that jurors and spectators alike usually became aware that the judicial system wasn't as exciting and dramatic as was portrayed on television or the big screen.

Throughout the several days his former forensics team testified about their findings for the various tests they performed, Daniel willed himself to stay positive and interested. Any demonstration of defeat in his manner or expression would be just as destructive as losing his temper. As each of the technicians performing the various laboratory tests described the procedures they followed, Daniel maintained a confident and erect posture with a look of unyielding concentration and purpose on his face.

Special Agent Frank Jimenez was the last witness to testify on behalf of the ERT. It was his job to summarize the results of the more significant tests performed. He explained that the only fingerprints found on the murder weapons were those belonging to the defendant and the ship officer who removed them from his possession. With regard to the DNA testing of the semen found at the crime scene, not only did it match Daniel's DNA, the autopsy results revealed he ejaculated inside of her minutes before she was murdered. Finally and probably most devastatingly, he described to the jurors and the millions of television viewers that no DNA evidence was found that would demonstrate that the serial murderer known as Damien Drysdale was ever in the Falcone suite or any other part of the ship for that matter.

To inject the horror of the murders back into the courtroom atmosphere after days of sleep-inducing, monotonous testimony, the prosecutor decided to call the FBI's photographer and the Chief Medical Examiner of Broward County. Through these witnesses, he introduced the gruesome photographs of the victims both at the scene and on the autopsy table. The medical examiner gave a grisly, detailed explanation of how the killings occurred and the cause of death of each victim. Most of the jurors could barely stand to look at the images for more than a few brief seconds. Heavy gasps, stifled squeals, outraged and repulsed expressions were some of the more predominant reactions. Every juror cried.

Exercising the adroitness of a seasoned story teller, Dallas brought the tension down a level by calling the expert in the field of photography he promised to produce earlier in the trial. The witness had an extensive and impressive resume establishing his proficiency in the field of cameras and film processing. He was an engineer who worked for the Kodak company practically since its inception, at times acting as a consultant in the film industry in Hollywood. He was a guru of special effects and the use of trick photography. When Dallas completed the presentation of the witness' credentials, Alan Shipman was well aware it was the prosecutor's intention to use this witness to introduce into evidence the videotape found at the Tyler home and the pictures of Daniel and Annie having sex. He stood up and reiterated his fervent objection to the lack of a chain of evidence. The judge decided to authorize the testimony, citing the witness' unimpeachable qualifications. The expert described his examination of the videotape and photographs stating in no uncertain terms that he found no tampering whatsoever. Based on this testimony, the judge granted the United States attorney's motion to show the incriminating images to the jury relieving the need to call the Tylers' neighbor. With the infusion of Daniel's motive to kill and perhaps a fair amount of anger toward him, Dallas' roller coaster was due to climb to its apex.

In order to get the degree of tension back up to a fever pitch, Norman Dallas saved the most emotive and affecting evidence for the closing phase of the prosecution's case. In the final days before he rested, he called Co Chi Cuyengkeng to relate to the jury his observations on the night of the murders. He was followed by Lee Andicoy, Security Chief Ted Hauser, Security Officer Brett Gerhardt, Lieutenant Stephan Johansson and Captain Lars Bjornson. Each man described in detail their participation in the events that took place that evening. Like a maestro conducting an orchestra, Dallas extracted the information from each of these witnesses in such a skillful manner that the jury was sitting at the edge of their seats. When the Captain testified about his initial search of the Falcone suite, there wasn't a dry eye in the courtroom. It was all Daniel could do to not look defeated and the perfect time for Dallas to rest his case. Daniel's moment to tell his side of the story was coming very soon. As the judge adjourned the proceedings for the night and the jury was escorted out of the courtroom, Daniel allowed himself a moment to be very scared.

* * *

The clicking sound of the footsteps of the night shift prison guard echoed through the halls of the tenth floor of the Federal Detention Center. They reminded Daniel of the macabre ticking of a clock counting down the final seconds before an execution. It was 3:00 in the morning and he had not gotten a wink of sleep. In six and a half hours, he would be taking the stand to perform the most important task of his life. If he didn't succeed in convincing the jury he was telling the truth, he could very well pay the ultimate price. He practiced his testimony ad nauseum with Alan Shipman and his legal assistant. His concern was less he would fumble over his words on the witness stand than that it was an almost insurmountable uphill climb to get the twelve people deciding his fate to believe him.

Before having Daniel testify on his own behalf, Shipman had presented evidence over several days detailing the murders that Damien Drysdale committed including Hannah Richards and the massacres in Europe. Dallas objected to its relevance. The judge allowed the testimony based on Alan Shipman's promise to tie it in to the subject homicides through subsequent witnesses and his closing argument. It was Leland who Shipman recalled to the stand to provide details of the Damien Drysdale investigation. There were also a few tricks up Shipman's sleeve. He wasn't considered one of the country's leading criminal defense lawyers for nothing. He deftly lead Leland through the specifics of each murder and the method in which the victims were slain highlighting Drysdale's penchant for decapitation and mutilation.

During the prosecution's presentation of its case, Dallas conveniently omitted introducing evidence as to how the photographs of Daniel and Annie came into Deborah's possession. In order to establish a link between Damien Drysdale, Annie Bryan and Daniel Falcone, Shipman convinced the Judge to accept into evidence the manila envelopes from both packages. He then called an FBI handwriting expert to the stand who offered his opinion that the names and addresses written on the envelopes were done by one and the same person. Shipman considered calling Jonathan Frazier to testify that the murderer's modus operandi matched that of the known serial killer. In the end, he decided against it, figuring it could backfire. One of the golden rules of both direct and cross-examination was to never ask a question without knowing the answer. Shipman feared that on cross, Dallas could ask Frazier his opinion whether Damien Drysdale actually committed the murders on the ship. The odds that the answer would not be in Daniel's favor were too great to chance. An opinion proffered by an FBI profiler that it was not Drysdale who massacred Deborah and her parents could be the nail in his client's coffin.

After two days of testimony from Leland and several other agents investigating the Drysdale murders, Shipman called Michael Munez to the stand. The purpose of Michael's appearance was to provide a description of the nature of his relationship with Annie Bryan and to prime the jurors with an initial example of the depth of Drysdale's jealousy. Shipman extracted from his witness a detailed account of the receipt of Hannah Richards' body parts. It drew a few oohs and ahs from the audience precipitating the judge to demand order. Shipman's hope was that the jury was finally seeing the monster, Damien Drysdale as more than just a figment of his client's imagination.

Michael was followed by Annie Bryan. Her testimony solidified the notion she was being stalked by Damien Drysdale just months before the murders on the ship, stressing her close relationships with Hannah Richards, Michael Munez and Daniel, all victims of the serial murder in one form or another. Annie told the jury how she met Drysdale in the course of her duties while visiting the Diamond and explained how on many occasions she caught him staring at her. In an attempt to evince the impression of his ever-present menace to Annie, Shipman had her recite the story of the day she searched her apartment upon hearing the creaking of her door. Norman Dallas objected vehemently to the intrusion incident arguing there was no way to prove anyone entered her apartment that morning, much less Damien Drysdale. The Judge sustained the objection and instructed the jury to disregard Annie's statement. Shipman expected as much. He was still pleased he was able to slip the story in. At least he had planted the seed. He never thought much of the disregard instruction and often invented novel ways to exploit it.

The conclusion of Annie's testimony was a risk, but one Shipman felt was necessary. Annie confessed her sexual interest in Daniel and her aggressive campaign to get him in bed, a rigorous effort that was ultimately successful. Shipman thought it might take some of the heat off Daniel. More importantly, he wanted the jury to realize that anyone stalking Annie not only had to be aware of her intentions, it was thrown in his face. At that point, Shipman was satisfied he had set the stage to argue that Drysdale had a fatal attraction for Annie and due to his insane jealousy for any potential competitor, framed Daniel for the triple homicide.

Shipman saved the recall of Ted Hauser for last to introduce the evidence of Terry Smithson's disappearance. He was surprised when Dallas didn't stand up to ferociously object. The defense attorney didn't know Dallas had made a conscious decision not to show his concern over the testimony. The prosecutor wanted the jury to believe he was confident the disappearance had no probative value whatsoever. He figured the judge would be consistent with his decisions to overrule the objection anyway based on Shipman's promise to tie it in later. Standing up and protesting would only give more importance to the event.

Perplexed, but pleased, Shipman led Hauser through Terry Smithson's time on the Joy of the Seas. The witness described Smithson's happy response to being transferred to the ship and detailed her long, loyal history of employment with King Cruise Line. Without the least bit of resistance from the prosecution, Shipman drew testimony from Hauser regarding his shocked reaction to Terry's failure to follow the normal procedures for terminating her employment. It just wasn't her way. When Hauser stepped down, court was adjourned for the day. After the jury was dismissed, Daniel had a brief conversation with his lawyer who notified him he would be the first witness in the morning and strongly suggested he get a good night's sleep.

Now, with the lights out order being announced over the prison's public address system, Daniel lay in the bunk of his cell staring at the ceiling without seeing. The temperature in the cell was a balmy 80 degrees, yet Daniel was helpless to control the fit of shivers that consumed his mind and body.

* * *

Waiting for sleep to come well after midnight, Daniel couldn't help but obsess about the nearly impossible task ahead of him. He was favorably impressed and truly grateful for the skillful way Shipman established a basis for a credible argument that Damien Drysdale was the mastermind behind the murders. Now, the ball was in his court to fill in the blanks in a reasonable and believable way. The unavoidable obsessive thinking about his testimony was far from a recipe for rest and relaxation. By 6:00am, he gave up trying to fall asleep. He reached over to the flimsy, makeshift table located next to his cot and grabbed the notes he took regarding his upcoming testimony. He had about an hour before they would come to allow him to take a shower and get dressed for the trial. Even though he had gone over the notes more times than he could count, he thought he might as well use his time constructively and review them one last time.

Two hours later, he was loaded onto the bus with twelve other inmates on their way downtown to the Wilkie D. Ferguson Federal Building. Daniel was scheduled to meet with Alan Shipman at 8:30am in the holding cell at the Courthouse for final instructions before he took the stand. Shipman was waiting for his client when he arrived. They were taken to a small room adjacent to the holding cell typically used for attorney/prisoner meetings. Although Daniel had testified in courtrooms on countless occasions, he felt a large lump lodged in the middle of his throat. Court wasn't scheduled to start for another hour and a half and already his palms were sweating. His hands were trembling so violently he had difficulty holding his notes. Normally, he was very comfortable speaking in public. This time, if he didn't get himself under control, he didn't think he would be able to construct a coherent sentence.

Before Daniel took the stand, it was Shipman's obligation to admonish him one final time that it was his constitutional right to remain silent. He wasn't required to take the stand on his own behalf. Testifying could bring about great benefits. At the same time, any false move on Daniel's part could be devastating. Shipman stressed that Norman Dallas was one of the best at what he did and Daniel would have to be careful not to get angry. To avoid any possibility of losing his temper during cross examination, it would be very important not to expound. He should keep his answers as short and concise as possible. If he could get away with answering a question with a simple yes or no, he should do so without adding a verbose explanation.

Though obvious, Shipman was duty-bound to warn Daniel if he chose to exercise his Fifth Amendment right, his story would not be told. He reminded Daniel the seed had been planted in the jury's mind that Damien Drysdale could have committed these murders. The million dollar question was whether it was enough to raise a reasonable doubt. With one small misstep Daniel could wipe away any uncertainty Shipman created. In the end, it was Daniel's decision whether he was willing to take the risk he would cause more harm than good. For him, the answer was simple. There was so much more to the story than what the jury had heard to that point. He didn't think he could live with himself if he chose not to testify and the jury found him guilty. He made it this far in life by taking risks that paid off and believing in himself. At this most important juncture in his life, he wasn't about to change things up. He would testify.

Shipman couldn't help but notice Daniel was exceptionally nervous. He recommended he take a deep breath after the completion of each question and take a moment to think about his answer. This was no doubt one of the most critical moments of his existence, but ultimately, he needed to remember he was telling the truth. If he stuck to the facts and spoke to the jury sincerely, he would do just fine.

The reminder he had truth on his side had a significant calming effect on Daniel. He could see why his lawyer was so successful over the years. He was doing an excellent job with what very little he had to work and brought out the best in his witnesses. As they concluded the meeting and the United States Marshall arrived to escort Daniel to the courtroom, he was beginning to feel much better.

* * *

When the parties and all court personnel were in their respective positions, Judge Jackson sat behind the bench and instructed the court deputy to bring in the jury. Once they were seated, he asked Attorney Alan Shipman to call his next witness. Shipman clearly pronounced his client's name sure to include his title, Special Agent in Charge. Daniel stood up, walked up to the stand, placed his hand on the bible and swore to tell the truth. His questioning began with the subject of his infidelity and separation from his wife. Daniel described his encounter with Annie Bryan, admitting he was just as much at fault. Both he and his lawyer agreed to get that bit of housekeeping out of the way at the onset. The jury would expect an explanation and could have lost respect for him if he allowed Annie to take the whole blame.

Next, Daniel defined his role in the Hannah Richards murder and how he and his investigative team were able to identify the killer and connect him to the slayings in Europe. After establishing that Damien Drysdale was an integral part of the saga, he began to tell the story of his encounter with Isaac Jefferson on the cruise ship. He gave a detailed account of their visit to Dunn's River Falls in Ocho Rios, Jamaica and managed to reiterate Terry Smithson's disappearance at the very next port. Doing his part as a maestro directing the flow of the testimony, Shipman had Daniel recite the story he and his family were told by Jefferson regarding his abandonment at the altar. Per his attorney's advice, Daniel omitted his initial feelings of uneasiness toward their new friend. Instead, he blamed his failure to see through Jefferson's lies on his focused attempt to save his marriage. He described his tireless efforts to win back his wife for the months before the cruise and Deborah's specific reasons for her hesitation. It helped establish a foundation for the confiscation of Daniel's cell phone and make the episode a more reasonable and believable consequence. Daniel was able to describe nearly verbatim his conversation with Deborah regarding his bad choice to devote attention to getting an investigation update. His concession of his cell phone was more than just that. At that moment, he realized it was either make a real commitment to reconciliation or let his wife move on. The choice was easy.

The moment he arrived at the part of the testimony where he was asked to recount the final night of the cruise, Daniel had to take a few minutes to collect himself. Having to admit his failure to protect his wife and in-laws to a crowded courtroom galvanized and reaffirmed his feelings of guilt, anger and incompetence. This was not a play of emotions for the jury or per attorney instructions. They came from a place deep within. Ultimately, after a short recess granted by the judge, he succeeded in calmly describing his actions on the last Saturday of the cruise up to his first contact with Isaac Jefferson that evening. He told the jury about his and Deborah's meeting with Isaac at the elevators and the invitation they extended to him to join them for a game of dominoes. His memory was somewhat fuzzy concerning the events that transpired once they returned to his suite after dinner and the show. He recalled that Jefferson brought the ingredients for a tropical drink to express his gratitude for his hosts' hospitality and kindness. Daniel specifically suggested it was Drysdale's means to drug them. That statement was followed by a vehement objection by Norman Dallas. The judge sustained the objection advising the jury it was their responsibility to formulate their own conclusion. It was just another of Shipman's successful exploitations of the ignore instruction. Waiting for Jefferson to deliver the cocktails while they were taking a break from the game was Daniel's last recollection on the ship related to the jury. The next thing he knew, he was waking up at Broward General Hospital wondering where he was and how he got there. By the time he completed his testimony, it was just prior to noon. Since Shipman had no more questions for his client, Judge Jackson decided to break for lunch and have Norman Dallas commence his cross-examination when they resumed at 1:30pm.

* * *

When the proceedings were formally recessed and the jurors were led out of the courtroom, Daniel was placed in handcuffs and taken to the attorney/prisoner interview room where he met with Alan Shipman.

"You did a great job, Daniel," said Shipman. "You stayed calm throughout your testimony and showed emotion at the appropriate times. You expressed yourself well and with confidence. I looked over at the jury several times while you were testifying. A few of the jurors were hanging on every word you said when you were describing the day of the murders. I'm hoping that's a good sign."

"I noticed the older female juror on the top row cried when I described my reconciliation with Deborah," Daniel added. "I couldn't read the male jurors, though."

"Daniel, that was the easy part. What happens this afternoon during cross will have a huge impact on the jurors. I can't emphasize more…you must, at all costs, keep your cool throughout Dallas' examination. You can be sure he's gonna try to push your buttons. You don't want the jury to see you angry."

"I understand, Alan. I'll be fine. It takes a lot for me to lose my temper."

"I can guarantee you Daniel, it's not going to be a pleasant experience answering his questions. It's his job to make you lose your temper and he'll try every trick in the book to get you to do it. Just don't fall into any of his traps."

Daniel had a lot of experience responding to questions under the attack of a defense attorney's cross examination. There were times he could recall when he wanted to jump out of the witness box and bust the lawyer in the jaw. This was a totally different situation. It was his life on the line. He prayed he would be able to maintain his composure.

"I'll do my best, Alan."

"You'll need more than that."

* * *

For the first ninety minutes of the cross-examination, Daniel's veracity was relentlessly challenged on a variety of issues. He was accused of inventing the character, Isaac Jefferson. It was insinuated he was a drug addict. His powers of observation as a law enforcement officer were mocked. The excuse regarding the cell phone confiscation was ridiculed on several levels. Not only did Dallas provoke Daniel by accusing him of being weak in his relations with his wife, the prosecutor made him out to be a lousy father for not insisting on checking the progress of the serial murder investigation on behalf of his children. Nor did Dallas pass up the opportunity to make Daniel look like a fool for not seeing through Jefferson's lame story about being abandoned at the altar.

Daniel fared well controlling his temper in that first hour and a half of cross, Dallas made great headway persuading the jury it was an absurd notion to believe one of the most highly regarded agents in the FBI could drop the ball in that fashion. Regardless of Falcone's ability to maintain his composure up to that juncture, Norman Dallas' instincts were telling him he was beginning to wear him down. When the prosecutor turned to the subject of Daniel's infidelity, he could sense he was getting much closer.

"Are you expecting this jury to believe the only reason you cheated on your wife was because you had too much to drink?" inquired Norman Dallas.

"What I'm saying, Mr. Dallas, is that I don't believe I would've behaved that way if I didn't have too much wine on an empty stomach. If you're asking me if I was aware of what I was doing, the answer is yes and it was a big mistake," responded Daniel.

"I'm not asking you if you were aware of what you were doing. That's obvious. My question is, would you have this jury believe your so-called altered state of consciousness was the exclusive reason why you had sex with that woman? Isn't it true you fornicated with her because you were attracted to her?"

"Annie is definitely a beautiful woman. But, she's just a friend. It was a mistake."

"Were you not involved in a very serious relationship with Ms. Bryan for many years?"

"Yes, that's true."

"And, in fact, didn't you live together as a couple for almost five years?"

"Yes."

"You even reached the point where you proposed marriage to the woman, correct?"

"Yes, I did."

"Yet, you expect this group of twelve intelligent and reasonable people to believe it wasn't your attraction to her that caused you to have sexual intercourse with her?"

"I didn't say Annie isn't an attractive woman. I stand by my statement. I would not have behaved that way under normal circumstances." Daniel was pissed off at himself for playing the alcohol card. On the one hand, it was bold-face perjury. He showed up at Annie's apartment wanting something to happen. But, there was no way he was going to admit that to the world, much less the jury. Now, he was just providing the prosecutor with ammunition.

"Isn't it true, Mr. Falcone, you're still in love with her and let me remind you that you're under oath?"

"Annie will always have a special place in my heart, but she's just a friend. I was in love with my wife."

Norman Dallas snatched the photographs of Annie and Daniel from the evidence table and spread them out on the witness stand for Daniel to see. Looking him straight in the eye, Dallas asked, "Does that look to you like a man who was in love with his wife? It looks to me like you weren't thinking much about her as you were putting your tongue in places too vulgar to speak of. Were you thinking about how much you love your children, too?"

Norman Dallas had struck a fragile chord. The implication that his wife and children meant little to him combined with the guilt of knowing in his heart it was actually true that he was never really in love with Deborah sent Daniel over the edge. His disrespectful reference to Annie as "that woman" only exacerbated his response. He stood up from the witness chair, pointed his finger within millimeters of the prosecutor's face and shouted, "First of all, Norman, that woman has a name and it's Annie. . ." Before Daniel could complete the rest of his sentence, two United States marshals grabbed him by the shoulders and forced him to sit back in the chair. Judge Jackson quickly had the jurors removed from the courtroom. When they were safely behind closed doors, he admonished Daniel that one more outbreak of that nature and he would spend the remainder of the trial in handcuffs.

When the gallery was sufficiently settled, Judge Jackson had the jury brought back in. He turned to Norman Dallas, who announced he had no further questions.

* * *

Closing arguments were heard the day after Daniel's testimony. The prosecutor took the entire morning and one hour of the afternoon to complete his presentation. It unsettled Daniel to see how attentive the jurors were throughout. Even more worrisome were the emotions Dallas evoked. He used his command of the English language to tug at the sensibility of every human being in the courtroom. The twelve jurors and three alternates wept for the last half hour of his argument as he described in detail the wasteful loss of life and the reality of two young boys who would be deprived the love of their mother at the hands of the man who sired them.

By the time Alan Shipman rose to speak, there wasn't a person in the courtroom, including Daniel who didn't think the case was already decided. Clifton Harris, sitting in the front row reserved for the media, was already formulating ideas for headlines for the next morning's paper. Shipman did an admirable job hitting the points hard that he felt could raise a reasonable doubt in the juror's minds. His professionalism didn't allow him to do anything but zealously defend his client, though even he lost a great deal of hope after Daniel's outburst. He felt their only chance was if Daniel had an impeccable performance on the stand and that didn't happen.

It took the jury a total of three hours to reach a verdict in a case that took several weeks to try. As the jurors marched back into the courtroom, there was a somber look on each and every one of their faces. Daniel looked imploringly for some positive sign. Not a single juror took a glimpse his way. It was an attitude with which Alan Shipman was not too familiar. In most cases of acquittal, at least two or three of the jurors will smile and look in the defendant's direction. At times they would even give them a nod of approval. There would be no such gestures on this day.

Daniel was mostly resigned to hearing a guilty verdict though he still held a small glimmer of hope. He always wanted to be a part of the American justice system as its defender and protector. Before this trial, he had the utmost respect for it. In his heart of hearts, he believed in the adage that the truth would prevail. After the judge had the opportunity to review the written verdict form and determine its legality, he instructed Daniel to stand and face the jury while the Clerk of the Court read the verdict. The only experience of terror he could compare to that instant was the moment he learned of the murder of Deborah and her parents. His knees were shaking so badly he was concerned when he stood up his state of mind would be apparent to the entire world watching.

Holding the shoulder of his defense attorney as support, he managed to stand. When he turned toward the jury, again not one member met his gaze. The clerk began to read the verdict.

"In the United States Court for the Southern District of Florida, Miami, Florida, in the case of the United States versus Daniel Falcone, Judge Clarence Jackson presiding, Case number 09-971, as to Count 1 of the Indictment, We, the Jury find the defendant Guilty of Murder in the First Degree of Katherine Tyler. As to Count 2, We, the Jury find the defendant Guilty of Murder in the First Degree of John "Jack" Tyler. As to Count 3, We, the Jury find the defendant Guilty of Murder in the First Degree of Deborah Falcone."

Daniel collapsed into his seat. He covered his face with his large hands and shook his head in disbelief. Despite his expectation of the guilty verdict, hearing the words pronounced in open court overwhelmed him. He didn't comprehend a word as the Judge silenced the courtroom then thanked the Jury for their service and advised them the sentencing phase of the trial would begin the following week. It didn't require the opinion of a trial pundit to predict Daniel's punishment. It was a foregone conclusion. Dallas had made it clear from the outset he would be seeking the death penalty. Based on the heinous circumstances of the murders, the judge and jury would have no choice but to side with the prosecution. Daniel couldn't even think about looking into the faces of his family and Annie knowing they would be devastated. The jury was dismissed for the week and Daniel, still in a fog of incredulity, was led out of the courtroom.

Chapter 23

An atypical dreary, wet January transposed into a beautiful South Florida winter in the first weeks of February. The sun shone bright in a cloudless, deep, cerulean sky. Tourists taking their early morning walk along Ft. Lauderdale Beach were greeted by the uplifting song of the Florida palm warbler. Pelicans dove elegantly into the Atlantic Ocean in the hunt for their first meal of the day. Sea gulls glided high overhead waiting for a scrap left behind by either the tourists or a clumsy pelican. Annie looked out at the scene that normally gave her an injection of cheer to start the day. That morning, it would take a lot more than a peek out her bedroom window to drag her out of a case of the profound doldrums. Since Daniel's conviction and death sentence, she felt as though all of her life spirit was thrashed out of her. Not only did she feel directly responsible for the horrific slayings of three innocent people, she might as well inject the lethal chemicals into Daniel's veins by her own hand. She was reporting to work every day but for all intents and purposes, she was just going through the motions.

She was scheduled to visit Daniel at the end of the week and couldn't afford to be depressed when she faced him. It was imperative to give him the impression there was hope even though her conversation with Alan Shipman after the trial didn't leave much room for optimism. Daniel's lawyer explained to her that in order to have a conviction overturned, it must be shown either the judge, the jury or one of the lawyers committed an egregious error that affected the outcome of the case. According to Shipman, the judge ran a very clean trial and the jury's decision was not based on a whim. There was no question they had both a legal and factual basis for their verdict.

The only slight chance Daniel may have would be the judge's ruling regarding media presence in the courtroom, however, in his opinion, the odds were not great. Shipman recommended several of the top appellate attorneys in the country. He suggested Daniel's only shot was to retain a lawyer who was politically connected and knew his way around the federal appellate courts. Annie already contacted all the lawyer's on Shipman's list and was going to discuss them with Daniel when she flew up to New York Friday morning. Unfortunately for both Daniel and Annie, she would never make that flight.

* * *

Daniel woke up to the ringing of the prison alarm which sounded at 4:00 every morning. Despite the frosty chill that pervaded in his death row cell on the tenth floor of the New York State Federal Prison, he was able to finally fall asleep around 2:00am. That gave him a total of two hours sleep. At least, it was an improvement from the previous night. This was his fifth day in his new home and he had probably slept no more than ten hours since he was transferred to the prison. Part of the reason for his sleep deprivation was the inability to get warm with the thin blanket provided by the penitentiary. The main cause was his continued self-deprecation over his behavior on the witness stand.

As things currently stood, he would most likely never know whether the jury would have believed him if he had been able to control his temper. Surely, the physical evidence was stacked against him. On the other hand, Alan Shipman did a masterful job shaping his case in an attempt to create a question in the juror's minds whether Isaac Jefferson was on the ship. How much Daniel's bad behavior affected the outcome would forever remain a mystery unless his appeals were successful. Annie was scheduled to visit today to discuss the hiring of an appellate attorney. This time around, Daniel would be responsible to pay the full fee. The hoopla surrounding the trial dissipated significantly after he was found guilty and sentenced to death. He hated to rely on Annie for financial support, but at this point, he didn't have much of an option. It was either accept her offer to pay for the appeal or a lethal injection.

Daniel stood up from his cot onto the frozen cement floor and stretched his aching back. His mattress was about as thick as a pancake and the pillow was even flimsier. Sleeping on the cot was probably just a step above sleeping on the stone cold, hard concrete floor. It did wonders for the neck and low back. The courtesy that was offered to Daniel at the Miami Federal Detention Center was not available at this prison, either. Although death row inmates were provided with private cells, he wasn't being separated from the general population. He was transferred to the New York prison where it was unlikely he would run into any of his former arrestees. Dealing with prison inmates as opposed to those in jail was a whole different ballgame. Meals and recreation time was proving to be a challenge. The stress related to avoiding fights was just one more obstacle to getting some decent sleep.

This time around, Daniel didn't allow himself to slip into a deep depression though his conscience was doing its best to bring him down in the first few days after his conviction. When the feelings of guilt and surrender reared their ugly head again, he quickly turned them into an emotion much more useful. He was boiling mad. He was pissed off for his pathetically weak response in the first place. Finally, real thoughts of revenge took the place of sorrow and defeat. The murderer became his mortal enemy. Daniel wasn't going to sit back and let this happen to him or his children without a battle. A week after his transfer to the New York prison, he had already developed a morning ritual of exercises that he completed before his breakfast of dry oatmeal and a pint of milk. Once he had access to the prison library, he planned to spend at least three hours a day precociously researching his options for appeal.

Visiting hours began at 9:00am. Daniel was expecting Annie sometime shortly thereafter. In the meantime, he wasn't permitted to leave his cell. The cell block was placed on lockdown before Daniel arrived at the prison. Drugs were discovered in three of the inmates' cells triggering a four week restriction on the entire block. Once he finished breakfast, Daniel decided to lie back down on his cot to try to catch a short nap before Annie arrived. The minute his head hit the pillow, he fell into a heavy, dreamless, comatose-like sleep. He was startled awake six hours later when the prison guard banged his night stick clamorously against the cell bars to wake him for lunch. Arising out of what felt like the sleep of the dead, Daniel was concerned about the time. He asked the security guard the hour who sarcastically replied, "What's it to you? You got a date?"

"Actually I was expecting a visitor at nine for a very important meeting."

The guard burst into a mocking guffaw and replied, "Yeah right, important business. I hate to tell you, buddy, but you got stood up. It's after 10:30."

"Are you serious? Is there a way to check if I missed the visit?"

"This ain't the Hilton, bud. Figure it out for yourself." The guard placed Daniel's meal on the floor and left the cell slamming the door behind him.

Daniel couldn't eat his lunch furious with himself that he slept through the time allotted for his visit with Annie. Since the cell block was on lockdown, he wouldn't be able to make any phone calls until the ban was lifted. Evidently, he wasn't going to get any cooperation from the staff. If Annie did show up for the visit, certainly someone would have come up to the cell to get him. He wondered if he slept through their attempts to wake him. His only option now was to wait to see if Annie showed up for visiting hours next week unless the sanctions were lifted before then.

* * *

It was great to be back in Ft. Lauderdale though his stay would be temporary. Shem would always have very fond memories of this area of the country. It was the site where he conceived the idea for his most brilliant masterpiece to date. To celebrate his return and to calm himself for what was to come, he took a trip to prostitute alley in Miami the previous day. The evening with the teenage prostitute in the Lycra Lame dress had its desired effect. He was as serene as a crocodile sunning itself on a chilly winter day.

The agent was sentenced to death last Tuesday. Shem was glued to the television set for the month and a half it took to complete the evidentiary and sentencing portions of the trial. The wait was well worth it. As he suspected, the look on the agent's face was priceless when the jury announced the guilty verdict. The expression was only to be matched by the hilarious, horrified contortion of his features when they decided to sentence him to death. He watched each of those clips at least a hundred times a piece, running it back and forth until the tracks on the DVD were almost worn out. Everything was finally in place for the most important undertaking of his life. There was nothing in his way left to prevent him from staking his claim. Munez and the agent were no longer in the picture. It was a long haul, but his patience was about to gift him with the most precious reward he could imagine.

The Birch Courtyard Motel advertised itself as "a tropical paradise just five minutes from the world famous Las Olas Blvd. and two minutes walking distance to the warm waters of the Atlantic Ocean on beautiful Ft. Lauderdale Beach." Yet, the main attraction for one of its guests was its location directly across the street from the Maya Marca Condominium high-rise. Tonight was going to be the biggest and most important night of his life. He was excited and more than ready to execute his plan. He pulled his cell phone out of his front pocket and dialed Annie's number. He made sure he dialed *67 so the call couldn't be traced then entered her digits.

She didn't answer on his first attempt. Having guessed that would be the case; he had practiced and prepared a detailed message. After the beep, using a voice altering device, he began, "Ms. Bryan, this is Special Agent Calvin Edwards with the FBI. You don't know me, but I worked with Daniel Falcone. Right now, I'm working under Robert Leland at the Miami Field Office. I have a very important message for you…I can't leave it on your answering machine. I can't afford to have my number identified, but I'll call you back in five minutes. Please answer. Daniel's life depends on it."

When he called back Annie answered on the first ring.

"Hello, Agent Edwards?"

"Yes, Ma'am. I'm glad you answered. I don't know exactly how to put this. I'm placing myself in danger by talking to you." After releasing an audible and dramatic sigh, he continued, "I just can't live with myself any longer with the information I have. Information that's been swept under the rug. I can't talk about it over the phone and I don't feel comfortable coming to your house. Could you possibly meet me at Birch State Park later on this evening?"

Annie felt an instant surge of excitement then almost as quickly switched back into a lower gear opting for a cautious approach. The metallic sound of the voice altering device spooked her. "Can we meet at my office? I'd feel much more comfortable with that. I can guarantee no one will know."

"No, No way. This has to be someplace private, out of the way. I can't risk being seen with you."

Annie thought for a moment then replied, "I don't want to do this by myself. Can I bring someone with me?"

"No. Maybe I shouldn't have called. Listen, I'm sorry I bothered you. It could cost me my job. Hell, it could cost me my life. Please don't mention to anyone that I contacted you. Good night."

"Hold on. If you have information that could help Daniel, you have an obligation as an officer of the court to reveal it."

"I knew this was a big mistake. I just thought I could get the information to you. They can't touch you. Ms. Bryan, if you tell anyone I called, I'll have to deny it. I gave you a false name and obviously you can tell I'm disguising my voice. I know you're not taping this call. I have to go now."

Feeling pressured, Annie made a spontaneous decision. "No wait. I'll meet you. What time and where?"

"I'm sorry. I changed my mind. I can't do this. It's too risky. I should have never called you in the first place."

"I promise I'll leave you out of it. You have my word. I can't just stand by and let Daniel be put to death if there's evidence that can prove he's innocent. Please."

Shem hesitated for several seconds to give Annie the impression he was mulling things over. After what seemed like a long enough pause, he said, "Alright, Ms. Bryan. I've heard great things about you. I know you're a straight shooter. That's why I chose you. I'm gonna trust you. I hope I'm doing the right thing. I'll meet you at 9:00 at the canoe rental pavilion. It's easy to find. Absolutely no one can know about this. You have to promise me you'll come alone."

"You're doing the right thing, Agent Edwards. Don't worry, I won't talk to anyone. I'll see you there at nine. I know where it is."

"Ok. Please don't be late. And if I see anyone else with you or if you contact the authorities, all bets are off. I'll know."

"I'll be alone."

Shem hung up the phone with a rare smile on his face beaming from ear to ear. He had to give himself a pat on the back for his acting performance. It was genius. With the rendezvous time set, he had an hour to prepare himself. The fat suit he purchased would help to disguise his look, though a potential problem could arise if she recognized his face. He planned to wear a baseball cap and lower the brim over his eyes to help prevent that contingency. The combination of the cap and the darkness should get him close enough to her for what he had in mind.

He wanted to be there well in advance of Annie's arrival in order to find a place to conceal himself as she drew near. Slipping into the fat suit then the dark blue suit he purchased for this occasion cost him barely any time at all. It took him only three minutes to drive to the park which was less than a mile from his motel. There was a parking lot for the canoe rental off the beaten path. The pavilion where he planned to meet Annie was situated next to the dune lake where the canoes were docked. The distance from the parking lot to the pavilion was approximately thirty yards. He parked his Crown Victoria which he purchased just two days prior, in the closest space to the pavilion. Since the canoe rental office closed at sunset, the parking lot was empty. He noticed a jogger when he first entered the park, however, saw no sign of any other presence since. There was the ranger to consider who was assigned to patrolling the park after dusk. He wasn't too concerned about that. After observing the park for the past week, he knew the ranger was most likely watching television at the office.

As Shem approached the pavilion, he decided he would stand next to one of the supporting posts so that he could hide his face behind it, if necessary. At three minutes to nine, he heard the sounds of a car's engine coming from the direction of the parking lot. Several minutes later, Annie walked up the pathway toward the canoe rental station at a brisk pace straining her eyes in the meager lighting to scan the area in search of the agent. She noticed what appeared to be a large person standing behind a post and wondered if Edwards was concealing himself to make sure she came alone. When she was about ten feet from the pavilion, a tall, heavyset man wearing a baseball cap, stepped out from behind the support pillar and pointed a stun gun at her chest. She turned to run while reaching for the pepper spray she had placed in the right pocket of her windbreaker. Before taking her first step, she was struck by an electric charge that initially sent her upper body into convulsions. Seconds after, everything went dark.

Chapter 24

The sounds of water rushing and the rhythmic chirping of what seemed to be thousands of crickets gave Annie the false sense she was dreaming of her younger days as a girl scout camping in the Green Mountains of Vermont. When she heard the voice of Alex Trebek from another part of the house, asking the contestant to respond in the form of a question, she knew she wasn't sleeping. At first, formulating thoughts didn't come easy. A thick haze seemed to shroud her brain making her head feel like it weighed five hundred pounds. The room was pitch black. She tried to get up out of the bed in which she was lying then realized she was bound to its posts. She attempted to slip her hands through the noose, but the harder she tried, the tighter the knots squeezed at her tender wrists.

When the cobwebs cleared to the point she was able to think rather than just react, she tried to recall how she got herself into this mess. She concentrated long and hard until finally she decided her last memory was the conversation she had with Agent Edwards. Going over the details of their discussion, suddenly the rest of the events that took place that night came back to her. She remembered driving to Birch State Park to meet him, parking her car next to his Crown Victoria and walking toward the canoe rental pavilion. When the man with the stun gun stepped out from behind the pillar, she had a split second to see his face before she turned to run. In that brief instant of time, a terrifying image was engraved in her memory. His features, especially the eyes could only belong to one man.

The realization that Agent Edwards was Damien Drysdale drove Annie to the edge of panic. She fought fiercely to free herself from the rope, but that just caused her more excruciating pain. The thought of being at the mercy of the psychopathic maniac sent violent shivers up and down her spine. When she could no longer stand the agony caused by the friction of the rope against her skin, she ended her desperate attempts to free herself. She came to the conclusion that if she wanted to think more clearly, hysterics would get her nowhere. Though she was unable to rid herself of an underlying sense of dread, she was able to calm herself enough to try to get her bearings. It frustrated her that the room was so dark she could barely see five feet in front of her. She listened intently to determine if she could hear evidence of the monster's presence in the house. As she lifted her head off the pillow, she heard footsteps climbing a staircase.

Seconds passed that seemed like hours when finally the door opened blinding her with light flooding into the room from the hallway. While her pupils constricted to a size small enough to clear her vision, she could make out the silhouette of a tall, statuesque-like man standing under the doorframe gazing down at her. If she wasn't in a state of terror when she first realized her predicament, the expression on her captor's face and especially in his eyes catapulted her into full scale panic. This man had no good intentions. That fact became even clearer when she noticed the gleaming butcher's knife in his hand. Annie tried to scream, but all she could muster was a barely audible squeak. Looking over her body in the direction of the knife, she realized for the first time she didn't have on a stitch of clothing. Her naked frame was totally exposed being there were no sheets or blankets on the bed. She didn't have the wherewithal at that point to notice that she was lying on a filthy, old, used, and mildewed mattress. Her exclusive concern was what the monster could possibly have in store for her.

For Annie, time continued to pass in super-slow motion. What felt like an eternity was actually mere seconds. The man she knew as Damien Drysdale stood in the doorway without moving a muscle. His menacing stare appeared to be fixed on her throat. She fought to free herself from the twine with all the strength she was able to convoke.

"You're not gonna get away. No one can hear you," he said.

Annie slowed her efforts to escape and looked up at the monster. The contorted smirk on his face made her tremble from head to toe. In a feeble voice that was hardly comprehensible, she muttered, "Damien, why are you doing this to me?"

That was the wrong thing to say. Referring to him by a proper name infuriated him. He was "Nameless." She had no right to address him, much less call him by his former alias. He was at her side before she even noticed he had moved and slapped her across the face without holding back any of the power of his exceptionally-muscled arm. The blow broke her cheek bone. His large fingers were imprinted in red on the right side of her face and her nose was bleeding profusely. She half-wept half-screamed. The acute pain from the fracture and the horror of her situation was putting her dangerously close to completely losing her mind.

"See what you made me do. It's your fuck'n fault. Don't even think about calling me that name again. Don't even speak to me unless I allow it…I'll cut your fuck'n vocal chords out. I wouldn't test me. I'll enjoy every second of it."

Annie always knew that Hannah's murderer was an evil, psychopathic maniac. It didn't prepare her for this. He was the devil incarnate. She was as good as dead. Feeling the crushing weight of her despair, she turned her face and attention away from him to grieve for herself. That was her second mistake. Shem grabbed her by the hair and violently tugged her head toward him so that he could look into her eyes.

"I wasn't finished," he bellowed. Annie didn't think the horror of the last ten minutes could get worse. She was mistaken. Shem laid his knife on a table beside the bed and began to disrobe. After he slipped out of his underwear, he retrieved the knife. With its sharp edge, he traced a circle around the nipple of Annie's right breast. Blood spilled down her bosom onto her stomach. The sight of the bright red, life-sustaining liquid gave him an instant erection. This time, Annie was able to scream at the top of her lungs. With a closed fist, he struck her in the mouth, chipping two of her front incisors and splitting her lip. He achieved the silence he was seeking. The punch nearly knocked her out, putting her in a state of semi-consciousness. The additional blood was also a benefit, but still not enough. He cut around the left nipple as he had done on the opposite side, this time piercing deeper into the skin to create a stronger flow. With blood oozing from her breasts, mouth and nose, Shem could no longer control his hunger for sex. He cut the twine binding Annie's wrists and ankles then flipped her over on her stomach. Over a period of forty-five minutes, he reached orgasm four times penetrating Annie from the rear. He wasn't aware she was unconscious after the first minute.

* * *

The sanctions were lifted on Daniel's cell block on his third Sunday in the prison. Monumental wasn't the correct adjective to quantify his relief. She didn't show up for visiting hours again that morning and he was worried out of his mind for her. At his first opportunity after lunch, he stood in line at one of the three pay phones on his cell block. When it was his turn, he stepped up to the phone, dialed the operator, and advised her he was making a collect call. Annie set up her phone system to allow any calls to her home to be redirected to her cell phone. So Daniel was confused when the operator told him there was no answer and he should try again later. He requested she give it one more attempt. She complied with no better luck.

Frustrated, Daniel slammed the receiver down on the hook and walked away. This was the second visit Annie had missed. Now, she wasn't answering her phone. He couldn't imagine one of the only people on his side might have turned her back on him. If he couldn't get in touch with her later in the day, he would try her Mom. Annie told him she instructed her mother to accept Daniel's call if he had any problem contacting her. If worse came to worse, he would have one of his brothers or mother try to touch base with Annie.

Two hours later, the cell block was given their second opportunity of the day to make phone calls. Daniel was too keyed up to wait. Just standing in line for the pay phone was about all he could bear. After what seemed like another two hours, but was really 20 minutes, it was finally his turn. He tried Annie's number for the third time that day with the same result. Coming to the conclusion that something was definitely wrong, he requested to make a collect call to Mrs. Bryan's number. When she answered, the operator made her required speech indicating Mrs. Bryan was receiving a collect call from the New York Federal Prison from Daniel Falcone, explained the tariffs, and that the call would be recorded.

"Do you wish to accept the call Ma'am?"

"Yes, please."

"Go ahead Mr. Falcone."

"Hello, Mrs. Bryan. I'm so sorry to…"

Cassie stopped him midsentence, blurting out in an uneven voice, "Daniel, my Annie is missing. She disappeared on a Thursday night more than a week ago and no one has heard from her since. I'm so frightened for her. That maniac either has her or… I can't even think about what he might have done to her."

"God damn it. I knew the bastard was biding his time. Mrs. Bryan I'm so sorry. I've been worrying about this for a while. It's no coincidence… just after I'm convicted of murder and sentenced to death, he's back to work." Having more than enough idle time in the prison, Daniel had numerous conversations with himself about the host of possible consequences of Annie's kidnapping. The case profiler, Jonathan Frazier, and he had also analyzed the issue together several times before Daniel was arrested. Daniel had formulated distinct opinions on how it would go down. They predicted that the killer had special plans for Annie. It wasn't his normal practice to spend months stalking and choosing a victim. Both men agreed Drysdale would most likely take his time with Annie. Daniel wouldn't share that part with Cassie. He continued, "I know it's not gonna put you at ease, but I really think we have time to find her. I've done a lot of reflecting about this. So did our profiler. We don't think his immediate intentions are to kill her. Who's handling this for the FBI?"

"What does that mean? What are his intentions? Daniel, you're scaring me."

Daniel had to say something and fast. Any hesitation on his part and Cassie would know he was lying. There was no way he could admit the truth to the mother of a daughter who would probably have to endure weeks, if not more, of pure hell.

"Our profiler says Drysdale thinks he's in love with Annie. That's why he was stalking her. Annie's smart. She'll know how to play him. She's a survivor Mrs. Bryan. Now please, who's handling the case?"

"Well so far I've spoken to Agent Leland and Agent Frye. I think Agent Frye is heading the investigation. Leland was promoted to some higher position."

"I can't say they're my favorite people in the world, but I know they're very competent agents. I'm sure they're doing everything in their power to locate Annie. Do they have any leads yet?"

"I don't know what that means. They found Annie's car at Birch State Park, if that helps answer your question. They assume she was kidnapped there. They tell me they have no idea where he might be. They still don't even know his name."

"This guy is slippery as an eel. If there's anyone who can get through something like this, it's your daughter. I've got to get out of this damn place. I feel so helpless. I would be searching the streets for her right now if I could."

"I know you would, Daniel. Please pray for my Annie. I just don't know what I'd do if anything happened to her."

"I don't know how I'm going to keep updated on what's happening. It's a sure thing Leland and Frye won't talk to me. Being totally out of touch with the rest of the world's been driving me crazy."

"Feel free to call me collect whenever you want. I don't mind. I could use someone to talk to who cares about Annie almost as much as I do." At that point, the damn broke and Cassie Bryan could no longer hold her emotions inside. She began to sob uncontrollably.

"I know it's not easy, Mrs. Bryan, but try not to get too upset. I'm telling you, I really believe they'll find her. We'll work through this. Are you sure you don't mind if I call you? It's not cheap."

Once Cassie was able to speak again, she responded. "I think I'm gonna need to hear from you Daniel. Call any time you want."

"Thank you. My time's up…I have to go. If there's anything you can think of that I can do from here, let me know. I'll be in touch soon."

"Take care of yourself, Daniel. Bye."

The frustration and anxiety Daniel was suffering was almost beyond his capacity to manage. He slammed the phone down and almost broke the receiver in half. He had to find a way out of this place. To be totally helpless while Annie was in the hands of the demented killer made him feel like a caged animal. He decided he had to get in touch with his lawyer, Alan Shipman. Annie met with him to obtain a list of appellate lawyers. Now he wouldn't be able to get his hands on it unless he was able to get in touch with his ex-lawyer. He hoped Shipman would accept his collect call. An appeal wasn't going to get him out of prison any time soon. At least he would feel like he was doing something. Perhaps these recent developments could get him a new trial.

* * *

The first snow of the season arrived late that February in the lower elevations of the Blue Ridge Mountains of North Carolina. Giant icicles hung from the eaves of Shem's front porch like the pearly white fangs of the Alaskan polar bear. The crystal clear spring water of the rapids ran through an endless field of pure white snow. Sunlight reflected off crystals of ice that cascaded down the cataract creating the illusion of a waterfall of diamonds. It truly was a winter wonderland outside the confines of Shem Chassar's hideaway cabin. Inside, the contrast couldn't be starker.

Annie never knew whether it was day or night. The room that was her prison was in perpetual darkness. Even when the monster left her door open, there was rarely any light coming from other parts of the house. She was in constant pain. The drugs he gave her to deaden her fighting spirit were no relief. Her cheeks were bruised and swollen, the broken bone left to heal on its own. The friction of the twine binding her wrists and ankles to the bedposts had rubbed the skin raw. The area surrounding her areola continued to sting as if she were being branded by a red hot poker, aggravated every time the monster entered the room by a reopening of the lacerations. Her anus, swollen and torn, ached constantly from the growing number of assaults. He was visiting her room every couple of hours to relieve his exceptionally high sex drive. Each violation was accompanied by a new infliction of pain. He had beaten her about the head and face, cut her in various places on her torso and extremities, thrown her on the floor and kicked her in the ribs managing to break two of them. Breathing was hard work. Maintaining the will to live was even more difficult.

She couldn't remember the last time she ate. He mentioned something about bringing her a meal. He hadn't kept his promise. She wasn't sure she would be able to get any food down anyway. It was excruciatingly painful just to open her mouth. He wasn't taking her to the bathroom often enough either. There were times she was forced to cope with the agonizing discomfort of a full bladder. He warned her that if she soiled or wet the bed, there were ways to make her suffering much worse. She couldn't comprehend that notion, but she wasn't about to test it if she could help it.

The few hours of repose between sessions were her only reprieve, if one could call it that. At least the pain and the drugs were preventing her from having any real clarity of thought. If she were able to use too much of her time to contemplate her misfortune and worry about her mother, she might have already given up. Sleep would have been all but impossible if it weren't for the sedatives. Every so often, she was able to catch a five or ten minute catnap. Consciousness was never far away. The pain was seeing to that. When she was able to formulate coherent ideas, they mostly dealt with escape. In spite of all the monster's attempts to smother her instinct to survive, Annie still held a primitive hope, no matter how slight, wanting desperately to flee.

Shem, on the other hand, was feeling like a kid in a candy store. The gorgeous winter wonderland outside only added to his good humor. They said revenge was sweet. It tasted better than he could ever have imagined. Since the agent's incarceration and death sentence, Shem had been riding on an unparalleled high. Now that Annie was his, life was about to get even better. The day he shook her hand upon their first introduction, he had to excuse himself promptly in order to avoid the public embarrassment of his obvious erection. Then, when he discovered he could reach orgasm by simply touching her clothing, it confirmed her unique ability to give him pleasure without blood. It was a done deal at that point that he must possess her. He could only imagine how pleasurable his orgasm would be when he felt her warm blood against his skin. At the time, he didn't realize it would be something that he would crave so badly. The rapture he experienced the first time he took Annie was almost spiritual. The second and third time was no different. He always knew he would keep her for a while. Now, he wasn't sure there was an end in sight, at least not until he thought about what it might be like to fuck her headless body.

* * *

The search for Damien Drysdale was still a priority though clues to his whereabouts were scarce. Special Agent Christopher Frye was now the lead investigator. Robert Leland was promoted to Assistant Special Agent in Charge, a necessary step for the grooming of a Special Agent in Charge. Frye's main concern at the moment was Annie. Though there was no substantive evidence to confirm it, he was certain she was kidnapped by Drysdale. They searched her apartment and found nothing to indicate he was there. Frye ordered Annie's phone records which revealed the last call she received was at 7:55pm from a payphone on Birch Street. As far as he could tell from other information gathered, she disappeared anywhere between one and two hours later. The night ranger for Birch State Park gave a statement indicating he first noticed her BMW parked near the canoe rental pavilion at 10:00pm. Frye was sure that somehow the wily Drysdale lured Annie to that location.

Nor did it seem much like coincidence to Frye that Annie was abducted shortly after Daniel was tried and convicted of triple homicide. He voiced his concerns to Leland who was adamant there was absolutely no evidence linking the two incidents. Leland reminded him that a jury found Daniel guilty based on a mountain of evidence and it wasn't Frye's job to question the American justice system. Leland's assurances weren't a great help to Frye. He was still ill at ease about the issue and became even more troubled when he did an extensive review of the Drysdale file.

Since the hunt for Drysdale began, all murders and disappearances occurring anywhere in the United States and especially within close proximity to South Florida continued to be reported to the task force. As Frye was reading through information stored on Leland's old computer records for the case, he came across a deleted file the new Assistant Special Agent in Charge neglected to remove from the recycle bin. Apparently one week before the cruise ship murders, two drug dealers were found murdered, shot at point blank range in Carol City. The deleted file was a copy of the Dade County Police Department's report alleging it was a drug deal gone bad and that traces of heroin were found in the apartment. In a note at the bottom of the file, it was marked, "Discussed with Dallas and discarded."

Frye didn't know exactly what he was going to do with the information. For the moment, he stored it in his own personal file requiring a password to access it. He couldn't imagine Leland and Dallas deliberately concealed potentially relevant evidence. Perhaps the drug murders were thoroughly investigated and it was determined Drysdale wasn't involved. Then again, it wasn't customary to delete or discard reports from the file. In any event, he wasn't sure he should discuss it with Leland. Not only was Leland his direct boss, he was being groomed for the Special Agent in Charge position. The office scuttle butt was that the agent who temporarily replaced Daniel in the interim was going to be transferred within the next few months and Leland would take his place. If anything fishy was going on, Frye didn't need to get himself in the middle of it. He wasn't sure about whether he could ignore the information either, especially if there was a possibility an innocent man, not to mention his own friend and colleague, was on death row.

Frye turned his attention to a woman by the name of Patty Lawson who was reported missing several weeks ago in the small town of Hazard in southeastern Kentucky. Her ex-husband had been harassing the local police to conduct a more thorough investigation after she wasn't returning any of his phone calls. It was eventually determined she disappeared more than six months ago. Frye decided it was time to send a team up to Hazard to investigate the incident further.

* * *

The visits to Annie's room were just as frequent. For a reason unknown to her, the beatings had abated. He continued to cut her and aggressively violate her from the front and rear, but the pain from the broken bones and bruises were beginning to subside. She was gaining some strength and more able to formulate lucid thoughts. It wasn't really a gift. She was that much more cognizant of her predicament. Her distress had increased exponentially. The fear of more abuse and the likelihood he would kill her was more real. She was now alert enough to even think about what was happening back at home. If her mother wasn't on the verge of a nervous breakdown, a fatal heart attack wasn't out of the realm of possibilities. She remembered her scheduled meeting with Daniel. He was probably worried out of his mind. There was nothing he could do from a prison cell and now his appeal would be put on hold. The fact that his problems were nothing compared to hers offered her no comfort. The psychological component was almost as unbearable as her physical suffering.

Tied to her bed, the muscles of her limbs stiff and aching, her mind working overtime, the sounds of the monster's footsteps coming up the staircase commuted insupportable stress to pure hysteria. When he opened her door, she froze.

"Ok, you're gettin' up. No more lying around like a fuck'n queen. I'm hungry. I want some breakfast," Shem ordered.

Annie was confused, to say the least. She didn't know what to make of this sudden change in the program. The last thing she wanted to do was speak and get smacked. While she wondered, Shem placed a bizarre mechanical device on her wrist then began to cut the twine tying her to the bed.

"I wouldn't think about escape if I were you. That bracelet on your wrist'll give you a hell of a jolt if you go outside the fence. I built it myself." He held up a pager and continued, "You try anything, this beeper'll go off. The shock'll put you in la la land for at least an hour. I'll know and you'll be sorry."

Shem finished untying her and dragged her out of the bed. The instant her feet hit the floor, her legs buckled from underneath her and she was down, landing flat on her rear-end. The lack of use of her limbs combined with being in the same position for days had rendered them temporarily useless. The constant abuse wasn't boosting her energy level either. Instead of giving her the thrashing Annie fully expected, Shem burst into laughter. He tugged her by the hair, his way of offering assistance to stand her up. When that didn't work, he used both hands to grab underneath her armpits and pull her to her feet. Once again, Annie tumbled to the ground in a clump and Shem roared. As quickly as he exploded into laughter, his expression turned severe, almost demonic.

"Alright, enough fun. I need to eat. We're gonna try this one more time. I recommend you do your best to stay on your feet. I don't want to have to break your face again. It's time for you to start doin' some work around here. Come on, get up. I'm not helpin' you this time."

Annie felt like the monster might as well have asked her to fly- there was no way she was going to be able to comply with his request. For a second, she thought about just bracing for another beating. Then, an instinct from deep within made her refuse to concede defeat. She reached up toward the bed to use it for support to help lift her body. The might she exerted just getting to her knees left her gasping for air. The muscles in her thighs burned like they did when she climbed the seventeen flights of stairs to her office in the 110 Tower. No matter how hard she tried to steady herself, her legs and arms trembled uncontrollably making it that much more difficult to achieve her goal. Time seemed to be getting away from her. She was sure he was about to deliver a blow for the excessive delay. Calling on sheer stubborn determination, the feeling in her arms and legs began to return. She felt an enormous sense of relief when finally she was able to stand without losing her balance. Her respite was short-lived.

"Come on. What's the fuck'n holdup? Let's go. I get in a really bad mood when I get too hungry." Shem gave her a violent shove toward the door. She remained upright for the first two steps. On the third, she stumbled and fell flat on her face. An excruciating shockwave of pain ran up her face to the crest of her scalp. Her nose dripped nickel-sized droplets of blood on the dusty, hardwood floor. Before she had an opportunity to think about picking herself up, Shem grabbed her by the hair and was about to strike her then saw the blood. He was in an instantaneous state of sexual arousal. In a split second, his pants and underwear were off and he was on top of her. Still naked and lying in the prone position, Shem's target was easy pickings. He wiped blood from the floor and rubbed it on his penis. Before he was able to enter her, his body spasmed in orgasm. It had absolutely no effect on his ability to continue. For the next thirty minutes, he plowed Annie's anus, not satisfied until he reached climax multiple times in his typical fashion. Because of the unusually large size of his penis, each stroke was like being impaled by a sledge hammer. The discomfort was worse than any Annie had ever experienced or imagined, yet she didn't dare make a sound. After he had enough, he took a few moments to catch his breath then shouted, "You see what you made me do. I made a simple request and you had to go fuck it up. Now look at ya. You're a fuck'n good for nothin' mess. Get up and make me some breakfast."

* * *

Shem sat at the dining room table watching Annie as she stumbled and fumbled her way around the kitchen trying to prepare his order of two perfectly poached eggs, two slices of lightly toasted Ezekiel bread with no butter and a bowl of mixed fruit cut in specific proportions. He could feel the stress and tension emanating from her body as she tried to get everything right. Even his power over her generated a sexual attraction to her. If he hadn't just climaxed multiple times, he would have considered taking her again. At the moment, he was giving it his best effort to control his insatiable urge to fuck her and feel the heavenly pleasure of her blood against his skin. His restraint had nothing to do with any concern he had for Annie. He was nowhere ready for this arrangement to end. If he continued to bleed her and abuse her at the current pace, her body could break down. He wanted her alive and vigorous. It was providing him with great satisfaction to have this woman at his disposal to service him and all his needs. Ultimately, it would maximize the bliss he expected to experience when he cut off her head.

The bracelet he made to prevent escape was a stroke of genius. It was the perfect back-up security measure if she ever happened to escape the room when he wasn't present. Her ability to get some exercise would also help keep her body from atrophy. Now that she would have more freedom around the cabin and perhaps if she behaved, outside, he couldn't be one-hundred percent sure she wouldn't find some way to sneak some tool to get loose when he locked her up. He would certainly keep his eye out for it and do whatever he could to prevent it. It gave him peace of mind to have the alternative stopgap. There were always the unavoidable times when it was necessary to leave the house to purchase food and other provisions. Those trips would have been a risk without his invention. The nearest shopping was a twenty minute drive. If she tried to go outside the boundaries of the property, the electric shock would knock her into next week. He would be able to make it back to the cabin before she regained consciousness. As a secondary deterrent, he had a special surprise for Annie. Shem was a firm believer in the old adage, "an ounce of prevention was worth a pound of cure."

In fact, no time was better than the present to put his plan B to the test. Annie's clumsiness in the kitchen only made Shem hungrier and more irritable. The eggs were overcooked, the toast cold and the fruit not cut to his standards.

"Come with me," he directed after he tossed the entire breakfast in the garbage. The calm, emotionless tone of his voice frightened Annie more than if he had shouted his command. She wanted to ask where he was taking her, but didn't dare open her mouth. The two times she had spoken without permission, she paid dearly with violent punches to her stomach. She followed him obediently to the front door ignoring the pain in her legs to keep up with his big strides. The thought they might be going outside nearly gave her the courage to protest. She was still naked. She had no idea she was in the mountains of North Carolina, there were four inches of snow on the ground and the temperature was less than thirty-five degrees. Whenever he let her out of the room up to that point, the few windows in the living area were sealed by locked, commercial grade, rolling, security shutters.

Shem opened the door. A blast of cold air struck Annie by surprise. It felt as though she had jumped into a pool of ice water. Her skin bloomed with goose bumps making it look like that of a plucked chicken. It didn't escape Shem's notice that the nipples of her breast were standing at attention. He had to concentrate hard to avoid looking at them so that he wasn't diverted from his purpose.

"What the fuck are you waiting for? Get the fuck out." Shem grabbed his coat from the rack beside the door and put the gloves on his hands that were in the pocket.

Once again, Annie considered asking his intentions then thought better of it. She had been through too much. Her body was weak and fatigued. She didn't know how many more beatings she could handle. If she made her punishment worse by speaking, she felt like it was possible she may not survive. She stepped over the threshold onto a pathway cleared of the snow that led to a driveway also recently shoveled. The lack of snow didn't seem to relieve the sting of the icy cement on the soles of her bare feet. She tried to focus on her surroundings to keep from obsessing about the discomfort. This was definitely not Florida. For the first time, she saw the mountainous landscape and the stream running within feet of the front porch. Shem had insulated the cabin so well, covering all windows with thick soundproof material, she was unable to hear the rush of the rapids from inside.

"Move it" Shem ordered. "Up the driveway to the gate. And don't even think about screaming for help. No one'll hear you and you'll have to deal with me." From where she was, Annie couldn't see a gate. The trees and hills blocked her view. She headed up the driveway not daring to speak, receiving a shove from behind every so often. Hugging herself, covering her breasts, she braced against the chill as she advanced. She didn't think it was possible to feel any colder until the icy mist from the rapids sprayed her body as they passed over its bridge. It nearly paralyzed her. Going faster was helping her keep her mind off her pain. She considered breaking into a jog then decided he might think she was trying to escape.

Due to the size of the property, it took almost ten minutes to get to their destination. Annie's fingers and toes felt like blocks of ice as did most of the rest of her body. She didn't realize she had been shivering so violently until she actually stopped just in front of the gate. Even her eyes were shaking in their sockets making it difficult for her to focus. She tried to memorize the landscape in spite of her blurred vision. Just outside the fence, she could make out an unpaved country road. She turned her head both ways to see if there was any adjoining property with neighbors or any vehicles approaching. A mailbox caught her eye.

"Don't even bother," Shem said. "There's no one around here for miles. This is a private road. It belongs to me. I'd shoot any trespassers…Give me your arm."

Annie held her left arm out toward the monster.

"Not that one, you dumb bitch. The one with the bracelet."

Suddenly, it dawned on Annie what he had in mind. In a panic, she threw all caution to the wind and shouted for help at the top of her lungs. Shem grabbed her right wrist, pulled her to the gate and forced the wrist through the iron bars. Annie received an excruciatingly painful discharge of electricity that sent her flying backwards several feet. She landed on her back, hitting her head on the rock-hard cement. She was unconscious before she hit the ground. Shem checked her pulse to be sure her heart was still beating. It was somewhat erratic though not enough to be of any concern. He knew she would survive. This test might have been counterproductive as far as her health was concerned, but it was necessary and actually quite fun. He doubted she would ever consider escaping during one of his excursions to town. He hurried back to the cabin to fetch two blankets to cover her and pull her on. Exposure in this type of weather was always an issue.

Chapter 25

No matter how hard Daniel tried to stay motivated to fight for his life in the New Year, circumstances were making it practically impossible. Over the past few months, his wife and in-laws were murdered, his children were taken from him and he had been sentenced to death, hardly reasons to be inspired. Although there were several lawyers willing to take his case, their fees were prohibitive. His brothers offered to help, however, they weren't wealthy. The amount they could muster up would barely cover the filing of the paperwork. His father would forbid his mother from contributing. He hadn't even attended the trial, not that Daniel expected he would. Daniel could count on one hand how many words they had spoken to each other over the past twenty years or so.

The icing on the mud pie of his life was that Annie was now missing for more than three weeks. From what Daniel learned from Mrs. Bryan, the FBI had absolutely no leads and weren't even sure she was still alive. Daniel maintained his belief that Annie's kidnapper had no immediate intentions of killing her. He just didn't know how long the maniac would keep her around. In the annals of the FBI's in depth research of serial murderers, those that showed the type of unusual, obsessive interest in their victim typically viewed them as a valued possession. Jonathan Frazier described the subject as a hybrid of a hedonistic and power/control serial killer. They derived pleasure from exercising dominion over their captives. There were enough examples in history where the murderer would keep the victim alive for extended periods of time to at least give Daniel hope. The unfortunate part was that some form of torture was often, if not always involved. His frustrations about being helpless to offer any assistance to Annie only made it that much more difficult to find the energy to work on his own behalf. The idea that the killer was winning was one of his few incentives. But, it was a big one.

He felt like his only chance was Annie's survival. If the FBI didn't find her, he would be forced to accept help from the state's inexperienced public defenders. Alan Shipman already advised him his only prospect of success was to retain one of the best and most influential appellate lawyers in the country. Without Annie, he was doomed.

* * *

The bone chilling cold front moving through the mountains of North Carolina was not the only reason why Annie couldn't keep warm. In spite of the hot air blowing directly on her face and torso from the central heating vent in her bedroom and the thick flannel pajamas the monster now allowed her to wear, she was shivering like a wet Chihuahua in a blizzard. Things had changed and Annie couldn't figure out for the life of her why. The monster was talking to her about particulars of his life she really wished he wouldn't share. After days of nothing but silence except for his commands, he was recounting with specificity his numerous, horrific slaughters of innocent people. The tales usually followed the brutal and merciless sessions he required to relieve his insatiable need for sex. It was obvious he considered his ability to commit these senseless murders a gift and expected her to be impressed. He told the stories as if he were giving a blow by blow account of a boxing match. At least, the beatings and the bleedings had been less frequent. He was only cutting her twice a week now. When he struck her, he avoided her head. Most of his blows were directed at her breasts. They were bruised and aching, but not causing her excessive physical distress. She could only hope the curtailed abuse wasn't a sign of the calm before the storm and that his stories weren't meant to prepare her for her own gruesome demise.

He had just left the room after violating her for more than an hour then describing the murders that would give her nightmares for the rest of her life. The fiend, beaming with pride, was eager to tell Annie about his capacity to outwit the most intelligent and talented law enforcement agents around the world. He boasted about the meticulous plans he devised for each killing and how he would leave just enough evidence to frustrate the police without leading them to him. It was evidently not his custom to save souvenirs from his murders. Almost as if he was instructing her on the logistics of a fine art, he explained it created a risk of being captured he wasn't willing to take. Annie had to stifle reacting out loud to the horror when he reported every last detail of the murders of Deborah Falcone and her parents. She would swear that her heart stopped when he promised to show her the surgeon's saw that just this one time he couldn't resist keeping as a trophy.

One of the most significant changes over the past few days was his willingness to allow Annie to move about the cabin and even go for walks outside. The exercise and decreased violence was the nourishment her mind and body so sorely needed. As her physical strength grew, so did her clarity of thought. Rather than obsessing over when the next bashing was coming, she had the wherewithal to give serious thought to an escape plan. She wasn't sure she had much time.

The monster was always attached to her hip never allowing her out of his sight, but Annie was sure he would eventually make a mistake. Just a brief detour of his gaze and she was confident she would be able to sneak a few necessary items either from the kitchen or his office and hide them in a private place on her person. It was certainly worth the risk. Lately, he had been leaving the cabin on a regular basis though he never failed to pat her down, tie her to her bed and lock the bedroom door behind him before his departure. With the right tools and a bit of luck on her side, it just might be possible to get herself untied and pick the lock. She definitely deserved the good fortune and had to believe it could happen. An immediate escape may not be in the plan due to the device on her wrist. There was a chance, however slight, she could get a letter out in the mail. She had been thinking about the mailbox just outside the gate since the day he shocked her. A note to the mailman explaining her predicament had the potential to save her and Daniel's life.

* * *

Annie would get an opportunity to put her plan into action much sooner than she expected. The monster had been behaving more and more erratically over the past few days. He wasn't visiting her room nearly as often nor expecting her to be his personal slave. She found herself locked in her bedroom for more than twenty-four hours at a stretch. One time, he actually forgot to tie her up. She was sure something was bothering him. Her assumption was confirmed earlier that morning when he visited her room to provide her with her first meal in a day and a half.

It wasn't until two days ago while she was scrubbing the kitchen floor that she heard a phone ring for the first time. Instead of answering it, he led her upstairs, tied her to the bed and locked her in the room. This morning, while delivering her breakfast, it rang for the second time, at least as far as she was aware. Once again, he neglected to tie her up leaving the room with the light on and an obvious sense of urgency, locking the door behind him. She quickly set her meal on the floor, jumped out of the bed and hurried to the door. Holding her ear up against it, she could hear every word of his side of the conversation. It helped that he was shouting.

"What the fuck? There has to be a way to reschedule it."

"No…impossible…find another way."

"I paid you a lot of fuck'n money. You lawyers are fuck'n useless. There's no way I can make it tomorrow."

"I don't have to do shit. Just handle it. Why do I have to be there?"

"Who the fuck do you think you're talkin to? I don't take threats well."

"It sounded like one to me. I can't be away that long."

"There has to be another way. What the fuck do I pay you for?"

After a long pause, Annie thought he might have hung up. She was about to high-tail it back to the bed when, in a much calmer voice, totally devoid of emotion he said, "How long is this gonna take?"

"I want it all done in one day. I want to be able to drive down there in the morning and be back before dinner."

"Fuck try. Make it happen."

There was another period of extended silence then, "Ok, tomorrow. This better take care of everything or you'll be sorry. I'm dead serious. Goodbye."

Annie bolted for the bed. Just before she was about to leap into it, her attention was diverted by a sparkling flicker in her peripheral vision coming from a point down low between the door and the bed. She turned her head to examine it more carefully and saw the flash was a reflection bouncing off the scalpel the monster sometimes used to bleed her. In his rush to answer the phone, it must have dropped out of his pocket onto the floor. It was only by dumb luck she didn't step on it. She didn't even want to think about what he was planning to do with it. Making a spur of the moment decision, she hurried to pick it up. It was either going to be her salvation or the dumbest move she ever made in her life.

Once back in the bed, she grabbed her breakfast, shoved the remainder of the overdone scrambled eggs into her mouth and chugged down the entire glass of milk. She almost choked at the sound of his footsteps pounding up the stairs. Normally, he was very light on his feet, usually surprising Annie when she heard the turn of the key in the lock without hearing his approach. He was most definitely agitated. Willing herself to stay calm, she used the short amount of time she had to evaluate the information she had just overheard. It was pretty clear he was going to be gone for most of the day tomorrow. This was a chance that would probably never present itself again. He was definitely off his game. His focus for the past few days hadn't been on her. The issue with the lawyer obviously had him distracted.

The idea she was contemplating would entail terrifying risk. Any one of a number of things could go wrong that would undoubtedly mean either the end of her or unthinkable pain and suffering. The sound of the stomping was getting louder by the millisecond forcing her to make another hasty choice. If she had the time to weigh the pros and cons, her decision might not have been so courageous. She tucked the scalpel safely down the backside of her pajamas not a moment too soon. Shem unlocked the door and burst through it.

Annie knew instantly she was in deep trouble. The look on his face was one she had seen too many times. There was a total lack of emotion or spirit. The blank, vacuous expression of his eyes would have sent a shiver up the spine of Satan. It was infinitely more frightening than the butcher's knife he was carrying in his left hand. With a clear purpose in his stride, he made his way to Annie's side. He reared back with his right hand and hit her square on the nose and mouth with a closed fist. Blood gushed from her nostrils and oozed down both sides of her mouth. Annie barely noticed it, half-dazed from the blow. Shem didn't bother with the buttons of her top or the snaps of her fly. He slashed through the pajamas with the butcher's knife exposing her breasts and opening a hole in the crotch. The tip of the knife had sliced into both breasts and several areas on her stomach. Blood was everywhere. The smell and the sight of it were too much for Shem to handle. He quickly undressed, his penis already fully erect. Though Annie was forced to live through the horror of another violent and bloody rape, later, she would thank the Lord he was too spent after the frontal assault to also take her from behind. She kept the scalpel tucked safely against her rear not taking the chance to use it and fail. His weapon was a lot larger. She had a much safer plan in mind for later.

* * *

It was the coldest day of the year to date in the Blue Ridge Mountains of North Carolina. Shem put on three layers of clothing before donning his parka. He wasn't totally comfortable with the idea of leaving Annie home alone for a whole day, but had taken every possible precaution to assure she was going nowhere. He had tied the knots of the synthetic twine extra tight and forced her to take a high dose of sedatives just minutes ago. She should be asleep for most of the day. None of this would've been necessary if his business didn't involve an issue of traceability. When the question of his anonymity came into play, there was no such thing as having too many checks and balances in place. He had employed an attorney who was well known for engaging in illegal activities and paid him an exorbitant fee to keep his mouth shut. Shem also wouldn't hesitate to use his knowledge of the shyster's connection to the mob to assure his obedience.

According to the lawyer, Shem's notarized signature was required by his personal bankers in the Cayman Islands on a stack of tax documents. A meeting with all parties involved had been scheduled months ago for today at the lawyer's office in downtown Atlanta. Shem was expected to attend and furnish an official form of identification. If everything wasn't filed by the end of the day, his funds would be frozen and subject to inspection by the United States government. Until just the other day, Shem had completely forgotten about the meeting. Perhaps it could have been delayed if he had requested a postponement a week ago. Now, according to the lawyer, it was too late. Shem's presence was unavoidable. The lawyer had prepared a falsified driver's license for Shem to present to the bankers who were already in town. All that was required of Shem was to show up and sign the documents.

Stepping out the front door onto the porch, his mind didn't register that the temperature had dipped below ten degrees Fahrenheit. His total focus was on the business at hand. It was pitch black at five o'clock in the morning. The sun would not rise for at least another two hours. He had a mile and a half walk to get to his car hidden in the woods just outside his property. As sure-footed as a mountain goat and seemingly with the night vision of an African lion, he negotiated the icy driveway without a slip or a slide. He had already calculated his trip to Atlanta would take at least four hours considering the icy mountain roads. His meeting with the bank representatives was scheduled for 9:00am. By one o'clock in the afternoon, he should be on the road back home. If all went according to schedule, he would be at the cabin by no later than 5:00pm. Just the drugs should keep Annie sedated until then.

* * *

Straining the muscles of her neck and shoulders, Annie lifted her head in the direction of her right hand securely tied to the bedpost. At the same time, she pulled her arm toward her mouth stretching the twine to its limit. She had already made two attempts to stick her index finger down her throat without success. The last time, she had gotten much closer, the finger reaching the middle of her tongue. The physical exertion required by the effort was starting to zap her strength. She was giving herself a second to rest, but couldn't afford to be too long. The drugs would pass from her stomach to her small intestine any minute. If that happened, her plan would go up in smoke.

After waiting a good minute, she took a deep breath then pulled her hand toward her mouth with all her might while compelling her neck to extend further than would ordinarily be possible. She could feel her finger glide against her tongue moving closer and closer to the back of her throat. At the absolute worst possible moment, a droplet of sweat from her forehead slithered into her eye causing a distracting sting. Her instinct was to close the eye, but with the determination that had gotten her through the hard times of her life to this point, she willed herself to ignore the reflex and continue her effort. With one final thrust of her head and arm, the sound of her neck cracking blasted in her ear as if transmitted through a loud speaker. Before her brain had the time to make the connection she was vomiting, she could smell the cheesy stink of the half-digested food from her stomach exploding out onto the blanket and the floor below. Never in her thirty-seven years had she been so happy about projectile puke. She prayed she was able to expel most of the drugs the monster forced her to take. She would know soon enough.

In the meantime, she had to think about getting her hands free. Since the room was almost completely devoid of light, she would have to work by feel alone. Yesterday morning, after the monster left the room, Annie had to figure out a hiding spot she would be able to reach with her hands tied. Luckily, the scalpel only superficially pierced the skin of her buttocks over the time it was hidden on her person. She caught a second break when, in his preoccupied state, he left her untied just long enough to find a suitable storage space. At least, she hoped she would be able to get to it when the time presented itself. It was a tense twenty-two hours until this morning, waiting to discover whether he noticed the missing scalpel or would find her cache.

Before attempting to recover her prize, she took a few minutes to allow her muscles to recover. The job would require a lot more stretching and straining both physical and mental. The sharp end of the scalpel was tucked in the groove just behind the bedpost where it met the backside of the head board. She had intentionally placed it on the side where she would be able to use her dominant right hand to retrieve it. Not only would it be necessary to distend her arm and wrist beyond their normal confines, she would have to deftly employ her fine motor skills to avoid dropping the scalpel all while keeping her cool. To top it all off, she had no idea exactly how much time she had to get everything she planned done. So many things had to go exactly right. Even then she may need a lot of luck, probably even a miracle to achieve each of her goals. The fact that the room reeked of her vomit just provided that much more of an unpleasant environment.

In order to succeed Annie knew she would have to take things one step at a time. If she allowed herself to think ahead, the stress alone from the enormity of her task would significantly work against her. When she felt she was physically ready to proceed, she inhaled and exhaled several breaths as a calming exercise. Her emotional fortitude would be just as important as brute strength and endurance. She had already tested several times to determine if she could reach the hiding spot during the day yesterday and a few times overnight. Every time, she was able to lightly touch the handle of the scalpel. Now, the twine was tied much tighter. As she extended her right hand backwards, she felt a tensing of her chest and stomach in spite of her work to control her nerves. She couldn't erase the thoughts from her mind that the twine's rigidity was going to prevent her from getting her hand behind the post. The first attempt failed almost as much as a result of her stress than the tautness of the twine. It only stood to reason that the more anxious she was, the less flexible her muscles would be.

She took a few more minutes to relax herself, employing a few yoga techniques she had learned from her college days when she was into that sort of thing. This time, when she extended her hand backwards, her fingers brushed against the back of the post. With all the tugging and jerking of the twine, it seemed to be giving her a little bit more slack. She flexed the twine to its limit several more times expecting to loosen it even more. On the next attempt, she was able to lay the palm-side of her index and middle fingers down to the second knuckle flat against the blade. A few more tugs of the twine and maybe she would have enough leeway to grasp it.

Just when she was ready to give it another shot, seemingly out of nowhere, her eyelids started to feel the heaviness of oncoming sleep. She tried to will her fingers to reach back toward the bedpost, but they rejected her command. Her entire body had turned numb. She fought with all her resolve to stay awake. It was turning out to be a losing battle. The realization that her efforts to expel the drugs must have failed was a devastating blow. Her determination to resist the urge to close her eyes was gone. She surrendered to a state of total relaxation. Before she could formulate another thought, she was asleep.

* * *

With no way of knowing how long she was unconscious, Annie woke up to full alertness in a panic. It seemed like only minutes ago she was struggling against the effects of the drugs, but for all she knew, the monster was already home. Unwilling to give up on what could be her one and only opportunity to escape, she stubbornly decided she wasn't going to worry about the time. If she didn't succeed with her plans, she probably didn't want to live anyway. She didn't think she could bear one more second of his abuse without a reason for hope.

As soon as the cobwebs cleared, she rededicated herself to the work of loosening the twine. Much more relaxed now that she was one hundred percent committed to her mission regardless of the consequences, she counted out at least fifty yanks of the twine. Her wrist was sore and raw by the time she was willing to call it quits. Blood dripped from torn skin adding to the countless red stains soiling the mattress. So long as she had done enough to give herself a shot to grip the scalpel, she could deal with the pain. A five minute break and she would be up to putting it to the test.

Closing her eyes, she visualized stretching her joints to their extremes and using the tips of her thumb, index and middle fingers to get a firm grasp of the handle. When it was time to execute, she didn't hesitate an instant, commanding the muscles of her right arm to unravel backwards, her knuckles to unhinge toward their target. She grabbed the edge of the handle just below the blade and pulled ever so slightly to coax it out from its crevice. With the dexterity of a surgeon, she teased the slippery surface of the handle, rolling it over her thumb and index finger until she was able to hold it reliably enough to transport it. Pulling it further out from the crack allowed her to add her middle finger to the mix.

With the scalpel free from the crevice, she slowly brought it around the post until her arm was in its normal position behind her head. For almost a minute, she allowed the limb to rest and regain some strength, though she didn't dare loosen her iron-clad clench on the blade. Dropping it was as good as shoving it into her jugular vein. It would be all over.

When she was ready, the next order of business was to move her purchase down the handle. She laid the bottom half of the scalpel against the palm of her hand and worked her fingers along the handle until she was holding it in a conventional grip. Confident the risk of dropping the scalpel was now minimal, she allowed herself a brief moment of relief.

Though her next chore shouldn't be as difficult, Annie was determined to maintain her intense focus. She was going to have to control the swaying of the twine while at the same time maneuvering the scalpel forward so that its sharp edge could do its work. Once she got that hand free, the rest should be a piece of cake. With the handle of the scalpel between her index finger and thumb, she pressed it against the twine. The blade sliced through it as if it were paper. The edge was honed so sharp, just a light touch was enough to bisect the synthetic material. There was an audible snap then her right arm was free. The tensile strength of the twine was so high, the back of her hand slammed against the mattress with enough force to send a bolt of pain through her wrist and up her arm. She didn't take the time to shake it off or allow the tight muscles to stretch before she cut the twine binding her left hand then both ankles.

The exhilaration Annie felt as a result of her liberation gave her a new sense of purpose and helped her forget how dangerously close she was to giving up all hope. Freeing herself of her restraints was a huge accomplishment, but it would be all for naught if she wasn't able to get out of the room. The ordinary person would think it would take an act of magic to open a locked door without a key or locksmith, especially since the lock installed on her bedroom door was the same used for the typical front door. Being a security expert, Annie was well educated in the field of commercial and home protection and more than capably familiar with the pin-and-tumbler mechanism of the common house lock. With the use of a pick and tension wrench readily improvised from conventional household items, they were relatively easy to open without a key. The scalpel blade was definitely thin enough to act as a tension wrench. It would leave enough room in the keyhole to facilitate maneuvering the pick inside the cylinder. The only trouble would be finding something around the room to serve as a pick in the pitch black. From her vantage point on the old, moldy mattress, when the monster did turn on the lights, she had been able to clearly see the room was vacant except for the bed. With a cutting tool however, she felt she could easily fashion a pick from the wood of the door itself.

Holding her precious scalpel, she climbed out of the bed and crawled on all fours in the general direction of the door, reaching out with her free hand every so often to test the space in front of her. Though she didn't know it, the first obstruction she came upon was the wall just six inches to the left of the door. She raised herself up on her knees and opted to run her fingers to the right along the wall. The cold bite of the metal hinge followed by the rough, grainy surface of the oak wood told her she had made the correct choice. She scooted over a few inches to shave a six by two inch splinter from the door with the scalpel then whittled the wood down to a perfect pick size gauging her progress with the tips of her fingers. Having only the use of the sense of touch at her disposal, like a seasoned cat burglar, she inserted the scalpel into the keyhole applying the exact amount of torque necessary to push the upper pins out of the cylinder and set them. Holding the tension wrench in place, she wriggled her makeshift pick into the upper part of the keyhole and exerted just enough pressure to the pins to overcome the friction and spring forces. When Annie heard the clicking of the tumbler, she knew she was home free. She squealed with joy as she turned the knob and the door opened.

Before making another move, Annie had to know the time. There was a clock in the kitchen. The challenge was to get there. The rest of the house was just as dark as her room. She just needed to get to the landing of the staircase where there was a light switch. Standing in the threshold of her doorway looking out of the room, the steps were located approximately fifteen feet to the right and seven feet straight ahead. She stepped into the hallway and turned right, placing her right hand against the partition between the hallway and her bedroom. Keeping her hand braced against the wall, she walked forward counting out exactly fifteen steps. She then got back down on her hands and knees and crawled in the direction she assumed would lead her to the stairway. After advancing approximately seven feet, she stretched her right arm out along the floor. She shouted out a joyous yelp once again when her hand slid down the riser of the first step. Creeping as close to the edge of the landing as possible, she felt up the wall until she found the switch. With a flick of her finger there was light.

Annie hurried down the steps as quickly as her sore legs would allow. As she ran to the kitchen, she flipped on every light switch along the way. She could hardly contain her excitement when she saw it was only 6:30am. She had only slept a short time. Her effort to rid herself of the drugs worked. Though she was as happy as she had been in weeks, there was no time to enjoy it. Now, she needed to get to the real work that would get her out of this godforsaken place and with a bit of good fortune save Daniel in the process.

* * *

The hopes, wishes, and resolutions of a new year did not translate into the type of good fortune Special Agent Christopher Frye was hoping for in the Drysdale case. He was working as hard as ever to uncover a lead that would give him some idea of the killer's whereabouts. The disappearance of Patty Lawson in Hazard, Kentucky provided just another small piece of the puzzle. When Frye and his colleagues visited the rural southern town, they took statements from two patrons of the bar where Lawson was last seen and the victim's ex-husband, all of whom claimed to have gotten a decent view of the suspected abductor. Two witnesses were inside the bar peering through the shutters of the front window watching the events unfold after the ex-husband dragged Patty out the front door. They saw when he crashed his truck into Patty's Camaro then her conversation with the man who pulled into the parking lot immediately thereafter. They were able to clearly see the pick-up driver's face after Patty opened the door to climb in and the overhead light switched on. Frye got a positive identification of Damien Drysdale after showing both witnesses a photo lineup of six photographs including Drysdale's King Cruise Line employee picture.

The ex-husband first saw the pickup truck as he approached the bar. Despite his agitated state of mind, he couldn't help but notice the vehicle parked on the swale across the street from Billy Bob's facing northbound. No one ever parked there because several cars were totaled after accidentally falling into the steep drainage ditch running along the highway. Intent on his mission at that juncture, the ex-husband didn't bother to pay the least bit of attention to the driver. However, after crashing into Patty's car on the way out, his headlights shined directly into the suspect's truck, giving him the look he needed to provide an accurate description. When presented with the photo line-up, he also identified Damien Drysdale.

Subsequently, the task force temporarily moved its base of operations to the FBI field office in Louisville, Kentucky. Frye was relieved to get away from Miami, at least for the moment. Leland was now the Special Agent in Charge but continued to pay unusually close attention to the serial murder case, closer than what Frye felt was appropriate for his new position. He was happy to have some space from Leland to work on clearing up a few matters. The murders that occurred on the Joy of the Seas were becoming an increasing source of concern for Frye. He took it upon himself to interview the residents of the apartment complex in Carol City where the two drug dealers were shot. On the third night visiting the area, he met with an older gentleman who lived in a small house adjacent to the apartments. A series of unusual circumstances helped the witness clearly recall that particular night. His dog had just finished giving birth to a litter of eight puppies. While taking her for a walk to stretch her legs, he caught a glimpse of a white man coming from the dealer's building, an extremely rare sight in that neighborhood in broad daylight much less at that hour. The bodies were discovered the very next day.

As far as the witness could remember, the stranger was driving an Acura Integra. It was too dark to be sure about the color of the car, but he thought it was red. At the time, he had no reason to memorize the license plate number. When Frye showed him the same photo lineup he showed the witnesses in Hazard, the old man identified the picture of Damien Drysdale. Frye then asked the man if he ever gave a statement to the police. His response was unexpected. No law enforcement authority had ever come to his house to ask questions. After the bodies were found, he didn't volunteer any information either. It was the steadfast rule of the community to keep one's mouth shut for fear of reprisal.

To a degree, the idea that Leland or Dallas hadn't interviewed the man alleviated Frye's concerns about foul play. It would have made matters much more complicated if they were aware of the witness. On the other hand, it didn't excuse a more in depth investigation by the task force into the Carol City murders. Frye felt compelled to add these killings to the list attributable to Drysdale. Clues could still be uncovered if the task force did its routine and thorough analysis of the drug murders. Before he had an opportunity to pursue matters in Carol City, the task force moved its base of operations to Louisville when the connection was made between the serial murderer and the disappearance of Patty Lawson.

Frye considered gathering a team in Miami to re-inspect the Carol City murder site for leads and conduct a more comprehensive search for witnesses without consulting Leland. The first time he approached the new Special Agent in Charge about his concerns, he was practically thrown out of his office. Frye would be asking for trouble if he went ahead with the investigation without his boss' approval. On the one hand, he didn't want to believe Leland or Dallas deliberately concealed evidence. The flip side of the coin was their obvious reluctance to authorize further analysis of the drug murders. They must have feared it would open up a whole can of worms that would disturb their otherwise rock solid case against Daniel Falcone.

Oftentimes ambitious men were guilty of tunnel vision. Frye really wanted to believe that was the case with Leland. It would be truly disturbing if exculpatory evidence was deliberately suppressed. Updating Leland with the new information from Carol City was probably the right thing to do. At the very least, Frye would be covering his ass. The question was if Leland refused to authorize further investigation, would Frye feel comfortable about leaving it at that?

* * *

Annie had already accomplished so much under incredibly difficult circumstances. The work left was going to require just as much physical effort and mental fortitude and perhaps even more luck. Her immediate goal was to find the keys to the shed she had noticed on the property during one of the exercise sessions the monster permitted outdoors. It was on the backside of the cabin, off the beaten path visible through the forest of evergreens from the trail where she and the monster were walking. Two heavy duty padlocks with an industrial strength chain prevented access. It was a much more likely candidate for a hiding place for the monster's prize possession he used to cut off Deborah Falcone's head. Finding a way in without leaving evidence of her entry was going to be a challenge. Once she had the murder weapon in her hands, she had every intention of placing it in the mailbox just outside the front gate with a note to the postman. Annie knew he delivered the mail in the mornings sometime after nine. Without fail, in the middle of her chores when the clock struck ten, he would lock her in her room for fifteen minutes or so. Later, he would come back to free her so she could continue her work and she would see him in his office opening letters. There were also times, in the hour or so before the postman was due, she would see the monster running letters through his postage meter. When she first saw it, she wondered why the heck a serial murderer would need such a thing. She had no way of knowing he was actually significantly more wealthy than she and that he managed his fortune himself. She was quite aware of the copious amounts of paperwork it entailed to oversee her own accounts just by the amount of mail she received daily. She left that to the experts. In any event, it was a stroke of luck he had a postage meter and she wasn't going to waste any time analyzing the reason for it.

The keys necessary to open padlocks wouldn't be the type one would carry around on a keychain. It was most probable he kept them somewhere in the cabin. Searching inside first was the best option anyway. It would save her a trip outdoors if the surgeon's saw happened to be hidden in the house. She decided to start with the office. Over the next two hours, she combed through every nook and cranny of the room where the monster spent most of his day, making sure she replaced everything she touched exactly where she found it. It helped, to a point, that he was a fastidiously organized person. It made the search easier to plan. At the same time, her job required astute attention to detail. He was sure to notice the slightest misplacement of a box, file or paper clip.

At 8:30am, when she was satisfied she had conducted an exhaustive search, she resigned herself to the fact neither the keys nor the saw were in the office. While she was rummaging through his paperwork, she was also hoping to find the address of the cabin or some information that could be used to locate her. Initially, her hopes were dashed quite comprehensively. He used white out to conceal each address and company name without exception on every last letterhead and document in the office. She strained her eyes in an attempt to read through the white-out to no avail. There was one piece of information, however, that could prove to be very helpful. He failed to erase the name to which one of the letters was addressed. She didn't know whether it was his real name or not, but it was possible he used it to purchase the cabin.

Annie thought the most logical place to search next would be his bedroom. Since the first day he allowed her access to the cabin, it had been her responsibility to clean it from top to bottom. His bedroom was the one exception. The door was always closed. She never dared try to enter and assumed it was locked. Prepared with her makeshift pick and tension wrench she had placed in the pocket of her pajamas, she tried the knob. She had mixed feelings about her chances to find what she was looking for when it turned in her hand and she was able to open the door. She was happy to get in, but wondered how likely it was he would keep something precious to him behind an unlocked door. There was only one way to find out. She sifted through every drawer of his dresser, taking each item of clothing out, then replacing it to its original position. She found some keys only to realize they were too small for padlocks. Then, she searched under the bed and every other piece of furniture in the room with no luck.

Inside his closet, the clothes were meticulously color-coordinated in order of the type of garment. She checked the pockets of each and every pair of pants, shirt and jacket and found nothing but empty space. Annie finally felt a ray of hope when she found a lockbox behind some folded T-shirts on one of the upper shelves above the hanging clothes. She used one of the keys from the dresser drawer and was able to open it. It was a minor blow that it contained only cash and quite a bit of it for that matter.

With her options running out in his bedroom, Annie was beginning to wonder if the key could possibly be hidden somewhere outside. If that were the case, she doubted she would ever find it. The property was way too vast to be able to search efficiently in the amount of time she had. There weren't many other places to look that she hadn't already scrubbed clean. The only other possibility was if he constructed some type of secret hiding place inside the walls or under a panel of the wood flooring. Before she even considered going out into the subzero temperatures, she would examine those areas.

Annie continued her work with unshakable resolve. She refused to give up hope until he walked through the front door. The master bedroom was as good as any other place to start. Once again, she scoured his private space, pushing, tapping and listening to every inch of floor and wall space. The inspection turned up zilch. She looked at his alarm clock on the night stand next to his bed and was shocked to see she had been in his room for more than two hours. At that point, she couldn't help but feel the tightness of anxiety in her chest. The cabin covered more than three-thousand square feet. The bedroom was maybe fifteen percent of the living space. To continue in this manner would mean it could take her well into the night to finish. If she could just find the key to the shed, everything would go a lot faster. Not ready to give up, she hurried back to the office and repeated the process of checking the floors and walls. After wasting another hour, it also proved to be fruitless. She was quickly arriving at the juncture where she might have to consider placing a letter to the postman in the mailbox without the murder weapon even though it wouldn't ensure Daniel's release from prison.

It was after noon when Annie's rumbling stomach reminded her she hadn't eaten all day. She didn't want to take the time from her search but had to concede that some nourishment for her body could help her think more clearly. It was time for a break anyway. She was exhausted and desperately needed it. The frustration of searching for hours and finding nothing would cause anyone mental and physical fatigue. She was fixing herself a turkey sandwich in the kitchen and still a thousand ideas were racing through her head vying for recognition. It didn't seem much like rest. Her head was throbbing and felt like it was stuffed full of lead. Just when she was about to try to clear her mind of the chaos to give herself a moment of relaxation, one particular thought won over all the rest. She dropped the butter knife in the mayonnaise jar and raced to the staircase. She was so used to the creaking step as she climbed and descended the staircase that she almost forgot about it.

The steps were constructed of thin wood panels similar to those of a parquet floor. With a closed fist, she knocked lightly on the culprit step from one end to the other. When she reached the far right side, she thought she heard a change in the timbre of the rapping noise. She pushed down on each of the panels in that area. To her thankful surprise, there was one that was looser than the others. She rushed back to the kitchen to fetch a clean butter knife to use as a prying tool. Without too much effort, she was able to displace the panel. It was too dark to see what was underneath, so she was off again to the supply room to grab a flashlight. She flew back to the stairway and aimed the beam into the hollow space. The light reflected off of two keys set on a wood plank just below the center of the step. Annie celebrated this time with a victory dance. Unknowingly, her revelry was premature. If she had reached further into the hollowed space, the events that followed might have turned out dramatically different.

* * *

The dark and icy gloominess of the forest couldn't diminish the excitement Annie was feeling as she tried the key in the padlock of the storage shed. Though she was wearing thermal underwear, a long-sleeved flannel shirt, a sweat shirt, a wool sweater and oversized parka given to her by the monster for outdoor exercising, the freezing gusting winds were able to penetrate through to her bones. With the wind chill factor, it had to be well below zero. After fumbling for several minutes trying to manipulate the key through her thick, wool gloves, the first padlock opened without any trouble. She repeated the process with the second with speedier success. Before she removed the chains, she memorized how it was looped through the padlocks.

Opening the shed doors, she was instantly taken aback by the number of nude photographs of her that covered all four walls of the structure. She hugged herself tightly, shivering not from the cold but as a result of what felt like a smack in the face by the insane obsession the maniac had for her. Quickly, she righted the ship, reminding herself there was no time for such concerns. She looked over the expanse of the large shed to see it was jam-packed with computer and construction equipment. It was already approaching 1:00pm. Considering the number of boxes in there, it could take up to four or five hours to complete the job. She had no idea when he would be back, but she was sure if things didn't go her way, she could be cutting it close. Hopefully, she wouldn't have to search that long. Even if she didn't find it here, she should still have time to write a note to the postman and place it in the mailbox. There was no use wasting time mulling over such things. If she was going to conduct a comprehensive search, she better get moving and fast.

Annie began her long and arduous task of going over the contents of the shed with a fine tooth comb. Though it was somewhat warmer inside, it didn't offer that much relief from the bitter cold. At 2:00, she was forced to return to the house for a few minutes for some sorely needed warmth. Her fingers and toes felt like ice cubes or popsicles that had been in the freezer too long gathering a sheet of frost. It was all but impossible to flex them. As soon as she arrived at the cabin, she started a fire in the hearth and sat directly in front of it for ten minutes. Excruciating pain coursed through her extremities as heat and feeling returned to them. After the pain dissipated, she ran upstairs, put on two more pairs of socks and an extra pair of gloves. Since her boots would no longer fit, she found a pair of the monster's snow shoes in the storage room and put them on.

By the time she made it back to the shed it was already 2:45pm. She decided she would give search until 4:00. For the next hour and fifteen minutes, she left no stone unturned. She searched above, beneath, between and inside of every object in the shed. She even tried to dig in the corners, but quickly came to the conclusion the ground was too frozen and he wouldn't have gone to that trouble. In the end, the saw was nowhere to be found. Refusing to let it get her down knowing there was still plenty to do, she scanned the inside of the shed to satisfy herself she was leaving it as she found it. That done, she walked out the exit, closed the doors, rearranged the chains in their original positions then secured and locked the padlock. It was time to get back to the cabin to compose the note. In it, she would include her statement of Daniel's innocence. Hopefully, if they never found her, it would be at least enough to reopen the case.

Annie had considered the monster could discover her plot. Really, her only hope was that his state of mind would still be distracted when he got home. She was going to try to tie herself back to the bed posts, though getting the last hand done would be next to impossible. Hopefully, she could convince him it snapped off. She had buried the excess twine cut from the one hand and two ankles in the snow deep in the woods on her way back from the shed. Thinking it through to its conclusion, the odds were he would realize the other knots weren't his. Her best and only chance was that in his diminished capacity, he would believe she may have gotten loose from the twine, but there was no way she escaped from the locked bedroom after all the drugs he gave her. Then, just maybe, he wouldn't check the mailbox. Whatever the case may be, she had no regrets she tried. If he killed her, at least she would escape the horror of his torture and abuse.

Once she repeated the process of warming her body at the edge of the fireplace, she went to his office, grabbed a piece of stationary from the desk drawer and contemplated how she would express her predicament to the postman. She wanted to keep it short, limiting herself to the most vital information. Whether it was a gift from above or simply the complicated way that memory works, as Annie collected her thoughts, she was struck by a sudden idea. She had been so fixed on the concept the saw was hidden in the shed, she never bothered to check the entire space underneath the step. Filled with a new sense of hope, she put the pen down, jumped up out of her chair, grabbed a butter knife and climbed the staircase to the offending step. She wasted no time re-dislodging the panel then reached in with her right hand feeling first to the right toward the wall. Her reward was a huge clump of dust. Next, she moved her hand toward the left and just as she attained the limit of her reach, her finger tips touched what seemed to be a cold, hard substance.

She forced her arm further into the hole and the extra inch she achieved allowed her to slip her fingers around the object and pull it toward her. When she abstracted the saw from the space, this time she let out a true victory scream. Fortunately for her, she blindly grabbed the instrument on its handle or she might have cut off a finger. It was extremely sharp. She was too excited to allow the dried blood stains on the instrument to make her sick. In order to ensure she didn't contaminate the object any further, she laid it down on the step and ran to the kitchen to fetch two large freezer bags and the rubber gloves for dish washing. Before she touched the saw again, she put the glove on her hand then delicately lifted it between the tips of her thumb and forefinger. She placed her precious discovery in the bag, sealed it then put it in the second bag for extra protection and sealed it. She replaced the keys where she found them and put the wood panel firmly back in place.

Carrying the double-bagged saw to the office, she searched for a packet it would fit in. She found an oversized manila envelope that turned out to be the perfect size. While preparing to write "For the Postman" on its face, Annie was unexpectedly but quite auspiciously afflicted by a fear she had overlooked to that point. She never considered whether she could trust the mailman to deliver her message. What if he thought it was some child's prank and spilled the beans to the monster? She obviously couldn't afford to let that happen. Her only other option was to send the envelope to a reliable person as if it were a normal piece of mail. It would take extra time to get a rescue operation together. In the interim, the monster could discover the missing saw and all would be for naught, except for the possibility of Daniel's exoneration. It would certainly mean an unthinkable death for her. All things considered, Annie felt she had no choice but to go with the plan most likely to succeed. She began to write.

Dear Mom,

First, I want you to know that I'm alive and holding up as well as can be expected. I don't have the time to write but a few lines. I'm being held captive by Damien Drysdale. As far as I know, I'm in a cabin somewhere in the mountains though I couldn't even tell you if I'm in the U.S. I obviously can't give you an address, but while searching through documents in his office, I saw a letter with the name Darryl Lee Presley. I'm hoping that's his real name or at least an alias he used to buy the property. I pray that information will help locate me. If not, maybe they'll be able to find me through the postmark on this letter. I'm enclosing a piece of evidence I found which I hope will exonerate Daniel. Don't unseal the bag. Please get it to Agent Christopher Frye at the North Miami Field Office immediately. Time is of the essence. Tell him the monster admitted to using the saw to murder Deborah Falcone. Please hurry, Mom. I love you.

Love,
Annie

She wrote her mother's address on the envelope, placed the saw and note inside and sealed it. She thanked God for the postage meter. In order to be safe, she set the stamp for $15.00. It would be devastating to go through all that trouble just to have the package returned for insufficient postage. She ran the meter tape through the machine then attached it to the envelope. It was now ready for mailing.

The sun had set leaving behind a moonless sky. With no lights on the property, it was as dark a night as Annie had ever experienced. The temperature had dipped to ten degrees below zero. The wind chill factor knocked off another fifteen degrees at least. The walk to the front gate would take about ten minutes if she could maintain a decent pace. Annie bundled up in the same four layers of clothing she wore to search the shed plus the oversized parka and three pairs of socks. She put the two pairs of gloves back on and added a scarf around her neck and a full ski mask to protect her face against the uncompromising cold.

Before she left the cabin, she grabbed a few extra batteries from the supply room for the flashlight. When she opened the front door, a blast of frigid air almost took her breath away. Telling herself it was almost over, she inhaled deeply, exited the cabin, closed the door and began the long trek to the gate. With the stiff breeze in her face, the walk to the mailbox was more difficult than she expected. Breathing was a chore. Placing one foot in front of the other was a battle. Several inches of new-fallen snow covered a solid sheet of ice that had frozen on the driveway surface. Slipping and sliding trying not to fall, Annie had to rest every two minutes or so just to catch her breath and replenish her energy. By the time she reached the last section of the driveway, she was exhausted. Toward the front of the property the path to the gate was paved over a thirty foot wide ravine which ran parallel to the fence separating Shem's land from the private roadway. The mailbox was located just outside the gate approximately twenty feet to the right of the driveway as Annie approached it. She couldn't go beyond the fence without setting off the bracelet on her right wrist. This meant she would have to stand on the five feet of flat land between the ravine and the fence and reach with her left hand to place the envelope inside the box. Careful of her footing as she walked along the fence on the narrow strip of frozen ground, she chose an area that was flat and free of ice. Turning toward the mailbox, she reached through the iron bars marking the confines of her boundaries. Using the arm without the bracelet, she was able to open the cover without too much trouble. She placed the envelope inside with just as much efficiency. Like most challenging tasks in life, this one would not go off without a hitch. In the open position, the lid laid just outside of her reach. There was no way she could leave it open for the monster to see. She had to give it her best effort to close it firmly. Fighting her exhaustion, Annie positioned herself as close to the fence as was physically possible and stretched her left arm out to the limit. Just as her fingers were able to grip the lid, her right wrist slipped outside the boundaries of the fence. A jarring electric shock knocked her off her feet and sent her tumbling down the twenty foot ravine. If the electric shock hadn't rendered her unconscious, the boulder upon which she struck her head when she came crashing to the bottom would have easily done the job.

Chapter 27

Traffic heading north on GA-15 had come to a complete standstill. Shem hadn't moved an inch for the past ten minutes. Normally, he wouldn't be bothered by such things, but recent developments were threatening to put him over the edge. Moments earlier, he had switched on the radio to see if he could get a traffic report. While scanning through the stations, he was interrupted by a loud pealing noise coming from inside his briefcase. Thinking it was his cell phone, he dialed the combination numbers for the lock to the case and opened it. Lucky for him he was already stopped when he discovered the real reason for the ringing or he might have driven himself straight into one of the large evergreens bordering the two lane highway. It was the alarm indicating that Annie went beyond the boundaries of the property.

After the initial shock, his first thought was that the pager had to be malfunctioning. He couldn't imagine that Annie would be capable of freeing herself from the twine much less escaping from a locked room. She had ingested enough drugs to choke a horse. The only other explanation was that the machine must have administered an inadvertent shock. Either way, he wasn't going to get an answer for quite a long time. The radio had settled on a station whose on-the-scene reporter was announcing from its traffic chopper that GA-15 would be temporarily closed for the next several hours. A semi-tractor trailer had flipped on its side and was blocking all lanes.

Any sense of nominal calm Shem had been maintaining after the past few days of nothing but trouble was gone. There was only one way to restore the peace and that option wasn't available in the middle of a traffic jam. Having no outlet for release, Shem was near what most people would describe as pure panic. His ego was incapable of accepting he could experience such a state. In his mind, it was a temporary lapse of concentration. In reality, he was gradually losing his ability to think rationally. Controlling his stress over his ignorance of what was happening at the cabin was proving to be impossible. He allowed himself to consider all kinds of scenarios, the worst being that Annie had actually escaped. The idea organized a full-scale, no holds barred attack on his psyche. It became real in his mind, developing into an obsession.

His biggest fear was that she had been zapped and she was lying unconscious outside the cabin. All weather reports for northern Georgia and southeastern North Carolina were warning people not to venture outdoors due to the extreme cold. According to his estimations, the voltage of a shock from his bracelet would cause Annie to be out of commission for more than two hours. If his machine's warning was accurate, she could be in serious danger of death from exposure. To be denied the opportunity of the climax he had been working toward for so many months was inconceivable. He racked his brain to call up everything he had ever read about exposure. The information he remembered brought no comfort. The length of time a body could sustain in extreme temperature varied greatly. There were cases where one hour of exposure to intense cold without proper protection proved fatal.

Waiting in this traffic mess was nothing short of torture. He thought about making a U-turn in the median and finding an alternate route then abruptly changed his mind. It would probably take less time just to wait it out. He inhaled deeply in one of his typical attempts to hypnotize himself into a calming trance though he knew deep down there was no way to mentally prepare himself for what was to follow.

* * *

Six hours later, he pulled through the gates of his property, raced up the driveway and almost skidded into the front door of the cabin as he came to a stop. Every single light in the house was on. He rushed up the steps taking them two at a time to her bedroom. She was most definitely gone. He checked the rest of the house like a whirling dervish and still no Annie. She was not inside the cabin. There was no time to figure out how this could have happened. If she had miraculously escaped the room, perhaps she was able to remove the bracelet. He refused to consider that option.

He had built a global positioning system into the device. When he was within ten miles from the electric shock instrument, the GPS was able to provide him with information indicating its location within a range of twenty to thirty yards. It was now after 2:00 in the morning and if it was still attached to Annie, she had been exposed to the cold for more than eight hours. He rushed into the house to dress more appropriately for the search and grab a first aid kit and a sonar device he had constructed that would increase in volume as he approached the bracelet.

During his drive home, he devised a plan for the search convinced it would be necessary. He would conduct a systematic perquisition beginning at the most obvious place, the front gate and working his way around the perimeter of the property. He hadn't advanced more than twenty feet up the driveway with his homing instrument held high above his head when its high-pitched squawk breached the dead silence of the night. The closer he progressed toward the gate, the louder it squealed. When he crossed over the ravine, it reached its highest pitch meaning she had to be nearby. He put the tracking device in the pocket of his coat and scanned the area around the gate with his portable magnetic floodlight. Unable to locate her anywhere on flat ground, he shined the light down into the ravine. Directing the beam downward along the ridge closest to the gate, he spotted Annie lying in an awkward position toward the bottom of the decline. Without thinking twice, he dropped all of his equipment except for his handheld flashlight and the medical supplies in his pockets and rushed as fast as the conditions allowed to her side. At the speed he ultimately attained, he was lucky to not have joined her in oblivion.

It was a minor miracle he arrived at the base still upright, though he almost planted the heel of his boot in Annie's face as he skidded to a halt. Shining the flashlight on her face, the first thing he noticed was a large scab on her forehead and dried blood running in a trail down her nose to the tip of her chin. He placed his index, middle and ring fingers over the radial artery of her wrist and could barely detect a pulse. It was quite obvious she had suffered serious injury besides exposure and was on the brink of death. He hurried to remove some chemical hot packs from his first aid kit and place them around her neck and hands, doing his best not to rustle the body. Having fallen such a great distance, there was always the possibility she fractured her cervical spine. Even more importantly, jostling of an exposure victim could cause cardiac arrest.

From what he could tell after a rudimentary examination of her neck, it didn't seem to be broken. As a precautionary measure, he carefully placed a brace around it. It was going to be a hazardous climb back up the ravine. He had to do his best to keep her body as still as possible as he carried her. Another fall would most likely be fatal. Leaving his flashlight behind, he gently picked her up and began the ascent up the steep incline. Several times, he lost his footing but was able to keep his balance. Upon reaching the top, he started toward the cabin moving as quickly as he dared keeping Annie's neck as secure as was feasible. Shem had left the front door open in anticipation that he would be carrying her. Once inside the cabin, he laid Annie on the sofa facing the fireplace and quickly started a fire. He removed all of her and his clothing and laid on top of her to transfer the warmth of his body to hers. Her skin was as cold as the icicles hanging from the eaves of his roof. After ten minutes or so, he ran to the supply room to get more hot packs and applied them to her neck, armpits, chest, side and groin. He then covered her with blankets and slipped a dry sleeping bag over her body up to her neck.

Shem was well versed regarding the recommendations that a person with severe hypothermia be taken directly to the nearest hospital. They had equipment far superior to his to elevate body temperature. He would do just about anything to keep her alive for his selfish purposes, but, emergency room treatment was obviously not an option. He was going to have to rely on his own abilities to care for her. His knowledge of medicine and especially the therapy for exposure to extreme cold was almost as sharp as any other subject he studied or read about in the past. Living in the extreme temperatures of the higher elevations and the nearest hospital being more than 100 miles away, he had the medical supplies for just about any health issue manageable by a layperson. They included equipment to administer care for hypothermia and start an IV. If anyone could nurse her back to health, he knew that he could. He would do everything in his power to make sure she survived even if it meant not leaving her side until she was on her feet again. When she was back to one-hundred percent, there would be no more risk taking, no opportunities for another attempt at escape. He would take her life his way, and experience the orgasm of a lifetime in the process.

* * *

"Sir, Attorney Alan Shipman is on the line for you," Director Bynes heard through the intercom located on the cradle of his phone. Bynes was in his twilight years as the top man with the Federal Bureau of Investigations. His plan was to announce his retirement before the year was out. So far, this wasn't the type of day he would miss. He had already been reamed by the President of the United States this morning for a botched mission to capture a high level drug dealer keeping his home base right under the President's and FBI's nose in the nation's capital. A call from former Special Agent in Charge Daniel Falcone's attorney wasn't what Bynes needed at the moment.

"Tell him I'm not available."

"I already tried that. He's insisting. It's about Daniel Falcone. He says it's extremely important."

"That's what everyone says. I don't have time for this shit."

"Yes sir, I'll do my best."

A minute later, Bynes' secretary was back on the intercom.

"Mr. Bynes, I can't get rid of him. He says you'll want to hear what he has to say. Better you first than the media."

"God Damnit, alright, alright, put him through."

Bynes loosened his tie hoping he wasn't wasting his time agreeing to talk to Shipman. Seconds passed then his phone rang. The Director lifted the receiver to his ear.

"Bynes here. This better be worth my while Mr. Shipman."

"I think it will, Director. I'll get straight to the point. Two hours ago, Cassie Bryan, Annie Bryan's mother received a package and letter purportedly from her daughter. I'm sure you're aware Miss Bryan's been missing for a couple of weeks now."

"I'm aware."

"Two things. First, there was a surgeon's saw in the package. The blade has red stains which appear to be dried blood. Second. In the letter, Annie wrote that she was kidnapped by the serial killer, Damien Drysdale and that he admitted to the murder of Deborah Falcone and her parents. She says the saw was the weapon used to murder Deborah Falcone. Cassie Bryan confirmed the handwriting as her daughter's."

"Where's the letter now?"

"I have it locked in my office safe."

"Are you trying to tell me a woman being held captive by a deranged serial killer made a nice little neat package and maybe took a stroll to the local post office to mail it? Is this some kind of a hoax? I have better things to do than listen to this crap. Try to sell your bullshit to someone else. I'm a busy man. You have a nice day."

"I wouldn't hang up, Director. I can't explain how Annie did it or guarantee it isn't some kind of a hoax. I can only tell you her mother swears the letter was written in her daughter's handwriting and showed me a sample. If it wasn't Annie who wrote it, it was someone who was able to copy her handwriting exactly. I can assure you I'm going to pursue this. If it is real, a woman's life could be saved and an innocent man is in prison. Do you want to deal with the repercussions later or look into it now?"

"You're barking up the wrong tree, Mr. Shipman. This is a matter for the local field office."

"Daniel asked me to take it to you. I had an attorney/client telephone conference with him at the prison after Mrs. Bryan came to my office with the letter. He believes Annie is perfectly capable of something like this. He wanted to give you a chance to get all your ducks in a row, if it is real. The media will go crazy with the story. He didn't want me to hand the letter and saw over to Agent Leland until you knew about it. His main concern is Annie. He wants to help."

* * *

Unlike the last time Daniel was in this courtroom, it was as calm and quiet as Saturday confessions at a Catholic Church. The room was occupied by a total of five people including the bailiff and court clerk. It felt like he had taken one on the chin when he saw Leland was attending on behalf of the FBI. If the new Special Agent in Charge was there for support of the motion, it was completely unnecessary and most definitely unwanted. If the message was we're truly sorry, Daniel wasn't interested in hearing it from Leland. The wound was too raw. Seated at the defense table, hopefully for the last time in his life, Daniel turned back toward the gallery where Leland was chatting with the federal prosecutor, Norman Dallas. Leland caught Daniel's movement in his peripheral vision and couldn't help but turn in his direction. The two men stared into each other's eyes. A weak smile formed on Leland's lips as blood rushed to his face. He barely nodded his head in greeting. Daniel remained expressionless continuing his stare. After a few seconds, Leland couldn't take it anymore and looked away. He had completely lost track of his conversation with Dallas who was not oblivious to the interaction between the former colleagues.

Since Alan Shipman had delivered the saw to the FBI's crime lab two weeks ago, many good things followed for Daniel. During their initial telephone conversation, Alan was able to convince Director Bynes to get involved. Daniel admired Bynes and was sure the feelings were mutual though it was pretty clear the possibility of horrendous publicity for the FBI had a great deal to do with the Director's decision to help. In the end, it was the right one.

The DNA test of the blood on the saw was placed on the front burner. Five days later the results came back as a positive match for Deborah Falcone. There were also fingerprints lifted from its handle matching the prints on file for the serial killer. An FBI handwriting expert compared a true sample of Annie's handwriting with the letter received by Cassie Bryan. The conclusion was that Annie did, in fact, write the letter enclosed in the package with the saw.

Daniel wanted to celebrate and feel the relief and joy such news would bring to a prisoner falsely accused. A dark cloud still loomed over his head preventing it. Annie, the woman responsible for proving his innocence, continued to be in mortal danger. The Bureau was doing everything in their power to find her with the new information provided by the postmark and the name she provided in her letter. So far, there were no further leads according to Cassie Bryan. The frustration caused by not being able to help was now tripled. Everyone knew he was innocent, but procedures had to be followed. It could be days, perhaps weeks before he was free. Director Bynes made a personal call to the trial judge and requested a special favor to expedite Daniel's hearing on his Motion to Overturn the Conviction. Daniel hoped the Director's influence would speed up his release from the prison. The federal prosecutor surely wouldn't be an ally.

Norman Dallas initially resisted the motion. It required a heated face to face conversation with Director Bynes and a phone call from the President of the United States to finally change his mind. Bynes enlisted the Chief Executive's help after his first attempt with Dallas failed. Together, Bynes and the President convinced Dallas that the consequences had the potential to turn out much worse. For now, he wouldn't be considered for the appellate justice position he so intensely coveted. If Annie became the serial killer's next victim and Daniel was ultimately proven innocent over Dallas' insistent objections, the federal prosecutor's chances to become a Supreme Court Justice would have been completely obliterated. Daniel shifted his gaze toward Dallas. The prosecutor did not reciprocate. He made his way to his table staring straight ahead. He was obviously not pleased to be a part of this process. The only apology he would eventually utter was brief, generic and on the record. He had no interest in approaching Daniel in a personal setting.

"All rise, the United States District Court, Southern District of Florida is now in session, Judge Clarence Jackson presiding."

Judge Jackson entered the courtroom through his private door and took his seat behind the bench. A man who had his own aspirations for advancement, he was more than pleased to grant this favor to the Director of the Federal Bureau of Investigations. It was always a very good thing to be owed a debt of gratitude by such a powerful man.

"I understand we have an agreement here on the Motion to Overturn the Conviction?" Judge Clarence inquired.

Alan Shipman immediately stood and responded in the affirmative.

"Mr. Dallas?" the Judge turned toward the prosecutor.

"We do, Your Honor."

"Before I pronounce my judgment, does anyone have anything to say?"

Robert Leland, now standing at the prosecution table with Dallas meekly raised his hand.

"Go ahead Agent Leland."

"I just want to offer my sincerest apologies to Agent Falcone personally and on behalf of the Federal Bureau of Investigations. I wish I could turn back time." Leland looked over at Daniel who did nothing to acknowledge the statement. Daniel actually had to stifle a powerful urge to tell Leland to go fuck himself. Shipman had already warned him against showing any resentment toward the participants in the courtroom. If Leland was waiting for a response, Daniel had no intentions of complying. Feeling Leland's discomfort, Norman Dallas stood and reiterated the apology on behalf of the prosecutor's office. He wasn't expecting any response from Daniel nor did he care. Later, he would say the right things for the benefit of the press. At the moment, there was no need to cater to anyone since the hearing was private and closed to the media. With the serial killer still at large and Annie in his clutches, it was a no brainer to keep the hearing top secret.

"Based on the newly discovered evidence which clearly proves my client's innocence, we're moving to overturn the conviction for all three counts of murder, effective immediately," declared Alan Shipman.

"I don't take the reversal of a jury verdict lightly," Judge Jackson responded. "However, I have read the entire motion and the brief filed in support and I have to agree with Mr. Shipman. Since the only living family members of the victims are Agent Falcone and his two children, there is no one else to consult. All parties having agreed, including the prosecutor and the arresting agency, I hereby order the conviction for all three counts of murder against Daniel Falcone to be overturned. I can't release you now Agent Falcone. There are procedures that have to be followed. You'll be returned to the Federal Prison in New York where they will process your release. On behalf of the federal government and the State of Florida, my heartfelt apologies for what you've been through. No system of justice is perfect, but I continue to believe America's is the best in the world. Good luck. I wish you and your family all the best."

* * *

The American Airlines Boeing 777 skidded to a perfect landing on Miami International Airport's runway four. The moment it arrived at its designated gate, Special Agents Christopher Frye and James Mancini were first in line waiting to disembark. According to the telephone call both men received from Leland earlier in the morning requesting their post-haste presence in Florida, they finally had a major break in the case of the nameless serial murderer regarding his whereabouts. For an unknown reason, Leland was unwilling to discuss the details over the secure FBI cell phone. As soon as the door to the airplane was lifted, the agents rushed through the jet way into the terminal and continued at a brisk pace toward the exit. A chauffeur had been sent to pick them up and was already parked outside the building's exit waiting for them.

Upon loading into the back seat of their ride, Frye instructed the driver to employ the rotating blue police light and siren for the trip to the field office then phoned Leland to warn him of their imminent arrival. According to the new Special Agent in Charge's secretary, Leland was on an important telephone conference and unavailable to take the call. Eager to get the information they had been anticipating for hours, Frye and Mancini encouraged the chauffeur to drive faster than protocol normally dictated. Less than fifteen minutes later, they burst through the entrance to Leland's waiting area to find the secretary's desk vacated. Frye was about to knock on Leland's door when he heard muffled shouts coming from behind it. Due to a healthy dose of curiosity and on a modest hunch Leland was up to no good, Frye surreptitiously motioned for Mancini to wait, placed his ear up against the door and eavesdropped on Leland's conversation. It became apparent rather quickly that the new Special Agent in Charge was on the phone.

"What the fuck Clifton? You owe me. I'm the reason you still have a job at the Herald. I need you to do this for me. It's imperative. Otherwise, our relationship is done." There were several seconds of silence then, "You wouldn't have had the Falcone story if it wasn't for me. I made you. Now, when this comes out next week, I want it written my way. I'm not gonna take the fall for this."

Frye had heard enough. Without knocking, he opened the door and entered Leland's office with Mancini following directly behind. Leland turned toward them and immediately hung up the phone.

"What the hell do you think you're doing? Have you ever heard of knocking?" bellowed Leland.

"Who was that on the phone, Robert?" Frye demanded

"I don't owe you any explanations. And I don't answer to you."

"I know exactly who you were talking to. It was Clifton Harris from the Herald. So now we know who the leak was you son of a bitch."

"Fuck you, Chris. I'm the boss here. You have no right to make those accusations. You're treading on thin ice."

"Bullshit, Robert. I know exactly what's going on here, and I can prove it. You've had it in for Falcone for a long time now. I know about the Carol City murders you and Dallas held back. If that case was explored, Daniel wouldn't have been prosecuted."

"I don't know what the fuck you're talking about. Get out of my office unless you can get a hold of yourself."

Mancini couldn't believe his ears. He always felt in his heart Daniel was innocent, but never would have believed his friend was set up by his own colleagues. Hearing this information, there was no way he was going to stay quiet.

"Now, come on guys," he said. "Let's have a civil discussion here. What's this about murders in Carol City?"

Frye explained what he discovered in Leland's computer recycle bin and the findings of his personal investigation. When he was done, Leland was the first to respond.

"That means nothing. There was no way Falcone was gonna get off with all the evidence against him. There was no reason to pursue those murders."

"You're just up to your ears in bullshit this morning."

"Come on, Chris. You know I admired Daniel. I was just as shocked as anyone else when nothing turned up on Isaac Jefferson.

I didn't know about the old man walking his dog. If I did, I would have been the first to get the ball rolling and look into it further."

"You're a fuck'n liar. You practically kicked me out of your office when I brought the drug murders up."

"Gimme a break, Chris. I had no idea. But the fact of the matter is, it doesn't matter anymore and we're wasting time here. The wheels are already in motion to have Daniel released from prison. Director Bynes called in a favor with the warden… something about getting him the job. They're letting him out today. We know where the killer is keeping Annie. The postmark on the letter finally paid dividends. The Director had some men he handpicked in Washington doing research in and around Asheville, North Carolina where the package was first processed by the post office. They traced it back to the original post office and mailman who collected it. They spent days searching through real estate records for mountain cabins in the area to check for property owned by the name Annie provided. Those little towns up there still store their information the old-fashioned way. Bottom line, we have an address. They also found the mailman who picked the package up. He confirmed they got it right. We're going in tonight."

"Well let's get busy then," said Frye. "Rescuing Annie and getting the prick is our number one priority. But just remember, Robert. The Carol City thing isn't over. Now, get back on the fuck'n phone and make sure that asshole Harris doesn't print a word about any of this. The news breaks and it could screw everything up."

* * *

By the time Daniel got to the pay phone that morning to get his daily update from Mrs. Bryan, it seemed the whole cell block was waiting ahead of him. After about forty five minutes, the line having reduced by less than one-half, a prison guard approached Daniel and told him the warden, Karl Schultz wanted to see him immediately. Daniel had a feeling this could be the good news he was expecting. A sense of excitement was abruptly smothered by his next thought. Something could have happened to Annie. He anxiously followed the guard to the warden's reception area for prisoners and was instructed to wait until his assistant came to get him.

Almost immediately, a beautiful, dark-haired, olive-skinned woman with a body of death and the personality of Medusa came out of the warden's office. With a facial expression of hostility and a tone to match, she advised Daniel that her boss was ready for him. When she stepped aside and pushed past him toward her desk, Daniel had hope that this was his last day in this godforsaken place. Agent Robert Leland, Christopher Frye and Alan Shipman were standing on either side of the warden. It didn't diminish Daniel's concern for Annie.

"Alan, what are you guys doing here? Is Annie alright?" asked Daniel.

"Before we get started, please everyone have a seat," said Warden Schultz motioning the men to the four seats facing him while he sat in the chair behind his desk.

"Please, Warden, what's this all about? Tell me Annie's alright," Daniel pleaded.

"We're not sure about that at the moment, Daniel, but we think so," said Agent Frye. Looking to Leland, Frye continued, "Robert."

"Daniel, first, I owe you an apology. I don't know how I can ever make it up to you."

"Robert, please just get on with it. Does this involve Annie? Have you found her?"

"I'm sorry," Leland fumbled. "You're right…Your release is effective as of today, the paperwork's done…"

"I'm happy to hear it, but what are you guys doing about Annie? Do we have any idea yet where she might be?"

Leland replied, "That's why Chris and I are here. Just last night, we got a big break. You might know the Director had some special agents working on locating the suspect. Well, they found him. They're in a cabin in the Blue Ridge Mountains. The records show it was purchased by a Daryl Lee Presley just three months ago. It's all confirmed. The cabin has been under surveillance since late last night. Through thermal imaging, we know there's a man and a woman. We're assuming the woman is Annie. A rescue operation is in the works. We're going in tonight. We'll be on the plane to Asheville in less than two hours."

"I'm going with you."

"You're right about that…thanks to Director Bynes. He granted your request. We're here to pick you up per his orders. We flew up here in a private jet to brief you and have you participate in the mission. I have to say, I'm against it. This is too personal for you. We can't afford to screw it up. It's a complicated operation with very specific maneuvers. Any rash act on your part could mean Annie's life. You know how slippery this guy is."

"You gotta be fuck'n kiddin' me," responded Daniel. "I don't give a shit what you think. I've been sitting in this shithole for months, special thanks to you, by the way. I've been frustrated as hell that I couldn't do a damn thing to help Annie. The fuck slaughtered my wife, left my kids without a mother, and framed me for it. I'm going."

"Alright, Alright, Daniel. This isn't the time to argue. You're in. How quickly can we get him out of here Warden?"

"Paperwork's done. I understand you have a change of clothes for Mr. Falcone. As soon as he's dressed, he's all yours."

"Thanks Warden. Let's get moving," barked Daniel.

Chapter 28

On the ninth day after her accident, Annie was showing the first signs of regaining consciousness. In her initial moments of awareness, she couldn't' tell whether or not she was dreaming. She was trapped in the cabin of a deserted cruise ship lost at sea. Then suddenly, she had the distinct feeling she wasn't alone followed by a sense of dread and hopelessness. When she opened her eyes, the light was dim, her vision blurred. She tried to move her right hand to wipe her dry mouth, but it seemed to be stuck behind her head. A voice she recognized and feared was pronouncing words she couldn't understand raising goose bumps along her spine. This was a nightmare, not a dream.

"I know you're awake. I can see your eyes."

Her immediate instinct was to flee. She tried to jump to her feet then realized they were bound to the bed she was lying in. The memories were coming back in waves of terrifying images of the abuse she had suffered over the past weeks. This wasn't a nightmare. It was reality.

"You're lucky you're alive. Then again, maybe not. Anyway, you can thank me. You owe me, bitch. For the past week and a half, every second of my day and night was dedicated to keeping you from kicking the bucket. Did you think you were gonna be able to die your way? Not a fuck'n chance. Were you trying to kill yourself?"

Annie didn't know what to do or say. This was the first time he had ever asked her a question. The few times she had spoken without his express permission, she had suffered dearly for it. Even if he did allow her to respond, she had no idea what she was going to say. In the brief seconds she took to analyze the situation and consider an answer, she abruptly recalled her last moments of consciousness.

"I want an answer. What the fuck were you doing?"

Annie didn't want to hesitate too long before she answered though she couldn't help but wonder what happened with the surgeon's saw. He said he had been taking care of her for more than a week. There were probably a million reasons why he would still want her alive if he had discovered what she was up to, none of them any less than horrendously terrifying. Her stomach twisted in a cramp at the thought of what he might have planned. Not daring to wait any longer and figuring there was no winning answer, she said the first thing that came to mind.

"I wanted to get out of here."

"Stupid bitch. Didn't believe my bracelet would work, huh? That was a big mistake…I am impressed, though. How the fuck did you manage to get yourself untied and out of the room?"

Annie didn't see how the consequences would be affected by her response so she just told the truth. She was rewarded with a backhand across the face. This time her nose held up. It didn't even bleed.

"That's just for now," he said. "I owe you a helluva lot more, that's for damn sure." Shem didn't want to inflict too much injury to her body until he was sure she was completely recovered. For the moment, she would have a reprieve.

To keep his hopes of the ultimate orgasm alive, he had spent the last nine days not budging from her side except to get supplies and food as needed from downstairs. His efforts to save her had become just as obsessive as his attraction to her. He was utterly and completely blind to the possibility that his fanatical fixation on his final plans for Annie could very well mean his downfall. The morning after his meeting with the lawyer and bank officials, he had every intention of mailing several business documents. If he had done so, he would have noticed Annie's failed attempt to close the lid of the mailbox.

"I got shit to do but I'll be back," said Shem switching off the lights and leaving Annie in the dark both literally and even more frustratingly, metaphorically with regard to the results of her handiwork.

* * *

The night was as still, silent and stygian as a black panther lying in wait seconds before it pounces on its prey. Regrettably for Shem, he was unable to profit from the serenity of the evening as disquiet overtook his normally self-assured demeanor. For the past couple of hours, he had the sense there was something altered about his surroundings. At first, he thought it was his imagination. Then, the incidents of finding personal items out of place reached the point where it could no longer be coincidence. As he was preparing some mail to take to the post office the next day, he noticed the postage meter was set at $15.00. He knew the last letters he ran through the meter all required standard postage. When he checked the postage history, he saw the meter was most recently set on the day he travelled to Atlanta just fifteen to twenty minutes before Annie set off the alarm.

His first response to understanding that Annie might have tried to mail a letter was a pullulating anger he feared he wasn't going to be able to control. The bitch had tried to pull a fast one over on him. She was probably laughing at him right now. The image of her hand-slapping, incessant snickering sent his thoughts into a tailspin. It evoked the infuriating memories of his mother and all the other whores cackling at his inability to have a productive ejaculation. If his emotions continued to viciously spiral in the same direction, he wasn't going to be able to lucidly analyze the situation. In order to figure out what he was going to do next, a sound mind was essential.

With colossal effort, he fought to retain his composure. He sat at his desk and surfed the net, an act that always brought him pleasure and serenity. It didn't completely resolve his unrest, but he managed to minimally calm himself to the point he could evaluate his options with more clarity. If she was successful in her attempt to mail a letter, it most likely already arrived at its destination. There was no telling how long he had before they came for him. It was a wonder they hadn't come already. He wanted more time to get every last ounce of pleasure possible from his possession of Annie, but these were desperate circumstances. "Desperate circumstances called for desperate measures."

Already his penis was fully erect with the thought of looking into her eyes as he sliced through her neck. He made his way to the supply room to fetch one of his sharper butcher knives. He considered the hammer and chisel then decided it would be too crude for her beautiful head. The surgical saw he used to decapitate the agent's wife would make a nice, clean cut. It would also be poetic justice. He quietly climbed the staircase to the step where he hid the saw. With the butcher knife, he loosened the plank and removed it. When he reached inside to retrieve his prized possession, he received the shock of his life. His face turned several shades of red, the rage inside his black soul building to a crescendo. Just when he was about to turn to make his way up the stairs, in his peripheral vision, he noticed a flicker of light penetrating the cabin through the front door's peephole.

* * *

One of the FBI's nine enhanced SWAT teams was called into action to assist in the rescue of Annie Bryan and the capture of the unknown serial murderer. A team of a total of twenty-two law enforcement officers was assembled for the exercise with the code name Operation Nameless. Special Agent in Charge, Robert Leland was leading the squad and would be stationed in a van at the back edge of the property. Agents James Mancini and Christopher Frye were following the lead of the SWAT team captains who were directing the maneuver from the field. Daniel was accompanying Agent Frye and his group on the backside of the cabin.

The consensus of those leading the team was to conduct the exercise under the cover of darkness. By ten o'clock on the evening that Daniel was released from prison, a perimeter was set up around the cabin with a radius of twenty-five yards. The agents were dressed in full winter nighttime combat gear which included a black assault vest and mask, a special operations H-Gear shoulder harness and tactical chest pouches. They were armed with lachrymatory gas grenades, a Boker Magnum Rescue folding knife, night-vision goggles, a TL-3 tactical flashlight, an ear piece and AR-15 semi-automatic assault rifles. All agents had a second pistol on their person and most had a third in a holster attached to their ankle or some other hidden part of their body.

Once everyone assumed their assigned positions, Agent Leland would determine the appropriate time to give them the signal to proceed. The plan was for the field agents to work their way to the edge of the dense forest and wait for Leland's command. When prompted, a swat team agent posted on the roof would drop the gas through the chimney then the agents on the ground would storm the back door. Meanwhile, the agents at the front would make their way across the stream and enter through the main door. Two men would be posted at each possible exit while the others were inside completing the mission.

The operation ended up being delayed for a half hour when one of the SWAT team agents was involved in a mishap. The offending agent slipped on some ice and broke his arm just as he approached the perimeter. When he lost his balance, the flashlight attached to his belt was accidently switched on and flashed across the front door of the cabin. Since it happened in a matter of a split second, it went unnoticed by his fellow teammates. After the injured agent was carried off the property in a stretcher, the mission was resumed.

Agent Frye was operating a thermal imaging scope which sent images back to the command center. He was scanning the cabin to detect thermal energy emitted from human bodies inside the structure. Just prior to the SWAT agent's accident, Frye was able to identify two live bodies inside the home. One was the shape of a woman lying in an upstairs bedroom with her arms sprawled back toward the bedposts. It was assumed she was tied to the bed. There was also a man moving about the first floor of the cabin. Frye assumed the woman was Annie Bryan and the man was the unknown subject referred to at the Bureau as the unsub.

When Agent Frye recommenced thermal scanning after the injured agent was removed from the scene, the man inside the cabin had disappeared. He swept the area outside the cabin between the structure and the perimeter without results. Daniel, who was watching the monitor on Frye's scanner, was having a bad feeling. Not a split-second later, a blast of semi-automatic gunfire originated from an area on the left backside of the home. By the time Daniel was able to shield himself behind a tree, every member of the SWAT team on that side of the house was instantly killed by a gunshot wound to the head. When Daniel peered around the tree to check on the agent who was standing next to him, the entire left side of his face was blasted away. He quickly surveyed the area for Frye, who managed to survive the onslaught by laying flat on the ground. Daniel watched as he scrambled behind a tree for cover.

Agent Frye attempted to communicate with Leland at the command center then noticed his head piece was damaged by his fall to the ground. When the gunfire ceased, Daniel grabbed the thermal image scanner Frye had dropped, picked up his rifle and without a second thought started on his way to the cabin, crawling on his stomach. Frye tried to order him back. Daniel paid no heed. In order to get to the cabin, he would have to cross a clearing of about thirty feet. As he advanced along the flat ground, more gunfire erupted toward the front of the property. Daniel took advantage of the opportunity to stand up and race to the rear entrance. With well-practiced speed, he pried open the lock with the Boker Magnum knife then opened the door and walked into the light-deprived cabin. Using his night-vision goggles, he quickly found his way to the base of staircase, raced up the steps and ran directly to the room where Frye had detected the woman's body on the thermal imaging scope.

Not bothering with the knife this time, he kicked at the door with such force, it flew open on his first attempt. Annie's head was cocked upward, her eyes squinting and straining expecting to see the monster.

"It's me Annie, Daniel."

"Daniel, Oh my God, I can't believe it. Thank God." Tears of joy and relief flooded her eyes and poured down her face. She knew something was up after hearing the faint sounds of what she thought was gunfire outside, but didn't dare allow herself to be optimistic until that moment.

"It's great to see you're in one piece. I can't tell you how worried I was about you. Are you alright?" asked Daniel.

"Well, I can't see you. Get me outta here."

Daniel cut the twine binding Annie's wrists and ankles to the bedposts then helped her get out of the bed.

"Can you walk?" he asked.

"I think so."

She took a few steps holding onto Daniel to confirm her answer. Her legs were a bit wobbly, but with a little assistance she thought she could make it.

"Just hold onto me. I'll be fine," she said.

"We need to get you out of here. Now."

"Where's Drysdale?"

"We don't have time to waste. I'll explain everything later. We need to hurry."

"I just don't want him to get away."

"There are others. At least I hope. I want to get you to safety. There are FBI vehicles parked on the street along the front of the property half a mile down the road from the gate. Do you think you can make it or should I carry you?"

"I'll do my best. I'll let you know if I have to jump on your back."

Daniel placed his right arm around Annie's upper back and hooked his hand under her right armpit. Holding her steady, he helped her descend the stairs and make it to the front door. He reached for the knob and turned it as a third barrage of gunfire erupted.

* * *

Special Agent in Charge Robert Leland was trying not to panic. His armored van was located approximately three quarters of a mile from the cabin on the western boundary of the property. He was receiving images from all of the thermal scanners and updates at twenty second intervals up until all hell broke loose. The maniac had taken them by surprise. Since the initial gunfire, he was unable to communicate with anyone out in the field. His only companion was an equipment tech who was maintaining the machinery. Every fifteen seconds he would attempt to establish contact with anyone who would respond to no avail. He heard rapid gunfire at least twice since the team took their first position. He thought about leaving the van to offer assistance then reconsidered figuring he could be a sitting duck.

There had been no gunfire for more than five minutes. Leland was hoping the team had gotten things under control. He turned toward the monitors to see if the images were back up when he noticed on the video screen one of the agents racing toward the backdoor of the van. Seconds later there was a burst of frantic knocking. In a muted voice he heard, "Leland, open the fuck'n door. Hurry. It's Frye. He's out here somewhere."

Leland looked at his monitor again. Frye was wearing a mask to protect himself from the cold and carrying one of the FBI issued rifles. As far as Leland could tell, it was his colleague. Pressed to make a choice, Leland feared taking the time to ask too many questions could get Frye killed. He didn't want to make a hasty decision that would put him in danger either. For a brief instant he contemplated that it might not be so bad to be rid of Frye. The hitch was that Mancini also knew of the Carol City murders and Frye could have spoken to a number of his buddies. The idea was crazy anyway.

Leland wouldn't live long to regret his decision. He unlocked and opened the door. The man he assumed was Frye jumped into the van pointing the semi-automatic rifle directly at the team leader's forehead. He shut the door to the van behind him, locked it then took his mask off revealing his true identity. Shem was well aware of the names of the agents investigating the Drysdale murders through the many newspaper articles he had read and television reports he had seen. His guess that Leland was in the command center turned out to be spot- on.

Leland tried to negotiate with the psychopathic killer, only to be ordered to shut his mouth if he didn't want to lose his head.

Alternating his aim of the rifle between Leland and the equipment technician, Shem first tied Leland to his chair with rope he brought from the house then the tech. When both men were secure, he removed a hammer from his utility belt and smashed every piece of equipment in the van. A familiar sensation in his loins was stimulated by the horrified look in their eyes, but he couldn't waste too much time here. There were still other goals to accomplish before the night was over. He pulled a hunter's knife from a sheath tied around his calf. It glimmered as he held it up in the light of the van. He slit the throat of the equipment tech first. Blood squirted across the vehicle dousing the already destroyed equipment. Next, he turned to Leland. The new Special Agent in Charge tried to beg for his life though his expression was resigned. Shem just laughed and stuck the knife upward through his right eye, into his brain, killing him instantly.

* * *

Daniel had waited until ten minutes had passed since the last gunfire to give the go-ahead to make a run for the front of the property. Before they had a chance to open the front door, he heard a crackle in his ear piece then the voice of James Mancini.

"Does anyone read me?"

"James, it's Daniel. Can you hear me?"

"Thank the Lord, Daniel, am I glad to hear your voice. It's a fuck'n mess out here. The son of a bitch opened fire execution style. I don't know how many other survivors there are. Right now, Frye and I are trapped at the command center. We had to find cover. We were dead ducks while he was using us as target practice. Leland and the systems operator are dead. The prick is relentless. He slit the kid's throat. Leland has a knife sticking out of his eye."

"Holy shit. How could this have gotten so fucked up? God damnit." Daniel took a moment then informed Mancini, "I have Annie here with me. I was just about to try to get her out of here. Is the unsub still out there?"

"I have no clue. He hasn't fired at us since we were able to get into the trailer. It's been about ten minutes."

"We can't leave you alone. I'm gonna have Annie wait in the cabin while I come out there to see what I can do."

"Like hell you are," Annie snapped. "You're not leaving me here. I know how to fire an assault rifle. I can help. You could use my help. I want the bastard just as much as you do, Daniel."

"We're on our way back there, James. Hold him off. Between the four of us, maybe we can kill the fucker."

* * *

After Shem Chassar murdered Leland and the equipment tech, he had taken a position in the woods within firing distance of the command center. Things were starting to get out of hand. He was outnumbered now and they knew his location. Besides Annie and the agent, five other agents survived his attack and they were now joining forces against him. He felt he had done just about all he could do. He was able to gun down most of the intruders. They had the upper hand now. His last chance to escape with his life was rapidly disappearing. There was one item left to check off his to do list before he made his getaway. The night vision, laser sight of his AK-47 was trained on the center of Daniel's forehead as he and several other armed agents approached the command center. Shem's brain was a fraction of a second from sending the signal to his finger to apply pressure to the trigger when a round of rapid fire from Annie's assault rifle whizzed by his left ear. Startled into a moment's hesitation, it provided just enough of an opening for a second round to strike his weapon sending the ten pound rifle flying out of his hands and causing the barrel to strike him between the eyes with significant force. If he hadn't been knocked to the ground, the next round would have struck him in the center of his heart.

When he regained his senses, he picked up his rifle and saw it was damaged beyond repair. Even though he was sure he could no longer prevail, he had delayed his escape so that Annie could watch when he blew his arch rival's head off. It wouldn't be possible now that he no longer had the element of surprise on his side and his rifle was rendered useless. One way or another, the agent's day of reckoning would come. It just wasn't going to happen that night.

There was no time to feel sorry for himself about the unfortunate events of the evening. They were only one-hundred and fifty yards away and closing in on him. The next rounds fired from their weapons would surely hit their mark. He disappeared onto one of the thousands of wildlife trails bordering his property. They would give chase, but would never find him. He knew these trails like the back of his hand. Twenty miles southwest of his property, he parked his Jeep on a secluded back road in the event an emergency escape was necessary. It was packed with supplies that would last for weeks. By morning, he would be well on his way to his next destination.

Epilogue

There wasn't a time when Daniel could remember having a more severe case of the butterflies. It had been many months since the last time he lived with the boys. He was nervous about how they'd receive him. He pulled his Crown Victoria into the parking space in front of his Hallandale Beach condominium, his hands clenched tightly on the steering wheel. As was their custom, the boys attacked their Dad before he could get out of his car. It was a very welcome assault and the perfect cure for his nervous stomach.

The condo would hold many memories of Deborah he was sure at times would cause him overwhelming heartache. He had finally agreed to see an FBI therapist and was working hard on his guilt issues. If the boys wanted to stay in the home where they were raised by their mother, Daniel wasn't about to deny them. His life would be very different now as a single parent. For the time being, he decided he would return to the Miami field office, but rejected the offer to resume his position as Special Agent in Charge. His passion had always been to solve crimes and put the bad guys behind bars. He felt at home again when Quantico granted his request to work murders in the criminal division. His goal was to hone up on his serial murderer profiling skills. The unfortunate reality that the monster got away was much more than a travesty of justice for Daniel. The name he used to purchase the cabin in North Carolina proved to be just another false identity. The unsub was still just that-a man without a name. Although he would give all of his cases their due attention, he made a private commitment to himself and his children. The day would come when the maniac who slaughtered his wife and in-laws would pay for his crimes.

Now that he was with his children for the first time since his imprisonment, it wasn't the time for dark thoughts. It was cause for celebration. The guests would be arriving shortly for his welcome home party Annie planned for him. When he walked into the living room with the boys clinging to his sides, it was great to see his mother, brothers, Mrs. Bryan, and Annie waiting for him to begin the festivities. Today, he wasn't going to allow his absent father to spoil the party.

* * *

March had come in like a lion with a blast of arctic air that chilled to the bone. Shem Chassar chose this place exactly for that reason. He wanted it to be cold year-round. The wintery, crisp air would keep him awake and alert and help him never make the same mistakes again. He was a fool to obsess over a woman. There wasn't a female on the face of the earth who deserved his attention. They were all a bunch of useless, filthy whores. They were objects, nothing more than play toys to use or abuse as he saw fit.

From this point on, he would practice his art without restraint. He had beaten the best the FBI could offer. There was no one who could stop him. Moderation would not be a part of his vocabulary, though his number one mission in life was revenge. Every last one of them would pay in ways they could never imagine. There would be suffering beyond human comprehension. When he was through with them, his story would go down in history. He would start with the agent's boys and family members, and then collect his dues from Annie, saving the agent for last. Patience, as always, was the key. It was what he'd lost when he let himself get involved with the foolish sexual attraction. That wouldn't happen again. Their worst nightmares would be realized when they least expected it.